D1408043

Also Available from Denise Little and DAW Books

Mystery Date

First dates—the worst possible times in your life or the opening steps on the path to a wonderful new future? What happens when someone you have never met before turns out not to be who or what he or she claims to be? It's just a date, what could go wrong? Here are seventeen encounters, from authors such as Kristine Katherine Rusch, Nancy Springer, Laura Resnick, and Jody Lynn Nye that answer these questions. From a childhood board game called "Blind Date" that seems to come shockingly true . . . to a mythological answer to Internet predators . . . to a woman cursed to see the truth about her dates when she imbibes a little wine . . . to a young man hearing a very special voice from an unplugged stereo system . . . these are just some of the tales that may lead to happily ever after—or no ever after at all. . . .

Front Lines

It is only since the advent of battlefront reporting, of turning on your television and seeing actual wars in progress, putting names to faces, "meeting" both soldiers and civilians who are caught in the day-to-day struggle for survival, that war has become more personal and the true price of combat has become real. Diane A.S. Stuckart, Laura Resnick, Josepha Sherman, Jody Lynn Nye, Dean Wesley Smith and others here visit the front lines of battle in stories that range from a chemical experiment gone horribly wrong . . . to a young recruit who may hold the key to "understanding" the enemy . . . to a US-Canadian conflict where the team attempting to broker peace is a joint Palestinian-Israeli unit . . . to a half-mortal knight trying to avert a war with the Elfin Host . . . to a Battle of Trenton fought against seven-foot tall Saurians. . . .

Hags, Harpies, and Other Bad Girls of Fantasy

From hags and harpies to sorceresses and sirens, this volume features twenty all-new tales that prove women are far from the weaker sex—in all their alluring, magical, and monstrous roles. With stories by C. S. Friedman, Rosemary Edghill, Lisa Silverthorne, Jean Rabe, and Laura Resnick.

The Magic Toybox

Thirteen all-new tales about the magic of childhood by Jean Rabe, Esther Friesner, David Bischoff, Mel Odom, Peter Morwood, and others. Here toys come to life through the love and belief of the children who play with them. A tiny Mr. Magoo yearns to escape the Old Things Roadshow and get home to the woman he's been stolen from. A child slave in Rome dreams of owning a wooden gladiator—could an act of magic fulfill his dream? Can a ghost who's found refuge in a what-not doll solve a case of unrequited love?

ENCHANTMENT PLACE

EDITED BY

Denise Little

DAW BOOKS, INC.

DONALD A. WOLLHEIM, FOUNDER

375 Hudson Street, New York, NY 10014

ELIZABETH R. WOLLHEIM

SHEILA E. GILBERT

PUBLISHERS

http://www.dawbooks.com

First Printing, August 2008
1 2 3 4 5 6 7 8 9

DAW TRADEMARK REGISTERED
U.S. PAT. AND TM. OFF. AND FOREIGN COUNTRIES
—MARCA REGISTRADA
HECHO EN U.S.A.

PRINTED IN THE U.S.A.

ACKNOWLEDGMENTS

CONTENTS

INTRODUCTION

Denise Little

Shopping is one of those activities that, depending upon the people involved, can split up a family, destroy a relationship, perfect a day, revive a shattered spirit, and/or save a marriage. It all depends on who's doing it, the company they keep, and the goal they have in mind. Pair a shopaholic and a mall hater for a crawl through a suburban shopping enclave, and the end result can literally be murder. On the other hand, show a depressed shoe lover a big spring sale at Macy's, and it may save that person from a life-threatening funk.

That dichotomy has particular meaning for me and my sister. My sister is a former beauty queen, and I ran retail bookstores for fifteen years. My sister believes in shopping as therapy. I avoid it like a contagious illness unless it involves food, books, or toys. On those things, I run wild. But as long as I get my bookstore fix, it's an activity that my sister and I can share—our tastes are different enough that we cherish the things we can do together. A few years ago, as my sister and I were crashing through the mall crowds together during a post-holiday sale, I wondered aloud what kind of people shopped for pleasure. My sister replied, "I wonder what kind of people don't."

At that point, my head filled with images of the kinds of people who might have trouble shopping in a standard mall. I've been immersed in speculative fiction since I was four, so the ideas that ran though my head shared a certain otherworldliness: vampires frying under the ubiquitous skylights and avoiding the mirrors everywhere (not to mention the wafting scent of garlic from the mall food court), werewolves put off by the unavoidable perfume squirters at the cosmetic counters, witches who needed the kinds of ingredients and pets that no standard mall stocked, and so on.

I shared my thought with my sister, who has no patience for whimsy. "Let them get their own mall!" she said.

That's where the seeds of *Enchantment Place* were born. Every time I read a paranormal romance, an urban fantasy novel, or a fairy-tale pastiche, I have a vision of the story denizens flopped out in their living rooms, wondering, "But where will we shop?"

This book's the answer to my silly flights of fancy. I think it may be a personal favorite. I hope you enjoy the mix as much as I did.

SHINING ON

Mary Jo Putney

A *New York Times*, *Wall Street Journal*, and *USA Today* bestselling author, Mary Jo Putney was born in upstate New York with a reading addiction, a condition for which there is no known cure. Her entire writing career is an accidental byproduct of buying a computer for other purposes. Over the years, she has evolved from Jane Austen-ish Regency romances to historical fantasy. Her releases in 2007 include a new historical romantic fantasy, *A Distant Magic*, and the paperback release of *The Marriage Spell* in June. She knows way too much about *Star Trek*, and she almost always has cats in her stories.

My Uncle Joe used to say that you could tell a lot about a man by his shoes. He should know—he spent most of his life shining shoes for businessmen who wanted to look spiffy for their next meeting.

Me, I chose combat boots. Thought I'd be brave and noble. Ended up in a place with too much sand and heat and things that went BANG! 'Nuff said.

When I got out of the service, I wasn't sure what to do next, since most of my job skills are frowned on in private life. And my family in Cincinnati was making me nuts. Nice folks, you know, but they kept hovering. Worrying about me. Like I was going to explode or something. Frankly, I could see their point. So I went to Chicago, where we'd lived when I was a kid.

Uncle Joe was long gone—he'd been a great uncle, maybe two greats. But being there in his home town made me think of him and of polishing shoes. So when I went to an employment agency, I put down "shoe shining" as one of my skills, since I used to help Uncle Joe, and he told me stories in the quiet times. He'd fought in The Big One. I fought in The Wrong One.

Anyhow, I got called in by an employment counselor, a middle-aged babe with a brisk tongue and nice eyes. She checked that I was really Roy Blake, then said, "Since you're a veteran, I could easily place you with a security firm."

I'd thought about being a rent-a-cop, for about two seconds. "No, thanks. What else do you have?"

She glanced down at a pile of papers. "If you're looking for something different, we have an opening for someone to run a shoeshine and grooming station at Enchantment Place. It's an exclusive boutique mall with very specialized shops and clientele."

"Grooming? Like combing dogs?" I liked dogs and critters in general, but I wasn't trained in fluffing them.

"The listing isn't very detailed. They do say that they want someone versatile and good at thinking on his feet." She handed me the paper. "You'd be an employee of the mall, with a base salary and a percentage of sales. The position includes an apartment if you need a place to stay."

I did, actually. I'd forgotten how expensive Chicago was. I studied the income estimates. "If they're telling the truth, this is really good money. But the listing is three months old. Why are they having trouble filling the job?"

"Because they insist on having a combat veteran." Her eyes glimmered. "Which you are. Plus, you know how to shine shoes. Are you interested, Mr. Blake?"

The job listing roused my curiosity, and the work sounded peaceful, so I decided to check the place out.

Which is how at the end of the afternoon I was standing in the living room of a really nice one bedroom apartment with an amazing view of the Loop and the lake. I'd passed the initial interview—apparently the combination of combat veteran and shoeshiner was rare—and now Missy LaFey, the assistant mall manager, was showing me the apartment that came with the job.

"Would this be satisfactory, Mr. Blake?" Missy asked. She was a cute little thing, so light on her feet that she hardly seemed to touch the floor.

I didn't reply at first because I was staring through the picture window at the setting sun. The location, twenty stories up in the high rise above the mall, was worth a million bucks, and the icy winter landscape made me glad to be inside and warm. "The apartment is great," I said. "But why are you offering housing to a low-level employee like me? I'd think this place could be rented for a ton of money."

"It could, but for the kind of work you're going to be doing, we need very special employees. No one is 'low-level' for that work. Enchantment Place is unique, and our customers expect a high level of service. People like you." Her smile was dazzling. "Giving mall employees special perks is a way of avoiding high turnover. Will you take the job, Mr. Blake?"

Sounded like I'd be a servant for a bunch of rich snobs, not my favorite kind of people. But the work would be easy, and I loved this apartment. I could always leave if I hated the job. "I'll give it a try. But why am I a member of the security staff?"

She chose her words carefully. "Some of our customers are very unusual. They need to be handled with care and sensitivity. It's expected that you will help out in whatever ways seem necessary in the course of your day."

In other words, there were rich spoiled brats who couldn't just be tossed out on their rear ends. Fair enough. I was good at tossing, but I could be patient for the kind of money and housing I would get at this honkin' upscale mall. Probably my size had a lot to do with being hired—at six four and with muscles on my muscles, I could quash a fight just by showing up and asking if there was a problem.

Missy pulled out a key ring. "Here are keys for the apartment, the employee entrance to the mall, and the shoeshine station. I suggest you take time familiarizing yourself with the materials. Some are quite unusual."

Shoe polish was shoe polish. So it came in fancy colors. Big deal. I was about to ask some more questions, but Missy's cell phone rang. She made an apologetic gesture and answered. Her expression changed. "I'll be right there."

She snapped the phone shut. "I'm sorry, but I have to go. Meet me at the shoeshine station tomorrow morning at 9:00 and I'll go over everything and introduce you to some of the shop owners. The station is part of the food court and easy to find."

Before I could answer, she darted out the door. And, swear to God, I *didn't* see her little feet touch the ground.

After Missy had whisked away, I studied the keys, thinking how weird this was. I mean, the deal was great, but for a shoeshine guy? Even a veteran? It sounded too good to be true. Maybe I should check the actual mall out before I moved my stuff here. So far, I'd just seen the management suite. I headed for the elevators.

Enchantment Place was in the late afternoon lull when I entered. Most of the day shoppers were gone, and the after work crowd hadn't rolled in yet. I could see a few people here and there, but no one was close by.

The food court was to the right, so I turned that way. Missy hadn't been kidding about the place being upscale—it seemed to be all specialty boutiques, each glittering like a jewel. Not a Gap or a tee shirt shop in sight. A place called "A Taste of Spice" had fancy cookware and crystal bowls full of fragrant spices, some of which were glowing faintly. Radioactive nutmeg?

The next shop—I halted. Whoa, baby! Did those discreet gold letters really say "Something different for the vampire who has everything?" I glanced into the shop, but the smoky glass made it impossible to see what kind of products the store carried. Probably it was some sort of gift shop for the rich and jaded.

The food court was amazing, designed like a tropical grotto with a cliff on one side and a waterfall several stories high splashing into a huge rock lined pool. The ceiling was designed to look like the sky, with sunshine and slow moving clouds.

I glanced into the pool. There were some very large ... things ... swimming around in the depths. Didn't look like carp to me.

The court had scattered clumps of jungly trees and flowers, and the seating wasn't just little tables and chairs. There were all sizes of benches and some couches that made me think of large, expensive doggy beds. I tried not to think of what spoiled teenagers might get up to in such places. Was part of my job to keep the public spaces decent?

I turned my attention to the food stalls. Again, there were no national chains in sight. One little stall called itself "Blood Wine." That must be where the Klingon wannabes stopped by for their tomato juice. The idea was a little creepy, but the place was spic and span, and the guy in the back polishing his glasses looked normal enough. Next to it was a coffee shop with the delectable sent of baking cinnamon wafting out.

Ah, there was the shoeshine stand, tucked between the coffee shop and "Kebabistand, for the carnivore in you." The stand was the old fashioned wooden kind like Uncle Joe had at the train station. Polished mahogany seats were set high so the shoeshiner wouldn't have to bend over, and brass foot rests gleamed like gold. This stand had been cherished for sure.

Supplies were stored in the ends, behind locked doors that opened with the old-fashioned iron key Missy had given me. Inside were neat drawers of different sizes with labels like "polishing cloths," and "black polish." I pulled that one out and sure enough, there were little jars of some fancy European brand of polish. I opened one and took a sniff. The familiar, astringent smell took me right back to Uncle Joe and me no higher than the old guy's hip.

Blinking a little too fast, I put that away and checked the other drawers. The shoe polish colors were what I expected, but what the heck was "hoof polish" doing here? I thought of cows being prettied up at country fairs, but this was a sparkly paste with a piney scent. Maybe it was one of those kid things—these days girls seem to sparkle a lot more than when I was in high school.

The next drawer said "beak polish." Now this was getting strange. I was about to check that out when a voice behind me said, "Finally! I thought they'd never get a new shoeshiner. I need the works right now."

The back of my neck prickled, because it was a voice, sort of, but I was hearing it inside my head, not with my ears. I turned warily and found a unicorn standing behind me. The size of a large pony, the unicorn—definitely male—was pure white, with a glossy mane and tufted tail. Prettiest critter I've ever seen, though that long, sharp horn wasn't just decorative.

I swallowed hard, wondering if I'd gone around the bend. But I had an aunt with the Sight, and in my travels I'd learned that there are more things under heaven and earth than most of us realize.

Given all the legends about werewolves, vampires, and more, maybe they really did exist and just preferred to keep a low profile. Certainly this unicorn looked as real as my own body. He also had a faint, horsey scent that convinced my nose as thoroughly as the sight of him convinced my eyes.

Missy had said employees needed to be adaptable, and now I understood why. Okay, I was adaptable. "I'd be happy to help, but I'm just starting right this minute, so you'll need to tell me what you'd like."

"No problem. The unicorn hoof and horn polishes are in there." The words rang in my head like chimes as the horn tapped a drawer. Then he stretched out on one of the doggy bed couches.

"There are a couple of different colors here." I showed

the unicorn the jars I'd found in the drawer. "Which do you prefer?"

"The silver. The gold is too formal for anything but gala events."

Right. Should've figured that out for myself. I spread the soft polish on the unicorn's hooves, which were indeed a little dingy. Shimmering particles brightened the hooves right up. While I waited for them to dry, I applied polish to that long, sharp horn. After buffing, the hooves and horn shone like rainbowed silver.

The unicorn sighed. "That feels so good. You have nice hands. By the way, my name's Bernie."

"Pleased to meet you, Bernie. I'm Roy."

Bernie rolled off the lounger and preened himself in the tall mirror on the side of the shoeshine stand. "I'm so glad you're here, Roy. My horn hasn't looked this good in weeks." He turned from the mirror. "Put it on my tab."

His tab? "Since you're my first customer, I'm not sure how that works."

"Ah, right." Bernie tapped a button with his horn and the largest panel in the shoe stand rolled up. Inside was a small computer, a cash drawer, and a credit card scanner. "I have an account at the mall that's linked to my bank account," Bernie explained. "All of us who don't have hands do that. Click the icon for 'rates' and you'll get a list that includes hoof and horn polishing. Then go to 'accounts' and look up Bernie. Write the job up with a 25 percent tip for yourself."

"You're generous," I said as I pulled up the rate screen.

A chuckle rang in my head. "I want us to have a long and happy relationship, Roy." With a jaunty twitch of his tufted tail, Bernie turned and trotted off.

So I was working for a mall that catered to magical customers. Maybe that shop I'd passed really did serve vampires. I suppose the idea should have freaked me out, but after dodging bullets and bombs in combat, pretty much anything was an improvement. If all the customers were as nice as Bernie, I was going to like this job just fine.

I scanned down the rate listings. Hoof and horn rates were straightforward. There were multiple prices for shoe polishing, apparently depending on size. And what was this "Claw sharpen and polish?"

I got serious about exploring the computer screens to see what I might expect. Maybe it would have been easier to wait for the morning meeting with Missy LaFey, but this was just too much fun.

A throaty voice purred, "Hey, sailor."

"Actually, I was a soldier." I turned—and froze solid at the sight of the most spectacularly sexy babe I'd ever seen in my life. She was curvy as a mountain road and twice as dangerous, with a black dress that must have been sprayed on. Ebony hair tumbled over almost bare shoulders, and her skin was so white that she must wear grade 500 sun block.

"I'm Monica," she said in that purring voice. "And I need my boots polished." She swung up onto a seat and set her foot on the rest. Her thigh high boots had six inch heels, and her skirt was slit up to *here*.

I swallowed hard, remembering when I'd had to defuse a bomb and me with no training. "Sure you need a shine, Miss? Your boots look perfect."

"I believe in preemptive polishing. And please, call me Monica. What's your name?" She had amazing eyes. I couldn't have told you the color, but I couldn't look away.

"R—Roy," I stammered. Though Monica was so hot that she made my palms sweat, my soldier senses were screaming that I should run in the opposite direction.

But I couldn't bolt, much as I wanted to. Feeling drugged, I pulled out a jar of black polish and applied it to the top of her left foot. "Higher, Roy," she breathed. "You're quite the hunk, aren't you?"

"Not really." Feeling suffocated, I stroked the polishing cloth over her ankle. She had great legs. Her black boots ended at midthigh, the soft leather slick below her silky skirt.

I was wondering if I could bring myself to polish over her knee to the thigh when a sharp voice said, "Monica, behave yourself!"

A woman charged out of the coffee shop. She wasn't a shimmering sex goddess. She was tall and brown-haired and looked . . . nice. Her gaze on Monica, she scolded, "You know perfectly well that you aren't allowed to hit on the employees here."

Monica looked like an embarrassed school girl. "But I just woke up and I'm *hungry*. I only would have taken a little sip or two, and a fresh drink is so much nicer than bottled."

"No rationalizing!" The newcomer's glare was stern. "Do you want to be banned from Enchantment Place forever?"

"I wasn't thinking!" Expression horrified, Monica yanked her boot from the footrest and leaned forward to say earnestly, "I'm so sorry, Roy. Will you promise not to give me away?"

She reached out and cupped my chin with one pale hand. I almost jumped out of my combat boots. Her fingers were cold. Not cool, like someone with poor circulation, but *cold*. Cold as the grave. And her persuasive smile showed a hint of fangs.

I gasped. "You're a vampire?"

"Of course." Monica stood and brushed the wrinkles from her dress. "Maybe you'd like to get together some night when you're off duty?"

I drew a shaky breath. "I don't think so."

"Wuss." She sniffed and walked away, hips swaying.

A hand closed around my arm. A pleasantly warm hand. "You look like you could use a cup of coffee. Come on over to my place."

I followed her and the scent of caffeine to the cozy shop next door. She was pretty, in a wholesome, girl-next-door way. "You're not a vampire or unicorn or something else weird, are you?"

She laughed. "I'm as human as you are. My name's Meg Rudolph, and I make a good cinnamon pastry. I'll bet you're the kind of guy who wants his coffee hot and black and nothing fancy added."

"Yes." I sank gratefully into a deep couch. "I'm Roy Blake."

She poured me a cup of steaming black coffee, then added a plate with amazing crumbly pastries. I wolfed the coffee and cakes down. I hadn't realized how hungry I was.

I finished the first cup, so she poured another. Drinking more slowly, I said, "This morning, I didn't know this place existed. Now I'm in the middle of things I never believed in. I'm not crazy, am I?"

"Not at all," she said serenely. "I was pretty startled when I started, but the place and the customers are real enough."

"Just checking." I decided to eat another pastry. "What's it like working here?"

"Great." Meg finished making some fancy coffee drink for herself and sat opposite me. "Sure, the customers are quite a mix, but most of them are very nice. They appreciate having a place where they can be themselves. Be normal. That's why the management is so particular about who's hired. You wouldn't have noticed, but you were magically scanned before they made an offer."

Now *that* was creepy. "Why did they do that?"

"To see how tolerant and adaptable you are. The owners don't want anyone here who will make the customers uncomfortable." Her voice softened. "A lot of our regulars have been persecuted, even hunted down. They deserve a place where they're accepted."

I glanced out at the mall, which was getting busier. A group of strangely shaped . . . beings . . . wandered by. Ugly as sin and with warts in places where most people didn't even have places. Trolls? Ogres? But they were chatting and laughing like any family having a night out. The mama ogre held her little daughter's hand, and the dad carried a baby in a chest sling. Having had too many people stare at the scar across my left cheek, I could understand why customers wanted to be treated like just folks. "Okay. But why does mall management specify a combat veteran for a shoeshine stand?"

"Sometimes things happen that you wouldn't see at a regular mall. Employees need to be able to calm trouble without hurting anyone and without freaking out themselves." She chuckled. "Keeps the job from getting boring."

A group of kids was entering her shop, and a man was approaching the shoeshine station, so I finished my coffee and got to my feet. "Thanks for the explanations, Meg. I'll see you later."

The fellow waiting at the stand was a big, burly guy, almost my size, with a restless air. His clothes were good but casual, and his shoes definitely needed cleaning. I said cheerfully, "Hi, I'm Roy, the new shoeshine man. May I help you, sir?"

"I need a shine pretty bad." He climbed into a seat and put one foot up. His dark brown shoes had been worn through snow and slush, so I pulled out leather cleaner as well as polish. As I went to work, he chatted away in a deep, growly voice. "I'm meeting my boy here in a few minutes, and I'll have to admit that I'm as nervous as a cat on a stove. Haven't seen him since he was a cub."

"You must have missed him." I'd learned from Uncle Joe that part of the job was listening if a customer seemed to want to talk, as this one did. And I liked to listen.

"I missed a lot while Johnny was growing up. My own damned fault." He flexed his knuckles nervously—and long, curving claws appeared in front of my nose, emerging from under his regular fingernails. As I flinched back, he said, "Sorry. If you haven't guessed, I'm a weretiger. Name's George."

A weretiger. Named George. Oooohkay. "I hadn't guessed. Just started here, and I'm still learning." I gave a final polish to his right shoe and gestured for him to switch feet.

"Then maybe you don't know much about my kind. Tigers are pretty solitary. We don't hang out in prides, like the lions, who are a bunch of furry extroverts. When I met my Johnny's mother, I figured she was just a fling, and I was free to move on. I wasn't going to have a permanent mate, not me. I've hardly seen Johnny since he was born. Now he's hitting adolescence, and soon he'll be going through his first Change. A boy needs his father then." George sighed. "I haven't been there for him, but I want to be from now on."

His claws flexed again, and he retracted them hastily. "I shouldn't be showing claws a week before the full moon. It's a sign of major nerves."

"Your boy will be nervous, too, but he's going to want this meeting to work as much as you do." Reassurance was another part of my job. "Things might be a little tense at first. That's only natural." I gave a last buff to his shoe. "But with good will on both sides, you'll work it out."

"If we do, maybe Deborah will be willing to give me a second chance," he said softly. "I've never met a female to match her in all the years since."

I didn't say anything about that. A woman who felt abandoned by her man would require some major convincing, "Do all weres have to change with the full moon?"

"There's a lot of variety, depending on the kind of were and the individual. Weretigers are usually moon bound, but as you can see, I'm so stressed that I'm doing some unintentional minor changing. A newbie were might change at any time if he's really terrified. But that's rare."

"Good luck with the family meeting. I'll bet it goes just fine."

Looking as if he wished he believed me, he paid up and left. A few minutes later, I got another unicorn customer. This one wanted iridescent gold polish on hooves and horns, plus a combing of her mane and tail. She giggled while I worked and said she was going to a club later for some dancing. I'd met my first unicorn teenager.

The mall got busier as the hour got later. With vampires and other nightwalkers among the customers, that made sense. I stayed pretty busy, too. The magical folk were a well groomed lot and liked to look their best. Plus, it was winter and the weather was messy, so there were others who needed snow and salt removed from their shoes before the leather was ruined.

Between customers, I'd wander into the coffee shop to see Meg. If she wasn't busy, she'd chat. When customers lined up, she showed me how to make mocha lattes. Sergeant Roy Blake, barista. Who'd have guessed?

I saw George meet his family on the far side of the food court, under a cluster of tall palms. The woman was a real looker—lean and taut and, yes, she moved lithely as a tiger. The kid was maybe thirteen or so, and he looked as nervous as his dad. I didn't have to be magical to see the tension among the three. I silently wished them luck.

My shift at the shoeshine stand ended at 9:00 PM, so I was ready to wrap it up by then. I locked the supply doors and headed over to see Meg. She was talking to a young fellow with the very pale skin I realized was a mark of a vampire. She waved when I came in. "Roy, meet Josh. He's my night guy." She covered a yawn. "I'm through for the day."

I greeted the boy, glad he wasn't eyeing my throat, and escorted Meg out of the shop. "If the moon was full, this place would be jumping, and I'd work later," she remarked. "But that's not for over a week. This is a fairly typical night. Do you think you'll like working here?"

My gaze went up the towering cliff. In the subdued evening light, the waterfall sparkled like crystal, and all kinds of tropical plants and flowers bloomed in niches. Amazing to find this in the heart of a Chicago winter. "I like it fine, Meg. Soothing." I cocked an eye at her. She was fine, too. Working over a hot espresso machine had made her brown hair curl into delicious little twists along her throat. She looked good enough to eat—in a nonvampire sort of way.

"Would . . . would you be up for a bite of supper? I still have lots of questions." I was startled to hear the words come out of my mouth—it had been quite a while since I'd been on the dating scene.

Meg gave me a smile that warmed my bones. "I'd like that, Roy. There's a nice little rib place near here. Quiet and great food and, if we're lucky, maybe a jazz musician or two."

I knew that my grin was goofy. This was my best day ever since Mary Jane O'Neill accepted my invitation to the prom when we were in high school.

A hair-raising sound between a scream and a roar blasted through the mall. I spun and looked down the east concourse, instinctively stepping in front of Meg in case something bad was coming down.

Meg wasn't the sort who wanted protection. She moved to my side as a tiger came barreling toward the food court. Customers scattered, and I saw the mama ogre yank her little girl from the tiger's path. An alarm began to sound, the mechanical blare adding to the air of panic.

Two people were chasing the tiger: George and Deborah. "Oh, damn! I'll bet that's Johnny," I exclaimed. "His dad met the kid and kid's mother here earlier. Said the boy was almost ready for his first Change, and that must have happened. But I thought it had to be a full moon?"

Meg whistled softly. "A new were who's terrified might change early if he's stressed enough."

Johnny entered the food court, skidding to a stop on big paws as he realized what a crowd was here. A few rags of clothing hung on his furred body, left over from his Change. He was kind of small for a tiger, but still pretty damned big, with teeth and claws that could kill as quickly as vampire fangs.

Two guards closed in on him, one from each side. They were packing stun guns, but I doubt Johnny noticed anything beyond how scared he was.

With a frantic yowl, he whirled and made a flying leap onto the cliff wall. There were plenty of cracks and crevices to support his weight, and he began swarming upward. Halfway up he skidded and almost fell, swinging precariously from his front paws. There was a sharp intake of breath from the onlookers.

He recovered and kept scrabbling up until he bumped his nose on the sky patterned ceiling. Shocked, he clung there, crying piteously.

As Meg and I headed for the cliff, she said, "Weres

heal really well, but a fall from that high would still be dangerous."

From her tone, I guessed she thought it might be fatal. We reached the cliff at the same time as George and Deborah. Johnny's mother growled at her former mate, "What the devil did you say to Johnny to freak him out like this?"

"Nothing!" George protested. "I was just telling him how great it was to be a weretiger and that I looked forward to us hunting together. How exciting it is to bring down a deer and sink your fangs into that fresh meat."

She looked like she wanted to slug him. "You idiot! Johnny's a vegan! He was already nervous about meeting you, and then you had to gross him out with hunting stories!"

"A vegan weretiger?" George repeated, stunned. He took a deep breath. "No matter, he's still my boy and we have to get him down safely." He stared at his hands, where the claws had extended from under the nails. "If I concentrate really hard, I should be able to Change and go up after him."

This time Deborah did slug him. I made a note to ask Meg about weretiger mating customs later. Her voice a dangerous growl, she snarled, "Don't you dare! You'd probably break your neck. Even if you made it up the cliff, you're the last person he'd want to see."

The security guards had joined us. One said, "The ceiling doesn't have any access panels near him and we don't have a ladder long enough, so we've called for a cherry picker. That will get him down."

Where would they get a cherry picker at this time of night? I doubted it would arrive before Johnny lost his grip. Time to make myself useful. I stripped off my jacket, shirt, and boots. "I'll go after him."

Deborah swung around and gazed at me with desperate golden eyes. "Can you get up there without killing yourself? Regular humans are so fragile."

"I was a Ranger, and climbing's a hobby." I flexed my fingers and toes to get them limber. I'd done my share of talking scared kids down under combat conditions, so this situation wasn't entirely unfamiliar.

Meg kicked off her shoes and coat. "I'm coming up, too."

"You're a climber?" I asked, surprised.

"Yep." She grinned, looking fit and ready. I hadn't noticed what a fine build she had—as strong as it was shapely. "Ready to ramble, mountain boy?"

"Yep." We started up, climbing in parallel. It wasn't too different from a climbing gym. I kept my eye on Meg, relaxing when I saw that she was as skilled as me. She wore knit slacks and top and moved as easily as I did in my jeans and tee-shirt.

I took one quick glance down and saw that the guards had cleared the food court. Probably didn't want witnesses if one of us went *splat.*

Once Meg slipped, and I grabbed a shrub and steadied her. Once she did the same for me. Maybe when spring came, we could go climbing together.

As we neared Johnny, Meg said quietly, "I'll do the talking. A female voice might be more soothing."

Smart woman. I nodded agreement. She raised her voice, "It's okay, Johnny. No one's going to hurt you. Just relax and we'll help you down." As we climbed the last few feet, she kept talking, her voice as rich and sweet as molasses.

Johnny was panting and his whole body was trembling. Even with weretiger strength, he wasn't going to be able to hold on much longer.

Keeping my voice light, I said, "I'm going to put my hand on your back for support, Johnny. Then we'll figure out how to get back to ground zero." I wondered how we'd do that. I'd rescued a few cats in trees, but I wasn't sure how good werefelines were at backing down. Hopefully better than their domestic cat cousins.

I reached out with my right hand and gently laid it on his upper back. He shuddered. Instinctively I began petting as if he were a cat, saying, "It's okay, Johnny. Everything is going to be all right."

Suddenly heat and light shimmered around his form.

I almost fell off the cliff, but I managed to keep my grip. Under my hand, the sleek striped fur transformed into bare, shivering skin.

Johnny cried out, and I thought we'd lose him, but Meg anchored herself on a small tree that grew from the cliff and wrapped an arm around his waist. "Don't worry," she crooned. "We won't let you fall."

He sobbed, "M—my father will hate me because I'm not like him. I can't run down helpless deer and rip their throats out, I can't!"

"You won't have to," I said. "Your dad doesn't hate you. He just wants you safe. And he wants to learn how to be a good father."

Johnny turned toward me, tears in his eyes but expression hopeful. "Really?"

"Really. He told me so. Now let's get down from here. It should be easier now with you in human form. Think you can find handholds if Meg and I steady you?"

He nodded, expression determined. A good kid. As we started to work our way down, applause broke out from below. Apparently the customers hadn't gone far.

If I ever had a more stressful descent, I can't remember when it was, except maybe that blizzard on Mt. Hood. But we made it to level ground safely.

Deborah leaped on her son with a hug that knocked him back into the wall, not that he minded as he hugged her back. George had found a blanket somewhere, and he wrapped it around Johnny, awkwardly patting the boy's shoulder. As the crowd drifted away, he said, "Come on, son. I'll buy you a tofu burger, and we can talk."

Deborah gave George a shining smile. If he was hoping for a reconciliation with her, he might just get lucky. Turning from her son, she shook our hands. "God bless you both! You're the best."

Thinking of old Westerns, I said, "Just part of the job, ma'am."

Catching the reference, she laughed and gave me a hug. After hugging Meg, she left with George and Johnny. The guards and onlookers were gone, so Meg and I were on our own. As I pulled on my boots, I said,

"I definitely could use a plate of ribs and a beer now. Are you still in the mood?"

She nodded vigorously. "You're on. I could put away a double rack myself."

As I buttoned my shirt, I said, "You sure know how to act in an emergency. Are you ex-military, too?"

She grinned and pulled down the neck of her knit top to expose the eagle, globe, and anchor of the Marine Corps on her shoulder. "Semper fi, Roy."

"Well, I'll be damned!" I stared at her, thinking she was as sexy as Monica the vampire, and in a way that didn't make me want to run like hell.

"Very likely." Her smile turned impish. "Ready for those ribs?"

"Rangers lead the way!" I offered her my arm and we left the mall together. I was wearing that goofy smile again. I was going to like this job just *fine*.

THE FACE IS FAMILIAR

Esther M. Friesner

Multiple Nebula Award winner Esther M. Friesner is the author of over thirty novels and over one hundred fifty short stories as well as being the editor of eight anthologies, including the popular *Chicks In Chainmail* series. Her latest titles include *Temping Fate* and *Nobody's Princess*, whose sequel, *Nobody's Prize*, will appear in 2008. Educated at Vassar College, she went on to receive her M.A. and Ph.D. from Yale University, where she taught Spanish for a number of years. She lives in Connecticut with her husband and two all-grown-up children. She's a harborer of cats and maintains a fluctuating population of hamsters. And boy, does she know where to shop!

"I always knew it would come down to this," Vivian told the ceiling. "Me, spending the best years of my life with nothing to do except talk to a hamster." She shook her head sadly, then rested it on the pet shop counter, pillowing her pale brow on folded arms. The counter was an all-glass model, with an array of doggie and kitty toys displayed haphazardly within. It ran the whole width of the store, rather like a barricade, with a gap at the left hand end to allow passage from one side to the other without the need to vault the counter itself.

The gleaming surface smelled faintly of cleaning spray, though the antiseptic scent lacked the power to eradicate the strong, persistent, underlying pong of incarcerated animals. It only took a few seconds of deep, applied self-pity before Vivian's nostrils could endure no more. She sat up straight and glared at the small, black-barred cage at her elbow.

"It's bad enough that you're a hamster, you know," she told the fluffy brown-and-white occupant. "But couldn't you at least *try* to be a good conversationalist? God knows, every other flea magnet in this dump blabs away at the least provocation. You just sit there like a hairy potato. A *cute* hairy potato, but still—! I thought that the whole point of a familiar was to provide his master with companionship!"

"Shows what you know, mortal," came a deep, melodious voice from one of the many display cages lining the back wall of Pet 2B Popular, one of Enchantment Place's premier providers of sorcerous familiars. The speaker, a black cat who rejoiced in the store-bestowed inventory name of Jupiter, stretched out with the regal grace of a panther and regarded Vivian with disdainful green eyes. "We familiars are more than mere companions. Bah! A visit to the nearest animal shelter could provide a wizard with something so commonplace as a . . . buddy. Nor is banal conversation our chief function. Any witch worth her salt can cast a spell of human speech on whatever she fancies, dog or dressing table, cat or couch, aardvark or armoire, chicken or—"

"I get the idea," Vivian said. "I'm not stupid."

"Of course not," Jupiter drawled. One whiskery eyebrow flicked ever so slightly.

Vivian looked long and hard at the black tomcat. She was indeed what Jupiter had called her—a mortal, and an unmagical one at that. Her knowledge of familiars, their ways and powers, was limited to basic maintenance and sale price. She doubted that the creatures destined to share the lives of witches, wizards, warlocks, and assorted enchanters possessed telepathy, in addition to their well-documented facility with human speech. And yet there were times she felt as though they *might* command in the power to project their thoughts into the minds of others. How else to account for the sneaking sensation that behind Jupiter's sweetly spoken reassurance lurked an unvoiced: *Darling, you're half as smart as a box of week-old sauerkraut—and that's a generous estimation on my part—but as long as you're the one in charge of feeding me and keeping this pesthole of a cage reasonably clean, I'll call you Einstein. You dork. Oops, did I say that? Prove it, I dare you. Oh, and while you're at it? Bite meeeeeeeow!*

The pet store clerk sighed. "Nice of you to say so," she told Jupiter. Her voice was flat as a deflated parade balloon. It didn't matter whether or not the cat's low opinion of her was true or a mere figment of her bored-to-tears mind. Thanks to a fairly nasty past, Vivian had so little self-esteem that she'd take that imaginary box-of-sauerkraut comment as a compliment.

Jupiter twitched his velvety ears forward. "By the seven La Leche Leagues of Lemuria, woman, what ails you? It's no fun lobbing sarcasm grenades at someone wearing a BLAST ME sign."

"Sorry I can't entertain you as you deserve."

"You're not sorry at all. I can tell. You smell insincere."

Vivian shrugged. "Have it your way."

The cat got up and began to pace along the bars of his cage uttering low, rumbling growls of dissatisfaction. "I *will* have it my way," he declared. "It's my birthright. Am I not a cat? How *dare* you dream you've got the authority to bestow or deny the fulfillment of my smallest whim!"

"Oh, shut up, you overweight dust bunny," Vivian said. She put her head back down on the counter and muttered, "I gave up daring to dream *anything* a long, long time ago. If I didn't need the money so much, I'd quit this job *yesterday*."

"You don't like serving me?" Jupiter tilted his head, bemused by the alien concept. "I can't understand why not. I haven't been unduly demanding. You, in turn, have not been unduly competent, but no matter. I learned to lower my expectations when dealing with mortals way back when I was still a kitten."

Vivian lifted her head and rested her chin on one fist. "What *is* it like being the center of the universe, Your Majesty? You must tell me. I already know exactly what it's like being the cosmic barf bucket, so you can skip that."

"Is your life so dreadful?" the cat asked. Then he yawned so hugely that Vivian could have counted every pink rib on the roof of his mouth had she been so inclined.

"I ran away from home, didn't I? In way too much of a hurry to finish high school, let alone go through college."

"Not a good choice," the cat said.

"Hey, after Mom died, my 'choice' was leave or stay home and go along with what my stepfather wanted me to do with—with—" She stopped, wincing at the ugly memory. "Never mind. I'll spare you the details. You've probably heard them all by now." She patted the small cage where the hamster sat contentedly munching sunflower seeds. "*Over*heard them, that is. At least Spooky's a good listener, even if he's a lousy conversationalist."

"Spooky?" Jupiter cocked his head to the other side, peering at the hamster in its cage. "Mistress Ardath listed him as 'Hammie' for inventory control. I know. I was there when she did it. She talks to herself when she's using the computer."

"Mistress Ardath can list him as anything she likes," Vivian said. "It's her store and she *is* the boss of me. But until he's sold, what's the harm in my giving him a name I like? And one that's a little more imaginative than 'Hammie,' God knows. I'm the one who takes care of him, after all."

"You really are . . . less than well educated as to the ways of familiars, aren't you?" the black cat observed.

"How much education do I need to shovel out a litter box?" Vivian countered.

"More than you have, since you did a slipshod job on mine last time." Jupiter puffed out his fur. "Silly mortal, how could you have worked here any appreciable length of time without learning even *one* of the basics? And the most basic of said basics at that! The Rule of Names states clearly that to name a creature is to limit, to claim, to forge a bond with the one thus identified. To know a creature's name is a magical force of great power. Why do you think witches' kids always lose their underwear at summer camp? Because their parents dare not risk losing the child himself should one of their enemies spy a *These skivvies belong to Merlin Ambrosius* name tag on laundry day!"

"Now wait just a minute," Vivian said. "Are you telling me that because I named this hamster, he's mine?"

"In essence, yes. In practice, not quite. Merely calling him by a different name than his inventory monicker is not enough, else I'd be bonded to the first sticky-faced human whelp who toddled in here and called me 'Kitty.'" Here the tomcat shuddered in disgust. "But bestow a name upon a familiar with whom you have established a *true* relationship, however small, and the deal is done."

Vivian blinked in disbelief. "So all the time I've spent talking to—*at*—this hamster did it?"

Jupiter nodded solemnly. "Well, you have been pouring out your heart to him for quite some time."

"Wonderful." Vivian's voice was flat. "I don't even know if my lease allows pets, and now I own a freakin' hamster."

"*Almost* own him. He is yours spiritually but not yet legally. He remains the property of this store until Mistress Ardath receives payment to sanctify his transfer."

"I've got to *buy* him?" Vivian eyed the hamster uneasily. The hamster continued to munch sunflower seeds, blissfully unperturbed by world politics, global warming, economic downturns, or the discussion currently in play over his fuzzy head. "Damn it, where's the store inventory? How much does he cost? Is she going to dock my pay over this? I can't afford that now! I can't afford that *ever*."

"Calm yourself." Jupiter licked on paw nonchalantly.

"Mistress Ardath never coerces sales. That would place her in violation of the Enchantment Place Chamber of Commerce rules. The customer's free will must be respected."

"That's a relief."

"However, there are no rules to prevent her from making your continued employment here as unpleasant as possible until such time as you bend to her will." A vole-eating grin curved the black cat's whiskers.

Vivian scowled. "If someone I could mention doesn't stop gloating, he's going to find a big dollop of dog food in his bowl tomorrow."

"Oh, boo-hoo, I'm *so* scared. Dog food, cat food, turtle snacks, lemur crunchies, it matters not. My life thus far in durance vile hasn't been a culinary pleasure cruise." Jupiter stuck his tongue out at Vivian, then became distracted and began licking himself. When he was spruced up to his satisfaction, he added: "Still, I suppose I shouldn't let you get away with insubordination. It's the principle of the thing. Very well, then: Mess with my food, and I tell Mistress Ardath that you've rendered our seed-stuffed friend unfit for sale."

"I'm going to let you in on a little secret, cat: you're not in a good bargaining position if you don't hold all the cards." Vivian went to the other side of the counter, where she began rearranging one of the store's floor displays of glossy black-and-silver feeding bowls. "It's not like we're alone here." She made a dramatic, sweeping gesture that took in the rows of cages lining Pet 2B Popular's back wall. Pair after pair of luminous, overly intelligent eyes leered out at the mortal girl from a dozen different breeds of familiar. "They all heard about Spooky, too, and most of them can talk. I've heard them. And the ones I think *can't* talk are probably playing possum about it. Especially that possum in the second row." She jabbed a finger at the specified marsupial, who gave her a dirty look before showing her his hindquarters. "Any one of them could narc me out in a heartbeat, so you can stop acting like you've got my fate in the palm of your—er, in the pad on your paw."

The big black cat merely began to purr. It was a resonant, compelling sound, one that slowly swelled in volume and intensity until Vivian was ready to swear that it had burrowed its way into the marrow of her bones and was now trying to shake her to pieces from the inside out. She opened her mouth to protest and discovered that her voice was gone. The purr had taken over her throat and was using her mouth as a secondary amplification system. Pair by pair, the glowing eyes of the other familiars began to close. Their breathing slowed, grew measured, and gently slipped into snores. Only the hamster continued to munch his sunflower seeds as though nothing had happened.

Jupiter stopped purring and met Vivian's astonished gaze. "I told you there was more to most familiars than companionship and small talk," he said. "Most of us have powers of our own. When a customer confers with Mistress Ardath, it's not to haggle privily over price. A wise witch knows that a familiar possessing just the right power of its own can be the difference between life and death for his mistress or master in a duel of sorcery. The skill I have thus so generously used on your behalf is my specialty. I am rather proud of it. It sends magical beings to sleep while it robs their minds of any . . . *inconvenient* memories. When my colleagues awaken, they won't recall our conversation about that little meatball." He flicked his whiskers forward, indicating the hamster.

Vivian peered into Spooky's cage. "Your power's slipping, Svengali. He's still awake."

"My power doesn't waste itself. If the hamster remains untouched, it must be because his memories are no threat to you," the cat replied smoothly.

"Really? Not that your power's imperfect?" Vivian shrugged. "Whatever. I've been working here for months and I still don't get all your little witchy rules."

"You don't even try," the cat countered.

"I've got better things to do. Okay, not *better*, but they're things I get paid for doing. That's all that matters to me."

"In that case, my money-grubbing friend, you should

have paid just a bit of attention to the Rule of Names. You'd have spared yourself all of the unpaid labor that's going to go with becoming my personal servant." Jupiter purred again, but this time it was a mundanely feline sound. "For starters, you will fetch me one can of sardines per day—skinless, boneless, and packed in olive oil. I will do my best to devour every morsel as quickly as possible, since you will have to clean up all vestiges of my daily feast lest Mistress Ardath catch wind of it. And believe me, even a nonwitch has little trouble catching wind of the presence of illicit sardines."

Vivian folded her arms and glared at Jupiter. "Did I ever tell you how much I hate blackmailers?"

"Did you ever do a price comparison on the cost of a can of sardines versus the cost of the hamster *you* made unsalable?" the cat replied sweetly.

Vivian sighed. "Skinless, huh?"

"And boneless." Jupiter licked his chops. "The Portuguese kind are the best, dear girl, and the best is none too good for me."

Vivian's indentured servitude to Jupiter had gone on for three weeks before everything went to hell in a hamster basket. The young Pet 2B Popular employee was taking her coffee break in the back room one fine spring afternoon when she heard a dreadful row from the front of the store. She emerged just in time to see Mistress Ardath, the shop's plump, elderly proprietor, confronting a tall, whiplash-slim man whose waist-length black hair and huge, violet eyes made him look like the illegitimate son of Elizabeth Taylor and the hero of one of the spicier *manga* epics.

"You'll regret this, Mistress Ardath, that much I promise you!" the man declaimed, dramatically laying a hand to the bosom of his nearly incandescent white suit. "This is not the way to run a successful business."

"It's the way I run *mine*," Mistress Ardath shot back. "*No* means *no*, whether it comes from the buyer's or the seller's lips."

"Then mark me well, there is *no* way I will be thwarted

in my desires. Good day to you, madam!" He spun on his heel and stalked out.

"Wow," Vivian said. "Who was that?"

"That was Master Jian, one of our more promising young warlocks. Unfortunately, what he *keeps* promising is to stop behaving like such an overgrown brat. He has yet to make good on that assurance. Just because he's young, handsome, powerful, and has enough charisma to make a supermodel eat a *whole* chocolate cheesecake, he believes that the world exists to give him his own way in everything." She smiled. "I didn't."

"So what did Master Jian want from you?"

"This." The witch rested one hand atop the hamster cage reposing on the counter.

"He wanted to buy S—the hamster?" Mistress Ardath nodded, her face serene. "But—but aren't you *supposed* to sell animals? Why'd you tell him no?"

"I was hoping that you would be the one to answer that question for me, Vivian, dear."

Vivian didn't need a dance card to know that the jig was up. She dropped her eyes, unwilling to meet her employer's kindly gaze. "I'm fired, aren't I?" she asked the floor.

"Do you deserve to be?"

"Don't play games with me. You're worse than he is. When did he tell you?"

"He?" Mistress Ardath sounded honestly puzzled.

"Jupiter."

Vivian heard a short, sharp intake of breath, then a strand of hastily muttered arcane syllables. She jerked her head up in time to see the effect of Mistress Ardath's spell: The black tomcat stood on the counter, his paws encased in glowing green booties. He shook them briskly, one by one, his whiskers quivering with wrath.

"What is the meaning of this outrage?" He raised a forepaw to his mouth and tried to bite the bootie, only to have a sharp starburst of white light sting his nose. He hissed his indignation.

"I apologize for the inconvenience," Mistress Ardath said in her most cajoling tones. "These are the esoteric

Chaldean Booties of Limitation. I wanted to bring you into the conversation without the affronting constraint of a cage, but I'm afraid I don't trust you enough to give you *unconditional* freedom. You might decide that it suits your purposes to use that hypnotic purr of yours on me, and I'm not in the mood for a nap."

"A wise move, madam," the cat said. "Now would you be so kind as to limit the witnesses to our little talk?" He waved one booty-sheathed paw at the back wall of cages where his colleagues crouched, eagerly listening in and observing the doings before them.

"But of course." Mistress Ardath rattled off a spell, and a gelatinous sea-green curtain fell across the entire back wall. A chorus of varied vocalizations rose up from the newly shrouded cages, but whether whimper, chirp, hiss, or mew, all were quite clearly the animal equivalent of *Aw, maaaaaannnnnn!*

"There." Mistress Ardath clasped her hands. "We can see and hear them, but they are unable to perceive us. Satisfied?"

"I suppose." The cat shrugged as well as he was able. "All right, let's get on with it. What's all this Chaldean be-bootied hugger-mugger about?"

"Our Vivian is under the impression that you've betrayed her trust in some manner."

The cat bristled. "And endanger my covert sardine supply? One whisper from me as to how the girl gave that seed-guzzling fuzzpuff a name, and I'd be back on a straight kibble diet! I'll thank you not to take me for a fool."

"Oh, you—you—you *fool*!" Vivian exclaimed, shaking a finger at Jupiter. "All she said was you'd snitched *in some manner*. She didn't say *how* you'd done it or about *what*, but you still went and spilled your guts so fast that—"

"Make one joke about violin factories, and I will smash your bones and drink the marrow in a milkshake," the cat said darkly.

"Vivian, dear, don't speak harshly to Jupiter." Mistress Ardath placed her hands on the girl's shoulders.

"Whether or not you laid claim to this creature by naming him, I never intended to sell him to Master Jian. I *could* not."

"Why?" Vivian packed her voice with disbelief, but privately she felt a surprising sense of relief that Spooky would remain in her life for a while longer.

"See for yourself." The proprietress of Pet 2B Popular stepped aside to give Vivian access to the cage. The girl stooped low and watched Spooky reposing happily on his fat rump, packing his face with food pellets, his eyes closed in gluttonous ecstasy.

"Hi, sweetie," Vivian murmured without thinking. At the sound of her voice the hamster stopped cramming food into his mouth and turned his drowsy gaze in her direction.

"So the bond does exist," Mistress Ardath remarked softly. Then, in a louder voice she said, "But it still makes no difference as to this beastling's marketability. Look at him more closely, Vivian. Tell me what you see."

Vivian wondered whether this was a trick question. She got her nose right up to the bars of the hamster's cage and stared. Spooky went about his business, oblivious. Straightening up, Vivian turned to Mistress Ardath and said, "Well, to be honest, there's not a lot to see in there. Just a hamster."

"Precisely!" Mistress Ardath looked as pleased as though Vivian had discovered the Fountain of Youth, the Hosepipe of Health, and the Spigot of Immortality, all wrapped up in one. "And because he is just a hamster, I could not in good conscience sell him to any of my magic-wielding colleagues. Pet 2B Popular sells *familiars*, and by official decree, every familiar must possess at least *one* supernatural talent of his own."

"Like my purr," Jupiter said proudly. "Before whose awesome might legions tremble and empires fall!"

"If you say so, dear," said Mistress Ardath.

"So that's why you wouldn't sell Spooky to Master Jian; because he's ordinary." *Like me,* Vivian thought.

Her boss nodded. "First I tried telling that snot-nosed

sorcerer that he simply wasn't the hamster type. Part of the qualifications for being a merchant of my sort is the ability to match the right witch with the right familiar. Compatibility is key to maximizing the success of all spells performed with the familiar's aid. The proper familiar can serve as a marvelous power amplifier for his or her human partner." She clicked her tongue. "I'm afraid he remained insistent about wanting the hamster, but I stuck to my guns. And it was true: Master Jian is not the hamster type. He's more ophidian."

"O-whatian? You mean he's Irish?"

"Ophidian," Jupiter repeated. *"Snakes,* Einstein."

"Indeed," said Mistress Ardath. "I offered him a lovely anaconda, but he'd have none of it."

"You should've just sold him the hamster and let him discover it was worthless on his own," Jupiter said.

"And ruin my commercial reputation?"

"Your *reputation?"* Vivian chimed in. "How about what that creep might've done to poor little Spooky once he discovered he'd been cheated?"

"You really *do* care about this creature, don't you?" Mistress Ardath regarded Vivian thoughtfully. "No wonder I sensed such a strong aura radiating from the hamster when that dreadful man first asked to see him! That was when I knew what must have happened between you two. As I told you, Jupiter is innocent of treachery."

"Does this mean I still get my sardines?" the cat demanded.

"No," said Mistress Ardath. Jupiter growled, but she ignored him. "Because there is true affection between you and—Spooky, was it?—I have decided to give him to you."

"Really?" Vivian hadn't known how much the little hamster meant to her until she heard his boss's offer and felt her heart rock with joy. "You mean it? He's mine for *free?"* A strange sound came from Spooky's cage. She saw the hamster standing on his haunches, holding onto the bars with his diminutive pink forepaws. Oddly, his cheek pouches looked slack and empty despite his recent food-stuffing marathon. *Probably unloaded them while I wasn't looking,* Vivian reasoned. She smiled at Spooky, who responded with a soft cheebling sound that was strangely encouraging.

Mistress Ardath chuckled. "Well, you will have to pay me *something*, else the transaction is not binding under the laws of Enchantment Place. Even a penny will do."

Vivian dug into the front pocket of her jeans and pulled out the fistful of change she'd been saving for her weekly visit to the laundromat. "Here, take it! Take all of it!" she cried happily, pressing the coins into her boss's hands.

"A princely sum, no doubt," Jupiter drawled. "Oh, for access to a word processor, that I might immortalize this touching moment into a Yuletide teleplay!"

"Jupiter, precious, if I approve a *small* sardine ration for you, will you stop being such a caustic kitty?" Mistress Ardath said. "You ought to feel happy for our friends. The affection between them is so intense, it creates cosmic emanations found only in the truest of witch-familiar bonds."

"Except Spooky's no familiar, and I'm no witch," Vivian put in.

"And you're probably not much of a witch yourself any more if you got stuck with a dud familiar!" Jupiter spat at Mistress Ardath. "A *small* sardine ration, forsooth? Pfui."

"Pish tosh," said Mistress Ardath, untroubled by the cat's snarkiness. "The truth is, telling good familiars from bad is not my calling. I am merely a merchant. I rely on others to provide my stock-in-trade. Within the society of witches, warlocks, wizards, and other practitioners of the magical arts are different levels of ability, prestige, and power, just as in the mundane realm. The lowest-ranking witch can sell familiars, but it takes one of far greater puissance to find and evaluate these talented creatures, to say nothing of persuading them to submit to the eventual bond of witch and familiar."

"What's so hard about that?" Vivian asked.

Jupiter laughed. "Are you kidding? Have you ever tried persuading an *ordinary* cat to do anything? Especially when it involves the word *submit?*"

"Such witches are known as Huntresses," Mistress Ardath went on. "They are very like those senior witches we call Dowsers, who go about seeking the hidden spark of magic in potential recruits for our own ranks. Dowsers and Huntresses both possess amazing skills and instincts, but they are not infallible. In their zeal to meet the ongoing demand for powerful yet amiable familiars, from time to time a Huntress will turn up . . . a dud." She looked at the hamster meaningfully. The hamster waddled back to the mound of pellets and sunflower seeds in his food dish and immersed himself.

"I'm kind of glad Spooky's *not* a familiar." Vivian looked fondly at her new pet.

"No creature that I sell *is* a familiar until it establishes a bond with its ordained human. Our Huntresses seek animals with familiar *potential*." She touched Spooky's cage. "Clearly *this* one's sole potential is to eat until he pops like a boiled cranberry. My goodness, just look at him shovel that food in!"

"He's not really *eating* everything that goes into his mouth," Vivian said. " 'Hamster' means 'hoarder' in German. Hamsters use their cheek-pouches like shopping bags. They pack them full of seeds and stuff, then unload them as soon as they're back in their homes." Seeing the astonished glances from Jupiter and Mistress Ardath, Vivian blushed a bit and added: "I've been reading up on hamsters ever since I started talking to—um, observing this one."

"That was a waste of time," Jupiter opined. "You could have been reading about cats." At this, the hamster made another of those weird cheebling sounds.

Vivian turned to Mistress Ardath. "Would it—would it be okay if I took him out of the cage? I won't let him get away, I promise."

"My dear, you needn't ask my permission. He's yours." Mistress Ardath jingled the handful of change Vivian had given her.

Very cautiously, Vivian unlatched Spooky's cage door and slid her hand inside. "Don't be scared, baby," she whispered. She gave a little cry of pleased surprise when the hamster hopped into her palm. The touch of his delicate paws was weirdly thrilling. *Man, if this is what does it for me, I have* got *to get out more,* she thought. She withdrew Spooky from the cage, cupped her other hand under him as well, and lifted him to eye level. She could have sworn she saw him smile, but it quickly turned into a vast, incisor-baring yawn. "If you're not the cutest thing I ever saw in my life—!"

"Which is over!"

A deep voice shook the walls of Pet 2B Popular. Sheets of iridescent blackness blossomed into being and swiftly flowed across the walls, ceiling and floors of the pet shop. Bronze fire flared from the spot where the front door once had stood. Backlit by that hellish radiance, Master Jian thrust his right arm straight at Vivian's heart.

"Hand over the hamster and no one gets hurt!" he declared. Then, in afterthought: "Except you. You, I kill."

"How *dare* you!" Mistress Ardath's hands began to glow pale purple, with silver sparks spitting from her fingernails. "This is a respectable place of business. Buy something or get out."

"I *tried* to buy something earlier, you cow!" Master Jian shouted. His raven hair writhed behind him like a nest of snakes. "Something I've wanted ever since I learned of its existence through my studies in forbidden lore. You turned me away, but I came back in hopes of . . . *persuading* you to reconsider."

"Persuading me or killing me?" Mistress Ardath gave him a cool look.

Master Jian's smile was as false as it was charming. "You must admit, madam, that death *is* the last word in any argument. But what have I returned to find? You, *giving* my prize to this—this—" he glowered at Vivian, *"—mortal."*

"She may be mortal, but she has established a bond with this creature," Mistress Ardath said huffily. "Something I doubt *you* ever could have done even if the hamster *were* good familiar material."

" 'Were'?" The man's dark brows met in perplexity. Then he threw his head back and erupted into laughter so loud that the black sheets of sorcerous malevolence sealing the pet shop shimmied wildly. "By the Spartan Municipal Abyss, and you call yourself a witch? Or has age dimmed your senses to the point where you have utterly no idea of the treasures under your own rent-controlled roof? Not good familiar material! Ha! That hamster holds the key to ultimate power, ultimate domination, ultimate—um, *ultimacy*! It must be mine!"

"If he says 'Mwahaha,' I'm going to hurl a hairball," Jupiter said *sotto voce.*

"What are you babbling about?" Mistress Ardath demanded. "This is a hamster like a thousand others. It's been in my store for twenty-two years now, and no takers. If there'd been anything extraordinary about it, you wouldn't be the first customer to come seeking—"

"*Twenty*-two years?" Vivian piped up. "Spooky's been in the shop for as long as I've been alive? But Mistress Ardath, *ordinary* hamsters only live to be two or three, at the most!"

Master Jian chortled. "Ah, Mistress Ardath, if your mortal minion knows more about your stock-in-trade than you do, you are getting too old for this business. You should give her a promotion. Oh, but wait. That won't work. You can't promote the *dead*." He hurled a bolt of killing energy at Vivian.

"You can in Chicago!" Mistress Ardath cried, deflecting it into a shower of harmless twinkling lights. Then she grabbed Jupiter with her right hand, seized Vivian by the back of her blouse with her left, and pulled them both down behind the counter. Vivian was so startled she lost her hold on Spooky, but the little hamster executed an amazing midair backflip and plunged into his new owner's cleavage before she could yelp.

No sooner had they all hit the floor than Master Jian launched a fresh barrage of fireballs, and the battle was on. Mistress Ardath filled the pet shop with the sonorous sound of a dozen shielding spells, setting up one mystic barricade after another against her opponent's attacks. Some crumbled at the first hit from the warlock's fiery assaults, others stood firm somewhat longer, resisting repeated hits, though in the end they, too, were smashed down. The counter itself transformed into a crystal wall studded with vicious-looking spikes, but Master Jian's unrelenting attacks soon blunted some and melted others clean away.

Knees drawn up to her chin, Vivian cowered at her embattled employer's side. When Spooky peeked up out of her neckline, she instinctively folded her hands over the hamster and turned her back on the crazed warlock. Hunching her shoulders, she tried to protect the tiny creature with her own body. "If he wants you, he's going to have to go through *me* to do it," she muttered into the hamster's petallike ear.

"I think that's the plan," Jupiter said. The black tomcat pressed himself against Vivian's legs. "Get these damned booties off me. Maybe I can purr that lunatic into submission."

"No—no use trying that." Mistress Ardath panted, on the brink of total exhaustion. "You'll only make him mad."

"Whereas *now* he's the picture of tranquility?" Jupiter said. "You know he's going to kill every living thing in this place except Spooky, then burn the store to the ground, and *then* build a new one just so he can go into it on opening day and kick all the puppies. Maybe I can't stop him, but I refuse to give up even one of my nine lives until I *try*! Now, get these bloody booties off me, woman!"

"Oh, for—!" Mistress Ardath barked out one more shielding spell, then grabbed for the laces on Jupiter's booties. She had barely touched them when Master Jian's magic pulverized both her spell and the counter.

Crystal dust filled the air, along with the young warlock's malicious laughter: "Bwahaha!"

"Was that 'Bwahaha' or 'Mwahaha'?" Jupiter asked. "Because I know what I said I'd do if he went 'Mwahaha,"

and I don't want to go to all the trouble of hacking up
a hairball if it wasn't—"

"Silence! You'll hack up your next hairball . . . *in
hell*!" Master Jian strode forward, his hands spilling over
with what looked like the madly burbling, unholy hybrid
offspring of sulfuric acid, white-hot magma, and boiled
okra. As he prepared to hurl this seething, reeking doom,
Vivian sprang to her feet, reached into her cleavage, and
pulled out her hamster.

"Stop!" she cried. "Here's what you're after. I give
him to you freely. Now kill me if you must, but leave
Mistress Ardath and Jupiter alone!"

Master Jian took a half step back and gave Vivian a
hostile look. "Who do you think you are, miserable
wench, to tell *me* whom to spare and whom to destroy?
How dare you presume to *give* me what it is my right
to *take*?"

"Have it your way, gerbil-brain," said the hamster, and
leaped from Vivian's hand. He landed at Master Jian's
feet and scurried forward, grabbing the toe of one blind-
ingly polished shoe firmly with both forepaws.

Then he opened his mouth.

It all happened fast, so incredibly fast that Vivian
blinked once and missed the part where Master Jian's
torso disappeared into Spooky's left cheek pouch, though
she did see the part before that, when the young warlock's legs shot into the hamster's right cheek with the
speed of an anchor plunging into the depths of the Mari-
anas Trench. She also had a clear view of the climax of
Spooky's uncanny stuffathon: With a last ditch effort
from halfway into the bizarre hamster's gullet, Master
Jian raised his hands, still fuming with the unflung destruction spell, and shot it at Spooky point blank.

The hamster merely opened his mouth a fraction wider
and the unspeakably devastating magic was sucked into
oblivion, followed almost immediately by Master Jian's
arms, neck, and frantically shrieking head. Then came
silence, punctuated by the faint, unique sound of a hamster belching.

The last of the crystal dust from the shattered shop

counter drifted to earth. The hamster sat on his haunches and began to groom his fur. His cheek pouches remained undistended, his cobby body the same. And yet, the warlock was gone.

"Oh, my," said Mistress Ardath. "That explains why Master Jian wanted *this* hamster. Such a wondrous power! Even the most potent, all-obliterating spell, gulped down like a sunflower seed! Any witch with *that* on her side could rule the world!"

"So that's why Jupiter's magical purr had no effect on Spooky," Vivian murmured. "He swallowed it." She glanced at the cat. "You're lucky he didn't swallow you."

"Can I go back in my cage now?" Jupiter quavered. "Where it's safe? Please?"

Vivian knelt before the hamster. "You can talk," she said.

"Among other things." Spooky sounded amused.

"Why didn't you talk before now?"

"Chatty familiars are a dime a dozen. Besides, *you* needed a good listener." The hamster stroked sparkling dust out of his whiskers, then groomed his belly ferociously. "Plus, I didn't have anything worth saying until now. Just because you *can* do something doesn't mean you *must*. You of all people ought to know that, or else why haven't you bothered to exercise *your* powers?"

"What powers?" Vivian felt as though someone had strapped her onto the world's craziest zero-G merry-go-round.

"Sweet lady, I'm a familiar; a familiar whose powers are now fully realized and complete. That doesn't just *happen* in the wild."

"It's true," Jupiter put in timidly. "When a witch finds the familiar that's her perfect match, their powers complement each other. Only then do *both* of them achieve their full potential."

"Our little Vivian, an undetected witch! How exciting!" Mistress Ardath sounded positively giddy with joy. "I've got a Dowser on speed dial. I'll have her come over right away to verify—" She dashed toward the back room, only to come up against the cloaking spells that

Master Jian had used to seal the room. Their posthumous durability was a tribute to their late master's skills. "Oh, my. Spooky, dear, I don't suppose you'd mind devouring these for me? I could do it myself, but I'd have to figure out the exact spell used to create them in the first place, and that might take some time."

The hamster made a courtly bow. "Your wish is my lunch, madam." The spells vanished down his maw in a heartbeat, followed by the sight-and-sound-baffling enchantment Mistress Ardath herself had cast over the familiars' cages earlier.

"Gracious," said the proprietor of Pet 2B Popular. "I've never felt so glad that I always fed you the premium brand of hamster chow." She ducked into the back room. Ears flattened, tail tucked, belly brushing the ground, Jupiter scurried after her.

Spooky looked at Vivian and smiled. "So how's it feel to know you're not a dud, either?"

"Pretty good." She offered him her hand. When he got aboard, she stood up again. "But not as good as I'm going to feel. Spooky, how would you like to come with me on a little trip?"

"Where to?"

"My stepfather's place. You remember hearing me talk about him, right? The one who said I *made* him hit me? The one who claimed that he had the right to do *anything* he wanted to me because he paid the bills? The one who said that the way I dressed and talked and acted all meant I was 'asking for it,' so whatever *he* did was all *my* fault?"

"You bet I do." The hamster gnashed his teeth and prickled up like a miniature porcupine. "I never understood how he expected anyone to swallow all those lies."

Vivian grinned as she carried her new familiar out the door. "Try."

HEART'S FIRE

Sarah A. Hoyt

Sarah A. Hoyt has sold over sixty short stories to such markets as *Weird Tales*, *Analog*, *Asimov's* and *Amazing*. These days her short-story writing takes a backseat to her novels—the magical British Empire series (starting with *Heart Of Light*); the Shifters series (starting with *Draw One In The Dark*); the space opera (starting with *DarkShip Thieves*); and, under Sarah D'Almeida, the Musketeers' Mysteries (starting with *Death Of A Musketeer*.) Sarah lives in Colorado and, when not typing furiously, can be found plotting (never mind what) with her husband, minigolfing with her teen sons, or rolling around with her pride of cats.

A cold wind blew in off Lake Michigan sprinkling a fine, freezing drizzle over the city of Chicago.

It was so overcast that the magically suspended El cars, riding the air above the city on a charmed path, barely cast a shadow on the buildings and bundled-up passersby below. Too cold for May, and local businesses were feeling the sting of the weather.

The Chicago Institute of Arcane Art, normally a hub of magician-artists the world over, looked empty and closed for the day.

And in a little jewelry shop tucked inconspicuously

between the familiar store and Steel Crazy, Ausenda Cuorefueco reached discreetly for the paperback romance tucked in her purse. She wedged it under the glass counter, at an angle, so no customers would see it. Should a customer come in, of course, she thought sullenly looking up and through the narrow door with its gothic lettering proclaiming *Heart's Fire—Enchantment From The Old Country.*

Around her, as she bent her head over her book, sparkled a fortune in jewels—pearls with a butter-soft sheen that would never fade; rubies that appeared to be on fire; diamonds that looked like a bit of sunlight captured and shown off to advantage against black velvet. The funny thing was that if those were the only ones in the store, her father would probably not have made Ausenda miss her classes at the university to sit here, on this dank, rainy day, waiting for customers who'd never come. Just because her mother was ill—or suffering from those hypochondriac complaints to which all great witches were subject—and her dad had to go to Gary to do something or other at their lapidary, it shouldn't have meant Ausenda had to be confined in the store for the day.

The store had adequate enough protection—both mundane and arcane. An alarm would sound at the police station if anyone so much as breathed on the glass cases while the store was closed. And through the Fate Protection Agency, an Erynis would follow the luckless thief until he returned what he'd taken or was driven mad. And besides, her father was a strong sensitive. He would be able to foresee danger. And plan for it.

But the problem was not with these beautiful and expensive trinkets so openly displayed. The whole reason for Ausenda's father to have her here was the door at her back. That door, which only opened to customers who asked specifically for the arcane jewels and who passed her dad's magical scan, led into a small dark room. There, more jewels were displayed on velvet cushions, each surrounded by a magical field to keep them from interfering with each other. These jewels, Ausenda's mother's work, were charmed. Charmed for happiness or wealth or who knew what else. And they could be sold only to people with magical power and, further, people with magical power who would know how to control it. Which meant people who could interfere with foretellings. People who could disguise a break in with magic. A good sensitive like Ausenda's father was needed to keep the trinkets from falling in the wrong hands. And even he might not be enough.

Which, Ausenda thought peevishly, glaring down at the book where the main character had just refused an offer of marriage, was a reason it was so stupid to leave her in charge of the store. She might be her parents' only child, but she was also the first Cuorefueco in generations uncounted to have not even a glimmer of magical power. Which was why she was studying accounting at college. She would be able to help with keeping the store going, but for the main part of it—for the charms and the attending at the store and all—her parents would need to hire someone.

And it was no use at all for them to continually try to match her with this sorcerer or another. So and so's nephew and such and such's cousin were always being dragged home for dinner by hopeful parents. And she knew it was no use at all.

Oh, it's not that she was ugly. Though she'd never consider herself pretty, she was small and neat enough, with a pleasing figure, oval face and long, straight dark hair. Her one beauty was her eyes, gray and soft, like evenly sparkling silver.

But even if she'd been the most beautiful woman to ever walk the Earth, she knew better than to get into a relationship with a sorcerer—even those who showed interest. A mortal in love with a magical being always got the short end of the stick. Always.

Ausenda started to lift her leg to cross it, and the movement—so easy in the jeans she normally wore—was arrested by the sight of the tightly cut gray skirt she was stuck with today. She sighed, putting her leg down, and was adjusting the skirt when the magical chimes on the door tinkled. And she looked up into the face of the most handsome man she'd ever met.

It wasn't an exaggeration, either, or one of those things that romance novelists said. The man wasn't very tall. Probably just on six feet. His shoulders weren't massive, though they were decently straight and square. And his body wasn't muscle bound, rather long and lank, like the statue of a renaissance shepherd.

The face, on the other hand, was aristocratic—longer than it was broad, with an aquiline nose, well-shaped mouth, and broad soft eyes like brown suede, all of it framed in golden brown curls and a neatly shaped golden brown beard.

He wore jeans and a sweatshirt and looked like a college student who had accidentally wandered in to ask for directions or to see if he could use the restroom. But even though the sweatshirt read, in garishly golden letters "Magicians do it enchantingly," he wore the broad platinum ring of a magus major. Which meant he was the sort of magician kings and presidents hired. And more than wealthy enough to buy the whole store if he wished, the room at the back included.

Ausenda dropped her book. "How . . ." she found her voice failing and called herself several kinds of stupid, even as she coughed to clear her throat and tried again. "How may I help you?"

He smiled widely. "I've come . . . in search of the fire in the heart."

She knew what the words meant. It was just the first of the long sequence that a shopper had to go through to gain admittance to the little door behind Ausenda. And yet the words themselves made her jump a little, and she told herself she was a fool and a total idiot. Fortunately, she was fairly sure her expression hadn't changed at all. She shook her head slightly and said, "I'm sorry. Not today. My father isn't here."

He came closer. She could smell his scent—pine with a hint of something spicy. "Why do you need your father?" he asked. "Can't you scan me yourself?" He smiled, showing very even teeth.

Ausenda shook her head regretfully. "No magical power at all, you see. I'm just a mortal."

"Ah," he said, as though doubting it. "But you're a Cuorefueco, aren't you?"

She shrugged. "Just a throw back," she said. "It happens." And then, defiantly, as though it helped explain everything, "I'm studying to be an accountant."

"Ah," he said again, and for a moment stood there, smiling at her, as though expecting her to give him the punch line to a joke he couldn't quite get.

But Ausenda could not explain it any better than she had, and she wasn't about to try. She'd heard the question many times, in many forms, since she was six, when her grandmother had despaired of finding any talent in her and had given up on teaching her. And there was no explanation for it. Yes, she was a Cuorefueco, and her mother came from one of the oldest lines of witches in Italy as well. Her ancestresses had foretold the future to Caesar himself.

And yet Ausenda, neat and small and not bad to look at, was perfectly normal. A perfectly common girl born of a magical family. And the problem was that no normal man would marry her. Her family would scare him off. And no sorcerer would have her—or rather many would, for the name and the business, but she knew they'd always see her as handicapped, and she didn't want to be pitied by the man she married.

"Well, my best wishes, then, signorina, for your accounting career," the brown-haired man said, and bowed a little, in an old fashioned, courtly gesture.

The door chime tinkled, and he was gone.

Ausenda looked at her book and frowned, wondering why he'd smiled so teasingly as he left. Perhaps he still thought her lack of power was a joke.

"Gone, Ausenda. The Heartbeat ruby is gone. Who did you let in, luckless girl?"

Father in a temper was not easy to take. He was a small man and as self-contained looking as Ausenda herself. In his dark, well cut suit, he looked like a diplomat or a chief executive. Not someone who should stand there, hands clasped to his distinguished graying hair, face flushed with panic. "Who did you let in?"

"To that room?" Ausenda asked, putting her book away and picking up her purse. "No one, Father."

"Someone you must have let in. The Heartbeat ruby is gone. Who was here? Who came? What customers?"

"No one," Ausenda said, then remembered the smiling man, with the brown curls. "Well, someone came in, but only one person, and he wasn't a customer."

Her words so managed to surprise her father that he was quiet for just a moment, and into that quiet, she said, "At least, he couldn't be, because he wanted to go into the small room, and I told him I didn't have the authority to open it."

"And yet you must have opened it, Ausenda," her father said.

She knew that was true. Only a family member could open that lock. But she also knew she hadn't. "But I didn't, Father."

"Did you let yourself be mesmerized? Did you open it while hypnotized?"

"No, Father. I didn't look at his eyes long enough for that, and I didn't stare at any jewel for him, and he didn't give me anything to read or . . . " She stopped and faltered.

Her father sighed. "You were reading your trashy romances again, weren't you?"

"Yes, but—"

"Did you buy it used?"

"Yes, but—" She said, reaching for her purse.

Before she could get it, her father had, and he'd pulled out the battered little paperback. He dropped it just as quickly on the floor and stepped on it. "It's dripping with mesmerizing magic, Ausenda."

"I'm sorry . . . I couldn't . . . I can't see it."

'Yes, but you brought it into the shop. When you know you can't see. This was a planned theft. Organized."

Ausenda thought of the man's teasing smile. An out-law? A rogue magician? A thief? She couldn't believe any of those. But then, no one was asking her to believe. The facts spoke for themselves.

"Well . . . I'm sorry. Was it worth . . . much?"

Her father looked at her as if she'd wounded him mor-tally. "It's not how much it is worth," he said, falling into a chair behind the counter and putting his face in his hands. "It's charmed jewelry, Ausenda. Charms are stupid. They tend to be very literal. The average witch, the way she'd spell jewelry . . . well . . . spell it for wealth, and the poor buyer would end up suffocating under paper money while the armored car passing through is emptied. But your mother . . . your mother doesn't spell things that way. Her charms are still flexible, but they work. They work well. Her charms in the hand of a dishonest man . . ."

Ausenda might not be a witch, but she had enough imagination to picture that. Her hair stood on end. "What was Heartbeat spelled to do?"

Her father shook his head. "I don't know. Your mother did it just last night, before she fell ill. It's a large ruby, shaped like a heart and set as a pendant on a chain. I don't know what she meant it for. Could be for any-thing. Healing illness of the heart or . . . anything."

What healed heart defects could also cause them. "Can you call the police?" Ausenda asked. "Or . . . the arcane detectives? Can you?"

But her father looked up, his eyes burning dark, "What good would it do us if he's a sorcerer and he covered his tracks? You must find him, Ausenda. You're the only one who saw him. It's next to impossible, but since you saw him and had contact with him, you might be able to follow his power."

Ausenda nodded. "Right. I'll got a fortune-teller and I—"

"No," her father yelled. "No fortune-teller. You must do all the arcane work yourself. Half of these witches around here are onto something shady. You must do the search yourself."

"But father, I have no power."

"I don't really care, girl. You lost the jewel, and you must find it. Think of what that man might do with it."

Ausenda stood outside the shop, the cold wind biting through her gray wool skirt suit. There had to be a way. There had to be something she could do. Her father said she couldn't go to a fortune-teller. And that was true. And she didn't have magic—oh, her grandmother had been furious at her and said she had magic and was hiding it, but that was just because Grandma refused to admit any of her descendants might be born without magic.

But there were things, after all, that even normal women did. Magic so simple even the mundane could do them. What she needed was a junk shop. One of those places that sold tarot cards and tea leaves and what not to those completely devoid of power.

Minutes later, she was sitting in her small studio apartment looking at the tea leaves at the bottom of the cup, while she looked in the small book she had bought, which showed her the configurations of the leaves and what they meant.

She swirled the three tablespoons of liquid left in the cup, and frowned at the results.

There were the oval shapes that she knew meant love, but what could that have to do with the situation at hand. And besides, she felt as if the tea leaves were being snide. She'd liked him very much, but it was far from love, and if he was a crook . . .

She swirled the tea again and wondered where the man was and who he was. This time the shapes that came up were what her grandmother had called airplanes. A little cross with the side arms a little bent. The man had either traveled recently or was about to travel. Both could be true. Perhaps he was hastening home to give a heart attack to his rich uncle. Perhaps . . . but let's assume no. Let's assume he had traveled here. That made sense, at least if he really was a magus major. She had never seen him before, and magicians of that rank were known—and respected—in the region where they lived. Which of course made one ask how he could be a crook. But then again, who could explain the quirks of men. She thought of his smile. He might very well be in it for the adventure. He seemed the type. Right.

For now she'd assume that ring was real. And she'd assume he was in town for a short time, maybe just to steal the ruby.

Her school friend Jack worked for the arcane crimes lab unit at the police department. She couldn't tell him the ruby was missing—well, at least if she didn't feel like being skinned alive by her father. But she could—and would—ask him about any new magus major in town. People above a certain level of power always registered with the police, in case their power caused disturbances on magically operated machinery.

She got him with the first ring of his private number. His rough, low voice calmed her some. They'd been friends since elementary school, and if Jack hadn't been snagged by a first class witch in the last year of high school, Ausenda would have taken him, difference in power or not. "Jack, it's Ausenda. Yeah, yeah, I'm fine. Just a question. Is there a new magus major in town?"

"Why? Is mama trying to bring someone over for dinner again?"

Ausenda opened her mouth to protest, closed it, put on her most bored, petulant tone, "She says he's Aunt Maria's first husband's sister's grandson and that he's a magus major, but I don't even know his name or if he's single, or . . ."

Jack chuckled. "They're never going to give you an out till you marry, you know? You should have married me while you could."

"Yeah, yeah," she said. "Missed my chance. How is Erin?"

"Fine. And the twins, they're so big. And starting to talk. Just yesterday, little Tristan—"

Ausenda listened for a moment to the adventures of Jack's twins, whom the proud father called *the redheaded monsters*. When she could get a word in edgewise without offending him mortally, she said, "So, the magus."

"Ah, him . . . His name is Zeus. Zeus Olympius. Don't laugh. Nice Greek family up New York way, and the parents clearly had a sense of humor."

"Okay . . . and what does he specialize in?"

"Ah . . . well, that might be why your mom has an interest. He works for the government. Spelling currency."

"Why would my mother have an interest in that?" Ausenda asked, even as she wrinkled her brow, wondering why someone who worked for the treasury department would need to steal a ruby.

"He makes it so that the currency can't be copied or counterfeited or altered. From there to spelling charms . . ."

Yeah, it was a step, and the question remained why he would need to get a jewel spelled by someone else. Unless, of course, he wanted to commit a crime with it and didn't want the magic traced back to himself.

She must find him without delay.

Sometimes the best magic was no magic at all. Ausenda had spent half an hour on the phone calling the best hotels in Chicago. He might be under an assumed name, but being a magus major might make that difficult. There were only a couple dozen of them, nationwide. The ring couldn't be removed, though it could be spelled invisible. But their power couldn't be hidden or damped. And there was a whole protocol they had to follow while traveling to avoid causing greater trouble. So chances were he was lodging under his very distinctive name.

The bet paid off. At the seventh hotel, the famed Four Seasons, she struck gold. Mr. Zeus Olympius was indeed renting a room there, but he had absented himself for a few moments. Would Miss like to leave a message?

Sure. Miss would like to tell the dirty stinky rat to give her back her father's ruby. But she couldn't do that. So she declined politely and hung up.

Now she must go see him at the hotel. Chances were

that he wouldn't want anything to do with her. That was too bad, as she couldn't hope to fool a magus major. No one could. However, if she could come to his room unannounced, before he could do a foreseeing . . . Of course, no hotel employee was going to let an unknown woman climb to the room of a man without calling him. And no one would give her a key. Unless . . .

Well . . . there were kits at the junk shop. For simple glamories and enchantments and even mesmerization. She went back.

"As you see," she told the slim, young hotel employee who looked, dazedly, down at the spelled note she'd put in his hand, "Mr. Zeus Olympius asked that you give me a key, so I can meet him for a very . . . confidential reason."

She batted her eyelashes a little, letting the hotel employee think it was a special meeting of *that* kind. Maybe it would stop him from thinking twice about the mechanics of the whole thing. That is, if the note worked at all. With junk shop kits, you never knew.

But the young man flushed and nodded and swallowed hard. He was maybe all of nineteen and clearly intimidated at the thought of aiding in a clandestine affair. Or perhaps only of aiding in a magus major's clandestine affair. He went to the counter and gave her the key, eyes averted. She took advantage of his embarrassment to grab the note and stuff it in her pocket. It had done its job, and, really, she didn't want someone finding it and its random combination of letters and asking the young man why he'd thought it said to give the strange lady a key.

It was a generic mesmeric note, copied from the kit. The boy had simply read the words she'd told him to read.

With the note in her pocket, she crossed the brown and gold marble atrium rapidly and headed up the broad staircase. The room, the employee had mumbled, was on the third floor. The elevator would be quicker, but an elevator was all too easy for a magus to jam.

Up and up and up, past opulent gold-leafing, across miles of Persian carpet, and down the corridor to room 333. She held her breath a little until the key worked, then went in.

For just a moment, she was breathless at the room itself, all brocade and ornate furniture. It had something of the regal about it.

What it didn't have was any of Zeus' personal belongings. No suitcase, no clothes. She looked, even in the closet. Nothing. The rat had flown the trap.

Sure she had lost him forever, she looked again, carefully. He couldn't have taken everything. He had to have left behind some clue or something.

She found it when she'd almost despaired of it, hidden almost completely beneath the rich red dust ruffle. A handkerchief. Fine lawn, elegantly monogrammed ZO.

As she picked it up in her hand, an image formed in the air, above the bed. It was Zeus, grinning—that infuriating grin. The words *Catch me if you can* formed in her mind.

For a moment, she was frozen in white-hot fury. He was taunting her.

She was no witch. Her grandmother had once told her she had as much magical sensitivity as a coal bucket. But if there was one thing Ausenda wasn't ready to do, it was let anyone mock her.

This handkerchief was supposed to give a real witch a clue to where the man had gone. Magus major couldn't help it. Their power was so great they left a mile-wide trail. But she was not a witch. And yet, she'd used those kits, and she'd discovered most of what she really, really needed to do, it was concentrate. Perhaps she only had vestigial power, but she could concentrate like nobody's business.

She sat, clutching the handkerchief and concentrating. After a long, long time, a picture of the Sears' tower Skydeck formed in her mind. Was it just wishful thinking, or had he really gone there?

Well . . . did it matter? If he hadn't, she'd lost the trail anyway. She stuck the handkerchief in her purse, closed it, and took the elevator down—if he stopped her doing that, at least she'd know where he was and what he was up to.

But the elevator went all the way to the lobby without disturbance, and, deciding that the occasion justified the expense, she hailed a cab to the Loop.

She got out in front of the soaring golden tower, ran into the lobby, bought a ticket to the Skydeck and took the levitating elevators up. All the while a little voice in her head told her she was a fool and was going only on an hunch and power she didn't have.

The elevators went up very fast. They were known for it. Slamming all the way into the Skydeck. The sky deck was one of the attractions of Chicago, and normally in May, at sunset, it would be crowded with families and cuddling couples. This time there was only one person there. His back was turned as he stood by the railing, looking out over the city.

The wind ruffled his brown curls.

"Thief," Ausenda said, under her breath. She hadn't meant to speak. The truth was, the word that had escaped her lips was the end of a thought that went *How can he be no more than a common thief?*

The word, spoken aloud startled her, but he only turned around slowly, comfortably. Mischief danced in his eyes, and his cheeks were reddened by the cold wind off the lake. Around his neck was a chain with the heart shaped ruby.

"So you found me," he said. "And I thought you weren't a witch."

"I'm not," she said.

"Well . . . that is terrible for you then, because you certainly cannot do anything to stop a magus major. I shall fly out of here and head home, where you can't follow me. You'll never recover the ruby." He touched it lovingly, with his hand, then got atop the railing and suddenly, effortlessly, spread his arms and . . . started floating away.

No. He couldn't get away. Not with the ruby. Blindly, madly, Ausenda reached for him and grabbed. Not with her arms. She could feel something else—a force, emanating from her and holding, grabbing. She didn't know what it was, but she felt as if her whole being were enveloping him, fighting him.

The effort of it, the mad effort brought her to her knees, panting and crying with tiredness and determination. She would never let him go. Never. And she didn't care if it was magus major power fighting her or not. She would die rather than let him get away.

As she thought this, there was a wrench, and he was pulled back, midair, to land on the deck full force, like a landed fish.

She put her hand out to the ruby and touched it. It felt warm, living, like skin. She opened her eyes.

The ruby was throbbing, shining, its light bathing the entire deck. Zeus was looking at her—and he didn't look at all as a foiled villain should look. He didn't even look like someone just forcefully plucked out of midair. He was looking at her, his eyes soft.

And the light of the ruby was doing something odd. She should feel angry. She should feel . . .

Zeus took a deep breath and extended his hand oh so slowly. She thought he was going to wrench the ruby from her hand, but instead he rested his hand atop hers. "It worked, you see?" He grinned. "You can have it now if you wish. It has done its job."

He reached up weakly, his hands trembling slightly, as from great tiredness, and removed the chain. He put it around her neck.

"I don't understand," she said.

He blushed a little and looked away. "Yesterday I came to your father. I wanted a jewel for a special purpose."

"What? No. You came today and you stole . . ." Ausenda paused. Everything that had made no sense in the day, from her father's leaving her in charge of the store to his insisting she find the ruby alone . . . everything seemed to make no sense. Unless there was something she didn't know.

"I came to your father. I am a magus major. I don't lack for women interested in me. All sorts of women. But they're interested in me for all the wrong reasons. For wealth or power or prestige. And none of them has a power to match mine."

"So your father did a foretelling . . ."

"And?"

"And then he told me who my perfect match was. And your mother charmed this ruby . . . to bring us together."

"But . . . I am not a witch. How can I have a power to match yours?"

"Ausenda, today you foretold and far saw. And you held back a magus major when he tried to fly away."

"But . . . I was just doing what I had to do," she said confused. "And it's not true, anyway. I mean . . . My grandmother tried. I had no power. She said I must have, but that was only because . . . I'm her granddaughter and she couldn't believe . . ."

"Your father says he's read the family history. Some women of your line don't get their powers until they find their perfect mate."

She looked at him, and her mind clouded with confusion. He was so handsome. Quite the most handsome man she'd ever seen. And yet . . . "You lied to me."

He nodded. "How else could I get you to see the lies you were telling yourself? That you weren't a witch, that you had no power, that no one would ever want to marry you for love?"

She got up. She had no answer for that, and not having an answer made her feel angry. And feeling angry made her embarrassed at her irrationality. She dusted her gray skirt angrily and went to stand by the railing. "I'm not going to fall into your arms just because my father and a ruby say I should."

He came to stand next to her, standing by the railing, looking out at the overcast skies over the city. "Of course not," he said calmly. "I would never expect you to."

"And I'd never have the slightest interest in you just because you're a magus major."

He made a sound that might be hastily suppressed chuckles disguised as coughing. "I'm not asking you to. On the contrary. I have had plenty of interest in the magus major. I want someone interested in Zeus Olympius."

"That," she said, "is a ridiculous name."

"Yes," he said, with heartfelt sincerity. "And you may tell my parents so when you meet them."

It was her turn to disguise a chuckle. She didn't need foretelling to know how this would end. But she would make him work for it.

THE DEVIL YOU KNOW

Susan Sizemore

New York Times bestselling author Susan Sizemore loves to shop, and she used to live in Chicago. So how could she resist contributing a story to *Enchantment Place*? When not shopping, or writing, she is knitting.

I go by the name Vicki McCoy. Mainly because had I wanted a career as a pole dancer, I would use the name my mother gave me, which is Vixen, but I became a law student instead. Now, I understand why Mom named me Vixen; it was in honor of a Japanese fox spirit that helped her out of a jam. I have nothing against the name Vixen except that it doesn't belong in the real world. Unfortunately, the real world was not the place where I was going shopping.

In case you haven't guessed by now, my mom's a witch. In the very best sense of the word. It's a family tradition that goes back to "time out of mind" as great grandma used to say. Now that old girl was one hell of a witch with no pun intended—but that's another story. One that we simply do not discuss in the family because, well—

Anyway, my shopping trip was related to the old girl in a way. You see, Mom's birthday was coming up, and she'd been pining for a new-fangled fairy-wing spell that's all the rage among the cauldron set. Mom's been

57

using a broom and great grandma's flying spell for as long as she's had an airborne permit. Brooms have become totally passé since the whole Harry Potter thing got going. Now, back in the sixties, when Mom was a teenager and *Bewitched* was on the air, brooms were considered cool. Not so now, and she wanted wings for her birthday.

I wanted to take her to a spa, or indulge her in any number of mundane activities, but no, all she wanted from me was a pair of wings. She couldn't ask my sister or brother who are both in the life for this present. For some reason it had to come from me. Apparently this was her way of making me show I'm not as mundane as I really am. She rarely pulls this sort of thing. Like I said, she's a good witch, and a great mom.

And because I love her, and I'd been putting it off, and her birthday party was that evening, I got in a cab and headed north on Michigan Avenue. I might live in the real world but I knew where I had to go, and it wasn't to Diagon Alley. They do things far more upscale in the witchy world my relatives hang out in.

There's a place near the Hancock Building. You have to cross a wide plaza to a building with a shiny gray marble façade. But instead of entering the wide and welcoming doors of this urban shopping Mecca you turn around widdershins as fast as you can. If you aren't dizzy when you come to a stop, you haven't done it right. Once your head is spinning look to the left out of the corner of your eye, and you'll see a green door. Approach it, and be prepared for anything. I did, and I was. I used to go shopping here with my mom when I was a kid, after all.

I was glad to see that the doorman was in human form today although I had brought dog biscuits along just in case. I used to be terrified when Cerberus stood guard at the portal when I was little. There's something about acid-drooling three-headed dogs that tends to bring out the tears in impressionable children—and nightmares for years to come. I hadn't been looking forward to facing the dog-glamour even as an adult.

"This is a private entrance, miss," the doorman announced when I approached.

I smiled pleasantly. "Yes, I know."

He gestured toward the mundane mall entrance. "I believe you're more likely to find what you're looking for—"

"I really won't." I continued smiling. Frustration and petulance might get some girls what they want in this life, but I see no reason to be unpleasant to persons who are just doing their jobs. "I know I must look a bit mundane." I gestured to indicate my outfit, which was sensible in the way no other member of my family would be caught dead in. However, the top couple of buttons of my pearl gray shirt were undone, so a bit of cleavage was showing for the doorman to notice. "You dog," I said when his gaze drifted to my bosom.

"Yes, ma'am," he responded with a grin. He stepped aside to open the door for me.

Once I sailed past this first level of security, I stood in the wide entrance atrium and took in the changes to a place I hadn't been to in years. It had changed, of course. It's a shopping center, stores come and go. Mind you, the very nature of this place is more chaotic than commercial. Magical duels had been fought over occupancy space, though I believe that sort of thing was better regulated these days. The merchants had decided that all that death and destruction and necromancy wasn't good for business. It did my heart good to know that the bottom line counted for something even in the heart of this strangeness.

The place had a sleeker look to it than I remembered, with a lot of copper and Southwestern pastels décor. There was a tiled fountain bubbling in the center of the atrium and a great many potted plants and palm trees around the edges. Bright colors flashed as tropical birds swooped through this landscape. I saw some frogs hanging around the edge of the fountain and quickly skirted the area. Who needed catcalls and lewd promises from a bunch of slimy amphibians with nowhere else to hang out?

Though I didn't recognize any of the stores I passed, I let my nose lead me to one very familiar first floor establishment. Dead Man's Bones is one of the finest bakeries on this plane of existence. Don't let the name turn you off; their product is made strictly from organic grain and honey and other natural ingredients, although what they use to grind the flour with I do not know and never want to find out. The warm, yeasty aroma that filled the air as I approached the place was heady enough to make me drunk. Many fine memories surfaced, and my stomach rumbled with desire at the thought of the ginger cookies I could hardly wait to purchase.

Only when I walked into the bakery, the place was empty. The lights were on, piles of crusty bread and tempting pastries lay locked away in the cases, but there was no one there to help me. I waited around for a while. I called out for help. I waited and called some more, but no one appeared to take my order. I was crushed, devastated, but I'm not one to allow nostalgia to get in the way of necessary errands. I reminded myself that all those magically delicious baked goods still contained enough carbs, fat and calories to paste aircraft carriers onto my hips, and I went about my business. Okay, I will admit to one momentary urge to break into a case and pull a snatch and grab, but I generally don't give in to my evil tendencies.

I found a mall directory and looked up the locations of the sort of stores that carried the kind of spell mom wanted. There were three, one here on the first level, one on the second, and one that kept changing locations. Magic shops that regularly pop in and out of multiple planes of existence may be the material for great fantasy stories, but they are no fun to shop in. Imagine the worst bout of nausea you have ever had, then pile a massive dose of seasickness on top of it and add the hangover from hell. That's how you're going to feel when you stagger out of one of those places if you're a magical amateur like me. So I immediately crossed that shop off my list and headed for the spell store on the first level.

I should point out that the mall was not busy. I saw a

few people going in and out of stores, but there was no crush of shoppers to make the place look like a weekend at Woodfield. There were a few people perusing the aisles of Magus Spells and Potions when I walked in, and each of them had a clerk helping them. Knowing exactly what I wanted, I went up to the main counter. There were three clerks standing behind it. None rushed up to ask if he or she could help.

I waited for a moment before I said, "Excuse me, I'm looking for a flying spell."

Nothing. Nada. Zip. No one even looked my way. This certainly wasn't customer service at its finest, or even at all. I waited around for a little while, cleared my throat, said, "Hello? Can anyone help me? Hear me?"

One of the other customers came up and got his purchases rung up, and wrapped, and a very pretty bow tied on the fancy silver paper while I waited and watched and fumed.

Eventually I tossed my head proudly and marched out into the mall. I guessed it was time to take my business elsewhere.

There are no escalators in this shopping mall, but there is a wide circular staircase that has a banister carved with fantastical creatures. The statues are all quite talkative, each one announcing the wonders and marvels of whatever shop pays for the advertising as you walk past. They're used to being ignored, poor things, so I made sure to nod at each of them or touch them as I walked up the stairs. I'd always felt sorry for the animated statues as a kid, and I found that my feelings hadn't changed.

The first storefront I saw at the top of the stairs was a tattoo parlor, and I couldn't help but stop and stare at what was going on inside the place. You see, spell and protections sometimes work best if they're in direct contact with the one using them. The process of getting inked with a magical tattoo is quite different than out in the mundane world. For one thing, the artists don't use ink, they use streams of colored fire. It's far more painful to sit through a magical tattooing session, but the results are far more spectacular, as well as useful. My brother

Samson (guess his twin sister's name) has a phoenix mark that covers his whole right arm. It's one of the most beautiful pieces of art I've ever seen. I remember how sick he was during the weeks it took to get the work done.

What stopped me in my tracks at the top of the stairs was the sight of a man with a wide bare back being worked on just inside the shop doorway. The artist was carefully crafting the image of a Greek trireme ship to his skin, in molten copper.

I was totally fascinated until the artist stepped back and turned in my direction. He looked past me rather than at me, but I certainly looked at him. Damn fine looking man, and shirtless to show off the work across his wide chest. Unfortunately, the artwork he sported was the head and glowing eyes of a red demon. I winced and instantly went on my way.

Listen, I wasn't overreacting, not exactly—it was just that I hadn't been reminded in years—

All right, you see, that great-grandmother my family doesn't discuss, when she died, she went straight to hell. Voluntarily. To be with her demon lover. Well, a demon dimension that's not exactly hell in the mundane definition of eternal damnation, but close enough. We've always been known as a family of good witches, so imagine this blow to our collective ego down the generations.

I pulled myself together and got my attention back on shopping after walking aimlessly for awhile. I discovered that I was standing outside a vintage clothing store. The items in the window display looked like a yard sale of Stevie Nicks' 1970s wardrobe, lots of beads and fringe and lace. Just the sort of stuff Mom liked. I stepped inside to have a look around.

The first person I saw was my brother Samson. I stepped up to him just as he picked up a pair of striped stockings.

"Do you think Mom would like these?" he asked, unsurprised at my sudden appearance.

"Wasn't the Wicked Witch of the East wearing those when Dorothy's house dropped on her?" I asked.

"I thought they looked familiar." He tossed them back on the counter. He smiled at me. "How's your birthday shopping going, Vix?"

Vix is the closest I can get anyone in the family to calling me Vicki. "Terrible, Sam," I answered. "Is Delilah going to make it to the party?"

He nodded. "She's flying in from Vegas this afternoon."

"Airplane or broomstick?"

"Fairy wings, of course. Have you gotten Mom's yet?"

"That's why I'm here. I'm making the effort," I said, and sighed. "But I couldn't get anyone to wait on me at the first place I tried."

He looked me up and down. "I can see why not."

I did not understand this comment. "Hold on," I said. "The covenants declare that anyone who can enter has the right—"

"Covenants aren't always kept," he reminded me.

This cynicism shocked me. Like I said, we're a family of good witches, but I'm also studying law in the mundane world, so the notions of deviousness and rule-bending should occasionally occur to me.

"Oh," I said. "So my business isn't wanted here."

"That would be my guess."

I was beginning to get angry, but I hate letting my temper get out of control, so I fought it down. Just because other people were being unreasonable didn't mean I had to be. That is, if Sam was correct about the salespeople not wanting to wait on anyone as obviously mundane as myself. I looked around the shop and considered asking my brother to help me pick out some more *appropriate* attire. After all he was wearing a leather vest but no shirt and had platinum white dreadlocks down to his butt. I envy Sam and Dee their hair, but I dye my unnaturally bright locks brown to fit in better in my chosen world. His look was a perfectly normal one for this neighborhood. It was a look I'd eschewed even before I transferred from Salem High to a public school environment. I'd always been the family rebel. Or the "Demon Child," as Mom had referred to me during those difficult adolescent mother/daughter relationship readjustment years.

I frowned as I decided that if I hadn't given in to peer pressure as a vulnerable teenager, I wasn't going to backslide now.

"I'll see you tonight," I told my brother, and I went back out into the mall determined to hold onto my integrity and do things my way. Or, as any member of my family would put it, *You are so stubborn, Vix.*

I glanced down at the atrium when I left the shop and noticed the tattoo artist picking up a mug of steaming liquid at a refreshment cart. He was on a coffee, or whatever, break after finishing up the copper ship artwork, I supposed. Despite not being enthralled by his own choice of body art, I took a moment to appreciate his very toned body before going on my way. If someone is going work out that much and go around shirtless, it's just rude for passersby not to ogle them. Mom raised us to be polite.

When I went on my way I soon found the second store on my shopping list. Can you believe it? There was actually a guard on this door. He looked rather like Shaquille O'Neal dressed as a genie and looked me over with an arrogant sneer I found pretty annoying coming from a guy wearing purple pantaloons and more body piercings than I had any interest in counting.

"Go away, mundane," he intoned.

"Listen," I said to this fashion victim, "I'm wearing a gray shirt, black trousers and sensible walking shoes because it's my personal choice. Respect for individuality is one of the foundations of the magical culture. Am I not right?"

He didn't even so much as blink. He crossed his arms and stepped in front of the doorway.

"Okay," I tried. "What if I tell you that I'm dressed for a costume party?"

This lame excuse set my teeth on edge, but the day wasn't getting younger. I had a birthday cake waiting at a bakery that I needed to pick up before the place closed.

The genie threw back his head and laughed. But he didn't move.

I took the gold coins I'd brought with me out of my purse and showed them to him. "Look," I said. "Real money, no fairy gold, no credit cards. I just want to make a purchase and leave."

"We don't want money from your kind," a woman said from behind him. "I do not want your business in my shop."

Prejudice. I hate it and always have. I doesn't matter whether it comes from the mundane or magical world, it's all about misunderstanding and fear and it's caused by pure laziness as far as I'm concerned. How much work does it take for a person to find out about those who are *other,* those who are *different*?

"Why do you people think Google was invented!" I heard myself shout.

Oh, dear, I was getting angry.

I took a deep breath and peered around the wide bulk of the guard. My voice was strained, but I tried to keep my tone pleasant. "I'm looking for a fairy-wing spell as a present for my mother's birthday. Perhaps you've heard of her, Meg McCoy? She's quite well respected in the community."

The proprietor of the shop ducked under her doorman's arm to stand in front of me. She put her hands on her hips. "Everybody knows about the cursed McCoys," she said. "And that Meg McCoy is a sloppy witch who couldn't even raise her kids properly, not that she knows who any of their fathers are."

Okay, that did it. Say what you will about me, I can cope, but *nobody* insults my mother. This time I let myself get angry.

When I get angry, *things* happen. If the world is lucky, it'll just be something as inconsequential as the queen winning an Oscar for playing Helen Mirren.

I felt my eyes start to blaze, which instantly vaporized the colored contacts I wear over my bright red eyes. My hair matches my eyes, by the way. My natural looks are the legacy of being a demon's great granddaughter. That, and my interest in becoming a lawyer. Once in every generation somebody in the family gets stuck with the looks, but we try not to give in to the beast twisted into our DNA. Nurture versus nature and all that.

Fury welled up in me, and the energy of it spread out across the area.

I began to yell. I saw every word as a spurt of flame.

I'm not sure what I said, but the metal in the genie's piercings began to melt. He yelped and ran off. I turned my attention to the shop owner, but a roar on the staircase interrupted me before I could get going on a proper tirade.

"Demon!" the banister creatures began to shout. "Help! Help!"

Oh, hell! What had I conjured up?

My temper cooled as though I'd been doused with ice water, but the damage was already done. I sprinted toward the stairs as another roar issued from an inhuman throat.

As I reached the top of the stairs, I saw the tattoo artist coming up. Only the red demon tattoo on his chest was the one in charge. It writhed, and it roared, and it had a life of its own.

It saw me and let out another ear-shattering howl. "I'm coming, honey!"

"Grandpa, no!" I shouted and started down the spiraling staircase. The steps shook with every step the demon took, and I almost lost my footing. I had to grab hold of the banister railing to keep from plunging headfirst downward. A wooden griffin holding up the rail beneath my hands whimpered in terror.

"Stop that!" I yelled down as the demon spit out a stream of fire.

But the demon didn't take any notice. He was really pissed off. My bad.

I knew where he was going as I vaguely recalled having shouted something like, "I'll summon the powers of hell to destroy you and all you hold dear!" when I began my tirade at the shop owner.

"I didn't mean it. Really. Thanks for the help. You can go home now."

The demon didn't listen. My great-grandfather was determined to spread hell on earth and carry out everything I'd threatened. I had to stop him before he reached the poor woman's shop. Only I didn't have any clue about what to do. I didn't think I could tackle the muscular tattoo artist when he was himself let alone when he was controlled by a spirit of supernatural evil.

"Help me," I begged the carved beasts.

"How?" the griffin asked.

"Slow him down. We have to stop this whole place from going up in flames."

There was muttering and squealing among the enchanted carved creatures, but they came through for me. The banister posts only had limited mobility, but they did what they could to defend their home and their very lives. A claw grasped at the demon's leg. A wing nudged him in the ribs. A unicorn toppled forward and blocked his way. The griffin wrenched itself free and rolled down the stairs ahead of me. The combined effort of the critters managed to bowl the demon over, and he tumbled all the way back to the first floor atrium and landed on his back.

I ran down behind him and jumped on his chest before he could rise again.

I grabbed the tattoo artist's shoulders and put all of my weight into holding him down. "Look at me!" I demanded. "Look into my eyes. Concentrate. Let the demon go. Be yourself again."

I repeated variations of this I don't know how many times while my great-grandfather's simulacrum gradually faded from this plane of existence and back into the ink. Ink mixed with demon blood marked this man's skin. Why would anyone want to do that?

I must have spoken out loud, because the tattooist answered, "It's the price I had to pay so I can do what I do."

I stared at him. "You *willingly* became a vessel for a demon manifestation?"

"Sure," he said. "It's a family tradition. My name's Adam, by the way," he added. "And you can either get off me now or kiss me."

He had a very winning smile, did the shaven-headed and muscular Adam. "I never kiss anyone on first possession."

His smile widened. "You're the one who brought out the devil in me."

I slid off of him and stood, but our fingers lingered when I gave him a hand up. "Listen, Adam, I'm sorry about—" Looking around I noticed that a crowd was gathered around, the atrium. When there should have been consternation and concern, there were mostly smiles and eyes bright with conspiratorial glee. I saw my brother looking down from the second floor. Suspicion nibbled at my temper, but I kept it under control.

"Samson McCoy!" I yelled up at him. "What is really going on here?"

He held up his hands. "I was here to stop you if anything went wrong, sis."

"What do you mean, *stop me? Wrong?*"

Behind me, my mom said, "It was what I really wanted for my birthday, hon."

She was standing in the doorway of a shop that hadn't been there a few minutes before.

I didn't understand. "I thought you wanted a fairy wing spell."

"I do." She gestured toward the migratory store's entrance. "I came along to help you pick it out."

"But—"

"I'll see you at the party," Adam said and walked away. The rest of the crowd scattered.

I boggled at my mother. "I really don't get it."

"I wanted to see you in action, darling," she replied. "You've been so—normal—lately that I was getting worried."

"What do you mean, *normal?*" A familiar ping of annoyance shot through me. "You said you didn't mind my living as a mundane."

"I don't," she answered. "But I do mind that to live in the mundane world you spend too much time closing off your emotions. You're practically an automaton lately. You need to come out of your shell every now and then."

"When I come out of my shell people can get hurt."

"No one was hurt today." She smiled in that winning, sweet way that lets her manipulate the hell out of all her children. "In fact, you saved the day. You were spectacular. It's my birthday," she added. "Indulge me, Vixen."

I had to admit that I did feel better somehow. The world was a brighter place. Catharsis is cleansing and all that. Besides, it was Mom's birthday. "I'm glad to give you whatever you want today."

"Good." She gestured toward the shop entrance again. "Now, about that spell you also promised me . . ."

I didn't want to go in there. I knew how I was going to feel when I came back out, but a girl's gotta do what a girl's gotta do. And the best spells always come at the highest cost. And Meg McCoy deserves only the best.

ALTAR EGO

Jody Lynn Nye

Jody Lynn Nye enjoys recreational shopping, particularly for books, cooking gadgets, art supplies (and who doesn't?) and esoterica. She lives with two black cats and one husband in the northwest suburbs of Chicago. Her latest book is *An Unexpected Apprentice.*

"**O**ne moment!" Abigail Cabot trilled, running toward the shop door at the ting-a-ling of the hanging bell. "Let me just cut you in, darlings. Just a moment."

The couple on the other side, a young woman with thick, dark hair and large green eyes and a tall man, about Abigail's lanky height of six feet, with blond hair and tinted glasses, virtually quivered with excitement, hardly able to wait while she swept her arm up, down and across, up and across, down and up. Abigail felt the warding spell recede to either side of the thick glass portal. She unlocked the door and encouraged the clients to enter.

"Welcome to Sacred Spaces," she cried, pumping their hands. "I am Abigail Cabot. And how may I help you?"

"Well," the young woman said, with a shy but vivacious look up at the man at her side, "James and I have just been given permission to form our own coven, and we need to furnish a new altar room. Oh, I'm Peggy Martel."

"How very nice to meet you. Tradition?" Abigail asked briskly, whipping a small notebook out of her cardigan pocket. She took a quick moment to close the circle that protected the store. At their startled glances, she smiled an apology. "Forgive me, but we have some very sensitive items, prone to malign forces. I have to keep a very tight warding spell in place, or it could cause some problems for my neighbors. You understand."

"I suppose," Peggy said, a trifle uncertainly. "We're New Wiccan Church, but we're willing to mix in other traditions if it works for us. I like to think I'm pretty open as a priestess."

"Excellent!" Abigail said, beaming at her. "If you come this way, I will show you a few things. I hope they will give you ideas about what you would like."

She hooked an arm through each one's elbow and led them in. She just hoped these nice people—these nice, *nice* people—couldn't hear the voices.

At the center of the round showroom, she halted and swung around so she could look both of them in the eye.

"Now, do you have any pieces you want me to work around? How's your altar room furnished at the moment?"

"It's a blank slate," James said. "We don't have a thing we want to keep. Not a thing," he repeated, with a sharp glance at Peggy.

"All right, James," Peggy said, with the air of someone who has had enough of an argument. "I can't help it if Delores made you so angry."

"I can't stand her. I don't know how we put up with working with her for so long," James said angrily. "She's a manipulator."

She's a bitch, a muttered voice whispered in Abigail's ear. She cringed.

"She's just strong-minded," Peggy said firmly. She turned to their hostess. "Abigail, we put ourselves in your hands absolutely."

"Yeah. All right. We do," James added.

"I assure you, I will be very sensitive to your needs," Abigail promised them. With a quick summing glance at her clients, she gestured at one of the open doors around her. "Please come this way. Let's just tour the vignettes I have on display here, and we'll see what you like. Please, let's start here."

"Ooh," the woman said, as they entered the first showroom. It had been painted pure white. A thin but plush white silk carpet, nearly wall-to-wall, lay on the inlaid rosewood floor. At the center lay a low table in rosewood with bronze stringing adding a golden thread to the warm, rich wood and complementing the careful arrangement of the altar set, ormolu antiques that Abigail had picked up in London a few years before for a song— though a fair song. At the directional points rose elegant brass candlesticks like exclamation points of pure gold. Narrow beeswax tapers, the natural wax slightly golden in hue, burned in them.

"Exactly nine feet across, very traditional, but all the furnishings are small in scale to allow for as much room to move as possible," Abigail explained, gesturing around the room. She was proud of the display. "Please notice the pentacle is woven into the rug. I have these custom-made in the Himalayas by trained mountain arachnaeds, eight-armed spider women, so you can order the colors and pattern to suit yourself. In fact, my husband is on a buying trip to Nepal even as we speak, so he could put in your choice almost *immediately*, if you order. I just love the purity of the white."

"What about candle wax?" James growled, but not as hoarsely as before. Abigail could tell he was softening in his stance. She was relieved. A grumpy attitude was not conducive to a large, one-of-a-kind investment like an altar room, or much else, for that matter.

"Spelled for resistance," Abigail chirped. She picked up the nearest point candle and tipped it. A thread of beeswax dripped onto the shimmering whiteness. The woman gasped. Abigail stooped and picked the slightly hardened wax up between thumb and forefinger and swept a hand over the pristine carpet below. "You see? It comes away without leaving a mark. Same for scuffy footprints, in case anyone comes in wearing dirty shoes."

"I don't allow anyone to wear shoes during ritual," Peggy said faintly. Abigail saw her mind was measuring up the space and deciding how close it came to her inner vision.

"There's more to see," Abigail said briskly, taking their arms again. "Men always love this next one. Please, this way."

Both of her visitors gasped with pleasure as she steered them into the fresh space. Living grass, green and perfectly manicured, covered the floor. The altar at the center was a sawn-off tree stump three feet across. Abigail inhaled the freshness of the atmosphere. It always smelled like a meadow after rain in this room. The walls were made of tree bark.

"A different species for each direction," Abigail pointed out. "Alder for the south—a species associated with fire, of course. Oak in the north. Colorado aspen at the east, and Venetian larch at the west. If you have a favorite tree you want included, you can choose from our catalogs. I have lists sorted by point orientation." She patted the walls. They almost thrummed with life. "Go on, touch them. They love it!"

"These are live trees?" the young woman asked. Abigail nodded. "How do you maintain them?"

"Oh, I'll show you how to water them. You'll have to trim them now and again—the same goes for the grass— but we do have a maintenance package, if you would prefer to have us take care of it. It's a good value for witches on the go!"

You must think I'm made of money, Abigail heard.

She clenched her fists. Positive attitude, positive attitude!

"Too pricey," James said automatically, though Abigail could tell he felt genuine regret. "Maybe someday. Do you have anything in a more moderate range?"

"Of course," Abigail assured him. "Let me show you three rooms that are all very affordable but that I feel are especially conductive to excellent magical work. Please, let's go this way." With an uneasy glance over her shoulder, she guided them across the atrium into the next showroom.

"Don't you think bronze is outdated for a cauldron?" Peggy asked her husband over a table full of catalogs in Abigail's snug little wood-paneled office. She thumbed through a handsome, leather-bound volume and pointed to a picture of a glimmering silver bowl. "Aluminum is a good conductor. Look at all these designs! I love this one with the embossed petroglyphs. It just *invokes* ancestral images."

"What's wrong with traditional fixtures?" James asked. Abigail pretended not to hear as she wrote up the order form. As she had predicted, they had chosen the first thing they had seen, the white-carpeted room. The promise of easy cleaning and the wow factor of the upscale furnishings had made it irresistible. Abigail quietly congratulated herself on her acumen. People did so often pick the first thing they saw, so she had to be very careful to show them just exactly the right arrangement. They were not taking the maintenance package, but she left them the option of annual aura cleansing and carpet re-spelling at a fixed fee. A fine morning's sale. Everyone was happy. She was glad. It kept the spirits peaceful.

"Nothing is wrong with tradition," Peggy replied. "It's just that the original owners aren't . . . our tradition. I mean, we don't know who they belonged to, or anything. Do you know what I mean, Abigail?"

"Of course I do," Abigail said. "I offer some vintage items and antiques as a service, but you are quite right. You should have tools that mean something to you both. I simply offer these for clients who have a feel for them. It is to your credit that you know those don't work for you. I am delighted to help you find that happy medium, if you'll excuse my little joke. For example, the thurifer above you on the right, James, belonged to my five times great-grandfather, Lawrence Cabot, of Salem, Massachusetts. With so many ancestors, I just find myself with too many artifacts in the house. I find myself using pieces I find comfortable to work with, or items of . . . especial sentimental value. The others I am making available. I include a guaranteed provenance of each item, so you can decide if they are compatible with your personal karma."

"Your great-grandfather?" James asked, taking the censer down from the shelf. He hefted the pierced bronze sphere in his hands. "How old is it?"

"Seventeen twenty-two. It was made in the New Forest, and it came to America with Great-Grandpa Lawrence's bride, Meghan Power."

"Very handsome," James said, turning it over. "How much is it?"

"No, Jim," Peggy said, with a hint of warning in her voice. James pouted. He and Peggy stared at each other for a moment, neither one wavering.

You never let me have anything! The whisper was just audible.

"No need for an argument there," Abigail said, infusing her tone with light warning. Peggy tilted her head.

Sighing, James put the thurifer back. "Nice, though. Thanks for showing it to me."

"You're entirely welcome. If you are still interested in it, please call me any time," Abigail said. "I always say that if something is meant to be yours, then it will find its way back to you one way or another."

That brightened James's face. The couple handed over a check. Abigail dropped it into a drawer after the briefest glance—it was bad manners to draw attention to money unless there was an error. In her business, there were seldom deliberate efforts to cheat her; the threefold return of bad karma was more than most practicing witches wanted to risk.

"Our installation team will be at your home in ten days," Abigail promised as she severed the wards and let James and Peggy out of the shop. "The magus who will do the magical setup is Alexandrian tradition, so I see no difficulty with compatibility of spells. Good luck to you!"

The young couple chattered excitedly together. Abigail waved as they walked to the elevator, then hastily redrew the protective symbols and threw her back against the door. Her fingers tingled. The wards felt weaker than they should have. She cast them a second time to make sure.

She was almost certain that the Martels had not heard the angry whispers. If they had, they ignored them. Abigail was relieved, but she just couldn't count on that happening every time a customer came in. Nor should she. She absolutely had to get rid of the source of the bad feelings.

"Mr. Howsfield?" she called. "Mr. Howsfield, where *are* you?"

Had it only been yesterday when the stout little man with the choleric complexion had come to her door brandishing IRS credentials? Abigail retraced her steps to the break room behind her personal office. There, in the neat, blue-painted, white-trimmed room, on the antique folding Pembroke table, was the severe-looking brown leather briefcase he had brandished at her at the door, demanding to see her books in the name of the government of the United States of America. Beside it, half empty, was the cup of black coffee she had poured for him. Between them was an immense pile of papers that she had gathered from her files at his insistence. Before them, in the chair, was no one, yet it was in that spot that she had last seen him.

You did this to me, a voice hissed in her ear.

"Oh, I didn't," Abigail said, clutching her hair with both hands. "I promise you, Mr. Howsfield, this isn't my doing!"

Damned witches! Causing more trouble than any other people I have to deal with.

Abigail clenched her hands. "Now, Mr. Howsfield, don't swear! It will only make things worse. Please, calm down, and matters might sort themselves out."

Your fault!

"It's not my fault! I will correct this problem, Mr. Howsfield, you have my word."

If only he had been the only person to have disappeared within the confines of Sacred Spaces. It had been bad luck, really, that she had lost track of him. Abigail had spent the entire afternoon sitting across the table from him, ignoring the doorbell and answering his questions with forced calm as he thumbed through her ledger. She had cooperated fully, even though she suspected that her audit was part of the ongoing government investigation of persons of magical talent. She knew he was uncomfortable in the presence of witches and warlocks. Not an uncommon sensation among the magically deprived, alas.

Historically, her family had kept its special abilities to itself. They had fought accusations of charlatanism, fraud, fortune-telling and a host of less savory crimes over the centuries. Abigail had defied her cautious and conservative family, and her husband Bernard's, too, to open her shop in Enchantment Place. She had seen it as joining those others brave enough to come out into the open about their talents. They would make the community more transparent to others, thereby taking away the strangeness, and, thereby, the fear of it. Bernard agreed that that path was best. She had always opened her doors to nonpractitioners. To those who were willing to learn, she explained the symbolism of the objects she sold. Most of them left with greater peace of mind than they had come in with. Some of it had to do with the calming spell that she refreshed daily, but the rest was just the unveiling of that which was "otherness."

If only she had not turned her back on Mr. Howsfield! Alas, the ringing of the telephone could not be ignored forever, not if she was to stay in business. With many apologies, she had excused herself. He had grunted at her, not looking up. To her relief, it had been Bernard calling long distance from Asia with some exciting news about Tibetan prayer shawls. When she had returned from taking the call, Mr. Howsfield was gone. She assumed he had left, until she found that the wards guarding the door had not been disturbed.

The local office had called looking for him. Abigail

could argue with truth that she had not seen him, but she could sense him. She felt his disapproving presence and heard his angry complaints. All her work to return him to physical reality, using chanting, incense, bell, book and candle, had so far been for naught.

She suspected she knew who had turned her in to the IRS, as well as causing other mischief with which she had had to deal. The other shopkeepers and merchants had mentioned a disaffected young man skulking through the shopping center just a couple of days after Bernard had gone on his trip. The young man had consulted numerous practitioners within Enchantment Place, all of whom had the same unhappy news for him: he was not a warlock, and no easy remedy for his condition was available. He had paid a visit to Sacred Spaces, a lanky, unkempt individual with intense, bulging eyes, festooned around the neck and wrist with faddish symbols from a dozen cultures and traditions. He'd handled nearly every artifact in the store, a habit that had Abigail frantic with worry. He had questioned her closely all the while as she dogged him around the shop.

"What's the secret to becoming a great wizard?" he asked, sliding a sly glance toward her. "The others won't tell me, but I bet you will."

Abigail had dived just in time to save Great-aunt Emma's cranberry glass chalice.

"There is no secret," she had insisted as her unwanted visitor turned from the cup to a priceless silver libation bowl. "You know, some things are inborn. You can work to become great at anything you do. It just takes effort. And time."

"What about the power?" the man had asked, fixing his burning hazel eyes on her. "I have to have it to make my plans work!"

"Well," Abigail had offered weakly, hoping to get rid of this uncomfortable and undoubtedly unprofitable stranger. "If none of the traditions you've explored have resonated with you, sometimes a course in Eastern philosophy has been known to connect those not normally magically inclined with the eternal. You should consider it. It's very balancing. You know, our goal is to maintain a balance with nature . . ."

He had been unsatisfied with the answer, as she feared he might be. He had thrust the silver bowl into her hands and stormed out. Abigail had hastened to lock and bespell the door after him. The bowl in her hands throbbed with discontent.

Abigail felt she could date the troubles she was having to that week, as had other shopkeepers in Enchantment Place. According to the owner of the shop that sold familiars, she, too, had been singled out for an audit, based on an anonymous call. Until the merchants had compared notes, some harsh words and unfounded accusations had been flung among them at a Merchants' Association meeting as they looked for the source of persecution—a witch hunt, as it were. Everyone used the forum as an opportunity to complain about everyone else. Little things seemed to go wrong after the meeting, like mail going awry, trusted cantrips failing, sensitive plants dying suddenly. Abigail suspected some retaliation at those they felt were responsible for their woes. Perhaps an unwary word, an unintended hex from an unhappy neighbor . . . ? She couldn't say.

Once the merchants figured out the real problem was probably mischief perpetrated by that same unknown caller, a few sheepish apologies had been offered around. Still, delicate feelings remained among the residents of Enchantment Place. Because of that, Abigail felt uneasy about broaching the problem to anyone else. She was embarrassed to admit that she, a Cabot, had been so careless as to misplace an IRS agent. Not to mention an electrician, a salesman, a feuding married couple, and a pair of door-to-door solicitors for a charitable cause she hadn't had time to determine before they, too, had disappeared. Certainly she had never again seen the poor woman who usually came in to clean at night. She had not quit, which is what Abigail told everyone, nor had she come to collect her wages. Instead, Abigail had the awful feeling that she and the others were still there . . . somewhere . . . in some form. She had been trying to get them all back. Nothing she tried worked, and she was beginning to feel desperate. To keep the problem from spreading outward and possibly capturing other innocent people, she strengthened the wards until the shop was virtually soul-tight.

She fretted each time clients entered the sacred circle of Sacred Spaces that they might not be able to leave again. Oddly, it only seemed to be people who came in with a disapproving attitude that vanished into the substance of the shop. Anyone with a good attitude left as they came, cheerful and optimistic. Abigail herself always sought to keep the positive at the uppermost. It was all the more important now. Business had not been as good as it could have been. She couldn't afford to have rumors go around, not that she wanted harm to come to anyone. She didn't dare tell Bernard. He would worry about her. The Cranes had a long history of unfortunate run-ins with persons of magical ill will, Washington Irving's misleading account notwithstanding.

Abigail returned to her office with the uncomfortable sensation of eyes upon her.

She turned on her computer and opened the blind e-mail account she had set up for confidential queries. Her independent searches on the internet had turned up no mention of disappearances based on bad attitude. She had opened the question to online magic-oriented chatrooms. The mailbox contained thousands of replies. Abigail opened one after another, hoping for some advice, but all of them ran along the same vein:

"Never heard of a problem like yours, Miss Mystery, but I'd love to hear how you fix it when you do."

"I'm on my own, then," Abigail said, pushing back from the computer.

With eight or nine tableaux from which to choose, she found herself falling back on the familiarly comfortable setting of the New England model. The stencils of the antique wallpaper had faded to rose gray over ivory. Every item in the room had belonged to one ancestor or another. She often fancied she could sense their personalities in them. Her majestic silver candlesticks at the

directional points had come from her great-grandmother
Rosamund Oresteia Miller, a handsome, Junoesque
woman whom Abigail admitted she resembled not at all.
But it was the focal object, a rough-hewn piece of gray-
brown wood shaped neither like a cross nor a pentacle,
that gave most visitors pause: it had been made by Lawrence Silas Cabot during the days just before the Salem
witch trials. He was the sole jurist to rule against death
for the accused witches. The nine-pointed block radiated
power. Abigail had always been taught that magic by
itself was neither good nor evil, but this object hungered
for justice, undoubtedly like the old man himself. Few
ever touched it, but Abigail could not bear to have it
hidden away. It was this and a few other pieces that
had forced her to surround the shop with such powerful
protective wards. Unshielded, Great-grandfather Cabot's
symbol of balance caused malfunctions in spells as far
away as a mile. During the few times she had managed
to contact his spirit, he had warned her about leaving
it unprotected.

The same went for a glass bottle she kept on the faux
mantelpiece in the room next to the box that held her
personal wand. It contained water gathered from a dark
well in Cornwall by an ancestress who supposedly went
mad and killed herself in a particularly disgusting manner. A few customers had asked to buy it, but Abigail
couldn't sell it with a clear conscience. It, too, was safer
here, inside the wards. It did make her feel a little uneasy. It glowed in the dark, especially when there was
no moon outside. To counter its malign strength, she had
a superb Herkimer crystal blessed by her great-grand-
aunt, one of the first female doctors in the colonies. The
double-ended gem, the size of her fist, absolutely glowed.
That, too, was highly sought by collectors, but Abigail
felt it was too powerful to let out of her possession. All
of these things were intended to aid in the eternal struggle against dark magic and the chaos of the void.

She lit candles around the room and settled herself in
a cross-legged position on the floor at the south end of
the antique occasional table. The honeyed scent of the

handmade candles warmed and calmed her. Tenting her fingers, she closed her eyes.

"Spirits of my ancestors . . ."

Pagan nonsense!

"Now, Mr. Howsfield, stop that," Abigail said crossly. Why of all the missing did he have to be the only one who could communicate with her? "It's not helping if I can't concentrate." She wriggled into a more comfortable position and tried to make herself one with the infinite.

"Spirits of my ancestors, aid me," she intoned. "Send me advice. What must I do to help those who have been lost? Give me a sign!"

Nothing happened. It was as though the spirits of her ancestors weren't even listening. The one time she had a truly important matter she needed to handle, and they were snubbing her.

"Please, spirits, I need you. Great-aunt Elsabeth, please!"

She concentrated until a tiny bead of sweat formed upon her brow and ran down to the end of her long nose. Suddenly, a gust of wind swirled into the small room. Abigail opened her eyes in wonder. She felt the enormous level of magic in the room drop like a tidal trough. The candle flames leaned sideways and were snuffed out.

"Helloooo?" a voice called.

Abigail frowned. "Spirits, is that you?"

"No, it's me. My name's Dahlia Maranski. I made an appointment? I'm interested in a personal altar room?"

Abigail unfolded herself and stumbled out into the atrium. A short, stocky woman with curly, dark-brown hair and a pink face full of freckles grinned at her.

"Sorry, but you didn't answer, so I just let myself in." The young woman held up a brass-bound athame. Abigail recognized it as an inexpensive commercial tool. "I hope you don't mind."

"Aagh!" Abigail cried. The woman had left the door unshielded! "Just one moment, please." She dashed to the door.

She was too late. The tall spring flowers in the vases by the winding staircase had begun to wilt at the gust of unleashed power. Across the broad hallway in the show window of the Wand Shoppe, a rosewood wand on a blue velvet pillow was writhing by itself. The Wand Shoppe's proprietor, a tall man in his fifties, stepped into view and snatched it up. When he noticed her watching him, he gave her a dirty look. Abigail hastily redrew the runes and reinforced the circle walls. The outflow stopped. Soon, the phone would be ringing with complaints from her fellow merchants. She returned to her visitor. Dahlia gave her a cheerful smile.

"Gods, this place is stuffy! It's really nasty in here. Sorry. My friends hate it because I always say what I think. I mean, it doesn't smell, but it's kind of . . . I don't know, *mean*."

"I beg your pardon!" Abigail exclaimed, horrified.

"I mean, you don't look mean . . ." Dahlia held out a couple of fingers toward Abigail, her face twisted in a contemplative grimace. "And you don't feel mean. It's in here. Like a pressure cooker. Really uncomfortable. You should, you know, air this place out." She looked rueful. "Sorry. I'm psychometric, and I was an only child. My mouth just does what it wants."

If she was uncontrolled, Abigail was not. She gathered her wits. This young woman was a customer, after all. Everything was back in place. No harm had been done— not much, anyhow. She moved to offer her hand to her visitor.

"That's quite all right. Now, you said you wanted to invest in an altar room?"

Dahlia returned the shake with tremendous energy and a sturdy grip. "Yeah, I did. I just moved into a new place. I've given it a good going over, purified the whole thing, and I'm ready to make a sacred space of my own. Just open to Mother Nature, you know. No ego involved. I'm in the city, but I really like the outdoors. I hear you've got some special stuff. I thought I'd take a look."

Abigail smiled. She was back on her own ground now.

"I have exactly the place for you," she said. With a firm hand on the shoulder, she guided Dahlia to the Living Trees tableau.

Half an hour later, she escorted the young woman to the door. The visit had not been a success, saleswise. Dahlia could not seem to relax in the store. She commented often on the tension she sensed. Nothing Abigail showed her seemed to tempt her past her uneasiness.

"Thanks," Dahlia said, with a rueful grin. "Maybe later, okay? You seem really nice, and I like your stuff. Maybe when you've got your negative energy issues under control, huh?"

"Thank you," Abigail said, doing her best to sound upbeat. Luckily, neither Mr. Howsfield nor any of the other missing people made any audible remarks. "I hope you will return soon. Thank you!"

The door swung shut with its customary tinkle. Mentally, Abigail reached out for the edges of the sacred circle and, with an act of will, attempted to pull them together with the warding spell.

They wouldn't close. She felt as though the lines she was drawing over the open space were being blown outward. Abigail threw all her skill at the leak.

"Spirits of my ancestors, aid me!" she cried. "Uncle Julian, Great-uncle Lawrence, help me!"

A wild wind pushed at her back. Rustling papers flew past her and sifted out under and around the frame of the closed door and swirled into the corridor at the feet of a couple of young witches pushing baby carriages. Abigail realized she wasn't going to be able to close the spell from the inside. Giving a moment for the two women to pass, she wrenched open the door and threw herself in the path of the outrush of power.

Feeling very much like a mime pretending to walk against the wind, Abigail leaned into the power. In the air of the atrium, it tasted stale and negative. Where had all this come from? She had given Sacred Spaces an auric cleansing at least once a month!

Clawing at the edges of her spell with her fingertips,

she concentrated on sealing it up. Under her palms the "chi" of the wards felt lumpy and ragged, not at all the seamless barrier she was used to. To her horror, the wall of power began to bulge out in invisible pockets. A gust of foul effulgence broke through and blew in her face. Abigail put both hands over the break and recited Solomon's ninth and most powerful chant of sealing. It held for a moment, then broke loose again. Magical energy gushed from a number of pinpoint holes. Abigail threw temporary seals over them, but she knew they would not hold for long. She could not contain the power brewing inside Sacred Spaces any longer on her own. It had achieved some kind of critical mass, and it was increasing all the time. At some point, very soon, it would burst through all her carefully laid restraints and explode in a gush.

What could be responsible for such a buildup of energy? The shop had acquired a personality of its own, and a very powerful one at that. Could one of the missing people hidden inside have latent powers? Could that unfortunate young man have sneaked back in and vanished? Could this be a way for her ancestors to let her know that they disapproved of her coming out to the community as a witch?

Her ancestors! Abigail's concern turned immediately to the artifacts in the New England room. She made the smallest possible slit in the wards and forced her way back into the store. Heedless of the psychic winds whipping at her face, she felt along the walls until she came to the room.

Dahlia had been right. The tension that filled the store was palpable, and it was coming from here, from the family treasures. Every one of them was generating an outward force, as if imposing its will upon its surroundings. She didn't understand. These artifacts were supposed to aid in maintaining the balance of good and evil, light and darkness, high and low in the universe.

But they *had*. Abigail stood openmouthed as she realized her folly. After the incident with the unhappy young man and the aftermath with the Merchants' Association, she had sealed up Sacred Spaces as tight as a drum. She had striven for perfection in her wards, never realizing that she had closed off the circle within from all other influences. It had begun to feed back upon itself, a "vicious circle," if one liked. The family heirlooms had reacted to what was inside Sacred Spaces: Abigail's own insecurities and anxieties, as well as the negative energy of the discontented people who had visited the store, including Mr. Howsfield. That protection was treating almost any incursion that was not completely positive as if it were a virus to be combated.

Abigail clenched her hands together. The power had built to a point at which she could not control it alone. Her only choice was to release it before it caused an overload. But how? If she left it to its own devices, it might wipe out Sacred Spaces and possibly half the mall along with it. If she did open the circle, the wave of magic would rush out like a tsunami. Her shop would be vulnerable to the elements, and the Merchants' Association would be angry with her all over again.

The answer was control. Abigail was not an exorcist, and she had no time to consult a specialist. She must handle this by herself. If word got out that she had caused her own magical circle to become a breeding ground for critical magical mass, she would be ruined. Too many important clients would take their business elsewhere, to a practitioner with a greater perceived level of control.

Positive thinking, positive thinking! Abigail thought, forcing herself to be calm as she settled at the end of the antique wooden table. She must break the circle, dismiss it completely, and redraw it the way she had always had it before. It would have helped if Bernard had been at home, to balance her feminine presence with his masculine one, but there were enough male symbols there, Abigail reflected, thinking of the walking cane made of the pizzle of a bull that Aunt Josephine Lodge had brought back from Spain, to fill in the deficit.

What's going on here? Mr. Howsfield's peevish voice interrupted her thoughts. *We're spinning in circles here!*

"Hold tight, Mr. Howsfield," Abigail said, feeling her way to retrieve her personal wand from the box on the mantelpiece. She, too, fought the maelstrom. "I fear it's going to get worse before it gets better!"

Enchantment Place could very well be blown off the map if she was not cautious. Sacred Spaces was situated on the west side of the building on the second floor. The mall itself sat foursquare to the four winds, which meant that if she unmade the circle in the traditional way, the power would release in the direction of the first point she opened. Therefore she had a terrible choice ahead of her: Which way would cause the least damage? Highrise buildings surrounded it on every side. She could flatten them with the power she needed to vent.

She had little time left. The power was becoming so dense that she could barely move or breathe. What direction would not cause destruction?

Ah, but there was one direction she could possibly use. It was highly nontraditional in magic from western Europe, but it was right at home here on the North American continent. Native Americans included not only north, south, east and west in their rituals, but also up and down. She would open the circle toward the ground. She cringed when she realized that beneath her store lay that of her greatest critic, the chairwoman of the Merchants' Association, but she would make amends to her later. Below the building's foundation lay nothing but reclaimed lake bottom. She pointed the wand at the floor, and hoped.

"Spirits of my ancestors, I thank you for your guardianship. In the name of the balance of nature, the source of all, I release this sacred space!"

Abigail heard a POP as the protective bubble broke. The power began to drain through the floor at her feet like a whirlpool. It caught Abigail and spun her helplessly around and around. Her hair whipped her in the face, and her clothes plastered themselves to her body like a mummy's bandages. Her lungs were pressed so tightly she couldn't breathe. It didn't matter what happened to her as long as no one else was hurt.

Control, she told herself. *Positive attitude!* She clutched her wand and concentrated. The winds of power receded from her shop door and rushed down the hole in the floor. Precious items crashed to the floor and crept in the direction of the outrush.

After what seemed like an eternity, the eddy seemed to lessen. In fact, the air in the room smelled cleaner and less fusty than it had in weeks. Drawing a deep breath, she lit candles in the brass holders on the old table. The flames leaned over, but in spite of the swirling winds, they did not go out.

"Spirits of my ancestors, return to me what was lost!" Abigail commanded.

As though she was watching a movie of soap bubbles popping in reverse, things began to appear in the room. First came a pair of blue argyle socks that Bernard had complained of missing. Next was a gold-plated candlestick Abigail was sure had been shoplifted. Then, one after another, people began to pop into being. She caught her cleaning lady, who appeared a foot above the floor. Mrs. Coral staggered into her arms and began to cry.

"I'm so sorry I've been a pain," Mrs. Coral wailed, wiping her nose on her denim sleeve.

"There, there," Abigail said, soothingly, patting her on the back. "It's all over now."

"No, it's not," said an unpleasant voice. Mr. Howsfield did not hesitate a moment on returning from the ether to advance upon her and brandish a handful of papers. "I don't care how, but you're going to be audited every year for the rest of your life, and I'm going to do it!"

After hearing him grumble at her for weeks when no one else could see him, Abigail was ready for him. "Are you sure you want to incur that much negative karma?" she asked, pointedly but gently. "It could happen again. Just like this."

Mr. Howsfield's choleric complexion paled to ashes. He clapped his mouth shut and scrambled for the door. Abigail felt relief as she helped the once-feuding customer couple to sit down on her antique settle and let the other returnees sort themselves out. She feared they would be angry, but they were all so relieved to be reembodied that no one was upset.

She felt more than relief, she realized, as she went to make tea for Mrs. Coral and her other unwitting guests. For the first time in weeks, the shop was serene, and so was she. She hummed a little song. The phone interrupted it.

"Hello?" she asked. The voice coming out of it was so loud she had to hold the receiver away from her ear.

"Are you responsible for the destruction, the havoc, the downright *mayhem* that has just gone through here? There isn't an unbroken light bulb anywhere on the first floor! Every one of my windows has been etched by shards of glass!"

"I am so sorry," Abigail said. "It was necessary. I'll replace them all. It was . . . spring cleaning. You know that every so often you have to clear out your sacred spaces. I'll be redrawing my wards in just a few moments. You have my word."

The voice on the other end snarled something unprintable, followed by a slam.

Abigail clicked her tongue and picked up the tea tray.

"It would be so much better for her karma if she had a positive attitude," she said.

FIRE AND SWEET MUSIC

Diane A.S. Stuckart

Diane A.S. Stuckart is a member of that proud
breed, the native Texan. Born in the West Texas
town of Lubbock and raised in Dallas, she
crossed the Red River just long enough to obtain
her degree in Journalism from the University of
Oklahoma before returning home to Big D.
Then, like countless others with a brand new
Liberal Arts degree, she promptly took a job in
retail. To her parents' relief, however, she eventually put that diploma to good use by publish-
ing several critically acclaimed historical
romances written as Alexa Smart and Anna Ge-
rard, as well as numerous works of short fiction
and fantasy under her own name.

Life beyond the Lone Star State continued to
beckon, however. Succumbing to a momentary
impulse, Diane recently pulled up stakes and
left the plains of North Texas for the beaches of
South Florida. There, accompanied by her husband, four dogs, and two cats, she now is finding
new sources of inspiration among the sand and
palm trees. Her most recent venture is an upcoming historical mystery series featuring Leo-
nardo da Vinci in his prime. Other fiction and
nonfiction projects are waiting in the wings!

When she's not writing or working at her day

job, Diane spends her time doing yoga, garden-
ing, and making sure the pets don't get eaten
by stray gators. She is always glad to hear from
her readers, who can email her at diane@diane
stuckart.com.

The blond man wandering the essential oils aisle was
different from her usual clientele. That was saying a
lot, considering the sort of people who normally fre-
quented *La Flamme du France* Perfumery.

Claire Delacourt followed his progress through her
small establishment by means of his reflection in a
baroque-framed mirror upon the opposite wall. Her uneasiness was growing, though why this man should raise
her figurative hackles, she was not certain. After all, she
was used to dealing with customers who were not quite
ordinary.

For the perfumery was located smack in the middle of
Enchantment Place, Chicago's premiere shopping desti-
nation for everything magical. As for her clientele, it
included magical humans as well as various otherworldly
beings in need of a special scent. Of course, that number
was interspersed with those of the mundane persuasion
who simply appreciated goods with a magical flair.

Not that Claire technically possessed any particular
magic, herself. What she did have was a "nose" . . . an
ability to distinguish a far greater number of scents than
the average person could. Along with that talent was the
well-honed skill that allowed her to blend said scents into
evocative perfumes.

While her core business was custom scents, the shop
carried expensive incenses and oils, as well as the more
typical soaps and candles. One moment, she might be
offering braided smudge sticks to a tourist from Kansas
City; the next, she was demonstrating the benefits of per-
fumed accessories to a pungent-smelling ghoul trying to
pass as human. She'd also come up with a line of scents
with her Wiccan clients in mind. In fact, several magic
practitioners had confessed to using her various perfumes
to jumpstart their rituals on difficult days.

Maybe not magic, her witch pal Jessica often joked about those products, *but they're the closest you can get straight out of a bottle.*

But this man, she sensed, was not looking for some simple *eau d'enchantment.*

Claire glanced at the oversized sports watch strapped to her wrist. Its digital display showed seven-thirty . . . half an hour past her closing time. Perhaps she'd only thought she had locked the shop's sole door and turned the hand-lettered sign in the display window. But why had she not heard the tinkle of the tiny brass bells hanging from door's knob, which should have announced this man's arrival?

As if hearing that last unsettling thought, he glanced up and locked gazes with her in the mirror.

Even though the convex mirror skewed his reflection, she could tell he was handsome. His strong chin and firm lips were clean shaven, while his pale hair rippled past his collar, gleaming against the somber black of the oddly outdated evening clothes he wore. With his golden hair and pale skin, he reminded her of the antique paintings of archangels hanging in the gallery across the way, save that he lacked the requisite snowy wings and flaming sword.

Feeling foolish at being caught gawking, she rose from her chair and made her way to the counter where he stood.

Up close, he was even more handsome, his strong features perfectly carved, his pale skin unblemished, his golden hair sleek as silk. His eyes were blue . . . not the pale blue of a winter's sky, but the deep azure of an unchecked flame. If not for his obvious air of masculinity, she might have thought him too beautiful, too perfect.

"Welcome to *La Flamme du France*," she greeted the man, deliberately assuming a more formal tone than usual lest he guess that last thought. "I'm sorry, but my shop is already closed for the weekend. If you would care to return on Monday—"

"Ah, but Monday will be too late."

The words were slow, seductive, disarming . . . just

like his smile. And he had an English accent straight out of BBC America. Damn it, she'd always had a thing for men with accents. Likely it was because she had been raised practically from birth by her New Orleans-born grandfather. Her late relative had never lost that French cadence that lingered in the speech of certain families from that city, no matter how many generations removed they were from European soil.

Suppressing an impatient sigh—many of her customers were males in need of a last-minute gift—she conceded defeat and stepped into her role as shopkeeper. "So, what sort of occasion is this, and who is the present for? Wife, girlfriend, daughter?"

She moved farther down the counter, pausing at the antique pomanders and vinaigrettes. She plucked one of the latter from the display and set the tiny metal box upon the glass.

"This is a lovely example of 19th century American silver work," she declared, turning the expensive trinket to show the intricate piercing in its lid. She opened it to reveal a gilded interior and wisp of dried sponge inside.

"Back in the good old days before everyone wore deodorant, every proper young woman carried a vinaigrette with her to ward off unpleasant odors. Why, you can still smell the original scent." She lifted it toward him so that he could breathe in the faint perfume. "Lovely, is it not?"

"Lovely," he agreed. "But I am not here to buy anything—or rather, I have purchased it already, and I am simply here to claim it."

"I don't understand. Are you saying you have been in my shop before?" Claire frowned. She didn't do layaway. Besides, if this guy had bought something from her previously, she definitely would have remembered him.

By way of answer, the stranger reached beneath his cutaway jacket to withdraw what appeared to be a parchment. It was rolled and tied in the manner of some royal missive, the faded ribbon held in place by a blood-red gobbet of wax. He set the unusual packet on the counter beside the vinaigrette and gestured her to pick it up.

Curious, she did so, and the scent of sulfur wafted from the roll, an angry, almost evil, odor that made her gasp in surprise. She dropped the parchment back onto the counter, but not before she'd gotten a closer look at the impression in the wax. What she saw brought a return of her earlier unease, for she was certain the symbol had some sort of demonic connotation.

After all, how else would one categorize a heraldic device that was a goat's head crowned with fire?

"I don't understand," she repeated, irritation tingeing her words. "I believe it would be best if you left . . . and do take that *thing* with you."

"That thing, my dear Claire, is a contract," he replied, the seductive smile vanishing like a flame snuffed out. "Read it, and you *will* understand."

"How in the hell do you know my name? And what is this talk about a contract? I own my place free and clear."

"Oh, yes, you own your shop, but what you do not own is your soul. That particular item belongs to me."

So absurd was his reply that she could only stare at him in silence for a few long seconds. Finally, she shot back, "Sorry, mister, but last time I checked, my soul was still mine. So why don't you leave, before I call mall security?" For emphasis, she picked up her phone and started punching in numbers.

A hint of his earlier smile returned. "You will not find it working, I fear."

And, quite disconcertingly, her call was not going through. Trying not to let her sudden alarm show, she set down the phone and glared at him.

"Fine, so there's trouble on the line. But in case you didn't notice, there's a lot of foot traffic outside my shop, and all the businesses on either side of me are still open. All I have to do is scream . . ."

". . . and everyone will rush to your aid," he finished for her. "Do not worry, I have no intention of harming you. I have simply come to collect what is mine. Would you care to see the proof?" he asked, breaking the parchment's wax seal and unrolling it upon the glass countertop so that she could read it.

The document appeared older than it had at first glance, curled at either end, its edges ragged. The page itself was densely penned with numbered and footnoted paragraphs written in black ink in an elegant hand. She snorted in disbelief at the document's title, *Contract for the Acquisition of a Soul.*

"Whereas the below-signed human, hereafter known as the Damned," she began reading aloud, and then gave a humorless laugh. "Cute. Did you pick this up at *Devil May Care*?" she asked, naming the Satanic-themed shop located in one of Enchantment Place's darker corners. Like most of the mall's stores, its inventory included a few souvenir items and gag gifts for the tourists.

"I assure you, my dear Claire, this document is quite genuine. Would you care to review the signature at the bottom?"

With an elegant finger he uncurled the final inches of the parchment, revealing the remaining text. At the bottom were places for two signatures. The first blank, entitled *Acquiring Demonic Representative*, had been signed in a harsh black flourish by someone named August Drake. The second name was penned in blood-red ink, and the title beneath it simply said, *The Damned.*

The signature, inexplicably written in her own hand, read, *Claire Delacourt.*

She stifled a gasp. Obviously, the signature was an amazingly accurate forgery, and the document itself some sort of demented joke, but to what purpose?

The man, meanwhile, gave a satisfied nod. "Legal and binding, in this world and the next," he told her. "The countersignature is mine, of course. Strictly as a formality, let me confirm that you are Claire Delacourt, daughter of Marie Delacourt, deceased, and an unknown father; born in New Orleans, now a Chicago resident."

"Yes, but—"

"Thank you, that is sufficient. Now, let us discuss execution of the terms."

Sliding his finger up the document, he indicated a blank that had been filled in with a handwritten date . . . the coming Sunday, which also was the day of her 25th birthday! He met her disbelieving gaze and nodded.

"My visit tonight is what one might term a courtesy call," he explained. "You have two more days before the contract becomes binding. You might take that time to resolve any pressing earthly matters with friends or family. Or, if your personal affairs are in order, you could do as many have and use your final hours to run the gamut of the traditional seven deadly sins. Or you may care to pick just one of them."

He shook his head. "I recall one woman who opted for greed. She spent her last day on earth buying designer shoes . . . one hundred and seven pairs, in total. But in the end, she learned she truly could not take them with her," he finished with an ironic smile.

It was that last comment that spurred her from her temporary vocal paralysis. "Enough!" Taking a steadying breath, she went on, "You can say whatever you want, but we both know I never signed any sort of agreement with you."

"Ah, but you did," he softly replied. "Think back, and you will remember."

At his words, she suddenly felt herself drifting in darkness, not quite sleeping, but somewhere far from wakefulness. She lingered in that state for several moments, until a memory began playing out before her mind's eye like clips from a silent movie.

A store that she recognized from old photos . . . the Delacourt family's original perfumery once located in New Orleans' French Quarter. A blond man, tall and handsome . . . the same man now in her shop who called himself August Drake. And across the counter from him stood a young woman with long black hair and thin pale features.

She looked uncannily like Claire. Indeed, Claire might have mistaken this person for herself, save that the dream woman clutched an infant in her arms. Her mother, Claire realized with a gasp, certain she was right, though she had never actually seen her parent before. And that must mean the dark-haired child was herself as a baby.

She watched as Drake withdrew from his jacket a rolled parchment similar to the one he'd showed her, though this one appeared quite new. Unrolling it upon the countertop, he took what looked like an old fashioned fountain pen from his pocket. With a nonchalant air, he used its pointed metal nib like a knife to stab his fingertip.

Blood, dark as india ink, shimmered upon his pale flesh. He dipped the pen's tip into the gleaming fluid and signed his name upon the parchment. That accomplished, he coolly handed the pen to Marie.

Claire felt, if not actually heard, her mother's thoughts, sensed her fear at the enormity of this blasphemy she was about to commit. She felt, too, the unspoken pain that ate its way through the other woman's frail body. All at once, she knew why her mother was making this decision to sell her soul.

Now she saw her mother juggle the restless child in her arms while awkwardly pricking her own finger with the pen. A sluggish red thread spun from her wasted veins, the blood hardly enough to dampen the shiny metal tip. Then, quite unexpectedly, Marie's expression changed from fear to determination. She clutched her fingers into a small fist, backing away from the counter and the parchment upon it.

Drake's handsome face now hardened into a cold mask, and Claire knew what he was thinking. He'd already signed the parchment; he could not leave without another name upon that page. She saw her child-self begin to cry in response to her mother's agitation, her tiny white arms pushing free of the confining blanket and waving wildly. Marie tried to comfort her baby even as she bravely stood up to the man before her.

And then it happened. The flailing hand of Claire's younger self slapped against the knifelike point of the black pen that her mother still held.

Claire winced in remembered pain as cold metal

pierced delicate flesh. In her mind, she heard the infant's shriek of pain. But what followed was even more chilling. A few drops of the child's blood, bright as rose petals, spattered onto the parchment. As if guided by an invisible nib, the blood thinned into a twisting red line that became Claire's adult signature upon the page.

And, at that, the memory faded to darkness.

Claire opened her eyes to find Drake coolly staring back at her. She tore her gaze away and glanced at the tiny white scar in the center of her right palm. The half-moon-shaped mark had been there ever since she could remember, so that she'd never had more than a moment's passing curiosity as to how it had come to be there. But now she had that answer.

Unwittingly echoing her mother's action, she closed her fingers into a swift fist to hide the evidence of that long ago injury. She could feel a slight burning there, however, as if she cupped a glowing ember in her hand. And she knew despite a protesting chorus of rational inner voices that everything Drake has said was true . . . that her soul had been sold to the Devil, if quite by accident.

Slowly, she raised her gaze again.

"Marie . . . my mother . . . she was dying," Claire said, taking the bits of her mother's memory she'd absorbed from the vision and slowly arranging the story into some semblance of order. "She knew my grandfather had not forgiven her for my birth, and she was afraid he would not take me in when she was gone, though he gladly did so when it came down to it. But that's why she was willing to sell her soul. She wanted to live long enough to see me raised to adulthood. In the end, though, she couldn't do it."

"She had great inner strength, despite her physical weakness," Drake agreed. "Had she signed the contract, she would have been restored to full health and lived the additional twenty-five years she had sought, rather than the six months that were left to her. But I am not in the habit of letting souls off the hook quite so easily.

The contract had been prepared; I could not leave without someone countersigning the agreement."

And so he accepted the soul of a mere baby.

Her dismay built into swift outrage . . . at Drake, yes, but also at her mother, a woman she had never known. Had Marie realized what she had done, that her abortive attempts at an unholy bargain had inadvertently snared her own child? Or had she watched in relief as Drake took his leave, certain the agreement was null and void? The vision had ended with blood spilt upon the parchment; she had not witnessed her mother's reaction. Of course, she could ask the question of Drake, but would she be able to believe his answer?

"How could you?" she demanded instead. "What you did was unconscionable. It was cruel. It . . . it wasn't fair."

"Life is not fair, nor is Death, nor much else of what happens afterward. If it were, I would not be in my current position."

Curious despite herself, she warily asked, "And your position is what . . . the Devil?"

He smiled slightly in return. "Hardly. I fear I am quite a bit lower on—what do you call it these days?—the chain of command. I was but a luckless human like you before I also sold my soul almost a century and a half ago. Now, I serve as Lucifer's representative here on Earth."

"Great, I'm stuck with a midlevel manager," she muttered.

He made some reply—something about Section 2B in the contract—but Claire barely heard those next words over her rapidly beating pulse. How could this be happening to her? She gave to charity, tried to treat everyone as equals, fed stray dogs and cats . . . hell, she didn't even cheat on her income taxes! So why had she been picked out of some random cosmic line-up to be damned? And this thing about contracts . . .

"There's got to be an opt-out clause," she abruptly exclaimed. "Most contracts have a provision that you're allowed to change your mind up to a certain number of days after signing. And since I didn't know until now that I signed the blasted thing, I ought to be able to invoke that clause!"

"I am afraid it does not work that way. Your contract law does not apply to otherworldly agreements such as this one. And as the contract was written to guarantee but twenty-five years, that is all you are allotted." So saying, he began rolling up the parchment again. "Do not worry, I will give you almost all of Sunday before I return for you. Shall we say just before midnight?"

He tucked the contract back into his jacket and then started for the door. Midway down the aisle, however, he halted and looked back in her direction.

"And I do suggest you reconcile yourself to your fate so that, when the time comes, you can make your departure with dignity. Believe me, there is nothing quite so distasteful as escorting a screaming, blubbering soul down to Hell."

"Oh, yeah?"

The retort which sprang reflexively to her lips was childish, but she didn't care how she sounded. Swiftly, she made her way around the counter and marched after him.

"You try dragging me off to Hell, and you're going to hear a lot more than screaming and blubbering," she sputtered, halting before him. "How about I throw in biting, kicking, and cursing? And suppose I whip up a few stink bombs to lob at you? You think that brimstone smells vile? You'll be the one screaming and blubbering when you get a whiff of what nastiness a professional perfumer can create."

She broke off her tirade, aware she'd gone from merely childish to downright infantile in her reaction but hardly caring. The prospect of eternal damnation did that to one. Drake, however, merely favored her with a considering look.

"Perhaps there is another option open to you, after all. I will concede your point that the circumstances surrounding the signing of this contract were—"

"Unfair? Reprehensible? Outrageous?"

"—unusual," he continued, as if she hadn't spoken. "And under Section 5D of our agreement is a list of conditions under which the Acquiring Demonic Representative may renegotiate terms with the Damned prior to contract fulfillment. One is the discovery that the Damned was not of sound mind at signing. Interpreting that broadly, one might argue that, as an infant, you did not possess the faculties to make an informed decision regarding the sale of your soul."

"So you're going to void the contract?"

He quickly dashed that hope, however, with a shake of his head. "I said renegotiate, not void. But as part of that renegotiation, you may be able to free yourself from the contract if you can meet my terms."

He glanced approvingly around the shop. "The fact that you have maintained a long-term presence in Enchantment Place demonstrates that your skill as a perfumer is beyond the ordinary. Your typical mundane would not last long among other magical retailers. Perhaps you possess a bit of magic that you don't even realize is yours."

"I'm good at what I do," she warily agreed. "So, do you want me to make you a custom perfume in return for giving me my soul back?"

"In a manner of speaking, yes."

A pensive look momentarily darkened his handsome features. "As I mentioned, I am not in my current position by choice. The Representative who recruited me did not follow proper protocol, and my human life was mistakenly ended before he fulfilled his side of the bargain. Thus, it was agreed that if I could recruit a certain number of souls, myself, I would be released from damnation and returned to human form to live out what would have been the remainder of my life."

"Interesting, but what does that have to do with me and my perfume?"

Drake idly picked up one of the scented fans from the display beside him and unfurled it, the action releasing a hint of gardenia. Oddly enough, the delicate lace and bone accessory did not look the least bit effeminate in his elegant hands.

"Understand that I have been acquiring souls for a century and a half. At first, it was a simple task, because the typical lifetime tended to be lamentably short and brutally harsh. The prospect of Hell was hardly more frightening than what most people faced every morning of their existence."

He paused and shook his head. "But as time passed, life became something to be enjoyed rather than simply endured. It grew harder to find people willing to bargain an eternity of damnation against some temporary earthly pleasure."

"Go on."

The otherworldly flame in his blue eyes burned more harshly as he replied, "Here is my counteroffer. You have until midnight Sunday to create for me a perfume so compelling that a single whiff of it will persuade a person to sell his soul to the Devil. Succeed, and I void the contract. Fail, and I will escort you to Hell on schedule."

Claire stared in stunned silence for a moment, still not quite believing she was having this conversation. Finally, she reached for the most logical argument she had.

"Two days is hardly sufficient time to create a memorable perfume," she protested. "There's the composing of it, which requires determining an appropriate theme, and then writing out the precise formulation. Then there's the compounding of the various oils and extracts, which can take weeks, or even months to get just right. Forty-eight hours is just about enough time to get you some cheap toilet water. And assuming I could even create such a perfume, why would I want to help you damn even more souls?"

"Because doing so is your only chance to keep from becoming one of the damned, yourself," Drake coolly replied. "I can assure you, that is a fate you will want to avoid. Perhaps a preview will convince you."

She opened her mouth to protest, and that was when her shop erupted in flames. The fire escalated into a roaring wall of orange, its light blinding. She cried out in fright . . . and then she shrieked in pain as the fire raked her flesh.

She should have been nothing but ashes now, given the way the fire burned with such fury. And yet she could see her raised hand before her, the flesh untouched even as flames danced along her fingers. Burned yet not consumed. Almost as bad was the fire's roar, the ceaseless sound itself sufficient to send a person mad. Beneath the deafening crackle, she could hear something else, too . . . heartrending screams of the other damned whose cries spoke of more untold pain and anguish.

And then the flames vanished, leaving behind no sign save the lingering stench of brimstone. Claire stared about her, amazed to find her shop still intact and herself alive. As for Drake, he stood nearby, once more watching her with detached interest.

"I can assure you, my dear Claire, that what you experienced in those few seconds was but a taste of what damnation is. But lest you find yourself thinking that you have seen the worst, let me assure you that there is more to it than eternal pain. From a biblical perspective, there is the whole 'removed from God' situation, which the Scriptures maintain is the ultimate punishment. But what they don't explain is that you are removed from everyone else, as well."

The blue fire in his eyes abruptly dulled. "For myself, I would rather suffer the physical pain. Loneliness is a far worse punishment than the flames. Though I still walk among men and women, I am not truly one of you anymore. Sometimes the solitude is such that I would weep in despair, save that the damned cannot cry."

Despite her fear, she could not help an unwilling surge of sympathy at the stark admission . . . an emotion that she ruthlessly tamped down as soon as it made itself known. No way was she going to feel sorry for this man . . . demon . . . whatever he was . . . not with what he'd done to her mother and, now, her. And no way was she going to let him send her back to Hell or wherever she'd just been . . . not if she could help it.

"All right, you've convinced me," she choked out.

Drake gave her a small, satisfied smile. "You have made the right decision. Remember, Sunday just before midnight," he said as he turned the deadbolt latch—she had locked it, after all!—and then called back to her, "And I do hope for both our sakes that you succeed with your task."

Claire did not wait to see if he vanished in some demonic puff of smoke or simply faded into the crowd but swiftly relocked the door behind him. For good measure, she pulled the display window's purple drapes, rather than leaving them tantalizingly open to allow late-night window-shoppers to look their fill. Then, shivering with delayed reaction, she collapsed into her chair behind her antique perfume organ.

Though, of course, it was not a true organ. That was but a fanciful term for the perfumer's traditional workstation, a semicircle of tiered mahogany shelves wrapped around a desklike worktable. The organ had been passed down from her grandfather, though it originally had been commissioned from a famous Parisian cabinetmaker by Claire's great-great-grandfather.

Upon those polished shelves were the tools of her trade: bottles of essences; jars of dried flowers and herbs and spices, glass vials of alcohol and fixatives, mortars and pestles. It was there at her perfume organ that she—like four generations of her Delacourt predecessors—created the custom fragrances for which her family had been known since they first opened for business more than a century earlier.

In fact, many of those who patronized the current incarnation of *La Flamme du France* knew nothing of magic. Rather, they came because their families had been customers of the original New Orleans perfumery. Locked in her safe was the shop's ledger filled with pages of custom perfume formulaes, many dating from the mid-1800s and the scent sold now only to the original customer's descendants. Perhaps among them was a fragrance persuasive enough to lure a person into damnation.

"Nonsense," she muttered. No way she was damned, just because some guy walked into her shop, showed her a strange parchment, and then pulled some bizarre performance art stunt on her. Why, she could name a dozen people in Enchantment Place who could create the same illusion by genuinely magical means, and probably the same number who could recreate it as a stage act.

She summoned a shaky smile, certain this was the explanation. Why anyone had done this to her, she could not guess, but eventually someone would spill the magic beans and tell all. In the meantime, what she needed to do was to call one of her friends. Talking could put the evening's strange events into perspective and maybe give her an idea as to the perpetrator's true identity.

Claire reached for the phone with one hand and started to punch in Jess's number with the other. In doing so, she realized that the earlier burning she'd felt in her right palm was replaced now by a different sensation, as if she were cupping a coin in her hand. Frowning, she turned her palm for a better look . . . and gasped at what she saw there.

The tiny half-moon scar was now the size of a quarter, the flesh red and thickened like a brand. But that was not all. Looking more closely, she saw that stamped into her palm was the same goat-headed symbol she'd seen imprinted upon Drake's parchment.

She set the phone back into its base without finishing the call. Her gaze remained unwillingly fixed on that angry crimson blemish that, more than any words or parchments, proclaimed the truth of what August Drake had told her. She was indeed damned. And that meant she had two days to create the magical perfume that would be her get-out-of-Hell-free card.

Claire made her way to the storeroom where she kept her safe. Her fingers trembled as she dialed the sequence of numbers that opened it . . . quite fittingly, the same numbers that were the day, month, and year of her birth. She pulled out the familiar ledger, its loose binding carefully tied so that no precious sheet might slip free and be lost to posterity. Not bothering to shut the safe again, she carried the musty book to her perfume organ and began flipping through its pages.

She had slept perhaps half a dozen hours since Friday night. Cloistered within her shop—door locked, sign turned to "Closed," and phone turned off—she had spent the remaining time seeking to capture the elusive scent that August Drake had requested.

Like every master perfumer, Claire had a repertoire of perhaps two thousand different scents, which she could mentally combine into a new fragrance without actually needing to blend them. It was a skill akin to composing music, using a combination of essences in three different parts. Properly compounded, the trio of various scents would harmonize to become a single, new fragrance, rather like a myriad voices becoming the solo sound of a well-rehearsed choir. And she was an accomplished enough perfumer that she rarely failed to create any scent that first bloomed in her imagination.

But this time, most of her attempts never made it beyond a tentative formula scribbled on a sheet of paper. Others, showing more promise, she'd taken to the next level, combining a few drops of oils on bits of white blotting paper. A few she actually did compound, only to dismiss them when finished as far too ordinary. And with each failure, she came closer to Sunday midnight.

After her first abortive attempt to call Jessica, she had sent a quick IM to forestall those of her friends she knew would come looking for her if she didn't call or stop by. *Sick aunt, gotta visit her in Tucson, back in a couple of days,* had been the excuse she'd used. Later, it had occurred to her that facing this frightening challenge alone might not be her best course of action. Perhaps she should find the nearest church and go pray . . . maybe even call upon a priest to help.

But she'd just as quickly dismissed both notions as futile. Assuming she could get a clergyman to believe her fantastic tale, he'd likely be little better equipped than she to battle her nemesis. As for the prayer part, she rather suspected this was one of those situations where God helped those who helped themselves—meaning her time would be better spent meeting the challenge Drake had given her than on her knees.

But could a perfume truly be blended that could lure a soul to damnation?

Friday had rolled swiftly into Saturday, which now had blurred into late afternoon on Sunday. Her back ached and her head pounded, while her fingers cramped with the effort of writing out line after line of discarded formulae. By now she was so weary that, while reaching for the bottle of May rose essence, she instead picked up the tiny vial that held her last rejected attempt. Before she realized it, she'd poured a few drops into the vial of the current scent she was composing.

Claire almost wept in discouragement at the time it would cost her to recreate what she had done. Grabbing up the flagon, she was about to dump its ruined contents, when a scent she'd never before imagined wafted from the vial. She promptly set down the small flask and stared at it in wonder for a few long moments. Finally, she shoved back her chair and wearily cradled her face with her hands.

"I did it," she murmured, hardly believing it could be true. Raising her head, she reached again for the vial and cautiously sniffed, praying she had not merely imagined what she had created almost by mistake.

A heady essence swept her, wrapping her in a fiery sensation that made her feel as if she were invincible, even while it seemed to fill her veins with an erotic song that spoke of both seduction and longing. Breathing its complicated symphony of power and passion, she knew this was a perfume that could induce someone to sell his soul.

Carefully, she poured the precious scent into a tiny crystal flask and stoppered it, then stared thoughtfully at the bottle's blank label. She must have a name for her creation. She grabbed up a pen and, with a flourish, wrote a few words upon the paper.

"Fire and Sweet Music," she read with satisfaction.

Handling the tiny bottle as if it were a precious jewel, she tucked it into a velvet-lined box. Then, she gently set it back upon her perfume organ and made her way to the storeroom for a well-earned nap.

Claire awoke to the storeroom clock chiming 11 PM. Groaning, she unfolded herself from her makeshift bed behind some boxes and freshened up in her small washroom. If this was it, she grimly told her pale reflection in the mirror, no way was she going to Hell without brushing her teeth first!

Several minutes later, she stepped into the dimly lit shop. If not for the loathsome scar on her palm, she would have had a hard time believing that any of this was true. But assuming Drake made his promised reappearance, it would be over soon. Surely he would agree that she had met her end of their bargain with her fragrance. She sat at the perfume organ and gently removed the bottle from its velvet cradle, unstoppering it for a final whiff of the special scent.

To her shock, it now smelled quite ordinary, an agreeable blend of floral and more exotic essences. Pleasant, yes, but hardly a perfume with the power to lure the unwitting to eternal damnation, she realized as the half-hour now chimed.

No more time.

In despair, she began to weep. She cried not just for herself but also for her dead mother, who unwittingly had brought her to this pass, and for all the poor souls who had ever believed the Devil's promise. She even wept for August, recalling what he'd told her of the loneliness and how he himself could not cry. And as she sobbed, a tear splashed into the open flask, momentarily filling the room with a wonderful scent. But Claire paid that oddity little heed, wrapped as she was in her own fearful misery.

By the time she regained her composure, the store clock was chiming three-quarters past the hour. Claire quickly restoppered the flagon and wiped her cheeks with a scented handkerchief off a nearby display. She would play this out to the end, she told herself. Let him make the decision as to whether or not the perfume met his approval.

Barely had she settled herself back in her chair when she smelled the now-familiar scent of brimstone. Drake was standing before her, parchment in hand, his other-worldly beauty overlaid by a frightening darkness that put to rest any doubts he was Lucifer's representative.

"We meet one last time," he coolly said. "Have you accomplished your task, or should we be on our way?"

Wordlessly, she offered him the crystal flask. As their hands brushed, she saw a flash of quite human hope play across his handsome features. The emotion vanished as swiftly as it had appeared, however, and it was with a casual air that he unstoppered the perfume bottle.

Once again, a wondrous scent spilled forth. Claire stared at the tiny vial, wide eyed. The perfume was even more compelling than the first time she had breathed it, offering the barest hint of roses and almond entwined with the faintest whiff of musk and overlaid with the subtle earthiness of forest and woodsmoke. It was a scent filled with memory and promise, a perfume that beckoned and compelled and was filled with power. Anyone under its spell would not hesitate to bargain with Lucifer himself.

"Fire and sweet music," August softly agreed as he replaced the tiny crystal stopper and smiled. Slipping the flask into his pocket, he added, "But we must give your perfume one final test upon a potentially damned soul. If the scent compels that person to make the Devil's bargain without protest, then I will free you from the contract."

"But where will we find this person?" she asked in a shaken voice.

By way of answer, he took her hand. "That, my dear Claire, is the easy part."

A heartbeat later they were no longer in her cozy shop, but walking in the cool night air along a dark, potholed street. From the boarded store windows, broken streetlights, and sounds of distant police sirens, she guessed they were in the less savory section of downtown Chicago.

It was not a place she would have dared venture into during the day, let alone after dark. Here, the buildings crowded together, their scarred facades forming a grim wall on either side. With the sidewalks broken and barricaded at intervals with overflowing trash barrels and rusted cars, she and Drake were forced to walk in the street. The single streetlight that had not been shot out or burned out illuminated a faint path before them . . . lit the shadows enough so she could make out human forms within them.

Claire allowed herself a bit of grim amusement. They were being watched, she knew, by a dozen or more pairs of eyes. Alone, she likely would have been raped, robbed, and left for dead in a nearby dumpster. Instead, the watchers seemed to hold back, perhaps sensing something about the man beside her that warned of a menace greater than any they could offer. Then one of them, less attuned to danger than his companions, leaped from behind a battered sedan by the curb and blocked their way.

She saw a glint of metal in his hand—a knife or gun—but the realization he had a weapon was merely an observation, not a cause for fear. In the meager light, she could tell only that he was young and dark skinned and angry. She'd never be able to pick him out of a lineup—the oversized sweatshirt he wore with the hood pulled past his brow guaranteed anonymity. With detached interest, she waited to see what he would do.

He raised his arm and waved what turned out to be a pistol at them, gangster-style, then burst out, "Hey, man, what you—"

He broke off, eyes widening abruptly, turned from an angry man to a frightened boy in the space of a heartbeat. *Guess you figured it out*, Claire thought with grudging sympathy. He turned to run, the slap of his sneakered feet echoing against the buildings as he fled back into the shadows. An answering rustle that was his friends trailing after him followed.

"Ah, well, perhaps he was not the best subject for our experiment," Drake said with a shrug. "Let us see if we might find someone else."

He gestured her down an alley that stank of things far worse than brimstone. Though it was darker there than on the street, she could make out five or six figures huddled against the wall. She sensed, too, a different atmosphere. While the street held anger like a carelessly leashed dog, hopelessness hovered in the alley like a baleful mist.

Drake's attention, however, was fixed upon a tattered man staggering toward them, a brown-bagged bottle loosely gripped in one hand. He gave Claire a satisfied nod. "I believe this is our man," he murmured, and then addressed him by name. "Good evening, Samuel."

"I don't know you," the man rasped, swaying as he peered at them with angry, unfocused eyes. His sunken cheeks and patchy gray beard made him appear past retirement age, but Claire suspected he was younger. He reeked of urine and unwashed body, but his clothes looked as if they'd once been expensive. Scrounged from a Goodwill box, or his own before some personal catastrophe had brought him to his current state?

Drake merely smiled. "You may not know me, Samuel, but I know you. I know how you lost your job, then your house, and then your wife. You began drinking to dull the pain . . . and then the drink became everything."

He carelessly gestured at the man's unkempt state. "But this isn't really you, Samuel. If not for that bit of bad luck with the tax man, by now you would have been president of that company that fired you . . . owned half a dozen cars. . . . had a million dollar house and a new young wife in your bed."

"Damn straight," the man spat back, shaking his head in exaggerated dismay. "Wasn't none of it my fault."

"But we can fix that, Samuel. I can give you all that—the house, the wife, the cars—and more," Drake smoothly persisted.

Samuel's eyes narrowed in suspicion. "Whadda you want me to do? Sell drugs? I can do that. Or off someone for you? I can do that, too."

"You need not do anything, Samuel. This would be more in the nature of a trade. I can give you everything we have discussed, and in return I simply want your soul."

The man barked a laugh. "My soul? Who do you think you are, the Devil? Well, let me tell you something, Mister Devil, I sold my soul once, and I ain't sellin' it again. Now get outta my way."

He pushed past them, heading for the street beyond. Drake reached into his jacket for the perfume bottle. He unstoppered it, releasing a wondrous scent that masked the alley's stench and seemed to lighten the very shadows.

"Samuel," he softly called after the man, "are you sure you would not care to reconsider my offer?"

The man paused in midstep; then, inhaling Claire's otherworldly fragrance, he turned. The expression of hopeless resentment fell from his face like a discarded mask.

"You're on the level . . . you can do it?" he demanded. "'Cause what happened to me wasn't fair. If you can turn it around, if you can give me my life back, damn right I'll sell you my soul. Just show me where to sign."

The man's words sent a shudder of horror through her. He would have kept walking, she realized, save for the magic worked by her perfume. How many others would Drake snare with that scent? And how could she enjoy her own salvation knowing that those victims were being damned in her place?

"You're right," she cried out to the man. "Life is not fair, but that's the way it goes. We can accept it and move on . . . or not. It's our choice."

She paused and turned to Drake. "It's my choice," she grimly told him and dashed the perfume flask from his hand.

The crystal shattered upon the concrete, the sound like a multitude of tiny cries. Samuel stumbled back and blinked as if waking from a dream. Then, with a sudden horrified look at Drake, he dropped his own bottle and fled the alley. As for the perfume, it spread in a tiny gleaming pool and then seeped into the countless small fissures in the broken pavement. A moment later, its magical scent was forever lost.

Drake stared at the broken bottle at his feet before raising his fiery blue gaze to meet hers. "A noble gesture, but I fear it was for naught," he told her and held out the flagon's crystal stopper. "A bit of your perfume still clings to this. I will take it to another perfumer and bid him duplicate the scent. Thus, I will have my perfume . . . and you, sadly, will be in Hell."

Claire gave a soft laugh. "Sorry, but no one will ever be able to recreate it, not even me. You see, my perfume contained one special ingredient no one can ever duplicate: my tears. And thanks to you, there will be no more tears to be had, since you told me the damned can't cry."

Before he could reply, a faint beeping from Claire's watch began to sound. "That was twelve," she said, feeling oddly calm as she finished counting the electronic chirps. "I guess it's time for us to go. I'm ready when you are."

"Very well," he replied and took her hand again.

In another heartbeat, they were back in her shop. The storeroom clock, which always ran a bit slow, finished chiming midnight. She stared about her in surprise and asked, "Taking the long way?"

"Unless there was someplace else you cared to go tonight, I believe you are back where you belong."

"I-I don't understand," she choked out, hope and despair battling within her. "If you're just trying to torment me awhile longer before we go to the real thing, I'd prefer you didn't. Let's be done with it. A deal's a deal, right?"

"Exactly." He reached into his jacked and pulled out the contract. Handing it to her, he went on, "We agreed if you created a perfume that could entice someone to sell his soul, this contract would be void. You kept your end of the bargain"

"But the perfume, it's gone."

He shrugged. "Our agreement was limited to the perfume's creation. And so it would appear that our contract is now null and void."

Barely had he said those words, when the parchment in her hand vanished in a puff of brimstone. She gasped and then glanced at her palm. The goat's head scar there had disappeared, as well, leaving behind only smooth flesh.

At her hopeful look, Drake nodded and favored her with a smile that was slow, seductive, disarming. "Actually, my dear Claire, sometimes life is quite fair, after all, especially for those who are brave enough to meet it head on. Which is a roundabout way of saying that our business together is concluded."

He was at the door when Claire finally regained her voice. "How many more do you have left?"

"How many souls? Actually, that man in the alley would have been my last. If I succeed in finding a replacement for him, perhaps we will meet again one day. Oh, and happy birthday, Claire," he added before stepping through the door, leaving behind the faintest whiff of brimstone.

It was her birthday . . . the big two-six, her friend Jess had joked.

"Party after work, right?" she'd informed Claire at lunchtime, not leaving the shop until Claire agreed to meet the gang at *Witches' Brew* for drinks. "I'd say bring a guy friend, except I know you don't have one," Jess had added with an exaggerated sigh.

Now, with the store clock chiming seven, Claire hustled out her last customers of the day—three middle-aged witch wannabees who purchased her entire line of beginner's ritual oils—and then locked the door and flipped the sign.

"Time to party hearty," she muttered in mock resignation. In truth, she was grateful that Jess and the others had convinced her to join them this night. Her memories of the previous year's hellish anniversary had faded over the months, with only the occasional nightmare to remind her; still, it would be awhile before she celebrated another birthday wholeheartedly.

She had turned off all but the usual single light and

was grabbing her purse from the storeroom, when she heard the faint tinkle of bells that announced her shop door had opened. *Damn, I could have sworn I locked it.*

"Sorry, I'm already closed," she called aloud as she walked into the shop again.

She halted at the sight of a tall, broad-shouldered man standing near the display of scented handkerchiefs and fans. His back was to her, so all she saw of him was his long blond hair that spilled past the collar of the black leather jacket he wore over tight fitting jeans. Then he turned, and she gasped at the familiar figure before her.

"August?" she asked uncertainly, a reflexive shudder running through her even as she took a few steps closer.

He nodded. "In the flesh," he answered with the familiar BBC America accent, "and I do mean that literally."

And she realized that the chill glow of otherworldly beauty that once surrounded him *was* gone. To be sure, he was still a handsome man, but now she could see quite human flaws in his appearance—a few faint lines in his face, a crescent-shaped scar along his temple, a sprinkling of gray hair in his golden locks.

"I guess you found that final soul to claim," she finally replied, unable to suppress the note of reproof in her tone.

He nodded again. "Do not worry, Claire . . . he was already bound for Hell. I merely formalized the eventuality. And, if it will make you feel any better, the vast majority of souls I acquired likely were hell-bound, as well."

"Yeah, except for me," she pointed out with some asperity. "So, why did you come back here? You couldn't resist checking out the one that got away, or something?"

"Or something," he agreed. "I suppose I wanted to make sure you were well . . . and to wish you happy birthday again. As I have done so, I will take my leave."

She hesitated until his hand was on the knob; then, tentatively, she called out, "Wait, you don't need to go yet. That is, I'm on my way to meet friends for my birthday celebration. Maybe you'd like to come with me?"

"I would be delighted," he replied, his smile disarming if not seductively so.

She grinned back and gestured him out the door—she hadn't locked it, after all—then closed it securely after them. "So let's show you how we party in the 21st century," she proclaimed. "But do me one favor, August," she added as he gallantly escorted her through the crowded mall. "Anyone starts talking about setting the town on fire tonight, and we're out of there, okay?"

MAKE-A-MORTAL

Pamela Luzier

Pamela Luzier is a voracious reader of science fiction, fantasy, humor and romance, and her stories usually include two or more of these elements. Four of her short stories have appeared in other collections and she has published romance novels under the name Pam McCutcheon. A former industrial engineer for the Air Force, she now lives in the mountains of Colorado with her terrier/poodle mix, Mo.

Ted Braun used his bulk to push through the wall of human protestors outside his store in the Enchantment Place Mall. They were brandishing placards with such slogans as "Make-a-Mortal Humiliates Humans," "Give Make-a-Mortal a Mortal Blow," and chanting "Make-a-Mortal is mortally wrong" over and over.

Great, just great. He didn't need a visit from the Mortal AntiDefamation League on the biggest shopping day of the year. Gift giving during winter solstice was a time-honored tradition, and he definitely wanted it honored—and then some—in his store.

A few potential customers looked on with curiosity from afar but didn't seem inclined to wade through the pack of human protestors, damn it.

A scrawny woman about his mother's age with short, wild hair stepped into his path and stopped him with a hand to his chest. An involuntary growl rumbled through him. How dared she? She was lucky the full moon was two weeks away.

She looked startled and took a step back, but it didn't deter her. "Are you Ted Braun, the owner of this store?"

He resisted the urge to let his growl deepen. "Yes."

"Your store is an insult to the mortal race," she declared in a ringing tone designed to be heard by as many people as possible.

Ted knew it was a mistake to engage these people in conversation, but he did it anyway. "Don't be ridiculous. I sell cute, fuzzy toys that bring joy to children." True, they were shaped and dressed like life-sized mortals, but how was that wrong?

"What kind of children want a toy that big?"

She must be the ringleader because the rest of the protestors had quieted to hear their conversation. He shrugged. "Lots of them. Ogres, trolls, dragons, unicorns . . ." That was why he had taken one of the double-height spaces for his store, to accommodate his primary customer base.

"You humiliate humans by making them figures of fun, making us appear small and ridiculous."

Some of them *were* small and ridiculous, like this feisty woman in front of him, but Ted knew better than to say that. Over the chorus of agreement from the protestors, he said, "You didn't hear werebears complaining when mortals opened those Build-a-Bear stores, did you?"

She looked taken aback, then he could almost see the pieces click into place in her mind. "You're a werebear?" She smirked. "Do they call you Tedd—"

"Ted," he said before she could voice the nickname he hated. "They call me Ted." If they knew what was good for them. *No one* called him Teddy. Not if they wanted their throat left intact.

And talking to this woman wasn't getting him anywhere. He tried to step around her, but she was as slippery as a naiad. She slithered back in front of him, and the league members started chanting again.

Ted sighed. "What do you want?" he shouted over the noise.

"Just listen to us."

Hell, he couldn't help but listen, they were so damned loud. "I can't—I have a store to run. You're blocking me from making my livelihood." And if she did it much longer, the security ogres would stop lurking and start dispersing—Enchantment Place didn't take kindly to interference with revenue.

She must have sensed that, too, for she raised her hand for the chanting to stop. When it did, she said, "If you'll just listen to us, we'll go away."

What a pain. He had a huge sale going this weekend and couldn't afford to waste time with her. Then again, he couldn't afford to lose clientele either. Lost customers meant lost revenue, and he desperately needed to get out of the red. He was counting on this weekend to do that for him. "Okay, I'll talk to *one* of you," he conceded. "If the rest of you back off and don't harass my customers."

The crowd cheered, and the ringleader raised her arms in victory. "Great. Now here's the problem—"

"Inside," Ted snarled. One of his clerks had already opened the store, and he wanted to make sure everything was in place for the big sale. True to their word, the league protestors had backed off and were no longer blocking the entrance—they just silently brandished their signs at anyone who came near. At least it was improvement. Of a sort.

Luckily, some of his larger patrons didn't seem intimidated. As Ted stalked toward the store, the small woman scurried along beside him. He glared at her. "If you annoy any of my customers, I'll have security throw you out on your butt. You got that?"

"Okay—"

"And no bad-mouthing what I do in front of any customers, either."

She scowled, but said, "All right."

Daisy had already opened the doors. For a human, she

was as big as an ox and twice as homely, but the unicorns adored her. And she loved working with the kids, despite the fact that she constantly had to watch out for horns in her lap.

"How can you work here?" the protestor asked Daisy, obviously recognizing her as human.

Daisy looked puzzled, so Ted explained. "This is one of the protestors . . ." He looked at the woman, realizing he didn't know her name.

"Susan."

"Susan, this is Daisy, my clerk. Please direct your comments only to me." Then, realizing something large and ugly was missing, he asked Daisy, "Where's Grunch?"

"He left a message saying he'd be in late."

Great, just great. The stupid troll had probably been out all night lurking under a bridge and was too tired to come into work. Well, he'd pin the kid's ears back for him when he finally made it to work.

There were only a few customers in the store at the moment so he sent Daisy off to deal with them and turned to Susan. "Okay, talk."

As she rambled on about how heinous he was for selling human look-alikes, he tuned her out and checked out his stock. The plush human figures ranged in color from pale ivory to dark brown, with the occasional green, blue and red. Each one had stitched facial features, making them look cute and adorable. At least his customers thought so. He rather thought they looked like oversized gingerbread men when they weren't clothed.

He carried a wide range of costumes to dress them in. Inexpensive human clothing was easy to come by, and he hired out to produce a number of specialty outfits in bulk. For those with special tailoring needs, he sent them to Zoë at Witch Stitchery to work her magic.

For today, he'd dressed some of his stock in his bestsellers—Shirley Temple, Maki Osa with his rubber Samurai sword, Merlin, and St. George. Plus, he'd let the staff each dress a couple of new samples last night after work, just to see how they went.

The boy in footed pajamas with the drop seat obviously reflected Grunch's sense of humor, especially since it was clutching a stuffed bear. The ballerina in its pink tutu must be Daisy's. But Ted wasn't sure which of them had created the Speedo-clad cabana boy or the hula girl.

He shrugged. It was worth a try. You never knew what would catch the public's attention.

There was a pause in the stream of noise coming from Susan's mouth. "Well?" she demanded.

"No comment," he muttered. Just to shut her up, he headed for the closest customer, an old crone who was inspecting the cabana boy sample—a witch by the look of her. Was he seeing right? Was she actually winking at the plush human? No, it must just be a nervous tic.

"May I help you, ma'am?"

Susan started to say something but he sent her a warning look, and she clamped her mouth shut in a firm line.

The skinny crone shook her head. "Nope. I just wanted to take me a look at this here cabana boy." She pulled open the elastic of his shorts and peered down inside. "Where's his parts?"

Ted closed his eyes for a brief moment. *Why me? Why now?*

Seeing that Susan looked as if she were about to explode from indignation, Ted said, "I think you have the wrong store. I think you want Spence's, two doors down."

"Hmph. I know what I want. I'll jes look around a bit."

She hobbled off to look at the undressed make-a-mortals on display, patting her pockets and muttering, "Where are them darned glasses?"

Susan grimaced. "That's disgusting."

"I agree totally. But I'm sure she's harmless."

Before Susan could respond, an ogress inquired about a princess doll for her daughter and Ted gratefully helped her pick out a costume to make her own cute fuzzy mortal, then assisted a dragon with a fire-proofed St. George.

"Did you see how happy the children were?" Ted asked as they left with their purchases. He just wished the witch would leave. If she didn't stop winking at the cabana boy, he'd have to escort her out. Customers were already skirting wide around her.

"Maybe," Susan muttered. "But what do you think that little dragon is going to do to that knight he just bought?"

"Play with it," Ted said defensively. Okay, he knew some of his customers might be using the figures as golems, punching bags, or as fodder in war games, but wasn't it better to take out their aggressions on an inanimate stuffed toy rather than a live mortal? *Don't ask, don't tell* was his motto. "It's all harmless fun."

A scream cut across the store, emanating from a two-hundred-pound ogrish toddler. They'd probably denied the little tyke the plaything his heart desired. Time for a little salesmanship.

But when Ted got closer, he realized the fuzzy make-a-mortal was moving, stalking toward the huge toddler. With that happy smirk and its arms outstretched, the human simulacrum did look a little crazed.

Was this someone's idea of a joke? Who was moving the toy and terrorizing the poor kid? A yelp from another part of the store showed that a troll had just been goosed by another moving mortal doll.

"What is the meaning of this?" the annoyed troll bellowed.

Great Ursa, what's happening here?

Susan, who had inevitably followed, narrowed her eyes. "What's going on?"

"I don't know." He was wrong—no one was standing behind them, they were moving on their own. "It must be some kind of spell. They're not supposed to do that."

"Are you sure you're not doing this?"

"Of course not. Why would I want to scare and annoy my customers?"

Another piece of his stock lurched into movement, waddling unsteadily on its round feet with a perky grin.

"Well, don't you have a spell suppression system in place?"

"Yes . . ."

"So use it."

"I'd rather not. If it goes off, it'll dump foam on the whole store and ruin all of my merchandise." Because it was designed by fairies, it would be pretty, but the glittery goo would be hell to clean up. He didn't even want to imagine the bill from the brownie cleaning crew.

"Then you'll have to close your store."

"I will not." Realization dawned. "*You* did this."

Her eyes widened. "No, I didn't. I swear. Besides, who would sell me such a spell?"

True, magicals didn't usually like to arm the mundanes against other magicals. "You're right. I-I'll have to think of some other way to stop this."

His mind spun as he glared at the magic mirror that should have warned him of this catastrophe. "Fat lot of good you are." That was the last time he trusted a traveling salesfairy.

Wait—the security fairies had also convinced him to buy a pair of portable spell suppressors, for just such a contingency. Daisy was busy trying to calm the customers and head off the stalking make-a-mortals, so he grabbed Susan's wrist and towed her toward a rack of clothes. "You have to help me."

"Ha. Why should I? You haven't even listened to a word I said."

He glared at her. "Look around you. Would you rather have these ogres, trolls, and dragons thinking of humans as cuddly and harmless . . . or as a danger to their children?"

She looked struck by his logic. "Okay, you have a point. What do you want me to do?"

He grabbed a couple of wizard outfits and thrust one at her. "Here, put this on." He skimmed the starry purple robe over his head and shoved the pointy hat hastily on his head. Forget the beard—it would just get in his way. Hurrying to the back room, he grabbed the suppressors.

As he moved toward the store microphone, he thrust one of the suppressors into her arms.

She stared at it in disbelief as she followed him. "A Super Soaker?"

He grimaced. She was right. The glittery pink and gold device looked more like a child's toy than a spell deactivator. "Fairy humor—they couldn't resist being cute. It's a portable spell suppressor. If you see any of my stock moving, shoot it." He hesitated. "Do you know how to use one?"

She took the giant squirt gun, pumped a round of foam into the chamber, and grinned. "Lock and load."

Ted suppressed a groan at her zeal. "Don't use too much—just a little dab will do it." The device magically replenished itself with unending foam, but the cost of the magic refills wasn't cheap. "Oh, and try not to hit any nonenchanted merchandise—or customers." Who knew what personal spells they might have on their persons?

"Okay," Susan said.

But first, he needed to do some damage control. Thinking fast, he made an announcement over the loudspeaker. "Attention, Make-a-Mortal customers. For your entertainment, we have enchanted a few of the dolls today. They may resemble an army of golems enchanted by an evil witch, but never fear, our wizards will save you!"

He leapt into the fray and pumped the suppressor, squirting a gob of gold goo and hitting a doll square in the chest. "Wizards, one, golems zero!" he yelled in triumph as it collapsed to the ground with its silly grin still intact, oozing glittery foam.

Thank Ursa, it worked. Suddenly, the fear on the children's faces turned to delight, and their parents' annoyance changed to amusement. Following his lead, Susan laid a big blob on another "golem" in the back of the head. "Wizards, two," Ted cried, though he hated seeing his stock depleted like this.

Daisy came running up, looking annoyed. "Boss, why didn't you tell me—"

He pulled her aside and spoke over the cheers as Susan nailed another one and the crowd yelled out the third score. "Someone else is doing this. I have to find out who. Here, you hunt golems." He pulled off the wizard outfit and handed her the suppressor.

She looked at the merchandise lying ruined on the

floor. "What are you going to do with them?" she asked as she donned the costume.

"Good question." He grabbed the mike again. "One day only, a special sale. Get a vanquished golem with every purchase, while supplies last."

There, that should help with clean-up, though he had to make sure supplies didn't last very long. "Go on, shoot some golems."

As she took aim and Susan scored another hit, Ted was distracted by snickering nickers coming from a party of unicorns. Susan's aim had been a little off and one had been hit with some stray foam—a gray spot appeared on its otherwise pristine white hide. It must have had a personal enhancement spell that had been ruined by the suppressor.

As the embarrassed unicorn galloped out into the mall, other customers realized what was happening and followed. Ted had no idea there were so many spelled folks out there. He was afraid he'd just lost some clientele, but thankfully most of those exiting stopped outside the store to watch the battle through the windows. Even the protestors peered in . . . and it looked as though some of them were laying bets.

"There's one, there's one," a dragonet said, squealing in excitement.

Daisy and Susan, really hamming it up now, caught the golem in a crossfire and gunned it full of goo. The red fuzzy doll collapsed. "Wizards, six!" everyone cheered.

Six already? He had to stop this! He could practically feel his money draining away as he stood there, doing nothing. And, though everyone seemed to be entertained, it wasn't selling any merchandise while they watched the show.

Who was doing this to him? And why? He was a good werebear—paid his taxes, changed only on the full moon, and took care not to eat his neighbors. Who had it in for him?

Wait, was that why Grunch was so late? Was the troll responsible for this? Maybe he was angry for being chewed out for being late all the time.

No, it didn't track with the troll's nature. He was used to being yelled at. A mischievous fairy, maybe? If so, Ted would have the creature's wings.

"Wizards, seven!"

Now everyone was involved in the hunt, except for that old witch with rheumy eyes who was winking madly at the cabana boy. She must really be senile if she thought he—or anyone—would respond.

Ted looked around quickly. Where was the culprit? Most of the lurching golems had come from the wall directly across from the mall entrance. The wards at his doors and windows should prevent destructive spells from crossing the threshold, so either it was a time-released enchantment set earlier . . . or the perpetrator was somewhere inside right now.

Well, he had to hope the scumbag was still here. Otherwise Ted had no chance in hell of finding and stopping the attack. He could call in mall security, but that would expose his "entertainment" charade and might panic the customers. No, he had to figure this out himself.

"Wizards, eight!" The score was slowing, because excited patrons were getting in the way of the "wizards."

Ted scanned the crowd rapidly, hoping to spot someone out of place, someone who might have it in for him. He didn't recognize anyone in the crowd. Unfortunately, the guilty party didn't have to be an actual spellcaster to cast the curse—he only needed to have an enchanted wand or object of some kind to point at Ted's merchandise.

"Wizards, nine!"

Ted winced at the score, annoyed that he hadn't seen any pointing going on.

"Stop that right this instant," a woman said.

Uh-oh. Ted whirled in the direction of the voice, afraid he'd find a golem molesting a customer. Luckily, he realized she was speaking to her preadolescent son who had partially morphed into a wolf. There were telltale signs of stuffing in the werewolf cub's claws and a golem lay with one leg shredded, spinning slowly around the floor on half a leg. The cub had probably lost control with all of the excitement.

"Werewolf, one!" the cub cried as another shout announced, "Wizards, ten!"

As she grabbed him firmly by the ear and shook him, he whined, "But, Mom, I just want to help defeat the evil witch's army."

"It's just pretend," she said in annoyance. "Control yourself."

As Ted squirted the squirming victim, the light dawned. Had Ted accidentally hit on the real offender when he'd made up his cover story? The only witch in the store was that batty old crone. Maybe she wasn't so harmless after all.

She was still staring at the cabana boy, who was clad in a tight swimsuit and unbuttoned Hawaiian shirt, holding a tray of colorful drinks. But this time she'd backed off to get a different angle of view. As she winked, one of the dolls in her line of vision behind the boy lurched into motion.

Bingo. The culprit wasn't an unknown enemy, just a senile old crone. She was probably trying to animate the cabana boy with her winks and kept missing because she couldn't find her glasses.

"Wizards, eleven!"

He strode toward her, his hands clenched into fists, and he felt his anger rise along with his ursine nature. When hair sprouted on the back of his hands and he felt claws dig into his palms, he forcibly calmed himself. He was no cub to lose control—he had to find a way to deal with this calmly and rationally. If *he* changed, it wouldn't be into a cute fuzzy toy.

The scrawny woman was trying another angle so he clamped his hand, mercifully free of claws, on her shoulder and said, "Don't you dare wink again or I'll call Security."

She screeched and whirled around, looking guilty. "What?"

"Your winking is doing this, isn't it?"

"Doing what?" She looked bewildered.

He sighed. So it really was an accident. But how in hell was he going to explain this to his insurance company? Was he even covered for acts of nonmalicious magic? "Look around. See all of those make-a-mortals walking around?"

"Y-yes."

"They're not supposed to do that. *You* did that."

"Wizards, twelve!"

He winced at the tally. "How many times did you wink, lady?" He grabbed her shoulders so she couldn't use her evil eye past his bulk and resisted the urge to shake her. Surely some of her winking spells had to have missed.

She still looked confused.

Susan came up, with her Super Soaker resting on one hip and wizard cap askew. "Is this the troublemaker?"

"Yes," he growled. "I caught her in the act."

The old woman squirmed in his hold. "I didn't do nothin'. Why you hurtin' poor old Agatha?"

"You turned half my stock into walking golems, Agatha. You scared my customers." Both statements were exaggerations, but it could have been worse. Much worse.

"Didn't neither. I was jes tryin' to get me a cabana boy."

Susan grimaced and looked as if she'd like to squirt the old witch right in the kisser. "Pervert," she muttered.

"Am not," Agatha said indignantly. "I jes wanted someone to help me in my old age. You know, bring me drinks, mebbe massage my bunions."

"Wizards, thirteen!"

Ted closed his eyes. All this bad luck and havoc because the witch wanted a servant? Why hadn't that damned magic mirror warned him? "Why didn't you just hire someone?"

She snorted. "Ain't no one want to work for old Agatha. Besides, how I gonna pay him? Fer some reason, all my spells have been goin' a leetle wonky lately, specially when I can't find my glasses."

The woman wasn't malicious, just incompetent and lonely. Ted's anger drained out of him, leaving nothing but frustration and sympathy.

Susan frowned, looking sorry for the old hag. "What are you going to do?" she asked Ted.

He sighed and released Agatha. "I don't know." He didn't want to call Security on the old woman, and he didn't dare ask Agatha to remove the spell. No telling what her bad eyesight would do then.

Already, her gaze was wandering back to the Speedo-clad boy toy.

He blocked her gaze with his large hand. "Hey, keep your eyes on me."

Agatha glared at him. "Why? You gonna work for me?"

"No, but I am going to help you."

"How?"

"If I buy you a servant, will you promise never to come in my store again?"

Agatha nodded, though she looked suspicious. "Iffen I had me a servant, I wouldn't need to go nowhere."

"Wizards, fourteen!"

I can't believe I'm going to do this. "Okay, then I'll get you one."

Agatha turned toward the cabana boy, but Ted said, "Not him. Another servant. A better one." He couldn't allow any animated merchandise out of his shop.

She pinned him with a glare. "I've taken a fancy to thet snazzy outfit of his'n."

"Okay, you can have the cabana boy costume." What little there was of it. "But not the boy itself."

Grunch arrived then, looking sheepish and a bit sleepy, though bewildered by all the commotion. The large hairy troll spotted Ted and tried to slip past him, but he wasn't made for being inconspicuous.

Ted raised his voice. "Over here, Grunch. *Now.*"

Daisy came hurrying up, too, her hair and wizard robe awry and her cheeks flushed. "Got 'em all, boss. I don't see any more moving."

"Good." With any luck, there wouldn't be any more.

Ever. Grabbing the mike, he said, "That's the end of our show, folks. The evil witch has been captured and her golem hoard defeated. Let's hear it for the wizards."

Cheers rang out as Daisy and Susan took their bows, then raised their squirt guns in victory.

"Remember," Ted continued, "for each purchase made today, you get one free defunct golem while supplies last. First come, first served."

The customers rushed to the golems and the register. "Can you take care of the customers, Daisy?"

"Sure, boss."

She headed off, but when Grunch tried to follow her, Ted stopped him.

Grunch looked contrite . . . and scared. "I'm sorry, boss—"

"Save it. I'll deal with you later. For now, take this witch to Spence's and buy her a magically programmable android, compliments of Make-a-Mortal. Make it a servant model, and charge it to the store."

Grunch's mouth gaped open. "Those things are *expensive*, boss."

"Yeah, I know. Just do what I say." It was worth it to get rid of the destructive witch once and for all.

Agatha poked him in the side. "Remember them duds."

"Oh, and give her the cabana boy outfit, too. But whatever you do, do *not* let her back in this store. Or allow her to wink at anything."

Grunch shrugged his massive shoulders, looking confused but compliant. "Okay, boss. Whatever you say."

Grunch trudged off with the gleeful witch hobbling in his wake.

Unfortunately, Ted's problems weren't over. He still had to deal with Susan and the protestors.

Unexpectedly, she said, "That was kind of you."

Relieved at her reaction, Ted waved away any claims to generosity. "Just trying to control the damage."

"Still, you could have had her arrested, but you didn't."

He grinned at her in hope. "Does that mean you'll call off the protestors?"

Her raised eyebrow showed his hope was in vain. "I helped you, now you help me."

His heart sank. "Come on, you can't expect me to close my store. It's my livelihood. Besides, can't you see how the little ones love the cute mortals?"

She snorted. "*Little* ones?"

"Okay, maybe not so little to you, but they are children. Would you take away their joy?"

Sighing, she said, "It's not the children I worry about. It's their parents . . . and others. You and I both know that your 'mortals' are sometimes used for target practice and . . . other unsavory things. Things that give your kind bad ideas about real mortals."

"I don't know that," Ted denied. "And neither do you."

Susan gave him a disbelieving stare.

"Okay, it's possible." He thought for a moment. "How about I change my advertising to more clearly emphasize that my toys are for children only? And no more clothing that would suggest anything . . . of an unsavory nature."

"You really think that will deter anyone?"

Maybe not. "What about a spell to make sure they can't be used for unwholesome purposes?"

She gestured with her spell suppressor. "And if they have one of these?"

Good point. He thought some more. "Okay, I'll ask Merle—a wizard friend of mine—to make it partly magical, partly mundane. If the spell is deactivated by outside means, he can set up an electronic device to make it explode."

He immediately rejected the idea. "No, wait—I don't want to hurt anyone who might accidentally cancel the spell." Especially a child . . . or any innocent bystanders. "Instead, I'll have an alarm go off identifying the location of the perpetrator. And I can have it set to notify someone if they try to remove the alarm, too."

"Notify who?" she asked suspiciously.

He grinned. "You decide. Would you like it to come to the league? That will help you identify antimortal sentiments among the magicals."

Her eyes gleamed, and he could almost see her mind churning over the possibilities. "Won't that be expensive, cut into your profits?"

"Probably." But he knew he could get a good deal from compassionate, ultraliberal Merle when he learned what it was for. "This no-tolerance policy might actually be good for business." He'd have to jack up prices to accommodate the increased expense. It might lose him some sales, but it would gain others. And earning the goodwill of the Mortal AntiDefamation League wasn't a bad idea either. "I'll even make sure Merle works with you to define exactly what will set off the spell."

"Okay, Ted, you've got a deal." She handed him the spell suppressor and took off her wizard robes and hat, then glanced over at the register. "Looks like your clerk needs some help."

True. Daisy was mobbed at the counter, and it looked as though his stock of wizard outfits was cleaned out. His spirits perked up. He might actually come out of this all right after all . . . even though that stupid magic mirror had been no help.

As Susan went outside to tell her cohorts the news, he glared at the mirror. "You were a waste of money," he growled. "Why didn't you warn me about this?"

A face formed in the mirror, appearing as the fairy that had sold him the defective rig. It grinned at him and wagged a finger. "Not nice, Mr. Braun. The specifications are working properly. I am set to warn you only in the event of imminent catastrophe to your establishment."

"And this didn't qualify?" Ted asked in disbelief.

"Not at all. As a result of this 'disaster,' you will develop a reputation for wholesome fun and become beloved of children and parents everywhere. Merle will make a lot of money from his patented antimortal sentiment detection invention, and you will form an alliance with Susan that will be the model for mortal-magical relations all over the world."

"And my store?" Ted asked.

"Your profits will skyrocket."

Stunned, Ted could only stare at the image in the mirror. *Really?* It had to be true—the mirror couldn't lie.

A dragonet tugged on his shirt. "Hey, mister, what was the final score?"

"Wizards, fourteen, werewolf one, golems zero," Ted said absently.

But that wasn't quite true. This time, everybody won.

FANG FEST

Laura Resnick

Laura Resnick is the author of such fantasy novels as *Disappearing Nightly*, *In Legend Born*, *The Destroyer Goddess*, and *The White Dragon*, which made the "Year's Best" lists of *Publishers Weekly* and *Voya*. Winner of the 1993 Campbell Award for best new science fiction/fantasy writer, she has published more than fifty short stories, as well as dozens of columns and articles. Under the pseudonym Laura Leone, she is the award-winning author of more than a dozen romance novels, including *Fallen From Grace*, which was a finalist for the Romance Writers of America's Rita Award. You can find her on the Web at www.LauraResnick.com

How I wound up going on the run, fleeing federal and local authorities, and being targeted for death by Chicago's major vampire syndicate . . . is a tale that began quite innocently.

To be candid, I blame my mother.

Admittedly, there were other factors involved. But it all began when my mother's incessant nagging drove me to do something so unusual, so extreme, so completely out of character that, had you known me before then, you'd have said it was impossible within the context of the universe as we know it.

In short, I got a job.

At the time, I had finished my education and was at loose ends, as the saying goes.

"*Finished* your education?" my mother shrieked at me one day as I lay on the couch in our den, with the TV remote in one hand and a box of fat-free snack crackers in the other. "You haven't finished your education, Lily! You've been kicked out of three colleges! Including my alma mater. Oh, the shame—the embarrassment!"

"That's why I don't claim to have 'completed' my education, Mother," I said, flipping TV channels. "But I am definitely *finished* with education."

Oprah was interviewing two tragically overdressed female vampires who had started a twelve-step group for those of their kind who wanted to give up drinking blood. After three years, the movement still had only a tiny handful of followers—and when you looked at the sunken, desiccated faces of these two founders, it was easy to see why. I flipped the channel again.

"I don't understand you." Mother paced back and forth in front of the TV, where sports pundits were debating whether horn size should be a handicap factor in the annual Unicorn Derby. As if anyone with a life really cared. "You've always scored so high in intelligence and aptitude tests. If only you would *apply* yourself."

"Mother, education is all about interpreting the symbolism of James Joyce and discussing why the Roman Empire split into two halves. Frankly, who cares? Why *should* I apply myself to that?"

"Perhaps you were just too busy applying yourself to drinking, dancing, and dating," she snapped.

"Well, that was the part of college I liked," I said reminiscently. In terms of lifestyle, college was definitely better than fleeing from room to room of my mother's luxury condo on Lake Shore Drive while she pursued me, nagging me about what I would do now—NOW, *right* now!—with the rest of my life.

I had been back home for two weeks, since being kicked out of my third college for failing every course I had taken there. In fact, I was the first student in the entire history of that school to fail "Alternative Belief Systems: Christianity, Judaism, and Atheism." It was that record-breaking achievement that convinced the administration to invite me to leave. Well, okay, that and also a few recreational opiates I was caught sharing with the hot new necromancy professor late one Saturday night. In his car. Naked.

But I digress.

Yes, I had been home for two weeks now . . . and it was beginning to feel like eternity.

"If you're not going to be a student," Mother continued, "then what exactly *are* you going to do? You can't just lie around here day after day!"

"Why not? That's what *you* do." Mom had married well. Twice. To men who were too stupid to get prenups and too law-abiding to have a curse or spell put on her when she divorced them.

Mother stopped pacing and turned to face me, hands on hips. "I *earned* everything I have."

Although I didn't acknowledge it, there was undeniably a sense in which this was true. If you had met my father or my stepfather . . . Well, suffice it to say that my memory of sharing a home with each of them, at various points in my youth, was precisely why I didn't view marriage as an appealing career alternative to college. I flipped the channel again.

"You can't sit around the house for the rest of your life," Mother said. "My astrologer says it's not your destiny."

She resumed her pacing, getting in the way of some CNN footage of an "equal rights for werebeings" rally in Washington, D.C. Hoping to drown out Mother, I turned up the volume.

"You're going to have to do something with yourself!" she shrieked. "Are you listening to me?"

"I'm trying *so* hard not to."

Some of the attending werecats had come into heat during the course of the three-day rally. This had resulted in a mass mating frenzy that, CNN said, merely confirmed widespread views that werebeings were not yet ready to assume the responsibilities that would necessarily accompany the legal rights they were demanding. Most of the camera footage was censored in accordance with broadcasting laws, but I could still see enough— even with Mom's pacing getting in my way—to be glad that all werefemales in Illinois were required, by law, to stay at home whenever their hormone levels were apt to incite such friskiness.

I like a little harmless fun as much as the next girl . . . but not in public and certainly not with TV cameras present.

"*Lily!*" Mother's voice was so shrill, I was surprised the windows didn't crack and shatter. "I'm *talking* to you!"

After a few more days of this sort of thing, I was desperate to get out of the house. So I did what anyone would do: I went shopping.

Enchantment Place, the most exclusive paranormal shopping mall in Chicago, was on Michigan Avenue, just a quick cab ride from Mother's condo. Catering to all manner of beings, Enchantment Place had every kind of exotic shop and service an ex-college student could desire, and it was open 24 hours a day, 364 days a year (closed for Halloween). The midnight-to-5:00-AM shoppers tended to be vamps, prowling weres, black-magic witches and dark wizards, Goths, writers, and musicians—in other words, not the sort of beings we typically saw on Lake Shore Drive. By day, the crowd was a bit more mundane, from society girls and trendy gays to day-trawling weres and licensed sorcerers.

I used cash from Mother's wallet, which I had grabbed on my way out the door, to tip the taxi driver. Then, with Mother's credit cards burning a hole in my pocket, I entered the mall in search of satisfaction.

Purple smoke and a peculiar smell was billowing out of A Taste of Spice, a culinary shop for chefs and spellcasters. This was too reminiscent of the chemistry class mishap that had hastened my departure from my first college, so I went right past the shop without looking in. I noticed they were having a sale at Walking On Air . . .

but floating shoes were already *so* last year, I decided not even to bother browsing. I tried on some cool leopard-print loungewear at Touch of Silk, but the way two dawdling male werecats started eyeing me made me decide against buying it. Personally, I don't think it's ever a good idea to look *that* interesting to a were.

I descended one level and headed toward my favorite shop, Fiery Finish, a store famous for its safety-guaranteed, spontaneously combusting accessories: bracelets, earrings, necklaces, rings, scarves, purses, collars, leashes, hand-cuffs, whips, anklets, etc. No guy ever forgets a girl who's got a ring of fire around her neck when they meet.

The shop, however, wasn't there. In its place was something called Fang Fest.

Realizing that Fiery Finish must have moved since my last visit to Enchantment Place (which had occurred be-tween attending my second and third colleges), I looked around for a mall directory. Not finding one, I went back to Fang Fest. The shop windows were so dark I could hardly see inside, and the place looked uninviting— maybe not even open for business. However, when I tried the handle, the door opened. So I went inside.

It was a gourmet deli catering to special tastes. But the shelves were sparsely stocked, and there were no customers. I spotted a guy behind the deli counter—an absolutely *gorgeous* guy—and headed toward him. On my way, I passed a haphazard display of bottles with names like Blood of the Virgin, Bloody Mary, Blood Lite, Heart's Blood ("100% Pure Ventricle Excre-tions!"), Bloodshot, Crimson Delight, and Red ("Accept No Substitutes!"). It was easy to guess who those bever-ages would appeal to—but given how lame the display was and how empty the shop was, I wasn't surprised to see some dust on the bottles. Merchandise was not mov-ing briskly through this place, I gathered.

"Hi, there," I said to the blond, blue-eyed, well-built guy at the counter. "I'm looking for—"

"The heart of a lawyer?" he guessed.

I blinked. "Uh, no."

He frowned. "You're not the one who phoned in the order for it? 'Cause I got the heart right here, on ice."

"No, that wasn't me."

"Hmph. I'm starting to think they're not coming for it. Damn. It's getting pretty ripe." His handsome face brightened with a fresh idea. "Hey, do you maybe want it at a good price?"

"No, thanks."

"I'll take fifty percent off the going rate," he offered.

"No," I said. "I'm not into hearts." Not into eating them, anyhow.

"No? Oh . . . wait, *I* know! You want some fresh feet, right? Something nice to gnaw on over the weekend?"

"No, thanks," I said quickly. "I was just wondering—"

"You're not into soft tissue? That's fine. We've got some lovely bones. A nice tibia, maybe?"

"I'm not a werebeast," I snapped.

"You're not?" His blue, blue eyes widened. "Oh! Sorry. My mistake. You just look sort of . . . I mean . . ." He peered at me. "Are you sure?"

"Positive." But if cute guys were going to mistake me for one anyhow, maybe I should have just gone ahead and bought the leopard-print outfit at Touch of Silk. "I came in here to ask about—"

"The job!" He slapped his forehead. "Of course!"

"Actually—"

"I'm sorry." He grinned at me. *Dazzling.* "I hope I didn't offend you?"

I was looking at his smile. "Huh?"

"The were thing. Honest mistake. You just look, you know . . . kind of sexy. I thought you must be one."

I forgot about finding out where Fiery Finish had moved to. "What's your name?"

"Taylor Vince."

"Taylor Vince," I repeated, watching him flick a lock of blond hair off his forehead.

"It used to be Vince Taylor. Then I changed it. I'm an actor. And a swimsuit model."

"I'm Lily White."

"Oh, you don't look *that* white," he said kindly. "Not like a vamp or something."

"My *name* is Lily White."

"Oh! Oh, I see." He reached under his cash register, fumbled around for a minute, then pulled out a sheet of paper. "Here's the job application, Lily."

"What? Er, I didn't—"

"You can take it home to fill it out, then bring it back."

My next attempt to protest died on my lips as I recognized a handy excuse to pay another visit to Taylor. "Bring it back?"

"Yeah, if you fill it out at home, you can take your time," he explained. "It's a little complicated."

I skimmed the application. It asked for my name, my address, my emergency contact number, and whether I was a felon. "I see."

"I'll help you," he said, "if there are any parts you can't figure out."

"Oh, good," I said, watching his biceps bulge as he folded his arms across his chest and smiled at me again.

"Do you think you can bring it back tomorrow?" he asked.

"Tomorrow?" I admired the way his thick golden lashes fluttered down over his sea-blue eyes as he glanced at his wristwatch.

He said, "I'd like to fill the position soon."

"Position?"

"Assistant store manager." He beamed at me as he added, "*I'm* the manager."

"And also an actor."

"And a swimsuit model."

"Is there a big staff here?" I asked.

"Just me."

That surprised me. "But . . . I mean . . . You can't work twenty-four hours a day, surely?"

"Oh, we're not open at night," he said. "I mean, I know the *mall* is always open. But we close at six."

"That doesn't make sense." I gestured at the display

of blood beverages. "Your clientele mostly comes out at night, I would think."

"I mentioned that to the boss."

"I thought *you* were the boss," I said.

"I mentioned it to the owner, I mean."

"Oh."

"I said, 'Boss, this stuff we sell is mostly for vamps and weres. And they mostly come out at night. But we're only open by day. That's why we're not making any money.' " Taylor tapped his temple with a forefinger. "I got a head for business."

"Obviously."

He shrugged. "But the boss didn't budge. So we close at six o'clock every day. Union rules, I guess."

"You're in a union?" I asked doubtfully.

"No."

"But if *you're* the only employee, then whose union . . ." Taylor looked at me blankly, and I realized it wasn't important. "Never mind. Anyhow . . . I'll be back tomorrow for sure. With this application, I mean." I smiled, thinking I'd better stop off at Fiery Finish today, after all. I wanted to make a strong impression when I came back the next day. So I asked Taylor if he knew where I could find the boutique that had been in here before Fang Fest took over this location.

"You mean Fiery Finger?"

"Finish," I corrected.

"They moved up to the top level. More floor space, more foot traffic. Closer to the fire hydrant."

"Maybe the safety guarantees in their products are a tad elastic," I said.

Nonetheless, I spent a few hundred dollars at Fiery Finish that afternoon. Then I went back to Touch of Silk and bought the leopard-print outfit. What the hell.

But Mother's nagging that night drove me over the edge.

I was trying to watch *Law & Order: Bloody Intent*, the *L&O* spin-off featuring an intuitive vamp detective and his partner, a plucky white witch with a dark past, when

Mom started in on me. Her obsession with my "utterly directionless life" was further fueled by her fury (all out of proportion, if you ask me) over learning that I'd charged about seven hundred dollars to her credit cards that afternoon.

"I needed a few things," I said, watching the TV vamp detective bare his fangs at an uncooperative witness.

"A flaming G-string?" my mother shrieked, waving around the bill as if it were evidence of my practicing illegal dark rites.

"It's not a G-string," I said, "it's a thong."

"What's the difference?" she snapped.

"Strippers wear G-strings. *I* wear thongs."

This reasonable explanation did not have the soothing effect on her that I would have liked. And by the time the plucky white witch was handcuffing this week's killer while the vamp detective reflected morosely on the human condition, Mother was weeping and wailing about my worthless father, and how I was just like him, and wondering what to do with me and what was to become of me and why Western civilization was in such a dreadful decline . . .

And I heard myself say, "Will you *stop*? I'm going to get a job, okay?"

She lifted her tear-streaked face out of her hands and stared at me. "*What* did you say?" She hiccupped.

"I've got a job interview tomorrow." And it was dawning on me that spending time at Fang Fest with Taylor was likely to be a lot more enjoyable than spending time at home with my mother.

"A job?" She frowned. "You're going to . . . *work*?"

"Yes. A job. Work."

"Hmmm." She stared off into space. "Interesting. A . . . *job*."

There was a sixty-second silence. I couldn't believe it. There was actual *silence*. In my mother's presence! For the very first time since I had come home.

"A job," she said at last. "Hmm." With a faint, thoughtful frown, Mother rose from her chair and left the room quietly.

When I went into the kitchen later, she was reading the newspaper. She looked up briefly at me, said something about the headline story—organized vampire crime was on the rise in Chicago—and went back to reading.

In silence.

That was when I knew I *had* to get that job.

You can perhaps imagine with what sorrow, what despair, what unmitigated horror I learned the truth about Taylor: He was a trendy gay.

Not even bisexual. And not into experimentation with his sexuality.

"I went through all that already, Lily," he said to me as we replenished the fresh blood supplies in the cold deli case, after I'd been on the job for about a week. "I gave girls a try. Human girls, vamp girls, weregirls . . . It's just not my thing."

His heart had recently been broken by a werecat. And before that, a werewolf.

"I've *got* to get over this thing I have for weres," he said desperately. "There's just no future with someone who's got to howl at the moon every month and who goes berserk around females in heat even if he *is* completely gay."

"Whatever," I said.

In addition to not having any interest in dating me (so that was seven hundred dollars of Mother's money down the drain), Taylor was not exactly the brightest bulb in the chandelier. He was no more suited to running a business than I was to getting a Ph.D in literature or history. At first, I also couldn't understand why I had been hired; the shop's weekly income wasn't even enough to cover my paycheck.

By the end of my second week on the job, though, I began to suspect what my true role was at Fang Fest. Taylor might be a tad slow-witted (as well as unavailable to the female sex of any species), but he was a very nice, amiable, sweet-natured person. I never met the boss—a vamp named Ernest Gore, who was in Miami for a while—but Taylor obviously admired and respected him.

And my guess was that Mr. Gore was too fond of Taylor to fire him, even though he was driving the business into the ground through sheer ineptitude.

My job, I realized, must be to compensate for Taylor. Given the level that Taylor functioned at, this wasn't that big a challenge. Also, it soon turned out that I had a real flair for making money. Figuring out how to get more beings into the shop and parting with their money—*this* was something that made sense to me, in a way that James Joyce and the Roman Empire had not. This seemed like something well worth *applying* myself to. In fact, I enjoyed it. I was also good at it—and being good at something is a real kick.

My being good at something also kept my mother amazingly quiet. Which was a major bonus.

I began by putting attractive stock displays in the windows, as well as signs—hand lettered in blood, which our target clientele found very nostril catching—that advertised special sales. And since fresh blood and organs spoil quickly, I started running special offers and two-for-one discounts several times a week. (Before I started working at Fang Fest, Taylor had simply thrown away all that stuff when it went bad. Such a waste!)

Then I redesigned the store's interior a little, using track lighting in red (for vampires), blue (for weres), and green (for practitioners of the Craft) to highlight different in-store stock displays. I also started hand selling some of the more expensive shelf items, since I had a good eye for who came into the store with money to burn.

And shoppers were indeed coming into the store by now. All it had taken to get them in there was a little business sense.

Next, despite Taylor's warnings that the boss (who was now in Vegas for a while) probably wouldn't like it, I rearranged the store hours. I scheduled Taylor, whom I seldom saw anymore (he had entered an intense new relationship with a vampire chef who'd become a regular Fang Fest customer), to work afternoons and evenings, and then I worked from ten at night until six in the morning. We were closed from six until early afternoon, since I'd studied sales receipts for the shop's first few months of business and discovered that no one had ever—not *ever*—bought anything at Fang Fest during those hours.

Now that foot traffic and word-of-mouth business had really picked up and we were turning a profit, I decided it was time to raise the shop's profile with the public at large. I held a few special events at the store, such as a white-tie exotic beverage party, where I served blood samples as varied as python, politician, okapi, Orthodox rabbi, Russian wolfhound, Mbuti pygmy, yellow-throated scimitar warbler, and Lithuanian.

Our next event was a July Fourth bash in which patriotic vamps and werebeasts came dressed as the Second Continental Congress; the event culminated in them signing a Declaration of Independence in blood. That party, which was an incredible success, got written up in the *Chicago Tribune*.

The next thing I knew, one of the local morning-chat TV shows decided to do a feature story on Fang Fest. But they asked a lot of questions about Ernest Gore (who was currently in Atlantic City for a while), which annoyed me. I was interested in promoting the store, not in answering questions about the boss—whom I still hadn't even met! In fact, it was starting to offend me that Gore hadn't even noticed all my hard work, never mind acknowledging that it was all thanks to *me* that his store was finally turning a handsome profit.

Taylor moved to the West Coast when his vampire-chef boyfriend got offered a job in Beverly Hills. With no idea where Gore was at the moment, I started paying the bills myself, using the Fang Fest checkbook I found in the storage room. With the shop so busy day and night now, I hired half a dozen store clerks, trained them, and began expanding into internet and mail order business.

By October, Fang Fest was the "hottest, hippest, most happening" business in Enchantment Place, according to *Chicago Magazine*, and CNN's new national *Paranormal Chic* program wanted to do a story on the shop.

Also in October, the authorities showed a sudden, intense interest in me, the store, and my boss.

One afternoon, two FBI agents in identical dark blue suits showed up at the shop with a search warrant that covered virtually everything in the store—the stock, the financial statements, the ordering and shipment records, and the safe. I had never been in the safe, since even Taylor hadn't known the combination. When the FBI opened it with a drill, they found $437,921, two guns, a disposable cell phone, and some diamonds in there.

"What do you know about this, Miss White?" one of the agents asked me.

"Maybe that's why Mr. Gore never calls," I said.

"Excuse me?"

I pointed to the cell. "He left his phone here."

While the FBI agents were searching the shop, questioning my staff, and hauling away all my stock and my records, some Chicago police showed up, too. Also some county officials. And a state prosecutor. It had recently come to their attention that Fang Fest wasn't licensed for, oh, *anything* we sold. And since I was by now selling my stock across state lines, too, the local authorities weren't the only ones interested in this oversight.

"I think I need to speak to Mr. Gore," I said.

"You need to speak to a *lawyer*, Miss White."

I went home that day wondering how I could contact Gore.

"Gore?" my mother said in the kitchen that evening, when I explained that I wasn't at work because the shop had been closed by order of law and everything in it had been confiscated or impounded. "Hmm. That sounds familiar. Gore, Gore, Gore . . ."

"Do we know a good lawyer?" I asked.

"My divorce lawyer is *excellent*," Mother said, leafing through the newspaper with a faint frown of concentration.

"No, I think I'll need a criminal lawyer."

"Ah, here it is! There's a fellow named Gore who's been in the news all week." She waved the newspaper she was reading. "The boss of Chicago's biggest organized vampire crime syndicate."

"No, no," I said, "my boss is *Ernest* Gore."

"Yes, that's the name," Mother said, squinting at her paper. " 'Ernest Gore, the most ruthless boss in the history of organized crime in Chicago, which is saying quite a lot.' Hmm. That doesn't sound good."

"*What?* Give me that!" I seized the newspaper and started reading. According to the *Tribune*, the clever financial machinations of vampire syndicate boss Ernest Gore had recently been blown wide open by the FBI, thanks to the steadily rising profile of a small Chicago gourmet deli he'd been using to launder money. "Oh, my *God*."

"I gather it's the *same* Ernest Gore?"

"I won't need a lawyer," I said, "I'll need an undertaker."

No wonder Gore had let Taylor run the shop so ineptly! It was *supposed* to lose money. Gore had *created* it to lose money!

"This is very bad news for me," I said.

The phone rang. Mother answered. The caller was Gore.

I took the phone from my mother and said into the receiver, "*Now* you're calling? NOW?"

"You've ruined me!" Gore bellowed into the phone.

"I've got local, state, and federal authorities crawling all over me because of you!" I shouted back.

Mother said, "Don't shout, dear—"

"Fang Fest was supposed to keep a low profile!" Gore said. "You were never supposed to *make money* there! Let alone become the most talked-about success story on the Miracle Mile!"

"How was I supposed to know that? You never once said anything to me!"

"I left messages for Taylor, telling you to stop doing what you were doing!" Gore shouted.

"When?" I demanded.

"Once a week for the past month!"

"Taylor moved West a month ago! I never got those messages, you idiot!"

There was a long, deadly silence during which I had a lot of time to regret calling a notorious vampire crime boss an "idiot."

When Gore spoke again, his voice was calm and firm. "You're a dead woman, Lily White. Every vampire in my organization will be looking for you by morning."

"In that case, I'd better start packing." I ended the call and threw the receiver against the wall.

Mother said, "What on earth—"

"Your astrologer is smarter than I ever suspected, Mom," I said wearily.

"What?"

"It turns out that sitting around the house for the rest of my life really *isn't* my destiny."

I was on the road before sundown, with enough cash to last me until Mother wires me a big sum of money from her post-divorce investments. I contacted the FBI to discuss trading information for protection. But since I don't know anything about Gore, and since my signature is all over the financial transactions of a money-laundering business that's broken a few hundred health and trade regulations, I have nothing to offer, and prosecutors are practically lining up to have a crack at me.

I also called my mother. She said, "You've lost a good job and you've got local, state, and federal authorities after you, as well as a lot of killer vampires. For goodness sake, Lily, what are you planning to do with your life *now*? What? WHAT, I ask you?"

I don't know yet. But I do know the moral of my story: *This* is what comes of mothers nagging.

MIRROR, MIRROR

Phaedra M. Weldon

Phaedra M. Weldon has written short stories for
several anthologies, as well as novellas published in shared universe fields such as *Star
Trek* and *BattleTech*. *Wraith*, her first novel,
was recently released in trade paperback.

"**S**iobhan, there's a dead body on the floor of your
shop."

She knitted her eyebrows together in concentration. It
wasn't the best way to start a Saturday night—especially
after just waking from the day.

Siobhan O'Donnell stood behind the counter of her
mirror store, a specialty shop situated in Chicago's Enchantment Place that gave the vampire population a way
to see their reflections. Small cameras built into every
mirror projected the vampire's image on a sheet of
crystal.

"And it's drained of blood."

She pulled the right side of her mouth into a smirk.

"You got something you want to tell me?"

With a slow nod, she looked up into the exotic face
of Captain Oberon Geld, one of Chicago's finest and the
former King to the Elven Seleighe court—as well as her
ex-partner and one-time lover.

But not anymore. On both counts.

"Ron," she said, using the nickname he hated most.

Just because he hated it. "I'm going to have to agree with you. There's a dead body on the floor drained of blood."

The tall elf opened his mouth to speak. Siobhan held up her index finger. "But I didn't do it."

"But you realize how this looks, don't you?"

She arched her eyebrows at him, fixing him with a look that said, "Duh."

Her last job—and life change—had been on the other side of the law. As a detective for the Chicago police, she'd been one of the best at investigating unconventional conventional homicides. Vampires did make good cops, as did the older, Seleighe Court Elves like Oberon. Both races were formidable, strong, intelligent, and long-lived. Both were attractive and sensuous in their own right, and both races possessed an irresistible sex appeal for mortals.

And they could both kill—violently.

Their differences were less obvious. A vampire held brute strength and the ability to shift to a second form, but an elf could wield magic—if he or she were properly trained. A vampire and an elf were a perfect team.

But the elves had one advantage over the vamps. They could move around in the daylight. She'd always wished she could invent some sort of magic potion to make day-walking a possibility. Just think of the money to made with that!

Oberon crossed his arms and nodded toward her. He was impeccably dressed as always, in a suit with his tie loosened and his jacket unbuttoned. His white-blond hair was cut short in a modern style, so unlike the long, braided locks he once wore as King of the Seleighe.

He didn't look any happier to see her now than the last time they'd met. Nor did she care for the angry glint in his bright amber eyes and their catlike pupils. His skin was flawless, as was her own. And he was as beautiful now as he was the first time the two of them had touched.

"Siobhan . . ." he started in that old, familiar patronizing tone. He held up the slip of paper the officers had found on the dead body. "What does this mean?"

"Oberon, how can I tell you when I haven't even been

allowed to see it? I told you, I came down here after rising to find a dead woman in the middle of my shop. I called the police right away—and your goons have kept me here for eight hours."

He handed it to her. Siobhan opened the folded piece of paper. In black marker someone had written YOU ARE IN DANGER. She didn't recognize the handwriting.

"Who is this from? What are you in danger from?"

She gave him a scathing look, hoping to hide her growing alarm at the note's message behind her terse manner. "How the hell am I supposed to know? And besides, is the message for me or for her?" She frowned at the body. "I'd say it was meant for her—albeit a bit late. I've been asleep all day."

"And the district attorney's going to say you got up and fed on some prostitute you found breaking into your shop."

"P'sshhhh." Siobhan moved away from Oberon to the body sprawled on her floor. She knew who it was— Melissa Broden, bartender and part-time donor over at *Chimeras*, the local vamp bar. The victim being a donor was the reason for Oberon's prostitution comment; he'd always hated to see humans selling their blood as boxed lunches.

Siobhan knelt beside Melissa and noticed the marks on her neck. Very round and very visible. There was little blood. She leaned in closer, careful not to touch. She was no longer a cop, nor did she have any gloves on. "Oberon," she said in a firm voice. Several of the officers nearby ceased their conversations. "This wasn't a vampire killing."

He moved closer and knelt down to her right. "Not a vampire?"

"No," she nodded to the wound. "Too perfect. Too round. Vampire teeth were human once—" she looked at him with arched brow. "No set of vampire bites is the same."

Oberon shook his head. "So how do you explain the blood loss?"

"Blood can be drained from a body in many ways," Siobhan sniffed. "I'd say this one was with magic. It's got that smell. The blood was completely removed from the body." She looked at Oberon. "Which, of course, would kill the human quickly."

"That's ridiculous." He stood. "There's no legal spell to remove blood from a human. That would be delving into dark magic, which is strictly forbidden, same as a vampire drinking from an elf."

"Well, that's just suicide." She stood up beside him. Elven blood was poison to vampires, causing them to burn up from the inside out. An elf could drink a vampire's blood with no other consequence than a trip to the hospital and a bad case of the runs.

She shook her head as she gazed down at the body. "I'd still look into magic. There's no instant punishment for using dark magic, Ron. Nor is there any way to prove the spellcaster's identity. Magic is strictly autonomous."

"Siobhan," he sighed, "I'm afraid you're going to have to do better than this. The district attorney's not going to blame magic. If she did, she'd incite the wrath of witches, mages, magicians, elves and the Goddess knows who or what else living in this world."

"Political suppression?" Siobhan narrowed her eyes. "What's going on, Oberon? Why are you so quick to count me as a suspect? You know I'm right. This wasn't done by a vampire."

When he didn't speak but looked away, she had her answer. "This isn't the first death."

Oberon didn't answer.

She moved to stand in front of him and search his beautiful face. "Why don't you tell me?"

"Whether you like it or not, Siobhan, you're not a cop. I don't report to you."

"What is wrong with you?"

But she knew that look. Had seen it many times. "You fought with Abyssinian again." The mention of Oberon's unseleighe brother caused the vein in his neck to pulse.

The two had never gotten along—though Siobhan

found the elven king's brother . . . amusing. Actually, he was a lot of fun where Oberon was stiff and unmoving.

"Damned vigilante." He turned a mask of calm toward her. "I made sure he stays out of trouble."

"You did what?" Come to think of it, she hadn't seen Abyssinian in nearly a week. Which wasn't like him—the unseleighe always stopped by. A few of her clientele tended to grab coffee at the local Starbucks and hang out, just to catch a glimpse of him. "What did you do to him?"

But Oberon wasn't going to tell her. "Don't worry about Aby. You're hungry. Maybe I can get you something at the station."

"No, thanks. You know my stomach can't handle pre-packaged food."

The elf winced. "Siobhan . . . you have to drink. It seems I'm forever telling you that."

And it was true. Others of her kind had learned to take only what they needed from several people a night. And it suited them. But she'd never been able to do that because each drink gave her a taste of her donor's life. And sometimes all the lives got jumbled up in her head if she drank from more than one a night.

Not to mention the drama to her stomach when she woke up the next evening. The banks were a fine substitute, all privately owned and operated for the sole purpose of keeping vamps docile. Each bank received its blood through well-paid donors. Then it was screened (even vampires get diseases) and sent out to distribution banks all over the city.

It was the anticoagulants they put in the blood these days. They made her retch for a day.

A siren blared outside, and the two of them glanced to their left to see the icebox arrive outside. In a few seconds several white-coated men would appear, give last rites over the body, and then sever the head to keep the victim from returning as a ghoul.

As they moved away from the body, Siobhan filled him in on what she knew about the victim. Female, in her late twenties, had come in to buy one of her mirrors. One of the higher end models with the AV option.

"AV option?"

Sometimes he was still living long ago with no real desire to learn the technology of the present. When they were lovers, he still couldn't turn a computer on. "Audio visual option. They all have cameras in them that project onto the crystal surfaces." She was proud of her mirrors, a project she'd started nearly twenty years ago when she was finally tired of not knowing what she looked like. "Some actually save AMVs."

"Recordings?"

"Uh-huh. Oberon, I didn't kill that child. And given a few days and a forensic examination of the body, I can prove it."

The white-coated men moved in through the front door. Everyone turned to watch, their conversations quieted. "Well, as for a forensic examination, that's not going to happen."

"Well, that's convenient, isn't it?"

Siobhan and Oberon turned to their left.

Abyssinian lounged in the doorway. Dressed in his usual long leather trench coat, his brilliant red hair in contrast to his pale skin, the unseleighe brought a bit of color to the room. He wore leather gloves, boots, and pants. Siobhan knew the coat hid a sword beneath it, and the rings on Aby's fingers were spelled with protection.

"How did you—" Oberon started, then glanced at Siobhan. "You stay the hell out of this case, Aby."

But his brother only made tsk-tsk noises as he moved to join them. He'd cut his hair recently, ridding himself of his familiar long braid. Where Oberon's eyes were amber, Abyssinian's were indigo. She and Aby had become friends since she left the force. She didn't exactly support vigilantes, per se, but she did think Abyssinian was a just and fair man. "Why don't you tell her about the missing unseleighe, Ron."

"Don't call me that."

But Abyssinian wasn't going to stop. He turned his bright, intense gaze on Siobhan. "Didn't mention the fourteen or so missing unseleighe. Vanished. Gone," he snapped his gloved fingers. "Oh, he's concerned for the dead humans, as well as any of the vampires or seleighe—but not for his own people."

"You're not my people."

Abyssinian looked down at the body. He glanced at Siobhan. "He think you did this?"

"It's what it looks like." Oberon balled his hands into fists.

"Like I said," Abyssinian folded his arms over his chest. "Convenient."

"Nobody asked you." Oberon rounded on his brother again.

"You really think I'm stupid enough to leave my food wrapper in my own business?" It was a crass statement, and her voice had risen some with her frustration. She especially detested the look of tolerance on the elf's face. His mask of superiority really chapped her ass sometimes.

"No, Siobhan. I don't. But my boss is going to come down on me if I don't make an arrest in twenty-four hours." He glanced back to the store where they were shuttling uniformed policemen out of the shop.

Siobhan could understand their caution. Sometimes the victims of a vampire's bite could go quietly. And sometimes it could get messy. But this wasn't a vampire bite. "I need time. Come on, professional courtesy."

"Sio, I can give you twenty-four hours before they're beating down my door for justice. But you'll have to leave the shop. It's a crime scene." He pointed at Abyssinian. "And *you* stay out of this."

Aby backed up, his gloved hands in the air.

"Twenty-four hours? Oberon, I can't do any amount of investigating in that amount of time. Christ, I can't go out in the sun for nearly thirteen of those hours." She glanced at her watch. "And it's nearly three in the morning now."

"That's what you got me for," Aby smiled.

Oberon moved Siobhan out of the way with a shove as he rounded on his brother. "So help me, Abyssinian

Geld, if I hear you've had anything to do with this case, I'll slap iron manacles on you and throw you into a dark room."

But Abyssinian only smiled. "Thanks, bro. I'll tell Mom and Dad you said hi."

"Hey, Captain," the burly officer stepped in close but knew better than to get involved in a family tiff. "The Last Rites team is ready."

Oberon glared at his brother before looking down at Siobhan. "Twenty-four hours, Siobhan. My own detectives will be working as well."

Yeah. Right. She took in a deep breath, dispelling the idea that vampires don't breathe, turned and left the shop through the back door with Abyssinian right behind her.

"Would he really put you in manacles?" Siobhan said as they walked down the Miracle Mile sidewalk, the store lights illuminating the entire strip.

"He already did." Abyssinian stopped and pulled down the left sleeve of his coat to reveal a nasty, puckered band of burned flesh around his wrist. "It only takes one manacle of cold iron to pretty much disable an unseleighe."

"My god," she touched the damaged flesh. "That's where you've been. I guess that hurt."

"Ever stepped into sunlight?" he asked as he pulled his sleeve back down. When she nodded, he nodded. "Then you pretty much know what it feels like. Only you can't get the manacle off."

"Why did he do that?"

"Because he's a creep. I keep telling you that. I told you that while you were dating him." He turned to walk and gestured for her to follow. "And you finally came to your senses."

"How did you get it off?"

"My brother has a very interesting set of friends. All girls." He beamed. "So I flirted."

"Where are we going?"

"To Sacred Harvest."

"The blood bank?" She reached out and pulled at his coat. He stopped and looked at her. "Aby, what's going on? And don't say you don't know 'cause you're a terrible liar."

"Melissa Broden bought a mirror from you."

"Yes. You overheard me tell Oberon that."

Abyssinian shook his head. "I already knew that because I asked her to buy it. Melissa was a friend of mine. And now she's dead, and the killer is trying to frame you."

"Wait," she shook her head. "Why did you ask her to buy a mirror?"

"Because I wanted to know what was really happening in Sacred Harvest. I've been watching it for weeks. A lot of vans go in and out of the back alley, and the other night I got a call from a friend, unseleighe. Said she met a really nice vampire and was meeting him at the blood bank for a night of dancing over at *Chimeras*. Well, then she vanished. Nothing. No body. No remains.

"Melissa got a job there and planted the mirror. My guess is that whoever is responsible for her death discovered the mirror—" he held up a gloved finger. "Noticed it wasn't a *normal* mirror."

Nodding slowly, Siobhan was catching on. "So we need to check out and see if the mirror is still there."

"Booyah." Abyssinian grabbed her hand. "Let's go. We've got about an hour and a half till sunrise."

Sacred Harvest was two blocks down from Miracle Mile near the Enchantment Place shopping center. The closer they got, the fewer people they saw.

Abyssinian paused at a door. A small sign to the right read "Sacred Harvest: Hours" and there were times posted below. "Do you hear anyone inside?"

Siobhan shook her head. "No."

He opened his right hand, splaying his fingers wide, and held it over the knob. A soft red glow surrounded the door, then a familiar click echoed in the alley.

"Neat trick," Siobhan followed him inside.

The place looked like any other doctor's office, with

industrial stainless steel sinks, sterile white counter tops, and aged vinyl couches where donors lay and made money while giving their life's blood to sustain the docile life of a vampire. Apparently elves could move easily in the dark as Abyssinian moved with a grace she'd only noticed once or twice with Oberon.

"Why did you break up with him?"

The question was totally unexpected in the dark. Siobhan paused. "What?"

Her companion stopped and looked at her. "Why did you leave him? What—what did he do?"

"Oberon? What did he not do?" She gave a stilted laugh. It was easy to laugh now, but two years ago when she and the elven king were partners in not only fighting crime but in the bedroom, she had—for the first time—feared another living creature. "In truth, Aby, I didn't love him. It's hard to love a man—mortal, vampire or elf—when they're so in love with themselves."

"I like you, Siobhan O'Donnel. You're honest. That's rare these days—no matter who or what you are."

He glanced at the front window before leading her into another room. This one was much smaller and filled with shelves of cabinets. The elf had his right hand out, and a small ball of light formed. It grew to the size of a baseball before he tossed it into the air. Sparkling light filled the room's tall ceiling and cast a glow over the two of them. "That'll give us light to see, but it won't alert any sensors."

But Siobhan caught the smell of something else. Something . . .

Sweet.

She had smelled it before—an hour or so earlier. And now she recognized it.

Elven blood.

She put a hand on his shoulder.

He paused. "What's wrong?"

"I smell blood. A lot of it."

"This is a blood bank."

"Well, duh. No, I smell elven blood." She spied a door on the opposite side of the room. Without a glance at her partner, Siobhan moved to the door. It was locked. Two powerful jerks and the mechanism broke under her strength.

The lemony smell of elven blood assaulted her when she opened the door. The ball of light started to follow them inside but hesitated and moved away. She could still see with her preternatural sight. In the center of the room lay an examination table, complete with restraining straps. It was smeared with blood. Buckets of it sat in the far corner. Thick, coagulated, dead blood.

"What the hell is this?" Siobhan took a step inside. "Is someone draining elven blood? What for?"

"Siobhan," Abyssinian said behind her. She turned to see him kneeling down over a pile of broken glass. He looked up at her. "I think we need to get out of here. Whoever it is found the mirror, and they probably took the recording."

"No," she moved to stand beside him. "The AV transmits packets directly to my FTP. But they're encrypted with a code set by the sender. That way the information is safe."

"Does Oberon know this?"

Siobhan threw him a hard stare. "What has Oberon got to do with this?"

"Nothing. Do you have a way of accessing the packet?"

"Yeah, from the computer in my shop. But I'd need to know what Melissa's code might be."

Abyssinian swallowed. "Try the note—the one Oberon found on the body."

She stared at him. "That note wasn't for me."

"It was for me." Abyssinian said. "Melissa called me yesterday. She was sure she was being followed. Said she was going to leave me a note at your shop—"

"Why are you in danger?"

"Because I already know what that recording is going to show, Siobhan. Like I said, I've been looking into this for a while. And let's just say I've pissed off the wrong people. I probably shouldn't have shown up at Mirror, Mirror, but I needed to draw my suspect out. Right now we need to get to your shop and get that packet to a safer place before the murderer does. He's not going to want this kind of evidence out."

Abyssinian turned abruptly, his eyes narrowing, his sword abruptly in his hands.

Where is he hiding that thing? Siobhan listened as well. "Someone's coming."

"We tripped an alarm," he moved back out of the secret room. "And I'd say there are lots of someones."

She followed him out, and the two of them made their way to the back door. Only now it was blocked by three humans. Two brandished swords, the other one a large book.

"Magicians," Abyssinian hissed, indicating the men with the books, and held his sword at the ready. He leaned back toward her. "Can you shift?"

"With pleasure."

In an instant Siobhan slipped into her wolven form, a beast with gray fur and bright silver eyes. She snarled at the men as they attacked—one sword after Abyssinian, the other after her. It was easy to dodge the sharpened blade in such a small space, and as the attacker tried to recover, she twisted around and sank her teeth into his left thigh. He screamed as he fell and tried to twist around to hack at the wolf with his sword.

Another lunge back and Siobhan was able to duck beneath the sword again and sink her fangs into the man's soft side. He lurched and was still.

The clang of swords told her Abyssinian was also engaged in a fight. The air buzzed around her as she felt the tingle of a spell and realized the magician was bringing the dead swordsman back to life beside her.

She moved away from the zombie and charged at the magician, but something kicked her back, slamming her into the wall. Dazed, she reverted back to her human form and sat blinking. Abyssinian parried several moves by his attacker, thrust up, then down, before bringing the sword up in a stroke that cut through the man from his left thigh to his right shoulder.

The new zombie charged the elf, but Aby twisted and cleanly sliced off the monster's head.

The magician began to chant again, and the two attackers came back to life again, completely whole.

"That is not sanctioned magic," Siobhan mumbled as Abyssinian bent down to help her. She saw he was bleeding along his neck where the attacker's sword had struck. It wasn't fatal, but it could cost him strength if he lost too much blood.

"Are you surprised?" he muttered as he grabbed her arm and pulled her in the opposite direction.

But there were two more swordsmen and another magician at the front and another set the filing room. With a curse, Siobhan took off toward the only unguarded room.

It was a back office, with an uncovered window facing the eastern sky. The dark was nearly gone, the dawn's colors quickly pushing aside the night's shade. There was no sign of a door or anything else save a single desk and chair. No closet.

"We're trapped."

Siobhan shook her head. "I am, you aren't." She nodded to the window. "In a few minutes I'm going to be a little bit less than toast. You can break that window and get away."

But Abyssinian was locking the door. "I'm not leaving you."

"Why not?"

"Because you have to know the secret. You have to know what it is these people are trying to do." He went to the window and braced himself against the pane. "If the murderer finds the files, if he destroys them, he'll come after you. You're vulnerable during the day, and he's a powerful mage in his own right." He looked out the window. "There aren't any attackers out there."

"Because they know I won't make it past sunrise."

"But I will." He lowered his sword and leaned against the window. He looked pale in the rising sunlight. "Unless they know I was wounded."

She saw the second hit—a wound in his lower left abdomen. "Abyssinian . . ." she moved to him, careful not to get her hands in the direct light from the window. He moved closer to her, staggering just a bit. She could only assume the adrenaline that had been pushing him was wearing off, and now his body was reacting to the damage.

The cut on his shoulder was deep, and it looked as if it had nicked the collar bone. He was going to need serious elven medical attention—and he was going to need to rest. "You're right—once I'm ash, you'll be at their mercy."

"I'm sorry," he said and pressed his back against the far wall. The sword fell to the ground with a clash as he lowered himself down against the wall. "I'm not strong enough. I was manacled . . . for too long."

"Manacled . . ." she knelt down beside him. "You said that was a long time ago."

"A day ago," Aby smiled. "I got in their way . . . I was taken and tortured . . . but I'm cleverer than he is."

"Abyssinian . . ." she touched his face. His indigo eyes focused on her. "I'm sorry I'm not much help either. Vampires are always painted as invincible and powerful. I wasn't those things even when I was a detective."

He leaned his head back against the wall. The light from the sun—now beginning to stream into the room on their right—illuminated his features. Oberon was beautiful—she would admit that. But it was a stagnant beauty, with no character or emotion.

But not his brother. Abyssinian's features were much harsher. Rougher, and yet, kinder. Abyssinian was exquisite. He touched her face with his gloved hand. "Do you trust me?"

"Trust you?" She shrugged. "Yes, I trust you."

"Then kiss me."

She blinked at him. *What?*

"Kiss me, Siobhan." He smiled. "Please."

She wanted to kiss him. Had wanted to since she first met him, years ago, a victim of a drug bust gone bad. Even now as he lost blood, she wanted to kiss him. And before she died . . . it would be nice to hold him.

Just once.

But as she came closer to him, she felt his right hand caress the back of her head, and then as she neared his face, he forced her head down, shoving her open mouth onto the wound at his neck and shoulder. "Drink!"

No! She struggled against him, pushing herself away. But he was strong—stronger than he appeared, and she felt her stomach growl as her lips and tongue tasted his life's precious nectar.

I can't drink! An elf's blood is poison! He's trying to kill me like this—to save me from a burning death! No!

The thick liquid filled her mouth, and she drank deeply, filling her belly even as the first morning's rays touched her bare hands, and then her arms, warming them. She drank . . . and drank . . .

"I loved . . . you . . . "

Too late she realized what she was doing—

Abyssinian!

She wrenched her thirst away from his neck. He was bone white, his eyes closed, dark circles beneath them. Siobhan pressed her fingers to his neck. There was no pulse. She yelled out at him, shook him, but his head lolled to one side, his life . . . gone.

Backing away, she left him on the floor and stood in the full sunlight.

Siobhan froze.

Slapping her hands to her face, she waited for the burning to begin as she stood in the light. Instead, it was warm against her skin. Tingling. Siobhan closed her eyes.

She began to laugh, deep in her throat as she spread her arms wide and drank in the sunlight.

Abyssinian . . . he'd known. He'd known this would happen! And he had given her a gift—but how long would it last? She had to use it well. She had to discover Melissa and Abyssinian's killer.

And she could do it in the daylight.

Walking the Mile in the daylight was different from the night. Darkness hid so many ugly things. Trash, cracks in the pavement, even the ugliness of neon signs with no light.

But to Siobhan, it was all so incredibly beautiful. She stopped in each of the shops along the way, admiring the colors, some faded and washed out, some vibrant in the sun. No one remarked about the beautiful, blood covered sword she carried in her hand.

It was Enchantment Place. Anything was possible.

It was close to eight before she reached her own shop. A yellow and black line of tape blocked the entrance, but she didn't detect anyone inside. Snatching the tape away, she opened the front door with her key.

The body was long gone, as was any remnant of what happened the day before. It wasn't until she ascended her stairs that she saw the destruction wrought on her place. She had been invaded, her possessions tossed aside as the killer looked for what Melissa had stolen.

But they hadn't found the secret room, hidden behind the mirror in her bedroom—though the mirror now lay in thousands of pieces. She tried to sieve through the wall but bumped into it instead. Had she lost her powers? She tried to shift into a wolf.

Nothing happened.

Siobhan ran to the bathroom and looked into the AV mirror.

She looked different. Her skin tanned, her eyes no longer holding the sheen of death. *How long will this last? And even if it were permanent, I would give it all back to have Abyssinian with me.*

Picking up one of the statues on the floor, she smashed into the thin wall and tore a hole so she could get to her computer. There she logged in and downloaded the packet from Melissa.

She typed in YOU ARE IN DANGER and sat back and watched as three seleighe held an unseleighe to the table she'd seen in the room and strapped her down. Then a tall, familiar elf entered and began to chant a ritual as the others shoved needles into the restrained elf's arms and neck and drained away her blood.

"It's old magic," came a familiar voice behind her.

She'd been expecting him. The instant she saw his face

on the recording. Siobhan stopped the playback and with two clicks sent the packet to a safer place.

She stood and turned inside the small room and stepped through.

Oberon sat on her bed, his hands folded in his lap. His eyes widened when she stood in the streaming sunlight. "I see . . . my brother finally unraveled it."

"Were you trying to create daywalking vampires, Oberon?" She was trying to understand everything.

"I was trying to make an elixir to allow them to walk in the daylight." He stood and took a step closer to her. "Think of the money to be made, Siobhan. No more working as a Chicago cop. No more skimping by—not if I had that kind of power in my hand."

Yep. A demoted king through and through. *Can't just live like the rest of us.* "Abyssinian figured out what you were doing."

"And he also discovered how to make it work." Oberon swallowed. "Pity. But tell me, what was it he did different? Was it a spell? Did he use an herb? Some amulet?"

"I drank from him. I drained him dry."

The elf blanched white. "Death? That is the missing ingredient?"

"Yeah, there's always a catch, honey."

"He loved you."

Siobhan swallowed. "I know that now." She turned and took up Abyssinian's sword where she'd left it by the bathroom door.

"You plan on killing me now, Siobhan? You think I can't keep my mouth shut? We might not have to kill another unseleighe again. We can use your blood to make the serum . . . "

"That's where you're wrong," she said as he held the sword high. Oberon started to stand, but he stumbled against a piece of wood and fell to the ground.

"Stop!"

Siobhan froze and turned to see a very pale and shaking Abyssinian standing in the doorway to her bedroom.

She stepped back, nearly dropping the sword. "You—you're alive!"

"Not for long," Oberon muttered as he started up from where he'd fallen.

Siobhan turned in slow motion to see Oberon pull his revolver from inside his suit jacket. He brought it up and aimed it at Abyssinian.

But she reacted with vampiric reflexes, brought the sword up, spun and cleanly cut him off at the knees.

Literally . . . cut off his knees.

Oberon screamed and dropped the gun. Abyssinian collapsed near the door, and Siobhan grabbed the gun as she backed up to where Aby was. She checked his pulse. Steady but faint. Why hadn't he had one before?

Confident Oberon was no longer a threat, she called 911 to report a burglary in her home.

"You know," Siobhan said as she and Abyssinian walked along the Miracle Mile, "I kind of miss the daylight."

"Yeah," he said. "Too bad it didn't last."

"You died."

"Oh, just for an instant. Then I woke up with the worst damned headache." He put his gloved hands behind his back. "It takes a lot more than two wounds to kill an elf. Though I probably should have told you that our bodies shut down like that."

"Yeah, you could have spared me some untold grief, Aby."

"You keeping the store open?"

"Uh-hm. You going to keep fighting the evildoers? Even if they turn out to be family?"

Aby gave her a wide smile. "Always. Oh, I heard from my bro's lawyer. They're using an insanity plea. I mean," he held out his hands to his side, his red hair flashing in the city lights. "Who ever heard of walking in the daylight by drinking an elf's blood? Sheesh." He shook his head.

She laughed at him. "It is crazy. But why didn't it

work for Oberon, Aby? Why wasn't he able to create a serum to do the same thing. Was it your death?"

He stopped walking and moved to face her. Abyssinian took her hands in his and kissed her knuckles ever so lightly. "Because the one element, the one thing my brother could never enjoy was the one thing that makes the magic work, Sio." He reached out and touched her cheek. "Love."

"He loved himself."

"Eh." He shrugged and stepped back. "Putz. And now, I have crime to fight, my dear."

"When will I see you again?"

Abyssinian held his hand out wide. "Just call me, Siobhan. You have my number." He bowed to her. "And my heart." And with that he vanished into the shadows of Enchantment Place.

THINK SMALL

Melanie Fletcher

In addition to writing, Melanie Fletcher does way too many things to be listed here—let's just say she is Hobby Lobby's beyotch and leave it at that. Her recent writing credits include "The Padre, the Rabbi and the Devil His Own Self" (Helix SF, http://www.helixsf.com), "Lost in Whitby" (*Fabulous Whitby*, ed. Sue Thomason,) and *Sabre Dance* (Double Dog #4, ed. Selina Rosen). An expatriate Chicagoan, she currently lives in North Dallas with a Bodacious Brit, a dollhouse addiction, and two fabulous furballs.

"**I** want a really big house in pink, with white ginger-bread and lots of gables," Emily Shelbourne said. "And real shingles, and lace curtains in all the windows, and the floors should be polished wood like a ballroom floor, and I want really pretty wallpaper on all the walls."

The shop owner, who had introduced himself as Mr. Silvanus, nodded as he jotted things down on an old-fashioned notepad. "And would you like us to electrify it so that you can have working lights?" he asked.

Emily gave him a disgusted look. "*Duh*. And I want pretty Tiffany lamps, not those stupid-looking modern ones."

"Of course." He wrote up a total, turning the pad

around and showing it to the elegant woman standing next to Emily. "This is the amount for the house, madam, plus wallpaper, carpet, paint, trim and labor. The estimate for the furniture is below it."

"Hmm?" Mrs. Shelbourne, who had a high-tech wireless headset in her ear and was arguing with someone named Stephanie, barely glanced at the high four figures on the pad. "Yes, whatever," she said, fishing in her Michael Kors purse and tossing a platinum credit card on the counter. "Really, Steff, just because we're raising money for breast cancer doesn't mean we have to do everything in candy colors," she complained into the headset. "There *are* other shades of pink, ones that don't blind at thirty paces—"

Mr. Silvanus pursed his lips and turned back to Emily. "If I may ask, is this for a special occasion?"

"It's for my tenth birthday," Emily said. "And I want it ready by then, otherwise my daddy will be mad at you, and he's a very important man with a lot of lawyers."

Mr. Silvanus smiled. "My dear child—"

"I'm not your dear child."

The smile turned wintry. "Ah. Well, then, young miss, let me assure you that Little Treasures has never missed a deadline. Even when it's," he peered at the pad, "only a month away, and we have to build a custom thirteen-room Victorian mansion in that time. Nevertheless, the dollhouse will be ready in time for your birthday."

"Good. Now I want to see the furniture and dolls. You *do* have Victorian dolls, don't you?"

The store owner beamed. "For you, young miss, I'm sure we can find the perfect dolls," he said. "If you'll follow me?"

He stepped out from behind the counter. Below his mellow tweed jacket was a set of well-muscled hocks covered in twisty black hair, descending to a pair of small, polished cloven hooves.

Emily blinked in surprise, and he chuckled. "You didn't know I was a faun?" he asked, peering over his gold-rimmed glasses. "I do need to get my hair cut—it tends to cover my horns. But many of the shopkeepers in Enchantment Place aren't exactly human, young miss. Surely you must have noticed that by now."

Emily made a face. "Of course I did. There's Madame Medusa on the third floor—Mommy gets some of her jewelry there. And there's the merman in Just Add Water."

"Indeed. Meddy and Lir aren't the only ones, of course, just the most," he paused, "*noticeable*. Now, about those dolls . . ."

A month later, the Shelbournes' elegant townhouse was decorated in pastel balloon sculptures and tasteful pink streamers for Emily's tenth birthday party. A group of girls from the prestigious North Side School (open to children of any sex, color, creed, IQ, or gender preference whose parents could stump up the truly astronomical tuition) gathered around her as Godwin, the Shelbournes' driver, rolled in a huge crate on a low, wheeled platform. The little girls didn't seem fazed by Godwin—employing a minotaur as a combination driver/bodyguard was the latest craze on the North Side, and the bull-men could be seen in all the best shops these days.

Mrs. Shelbourne came into the room, all smiles for the daughters of potential donors (Daddy was in Japan this week on business; he'd faxed Emily a happy birthday note that bore a striking similarity to his assistant's handwriting). "Are you ready, dear?" she trilled. "All right, then—on three."

As the girls yelled out the count, Godwin grasped the sides of the crate and lifted.

Emily squealed and clapped her hands; sitting on the wheeled platform was a huge, beautiful Victorian dollhouse. The house's central tower stretched up for a full three stories, ending in a mansard cap with a tiny widow's walk at its peak. Wings branched out from either side of the tower, and a wraparound porch graced the right side of the building, perfect for dolls to promenade around on a pleasant spring day. The clapboard walls were painted a beautiful shade of pink, with dove gray shingles, and all the railings, window frames, gingerbread and other trim were finished in white with mauve accents.

She dashed around to the back. Each one of the house's thirteen rooms had polished wooden floors, white crown molding and baseboards, fully functional doors, and lovely wallpaper. The furniture was equally precious, right down to the miniature Persian rug in the parlor and the tiny dollhouse in the upstairs nursery. As a final touch, a family of four dolls—Mr. and Mrs. Havencrest, according to Mr. Silvanus, and their children Grace and William—sat in the parlor.

"It's perfect!" Emily cried, throwing her arms around her mother's waist. "Thank you, Mommy!"

Mrs. Shelbourne gently unwound her arms. "Don't wrinkle Mommy's dress, dear," she murmured. "Now, why don't you play with your little friends?"

She nodded at Godwin to remove the crate and left for her home office to harangue the caterers over an upcoming Equality for All Species benefit. The girls crowded closer around the dollhouse, oohing and aahing over all the marvelous details. And when Emily plugged in a cable snaking out from the house's base, the dollhouse lit up like Christmas, tiny glows twinkling from lamps throughout all the rooms.

"Isn't it the absolute best?" she crowed, basking in the sure and certain knowledge that none of the other girls had a dollhouse even half as nice as hers.

Hannah Madison, an alabaster-skinned redhead and the social doyenne of the fourth grade, shrugged. "It's okay if you like kid's stuff," she said.

Emily switched gears faster than Lance Armstrong and glared at Hannah. The tall girl already had tiny bumps on her chest and was allowed to wear makeup by her mother, an executive for a major advertising company. "It's not kid's stuff," she spat. "Colleen Moore's dollhouse is in the Museum of Science and Industry, and she was a famous actress."

"Never heard of her." Hannah smiled, cherry pink lips gleaming. "I let Tyler Brandon kiss me yesterday."

The girls looked from Emily to Hannah, trying to judge the balance of the social power. Tyler Brandon was, without a doubt, the cutest boy in the fourth grade, even if he did tend to grow hair around the full moon. "What was it like?" one of the girls asked.

Hannah thought. "Kind of meaty."

The guests crowded around Hannah to hear more about Tyler Brandon and what the future had in store for them in re: kissing. With the spotlight gone, a smoldering Emily clenched her teeth until her delicate jaw muscles stood out like rocks, and proceeded to do what any child raised by distant, permissive parents would do in her situation.

The screams could be heard all the way in the garage.

Later that night, after the carnage was cleared and an embarrassed Mrs. Shelbourne finished apologizing to the parental cream of Chicago society, Godwin carried the dollhouse up to Emily's bedroom, where she would be grounded for the next two weeks (laissez-faire parenting was one thing, but Abigail Shelbourne was not about to lose her place on various charity boards because of a ten-year-old's emotional rampage) and set it up in a corner of her room. "Good night, miss, and, er, happy birthday," he said with an embarrassed snort, before closing the bedroom door.

Emily glared at the dollhouse, a bright pink symbol that she wasn't nearly grown-up or popular enough to deserve a kiss from Tyler Brandon. "Stupid dollhouse," she snarled. "I didn't want you anyway."

In a sudden rage, she kicked at it. Her foot connected with the parlor window; the trim cracked and split under the blow, and the thick plastic of the window bent inwards. "Stupid party," she added, knocking out a porch post and section of railing. "Stupid Hannah. It's all STUPID!"

She slapped the tower roof cap. The railing crumpled and the cap slid sideways, held only by a thread of dried glue. Feeling better, Emily tossed her party clothes on the floor, pulled on a nightgown and threw herself into bed, plotting future humiliation for Hannah Madison and her stupid breasts.

In the corner of her room, the dollhouse sat in its damaged glory. Someone with a keen imagination (not a valued skill in the Shelbourne household) might have seen a flicker of movement through the lace-curtained windows.

And then the front door creaked open.

Emily was in the middle of a wonderful dream about a bald, poor Hannah Madison begging her for money in the middle of a field trip, when something sharp poked her shoulder.

"Hrrmdonwannagetup," she mumbled, turning over. Another pointed poke landed between her shoulder blades.

"Ow!" She jerked awake, blinking at the dark room, then turned over and froze.

Standing on her sheets, not five inches from her nose, was Mrs. Havencrest. The doll held a piece of the cracked porch support, with the jagged end towards Emily. "And what, may I ask, is the meaning of this," she said in a tiny but perfectly audible voice, flinging her free hand at the dollhouse. "How dare you ruin my home, you little hoyden!"

"Your—but—" Emily rubbed her eyes. The doll was still there, glaring at her. "You're a *doll*," she said stupidly.

"And you, young lady, are a hooligan of the highest order," the doll snapped in an aristocratic voice. "What on earth possessed you to go on a rampage with my house?"

"Your—" Emily glanced across the room at the Victorian mansion. "That's *my* house. My dollhouse, I mean."

"Rubbish—it's my house, and I was very proud of it until you came along." The tiny woman planted her free hand on a hip. "I have no idea what gave you the idea to destroy someone else's home, but I'll have you know I won't stand for such behavior. You *will* repair everything you damaged."

Emily had heard about things like this at school; it was why Megan Gallagher had to take those colored pills at lunch and napped on her desk all afternoon. She bit her lip, willing herself to wake up. "I'm not crazy," she whispered. "This is just a dream, and you're not real."

The little woman snorted. "I have my doubts about your mental well-being, but if this is just a dream, you won't feel this." Hoisting the porch upright like a lance, she poked Emily in the side.

"OW!" The girl scooted to the far edge of the bed, tears in her eyes. "Stop that!"

The doll crossed her arms, a tiny Valkyrie in Victorian garb. "Do you still think this is just a dream?"

Grimacing, Emily lashed out with her foot, trying to punt the doll across the room. She didn't expect the tiny Victorian mother to move like a lightning bolt, thrusting the upright's sharp end into the girl's soft instep.

Emily yanked her foot back and howled. *"Stop it!"*

"With pleasure," Mrs. Havencrest said, "just as soon as you promise to repair what you did to my home."

Sniffling, the little girl glanced at the dollhouse. Even in the dark, she could see the damage from her kicks. "I don't know how," she whined.

"Then you'll have to learn," the doll said firmly. "And no shoddy workmanship, my girl. I expect everything to be repaired and looking like new. Or else."

"Or else what?" Emily whimpered.

A miniscule eyebrow arched. "Or I will be forced to take action," the doll announced in ominous tones.

And with that, she shimmied down the blanket and marched back to the dollhouse. As soon as she was inside, Emily yanked up her blanket and cowered underneath it. After all, the house came with three other dolls—who knew what else was waiting for her on the floor?

The next morning, after a prudent peek under the bed, Emily warily approached the dollhouse. The dolls were in the same position she'd left them in last night—Mr. Havencrest in the chair with his paper, Mrs. Havencrest with her embroidery, and Grace and William playing on the floor. There was no evidence of life, movement, or execution of threats that she could see.

Her lower lip crept out, and she nudged the house with her toe. "You're just a bunch of dolls," she muttered. "And it was just a stupid dream. I'm not fixing anything."

The dolls didn't offer a reply. Relieved, she went downstairs for breakfast.

The trouble started when she went into the family room (aka the smallest of the three cavernous public rooms) to unplug her Wii and sneak it up to her room. But the small white game controller was missing. Annoyed, Emily searched between cushions, peered under chairs and looked on every shelf of the massive entertainment unit. Nothing.

She went to the door. "Frieda!"

A plump woman in a uniform and apron peered out from the front room. "*Ja*, Miss Emily?"

"Where did you put my Wii controller?"

The housekeeper looked confused. "Your wee what?"

Emily rolled her eyes. *Servants.* "My *Wii controller*," she enunciated. "You know, that white thing I play computer games with?"

Frieda frowned. "The last time I saw it, it was in that box next to the television."

"You didn't move it somewhere?"

"No. I don't touch the electric things."

Emily went cold. An unbelievable suspicion was beginning to form. The confirmation came when she went back to her room and found both her cell phone and iPod missing from their respective chargers. Three small things, easy enough for a tiny creature to carry off.

Swallowing hard, she went to the dollhouse. As she feared, the dolls were moving again; Mr. Havencrest was examining the shattered parlor window and shaking his head, and Mrs. Havencrest was in the kitchen with Grace and William, cooking breakfast.

Emily crouched down, ready to jump if anyone came at her with a porch upright. "Where are they?" she said.

Mrs. Havencrest gave her a placid look. "Where are what, dear?"

"My *stuff*. My phone, my iPod and my Wii."

"Those electronic things?" The doll pursed her lips. "Oh, dear. Were they important to you?"

The light of cause and effect dawned. "You broke my stuff?" Emily whispered in horror.

Mrs. Havencrest held up a spoon. "Don't be ridiculous. Unlike you, I do not wantonly destroy other people's property," she said. "I simply removed them to a safe place. They will be returned, eventually."

"Eventually when?"

"When my house is repaired, of course."

Emily gaped at her. "I can't go to school without my phone!" she wailed. "And I can't play games without the Wii, and how am I supposed to listen to music without my iPod?"

"I haven't the faintest idea," Mrs. Havencrest said calmly. "All I do know is that the sooner my home is returned to its original state, the sooner your belongings will be returned to you. The ball, as they say, is now in your court." And with that, the doll returned to her cooking, as Emily stared at her in misery.

The next day, Godwin picked her up from school as usual. Emily had plotted her question all afternoon, and the moment she was in the car she launched her very best smile and said, "Godwin, could we go to Enchantment Place?"

The minotaur turned around, giving her a quizzical look. "Your mother said you're grounded, miss, and I was supposed to take you straight home after school," he rumbled.

"I know, but—I need to stop off at Little Treasures. It's really, really important." She didn't realize until she felt the twinging pain that she was wringing her hands. "I . . . kinda did something to my dollhouse, and I need to fix it."

Godwin studied her for a long moment, then sighed.

"I don't need to pick Mrs. Shelbourne up until 6:00 PM. I suppose we can make a side trip to the mall."

Twenty minutes later, Mr. Silvanus looked up from an old-fashioned accounts book. "Can I help you?"

Emily scuffed her shoe along the store's spotless floor. "I, um, I need to fix my dollhouse," she said. "I kinda kicked in a window. And broke the porch. And knocked the cap off the roof. And I have to fix it fast. Or else."

"Ah." The faun looked over his glasses at her, a glance that spoke volumes about spoiled little brats who ruined their toys. "Well, we do offer classes in building dollhouses. They're every Wednesday at 4:00 PM—"

"I have soccer practice then," Emily said. "And I couldn't come anyway because I'm grounded. Can't you just show me how to fix a dollhouse now?"

Mr. Silvanus waited.

Some faint memory of good behavior kicked in, and she blushed. "Please?"

The faun smiled. "In that case, I do believe something can be arranged. If you and your gentleman friend would follow me?"

He gestured them behind the counter and through a small doorway. Unlike the brightly decorated shop, this second room was painted in plain white and filled with long wooden tables covered with dollhouses in all stages of construction. Emily felt as though she were getting a sneak peek at Santa's workshop during dollhouse season. "Wow. Did you make all these?" she said.

"Not all of them," the faun said. "Some of our clients are hobbyists with no workshop space of their own, while others are professionals who do in-house work for our shop." He led them to a nearby house that was similar to Mrs. Havencrest's Victorian mansion. "Now, if you can show me what exactly was broken?"

Embarrassed, Emily pointed at the tower cap, the porch and the parlor window, while Mr. Silvanus tapped his lips. "Hmm. Well, it's not too terrible," he said. "We carry porch kits, and I can order a replacement window

for you. The cap would probably be the easiest thing to
fix right now. All you need is some glue, paint and a
new railing set. You can buy what you need and get
started on it today, if you like."

Emily imagined her treasured electronics buried somewhere dark, wet and smelly. "Yes, that's what I want to
do—" Her face crumpled. "But I don't have any money
on me."

Godwin harrumphed. "I can buy what you need, miss.
You'll probably need a miniature tool kit, as well, and
some fine grit sandpaper."

Mr. Silvanus smiled. "Ah, a craftsman. Let me assure
you, sir, that Little Treasures has everything for your
miniature needs. Let's go back to the main store and get
the little miss outfitted, shall we?"

That evening, while Mrs. Shelbourne was at a benefit
for the United Way, Emily donned a kitchen apron and
sat at the kitchen table, now spread with sheets of the
Tribune. Frieda had fussed about her kitchen being invaded by miniaturists until Godwin explained something
in low tones; the housekeeper gave Emily a quizzical
look, but she finally retreated to her chair with the rest
of the newspaper.

In front of Emily sat the tower cap, remnants of the
broken railing still attached to the top. Alongside the
cap were a pencil, paint bottle and brush, a sheet of fine-
grade sandpaper, a ruler, a saucer from an old china
pattern Mrs. Shelbourne didn't like, and the matching
cup now full of water. Nearby, a small beige box held a
collection of craft tools. "What do I do?" she asked in
a small voice.

Seated next to her, Godwin gave her a reassuring
snort. The minotaur's black suit jacket hung on the back
on the chair, and he looked moderately ridiculous in another kitchen apron. "I think you'll need to cut off the
posts, then sand the top smooth for the paint."

Under his guidance, she used a craft knife to slice at
the bottom of the posts until they could be peeled away

from the roof. Next, a folded square of fine sandpaper scoured away the last bits of wood and glue.

"Now, we'll paint it and let it dry while we work on the railing set," Godwin said. He showed her how to stroke a thin layer of white paint across the roof; while that dried, they cut strips of railing to size using the tiny silver miter box and saw blade from the miniature toolkit.

When the balusters were in place, Godwin had Emily glue the completed railings to the elegantly carved corner posts. "Now we let that dry, and we can paint it tomorrow," he said.

Emily groaned. "Tomorrow? But I want to paint it now!"

The bull-man shook his head, his nose ring flashing under the kitchen fluorescents. "The glue needs to dry in order to be strong. If you painted it now, it'd fall apart in your hands the first time you touched it. Why don't you go take a look at your dollhouse and see what you can do next?"

Emily sighed noisily but headed upstairs to her room. When she plopped down in back of the dollhouse, she saw Mrs. Havencrest tucking the children into bed.

The doll nodded at her. "Wait downstairs, dear. I'll be right along," she called.

Emily wiggled down until she was lying on her side. In the parlor Mr. Havencrest gave her a polite nod, then went back to his paper. Soon, Mrs. Havencrest glided down the polished staircase. "How are the repairs going?" she asked, taking a seat in the parlor.

Emily shrugged. "We took off the old railings and sanded the roof down, and now I'm waiting for the glue on the new railings to dry so I can paint them."

Mrs. Havencrest beamed at her. "Splendid! Now, please make sure that you put at least two coats of paint on the railings—the wood simply drinks in paint, you know, and I don't want anything showing through."

The little girl sighed, ruffling the doll's hair. "But that's gonna take hours," she complained. "It won't be finished until tomorrow night."

"It takes time and patience to do a job well," the doll said primly. "Which is a useful lesson to learn. Speaking of lessons, shouldn't you be doing your homework?"

Emily stared at her. "How did you know I had homework?"

"Mothers always know," Mrs. Havencrest said, waving one porcelain hand. "So, what is it?"

"A stupid book report."

"And I presume that you haven't even read the book yet, hmm?" Emily shook her head, and the doll tsked. "Well, then, you can read to me while I sew."

Emily blinked at the request. To have someone *want* to listen to her talk was an odd novelty. She got up and fetched the book from her dresser. As she sat back down, she spotted Grace and William scooching up in their beds, waiting to hear the story. Both of them made the universal children's gestures that translated to, "Don't tell Mom we're up!"

With an almost imperceptible nod, Emily began. "Once upon a time, sixty years ago" she read, "a little girl lived in the Big Woods of Wisconsin, in a little gray house made of logs . . ."

The next evening, she brought the now finished porch cap up to her room and glued it into place. Mrs. Havencrest stood outside the house, making sure the cap was positioned properly. "Capital! Now you may have the first of your belongings back," she said. "Your iPod is in an empty jar underneath the kitchen sink."

"Yes!" Emily jumped up and went downstairs. Mrs. Shelbourne was at the spa getting her pores expressed, and Frieda was busy cleaning the powder room, so the kitchen was empty. It only took a moment to rummage through the cleaning supplies under the sink until she found the empty jelly jar and her iPod.

She headed toward the game room, then paused as an unfamiliar feeling stirred in her mind. There were still two more repair jobs to do, fussy ones, and the sooner they were done the sooner she'd have her phone and iPod back. Besides, she sort of liked working on the house. And it was nice to talk to the Havencrests, and there were still three more chapters of *Little House in the Big Woods* to read to Grace and William.

Unaware that she was smiling, she went back upstairs.

The second repair job was the parlor window. Since this was going to be more complicated than the roof cap, Godwin suggested that they move the entire house to a small card table in the corner of the kitchen.

As they worked on the window, Emily asked the minotaur where he had learned how to fix dollhouses.

Godwin chuckled. "I never worked on one before now, but it's just wood. My father taught me how to carve things out of wood when I was just a calf," he said. "I made a complete set of cups for my family when I was your age."

Emily bit the inside of her lip. "I never made anything before—nothing useful, I mean."

Godwin gave her a thoughtful look. "That's only because you were never taught how. But you're making something now."

She shrugged. "I'm just fixing stuff."

"It's the same thing, if you think about it. Someone else may have made the rest of the house, but you made this window."

"Yeah, I guess you're right." Emily peered at the ruins of the parlor window. "But how are we going to get it off?"

"Good question."

Frieda, who had been watching them, now appeared with a small glass and an eyedropper. "It's glued on, ja? Soften the glue with some warm *wasser*, and the wood comes off easy. Here." She drew up a small amount of water with the eyedropper, then dripped it along the top of the trim. "Try pulling it off."

Godwin did, and the window frame popped out of the house side with a gritty slurping noise. "That worked!" Emily squealed. "Frieda, you're a genius."

She examined the raw window hole, not noticing the look of pleased surprise that passed across the housekeeper's face. "The inside frame doesn't look too bad," she announced. "I think it just needs some sanding and paint."

The minotaur snorted in approval. "Then you know what to do."

Nibbling her lip in concentration, Emily folded up a piece of sandpaper and went to work. The hours flew by, and she was yawning by the time she got back to her room.

As it was too dangerous to move the house with everything inside, she'd removed all the doll furniture and arranged it on her desk. Mr. and Mrs. Havencrest were busy with their newspaper and embroidery, while Grace and William waited for the last few chapters of *Little House in the Big Woods*. Emily finished reading the book to them, then changed into her nightgown and drifted off to sleep as the Havencrests chatted, images of a snug little house in the middle of tall, waving grass drifting through her head.

"No, Patsy, you cannot seat werewolves and elves at the same table," Mrs. Shelbourne sighed into her headset. "Elves are vegetarians, and werewolves—well, they aren't. Put the elf with Dr. Pearlman and Mrs. Drake and the werewolf with Mr. De La Hoya. I'm sure he'll be delighted to be seated with someone even hairier than he is—oh, hold on."

She put a finger over the receiver and glanced at Emily, who was just coming down the stairs. "Dear, what *have* you been doing in your room? You're absolutely filthy."

Emily glanced down at the paint smears on her apron. "Um, fixing my dollhouse?"

Her mother blinked. "Whatever for? Oh, I know you're grounded, but I'll have it taken back to Little Treasures—"

"No! I mean, please don't," Emily said. "I'm the one who broke it, so I should fix it."

If they hadn't been Botoxed into submission, Mrs. Shelbourne's eyebrows would have reached her hairline. "Hmmph. Well, if that's what you want—"

"It is, honest."

"All right. Then go get cleaned up for dinner—your father's finally home, and I would like to have a nice family meal tonight."

A nice family meal, in Mrs. Shelbourne's lexicon, meant one where she only answered her cell phone two or three times, and Mr. Shelbourne ate while studying the latest market returns on the laptop next to his dish. Emily drew a pattern in her mashed potatoes as her mother explained to someone named Muffy why there couldn't be more than four gargoyles at a table due to wingspan.

She turned to her father. "Did you have a nice trip, Daddy?"

"Mm-hm," he said, eyes focused on the laptop screen.

Emily tried again. "I'd like to go to Japan someday. It looks really cool."

"Mm-hm."

"Maybe you could bring me back a kimono on your next trip?"

"Mm-hm."

Something small and very frayed snapped in the little girl's head. "Did you know that the dolls in my dollhouse are magic?" she said brightly. "They come to life and help me with my homework."

"Mm-hm."

"They stole my iPod and phone so that I'd fix their house, but now we're friends, and I like them a lot."

"Mm-hm."

Emily stopped. There comes a time in every child's life when he she realizes that parents aren't towering gods who are all-knowing and all-seeing, that Mom and Dad are human and prey to the foibles and failures of humanity. This epiphany descended upon her now, and for the first time in her short life she understood, she *truly* understood, that she'd been born to a couple who had no idea how to raise children and thought of her mainly as a fashion accessory.

She sighed. "May I be excused?"

"Mm-hm."

As her mother tried to find a catering service that could provide pigeon tartare, Emily headed for the kitchen and her last task on the dollhouse.

The porch kit proved to be trickier than it looked. She had to take out the entire front railing set, build a new one, and shore up the cracked roof. While Godwin tucked into dinner and Frieda fussed at the stove, she worked on gluing balusters into the railings.

She suddenly stopped, biting her lip. A shine welled up in her eyes.

The minotaur looked up from his vol-au-vent. "Is everything all right, Miss?" he rumbled.

"No."

"Is it the railing? Everything's spaced correctly, and it should fit just fine—"

She shook her head. "It's not the railing," she said. "It's—"

She blinked away tears, trying to figure out how to explain. "I didn't want to do this at first, but now I kinda like it," she said, hesitant. "And once this is done, there won't be anything else to *do* on the house."

Godwin looked confused. "But that's a good thing, isn't it?"

Frustrated, Emily burst into tears, a child's tears of loneliness and grief. "B-ut then I w-won't be able to come down here anymore," she sobbed. "And I *like* being down here!"

The housekeeper caught on faster than the minotaur and bustled over, taking Emily into her arms. "Oh, *mädchen*, don't cry," she soothed. "You don't have to stop coming here just because your *poppenhusen* is fixed. We like having you here, don't we, Godwin?"

"Of course we do," the minotaur agreed hastily.

Emily sniffed. "Really?"

"*Ja!* And if you need a reason to come down here and see us," Frieda thought for a moment, then snapped her fingers, "I'll teach you how to knit. And after that, crochet, and needlework. And baking, just like Martha Stewart!"

"And I can teach you how to carve wood," Godwin added. "I'm sure you could be making things for your little doll family in no time."

Frieda patted her on the back. "Now, blow your nose and finish your porch," she said. "Your dolls must be lonely for their house, *ja*?"

"Yeah." Accepting a clean white hanky, Emily blew her nose and let out a deep, shuddering sigh. A strange and wonderful feeling crept through her; for the first time in her life, in her very own home, she felt—*welcome*. Not tolerated, or paraded at charity events, or kept around for photo opportunities, but wanted, and loved, and truly welcome.

And it didn't matter that she was welcomed by a minotaur, an Austrian housekeeper, and four Victorian dolls. You couldn't pick your family, after all.

She wiped her nose one last time. "I guess . . . I guess I'd better finish that porch."

"Hi, Mr. Silvanus!"

The owner of Little Treasures looked over his counter and smiled. "Ah, Miss Emily. And what can I do for you this fine morning?"

"I'm redecorating the children's room," Emily said, pulling out the list Mrs. Havencrest had approved after some wrangling with William and Grace. "Could you please order this wallpaper and carpet for me, and that furniture set, and let me know how much it'll cost?"

"Certainly." As he worked on his notepad, he glanced at her. "So, are you enjoying your dollhouse?"

"Uh-huh." She tilted her head to the side, considering him. "Mr. Silvanus, you know about the dolls, don't you? What they can do, I mean. Did you give them to me on purpose?"

The faun smiled. "In olden times, a dollhouse was given to a little girl as a teaching tool so that she could learn how to run a household," he said. "In your case, I thought you needed to learn certain things, for your own well-being. The dolls were a means to that end."

"Oh." She nodded slowly. "I *think* I understand."

Silvanus glanced up at an indulgent Godwin, waiting at the door for his charge. "I'm sure you do, Miss Emily. Here is your estimate," he gave her a slip of paper, "and I will call you when your items arrive."

"Okay, thanks. Bye!"

He waved as she took the minotaur's hand and left, then turned to a dissatisfied-looking little girl who was tapping her Mary Jane-clad foot. "And how may I help *you*, young miss?" he asked.

A falcon could have landed on the girl's pout. "I want to buy a big dollhouse, with a front porch, and wood floors, and curtains in all the windows, and a place where I can put a pond out front," she announced. "And I want real porcelain dolls—no plastic stuff, okay?"

Mr. Silvanus smiled. "I have just the thing."

CUPID'S CRIB

Christina F. York

Christina F. York was once a closet romantic. She is learning to embrace her "sappy side," and it shows in her work. Her stories in anthologies like this one and *Fantasy Gone Wrong*, as well as romance novels like *Dream House*, display her belief in the power of love stories. But romantic doesn't mean weak, as her *Alias* novels clearly illustrate—girls can kick ass, too! Chris is living her own love story with husband and fellow writer, J. Steven York, on the romantic Oregon coast, where the couple is supervised by the obligatory writers' cats, Oz and Sydney.

"They don't want it." Coop slouched against his desk, a stocking cap pulled low over his tightly curled dark hair, a sneer twisting his full lips. "I'm tellin' you, Allie, these jive-ass people do not want true love."

Allie, her shift in the love boutique over, settled into the worn sofa Coop kept against the opposite wall. Her mouth lifted in a tired, resigned smile that quickly disappeared. This was their nightly ritual, her and Coop. Going over the day's receipts and having this argument.

Coop popped the top of a tall one and glared at her, daring her to say anything. He was a walking cliché, but there wasn't anything she could say that would make him change his behavior. Rather, he relished his persona as a disaffected black man, even though she knew differently. She knew how much they pulled down every day, and she had seen the elegant townhouse Coop called home. Still, he put on the attitude, and tonight she was too tired to give him the fight he so obviously relished.

But somehow she couldn't stop herself. "You are so full of shit," she said. "No wonder your eyes are brown."

Coop rolled his dark eyes and shook his head. "Didn't nobody tell you it ain't a good career move to dis your boss like that, girl? It's trash talk like that gets a person fired."

Allie smiled, for real this time. "Yeah, right. Like I don't tell you that most every day. And it's not like you've got people beating down the door to work for you. Not after the last three clerks you chased off."

Coop shrugged elaborately. "I could find me another 'retail manager,' Miss High-and-Mighty. I could find me another manager in a heartbeat, and you'd be out on your sweet little ass."

"You know, Coop," Allie sat up, putting her feet flat on the floor. "There are still sexual harassment laws in this country. You aren't supposed to talk to me like that."

"Aw, girl, you know I'm just kidding." His voice dropped into an attempt at sweet-talk, though it came out more like a whine. "And that is a sweet little ass you got there."

Allie laughed. "Coop, you are still full of shit, and I am still tired. I am gonna show you my sweet little ass, going out the door." Her actions followed her words, and she walked out of the office.

Pulling her keys from her purse, she called back over her shoulder. "I'll see you in the morning, Coop. Don't piss off any customers in the meantime, okay?"

She walked out the door, bolting it behind her, and walked past the display windows, with their array of lingerie and lotions. The loopy script that spelled out "Cupid's Crib" across the window was so brilliant pink that it nearly glowed in the streetlights on the deserted sidewalk. Coop would go out the back and check the lock there before he left. It was part of their comfortable pattern, the rituals they had developed in the six years she had worked for him.

Didn't seem that long, though. Allie walked toward the El, shrugging off the uneasy feeling she got when she thought about Coop. She didn't want to examine the reasons she stayed at a job with a sexist, foul-mouthed poser.

She told herself it was because she knew he was a poser. He wasn't any of the things he claimed to be, although she supposed the black part was for real. You couldn't hardly fake that, could you? Then again, if he was really Cupid, as he claimed he was, maybe he could.

She gave a harsh little laugh as she boarded the nearly empty train. God of Love, my sweet little ass. More like the God of Bad Attitude. She just hoped he wouldn't open early tomorrow and scare away the customers before she got there.

He'd done that a couple times lately. Scared customers away. Most of the time it was okay, he stayed in the back, behind the one-way mirror behind the register, and left her alone. But once in a while, when he was in a particularly foul mood, he'd come out, and "help" her with a customer.

Mostly, his help meant bad-mouthing the customer's choice of goods and harassing them about why they had come in his shop. Sometimes they got angry and told him they had no idea why they had come in, since he was so obnoxious, and stormed out. It lost Coop a sale, which he richly deserved, but it also lost Allie a tiny piece of her profit-sharing, and that pissed her off.

But the worst were the women, mostly women anyway, who cried. After Coop yelled, and badgered, and asked questions that were really none of his business, after he stalked back into his office, dismissing the customer and her concerns—then came the tears.

They always had a reason to be there, which usually boiled down to, "If I can just make him love me," and the fact that it was weak and pathetic didn't make it any less sad. And she didn't need to see sad. She'd seen enough of that already.

Working at Cupid's Crib wasn't all bad. Really. She made enough money to afford a condo within walking distance of the El and a red convertible, the kind her mom had called a "zip-zap" car. She kept the Miata garaged most of the time, preferring the convenience of the train, but a drive along Lake Michigan was a sweet reward on her rare days off.

And it wasn't just the money. She wanted to help people find love, and if the potions and lotions and candles she sold helped them, that was good enough for her.

By morning, her argument with Coop was old history, as it was every morning. She unlocked the front door, booted up the cash register system, ran a stock report, and put it on Coop's desk. He did most of the ordering, since he usually didn't insult the suppliers.

As she waited, watching the early shoppers stroll through Enchantment Place, eyeing the shop windows and occasionally venturing inside one shop or another, she worried about Coop.

He had been getting worse, she was forced to admit. It had happened slowly, almost imperceptibly, but she had noticed. Maybe his attitude problem was *his* problem, and none of her business, but if it drove away enough customers, it would become her problem, too. And that made it her business.

Not that she gave a damn if Coop wanted to act like a jerk. Let him. Just don't destroy Cupid's Crib in the process, that was all.

But what if there was a way, some way to convince him that people *did* want true love? Would that change his attitude? Probably not. Coop seemed real fond of his attitude problem.

The thought continued to nag at the back of her brain all day. Coop stayed out of the way, dealing with suppliers, she waited on customers, and at day's end Allie still hadn't made a decision.

At least, not a conscious one.

But when Coop started his usual rant after running the totals for the day, Allie took a different approach.

"Why do you say that, Coop?" she asked earnestly, her eyes begging him for an honest answer. "Really. You give me some jive-ass answer about how people want an easy out, they don't want real love, but you have never given me a real answer about why you feel that way."

She looked him over, waiting for an answer. Baggy pants slopping over his expensive sneakers, flashy gold jewelry, the permanent sneer that curled his mouth—his costume was a part of the attitude, and as far as she was concerned, it was time for a major change.

"Girl," Coop said, "that ain't none of your business."

"You made it my business when you started driving away customers, Coop. Look at today's totals," she pointed at the reports spread across his desk. "Then look at last Tuesday, the day you decided to help out front. We lost, what, thirty percent of the sales that day?"

Coop raised his hands in mock surrender. "So I should stay out of the store. I'm down with that, okay?"

"Not okay. You promise that every time, and every time you end up back out there, bad-mouthing a customer, making trouble. You make people *cry* out there."

"It says 'Cupid' on the door, girl, not 'stupid.' People gotta know when it says Cupid, it means love. But no! They're all up in my face, saying they want to meet somebody, but what they really want is to score, to get lucky."

"You really believe that, Coop? Do you?" Allie thrust her chin out, challenging Coop. "Care to put your money where your mouth is?"

Coop slouched behind his desk and dropped heavily into his chair. "Money ain't no big thing. I got enough. And you do, too."

"I won't have for long if you keep going the way you do." Allie's irritation boiled over, and she sprang to her feet, pacing in front of the desk, her hands balled into fists. "I mean it, Coop. I've had it with your attitude. I can't take it any more." She stopped, planting her fists on the desktop and leaning over, getting in Coop's face. "Serious. Dead serious. This shit has got to stop."

He looked up at her, feigning boredom. She knew better, knew he was masking his true feelings, but she couldn't get through to him. But as she stared him down, she saw a subtle shift, a chink in his mask. For an instant, she saw fear and hesitation.

"So, what's it going to take?" she said quietly, pressing her advantage. "What if I prove to you that people want love, would that make any difference in your crap-ass attitude?"

He relaxed, the fear replaced by arrogance. He laughed, a harsh, hard sound. "You can try, girl, but no way can you prove it, 'cause it's not true. No way, no how. Nobody wants the real thing. It's too messy, too hard, and too damned much work."

Coop stood up, straightening from his usual slouch to tower over her. At six-foot-five and whip-slender, he was an imposing figure, but she wasn't going to be intimidated. She held his gaze, leaning her head back to maintain eye contact.

When he continued, his voice was soft and sad. The brittle shell had been pierced for a moment, and he looked steadily into her eyes. "I've been doing this job for hundreds, no, thousands, of years, girl. I've offered mortals love again and again and again, only to have them throw it away, in search of—something. I could give you a list—Henry the Eighth, just as an example. There's true love out there," he gestured through the one-way window, into the store, "but I guaran-damn-tee you, nobody's gonna buy it."

"If it's out there," she replied, "where is it? Which bottle? Which jar?"

"If somebody wants it, it'll turn up." Coop's harsh laugh returned. "But ain't nobody going to want it."

Allie began her campaign the next morning. With each customer, she made an extra effort, offered a little more. By two o'clock, she was exhausted, and she was beginning to think Coop was right. They all wanted the sizzle, but nobody wanted more.

She was straightening incense and candles, not looking for anything special, not really. Just cleaning up, making the place inviting, when she spotted a little heart-shaped candle she didn't think she'd seen before.

Her heart leaped, in spite of herself. Maybe this was the thing Coop had talked about. And if it had appeared, then the customer who wanted it would be the next one.

She watched the door expectantly, waiting for the person who would prove Coop wrong, who would force him to reconsider his bad attitude. But when the sensor on the door beeped, it was a hard-looking thirty-something woman, and she was in a hurry.

"Music?" she asked brusquely. "Something kind of, you know, sexy."

A few minutes later, she left, clutching a CD of Ravel's Bolero and assuring Allie it was exactly what she wanted. Allie didn't have the heart to tell her she was a walking cliché, and any man who responded to such an obvious ploy wasn't worth the effort.

She looked at the candle sitting on the counter, abandoned while she rang up Bolero-woman's CD. She shrugged and shoved it under the counter. She'd have to find the manifest and get a proper price on it before she put it back on the shelf.

The phone beeped, and Allie picked up the inside line.

"It's not the candle," Coop said, from the other side of the window. "That came in last week, must have lost the price sticker. Five-ninety-nine, if you want to put it back in its place. And true love? I'm telling you, nobody wants it."

Two days later, she once again thought she'd found her chance. An older couple, well past retirement age, came through the front door, hand-in-hand. The woman reddened as she looked over the array of merchandise, and her companion seemed flustered. But they exchanged a glance and approached Allie.

She smiled at the woman, trying to put her at ease.

Cupid's Crib could be a little daunting the first time you came in. Allie noticed that neither the man nor the woman wore a wedding ring, and the woman quickly stuck her left hand in the pocket of her sweater when she caught Allie's glance.

It was sweet, really. Love could find you any time, at any age. Allie remembered the rose-scented lotion she had stocked earlier that morning. It seemed like just the right thing for such a sweet couple.

The man moved a few steps away, leaving Allie with the blushing woman. Allie smiled again, and said, in her sweetest voice, "Can I help you?"

The woman hesitated, and Allie went into her sales pitch. "I know this can be a little overwhelming, the first time you come in. We have so many lovely things! But perhaps if you give me some idea what you're looking for . . . ?" Her voice trailed off delicately, inviting the woman to share the secret longing that had brought her through the door.

"I don't know if you can help me, dear. I'm not even quite sure why we came in here. But I suppose you might have something," she turned her head, taking in the shelves of lotions and racks of lacy gowns and robes. She continued to turn, looking toward the back of the shop, where the naughtier merchandise lurked, away from the casual glance of a passerby, and blushed again.

Allie touched her arm and steered her toward the lotion display, away from the back of the shop. She put a drop of the rose lotion on the woman's hand. "Very smooth and silky," Allie said, "makes your skin soft and so touchable."

The woman hesitated, glancing back at her companion with a fond smile. He was engrossed in a display of videos and already had a couple in his hand, Allie notice.

"You're a lucky woman," Allie said. "To have someone you care about so much."

The woman sighed and moved toward the register, the lotion in her hand. "I suppose." She turned her back to the man, and dropped her voice to a whisper. "I just wish he'd go ahead and propose already. I know he wants to, and I am sure as hell tired of trying to live on a single pension. When we're married," her whisper carried a tone of desperation, "at least we'll only have one household to support."

"But you love him, don't you? I can see it," Allie insisted.

"Maybe." The woman shrugged. "Doesn't matter. We need each other, and that has to be enough."

"I might be able to help you." An idea took hold of Allie. If the woman just said she *wanted* love, then the thing, whatever it was, would appear. That's what Coop had said.

The woman shook her head. "Tried that once, didn't work out so well. What we have is fine." She looked over at her companion, who had turned her direction. "You about ready, Norman?"

"Right there, honey," he replied. He glanced down at the videos in his hand, then set them back on the rack with a shrug. "Ready whenever you are."

The couple left the store, holding hands, the small plastic bag with the lotion bottle tucked carefully in the bottom of the woman's handbag.

Strike two.

"Admit it," Coop said, smirking. "You can't find anybody says they really want true love. You've been trying with every customer." He nodded toward the window. "I can see you, all day, trying to convince people, but you got no takers."

It had been a long day, a typically busy Saturday. Lots of twenty-somethings in pairs and packs, looking for an edge for their Saturday nights. Quartets of thirty-somethings, fueled by reruns of "Sex and the City" and a couple of rounds of pomegranate Cosmos, trying to convince themselves they were hip and happening.

And not a one had asked for love. They asked for sexy lingerie, spicy cologne, scented candles, bubble bath, body paint, and bath oils. The Cosmo-driven career women dared each other to try on the skimpiest lingerie and shrieked about how this boyfriend or that husband would react. They even bought love potions, which Allie knew were mostly sugar water and food coloring. But nobody asked if they really worked. They didn't want to know.

Late in the afternoon, Coop wandered out into the front. He sauntered up and down the aisles, looking at the displays, occasionally rearranging merchandise or stopping at a discreet distance to listen to customers discussing their purchases.

Allie held her breath, waiting for the chaos that would inevitable follow. He was going to wreak havoc, he couldn't help it. She just didn't know what form it would take today.

But instead he wandered back to the office.

It was nearly closing time when he emerged, and she could feel his attitude from across the shop. There weren't any customers, and he stalked up and down the aisles as though looking for something to complain about.

Allie considered flipping the "OPEN" sign over and locking the door, pretending that it was time to close. But she knew she couldn't get away with it. Coop would not only notice, he'd badger her about losing business, turning her own arguments about lost sales back against her.

She eyed the clock warily, as Coop continued his inspection. Fifteen minutes to closing time, maybe eleven or twelve until she could lock the door with a clear conscience.

It wasn't to be.

The door buzzed, and Allie hurried to wait on the man who walked in. But she wasn't fast enough. Coop got there first, greeting the guy as though he were an old friend, though it was clear they had never laid eyes on each other before. Still, the guy responded with the same show of camaraderie.

The two men moved toward the back of the store, where the raunchiest merchandise lurked in subdued lighting. Their laughter drifted back to her, a sound that made her feel as though she needed a shower.

The man made his selections quickly. As he approached the counter, Coop caught Allie's eye and motioned forcefully for her to come over and handle the register. He was grinning in triumph, confident of his victory.

Dismay flooded through Allie as she bagged the toys and lubricants. He leered at her as she rang up the merchandise, wagging his eyebrows in what she supposed was meant to be a suggestive manner.

"Sure you don't want to join my little party?" he asked, as she took his credit card. "Platinum card means never having to say 'No,'" he added, as though that made him something special.

Allie's stomach churned, but she forced a polite smile. "Sorry," she said. "I never socialize with the customers. It's kind of a store policy."

A policy that she had instituted in the last fifteen seconds and that caused Coop's eyebrows to lift in surprise. The accompanying grin told her he could barely contain his glee at her response.

The customer took her rejection with poor grace, trying to insist that he was different, that she should break her policy "just this once" for him. It took her another ten minutes of increasingly adamant refusals before she could get him out the door.

As she swung the door behind him, he turned around and threw her a kiss. "You don't know what you're missing," he said.

Allie slammed the door. "Oh, yes. I think I do know," she muttered. "I think I know all too well."

Across the shop, Coop was practically vibrating. His eyes were bright, and his straight, white teeth showed against his dark skin in a wide smile.

"Give it up, girl. I'm right. I am sooo right. There isn't even a word for how right I am. Admit it, now. " He shook his head, and the diamond stud in his ear caught the light, twinkling at her. Even his *jewelry* was mocking her.

"You think he was looking for love, Allie? Think that stuff was to help him find true love?" Coop's laughter spiraled up, bordering on hysteria. "You think that was about love? The guy wanted a lot of things, girl, and he was pretty clear about what they were, and not a one of them came anywhere near love."

Anger flashed over Allie. She felt the heat climb through her body, flowing through her arms and legs, spreading outward from her core.

Her vision narrowed, until all she could see was Coop's mouth, his lips and tongue laughing and mocking. There was no sign, no hint, of the man she once thought lived inside that shell, the man behind the mask.

He'd gone too far.

She started across the shop. She had to stop him, stop the laughter. If she couldn't break through, couldn't get through to him, then she was done. Her profit sharing, her condo, her zip-zap car, none of it was worth the pain that stabbed at her heart and blurred her vision with tears.

As she walked toward Coop, not knowing what she would do when she reached him, she brushed her hand along a counter of decorations.

Instinctively, she grabbed a dusty plastic toy that threatened to fall off the shelf. It was a miniature bow and arrow, a cheap plastic imitation of Cupid's traditional weapon, that had been placed on a clearance rack months earlier. But no one wanted it, and it had been pushed aside many times, until her unintentional touch had pushed it over the edge.

Holding the bow, with the arrow dangling loosely from the string, she planted herself in front of Coop, craning her neck to look up at him.

"Stop!" she commanded.

He paused to look at her, surprise at her harsh tone registering on his face. He tried to hold back his laughter, biting his full lips in an effort to appease her.

"That's it, Coop. I quit. I can't take any more of your shit, and I can't stick around here and watch you destroy this place and yourself."

She shoved the bow and arrow against his chest and

let go. It snagged on one of his chains, and he reached up to yank it free.

As he did, the plastic tip of the arrow nicked his finger, drawing a tiny drop of blood.

Well, that was really it. Not only had she quit, she'd managed to injure Coop before she could get out the door. Now she was done for sure. Allie whirled around and grabbed her purse from under the register. She could send for her final check and anything else she'd left behind.

She ran for the door without looking back. She'd seen enough of Coop's triumphant smirk, heard enough laughter to last her forever.

But before she could open the door, a hand closed over her arm, gently pulling her back, and turning her around.

Coop looked down at her. The laughter was gone, his eyes were wide, as he stared at her in amazement. There was a spot of blood on his shirt, and the bow and arrow were still tangled in his gold chains.

He looked from her to the arrow and back again, as though he couldn't quite grasp what had happened. Then a slow grin broke over his face.

"Allie," he said, "do you believe in true love?"

WITCH STITCHERY

Deb Stover

Once Upon a Time, Deb Stover wanted to be Lois Lane, until she discovered Clark Kent is a fraud and there is no Superman. Since publication of her first novel in 1995, Stover has received dozens of awards for her unique, cross-genre work. Deb's twelfth full-length novel, *The Gift*, will be a paranormal romantic suspense. For more information, visit www.debstover.com

Zoë Zykowski was a late bloomer—in more ways than one. She missed her senior prom, for one thing. Because of the full moon, her date—a werebear—had far more urgent matters that night. Her entire life has been spent serving others, or, at the very least, she'd sacrificed her own needs to allow others' to be met.

She should've been born a brownie . . .

Witch Stitchery was a dream fulfilled, a store at Enchantment Place where she used her gift on a daily basis, at her discretion, placing her special stitches only where and when she saw fit. Yes, okay, so that probably made her a magical snob—so be it. She could live with that.

Over the years, she had learned to exercise enough control over her gift to serve only those she deemed worthy. Did that mean she was playing god? Maybe a little. So what? With so many jerks and unworthy people waltzing through her door demanding magic or role-playing costumes, how could she not? Otherwise, she would have become an unwitting accessory to numerous crimes over the past decade.

Her most recent customer was definitely unworthy, though certainly not a criminal. Britney was a high school cheerleader and a mundane, of course, who'd had life handed to her with sugar and maple syrup. She was selfish, conceited, shallow, and beautiful—pretty much everything Zoë was not.

One morning some weeks ago, Britney had bounced into Stitch with a design in mind for her perfect prom dress expecting—make that demanding—that Zoë use magic to make Britney a shoo-in for prom queen.

Heh . . .

Oh, Zoë would never curse anyone—not that she had that kind of power anyway—nor would she use her special stitches for anyone so blatantly unworthy. One could only hope the girl would mature enough over the years to become worthy. Zoë looked forward to making the lovely young lady's wedding gown one day. Perhaps . . .

Zoë was just pressing the very normal, nonmagical, neat, expertly sewn hem of Britney's beautiful blue silk gown when the seventeen-year-old flounced into the store on Thursday afternoon, tugging a wide-eyed girl of eight or nine along.

"Is it ready? Is it magical? Is it wonderful?" Britney asked in her annoying teenaged way.

Zoë merely smiled. "You'll be beautiful and perfect, of course." And she would. Nothing could make the bouncing, blue-eyed blonde anything less, at least on the surface. Inside was another matter . . .

Britney's gaze drifted down the expanse of blue silk. "Oh, it's gorgeous. And magic, of course."

Zoë smiled again. "I'm sure you'll be satisfied. Diana will assist you in the dressing room."

Britney grabbed the hanger and headed for the dressing room with Zoë's assistant, Diana, leaving her young charge behind. The girl heaved a weary sigh. "That's my sister for you—always forgetting I even exist."

Zoë blinked, though not surprised. "She's a little distracted, I think. I'm sorry. I didn't catch your name."

"Brenna."

Looked as though Zoë was babysitting, whether she'd offered or not. "I'm sure your sister won't be too long."

Brenna rolled her eyes. "Yeah, right. She'll prance around in front of the mirror admiring herself for an hour or so."

Zoë bit the inside of her cheek, already liking Brenna a lot more than her big sister. "What grade are you in?"

"Third." Her short blonde curls stuck out helter-skelter, but her narrow chin didn't deter from the hint of vulnerability her large blue eyes revealed—the only clear family trait she shared with Britney. "Our dad's a Reservist, and he's in the Middle East right now. Mom's always busy with work. She's a doctor at Providence Medical Center. So that means I get hauled around by you-know-who."

"Oh . . ." *And big sister is busy playing big cheerleader on campus, so where does that leave you?* "I'm sorry." Zoë stepped around the display case of buttons and gewgaws to eliminate the physical barrier between herself and Brenna. "How long has your dad been gone?"

Brenna's pointed chin jutted out even farther. "Seventeen months, three days, twenty-two hours . . ." She glanced at her watch and counted on her fingers. "And seven minutes." Threatening moisture glistened in her eyes.

"Wow . . . that *is* a long time." Zoë reached out and touched the girl's shoulder, tentatively, sensing an underlying pride she should not and would not breach. Brenna needed to keep that defense mechanism in place. *Important stuff* . . . "You must be very proud of your dad."

"Yup. He's a real hero. Has lots of medals, awards, ribbons, and stuff."

Zoë nodded, swallowing the growing lump in her throat with difficulty. She was fortunate to still have both her loving, doting parents—both powerful witches in their own right—alive and well and present. "Do you have . . . anything that belongs to him? A piece of clothing, perhaps? Something special you can wear or carry when he's not around?" She shrugged, trying to appear nonchalant, though she was already on a mission—shame on her. "Anything at all?"

"Yeah." Brenna heaved another of her sighs, far too large for her small frame. Appearing hesitant, she reached into her small backpack and withdrew a worn cap, a tear trickling down her cheek before she could capture it. The girl scrubbed at it with the back of her hand and sniffled before showing Zoë the hole in the side of the wool beret. "Daddy left this with me when he shipped out, but our stupid dumb dog, Kookie, chewed a hole in the side of it."

Zoë reached toward the worn wool, knowing only magic could possibly mend this type of damage. The tear wasn't in a seam, or a simple matter of wear, but a ragged, chewed gape in the fabric. "Would you like me to try?" she asked. "I'm pretty handy with needle and thread."

Brenna's eyes grew round and hopeful. "Yes—oh, yes!—very much." Her lower lip trembled. "I miss my dad. He always made time for me, even when Mom was busy with her patients." Guilt etched itself across Brenna's petite, pixielike features, and she hurried to add, "My mom means well, but she *is* very busy . . . and important. People depend on her."

And so do you. "I understand," Zoë said, and she did. Her own well-meaning parents had often been too busy when she needed them most.

She took the soft boiled black wool beret and examined the hole. "Do you mind if I take this into my workroom for a few minutes, Brenna?" She gave the girl an encouraging smile. "This will require some extra special thread and a fine needle I have back there."

The girl chewed her lower lip for a moment, clearly reluctant to let the special item out of her sight, then gave a solemn nod. "You'll be careful. I can tell."

"Yes." Zoë again swallowed the lump in her throat. "I will." This child and her need personified the very reason Zoë had opened Witch Stitchery. Brenna was the reason Britney had found the shop—the purpose. Everything happened for a reason, and this was Zoë's ultimate mission—not Britney's lovely prom dress . . .

She hurried into her workroom and retrieved her special mending kit—reserved only for particular customers with extra special needs. She stroked the fabric, inhaled its essence, then made several quick stitches near the edges of the chewed wool. Gold and silver sparks appeared over the hole, magically reweaving it until the beret looked almost new. She tilted it and looked inside, noting the name embroidered on the hatband. *Captain Peter Hansen.*

Perhaps Zoë could do nothing to protect Captain Hansen from this great distance, but she could at least ease his little girl's pain this small bit. She brushed her fingers across his name, smiling to herself as the crisp, white embroidery thread transformed to gold before her eyes. Deftly, she clipped the thread and returned to the front room with the mended beret just as Britney emerged from the dressing room to show off her blue gown.

"It's perfect." She spun in front of the mirror, sending the silk into a swirling circle. "Mother already paid you. Right?"

"Of course." Zoë handed the beret to Brenna with a wink.

The girl's eyes grew round. "Thank you," she murmured. "How much—"

"No charge." Zoë grinned. "Just keep it away from Kookie-Monster."

"I will." Brenna put the oversized beret on her blonde curls. "I promise."

"Was your prom here at Enchantment Place, too?" Britney asked as Diana unzipped the back of the gown. "Even way back then?"

"It was, indeed." Britney didn't need to know that Zoë had been jilted by a werebear under the control of a full moon that night. The memory still stung, even after all these years. "Even *way* back then." She couldn't suppress a smile at that. To a seventeen-year-old, twenty-eight probably seemed ancient and decrepit.

Diana and Britney returned to the dressing room just as one member of Enchantment Place's brownie cleaning crew delivered a stack of flyers. "They're lookin' for chaperones for the prom, Zoë. You oughta go," the faerie said, giving her a thumbs-up on his way out the door. "What a babe of a chaperone you would make. Take Ted. 'Bout time for that. Ya think?"

Oh, just what I don't *need.* Zoë leaned her elbows on the glass counter, chin in her hands, remembering the perfect dress she'd made for herself ten years ago to wear to the Prom at Enchantment Place. *A matchmaking brownie . . .*

Ted—*her* werebear prom date—was a great guy. He never would have stood her up on purpose, but the pull of that decade-old full moon had been too powerful for him then. Now, of course, he had more control over his . . . changes.

Just as Zoë had control over when and for whom she imparted her magical stitches. Once upon a time, her magical stitches simply worked—or didn't—sporadically. Now she was in command, thank goodness.

"Why don't you want to go?" Brenna asked.

Zoë shook her head, so lost in thought she'd forgotten the girl's presence. "I'm sorry. I . . ." She sighed and gave Brenna a gentle smile. "It's a long story—kind of a sad one for me."

"Oh . . ."

"Besides, it's silly to keep thinking about it after all these years." Zoë moved to the end of the counter, planning to distract Brenna by showing her some of her handmade dolls, when trouble flew through the door.

Pint-sized, winged trouble . . .

"You're not welcome here," she said before the pixies could even get started with their usual extortion attempts. "Fly away."

Brenna stared silently from the fluttering pixie thugs to Zoë, then back again. "What . . . who . . . huh . . . ?"

"Don't let their size fool you, Brenna." Zoë folded her arms and cocked a hip. "Tom and Jerry are crooks through and through."

"Tom and Jerry? Faerie crooks?" A giggle bubbled up from Brenna, but she seemed to sense her error and covered her mouth.

Too late. Tom and Jerry buzzed Brenna's head like bees on honey.

"Scram or I'll call security, you sleaze-fae." Zoë reached for the button on her intercom. No one wanted to face the vampire security guards. "I mean it."

"Lighten up, doll," Tom said, close—too close—to Zoë's face. "One of these days, you're gonna regret not playing along and forking over the magic cloak for the queen."

Jerry joined his cohort. "Yep, you've been warned for the last time."

"I'm *really* scared." Zoë rolled her eyes, but didn't back away from the hovering menaces. "Get . . . out . . . of . . . my . . . store *now*!"

Tom and Jerry finally left the store and Zoë released a sigh. The pixie gangsters had been demanding she create a magical cloak for their queen for years, but she always refused. Oh, sure, she could sew a cloak, but it wouldn't contain magic—not for a gangster leader.

"That was weird," Brenna said. "Really weird."

"They always are."

Britney bounced out of the dressing room with her new gown bagged and ready. "I need to pick up my shoes, Brenna. Let's hit the road, kid."

Brenna grimaced, and Zoë grinned, tapping the girl's black beret. "Keep it close."

"Will do." The girl trudged along behind her big sister, but she paused at the door to look back and wave.

"Sweet kid," Diana said. "The little one, not Britney the Barbarian."

Zoë couldn't help herself. Laughter burst free before she could prevent it. Typically, she was the model of professionalism, but Diana's description of Britney was simply too perfect.

"Did I hear Tom and Jerry out here?" Diana asked, her expression growing solemn.

Zoë sighed and busied herself with straightening a display of lace that already looked perfect. "Yep. The little farts have been and gone."

Diana touched her sleeve. "Zoë, they're dangerous. Why don't you just give them what they want so they'll leave you alone?"

Zoë shook her head and met Diana's gaze. "Who knows what their queen would do with a magical cloak?" She dragged her fingers through her sleek black hair. "That's a risk none of us should be willing to take."

"Mab will have our wings clipped if we don't bring back that damn cloak," Jerry said as the bartender slid him another shot of fermented nectar.

"Tell me about it." Tom tossed back his third dandelion ale and belched. "That Zoë is a hard nut to crack."

"She always has been." Jerry leaned close to his partner. "Did you see the kid in there?"

"Sure, I saw her. Mundane, if you ask me."

Jerry rubbed his chin, thinking back to the protectiveness he'd sensed between Zoë and the kid. "I got a hunch the kid could be Zoë's weak spot."

Tom snorted, then fell silent. "Ya think? Really? A mundane like her?"

"It's worth a shot."

"What have we got to lose?" Jerry sighed and drained his nectar.

"Besides our wings?"

"Bingo, brother. Bingo . . ."

Prom day was hectic at Witch Stitchery, as always. Zoë and Diana pressed, hemmed, steamed, and made various last minute alterations to dozens of gowns for high school juniors and seniors. All of Enchantment Place was abuzz—literally and virtually. Not a single shop was immune to the annual extravaganza.

Though Zoë wished she *could* be immune.

After all these years, she should have forgotten the heartache of being jilted for her senior prom, but—sigh—she couldn't lie, even to herself. The memory still had the power to sting when she least expected it—probably because she had, and still did, care more for Ted than she should . . .

She drew a deep, cleansing breath, envisioned a protective circle around her emotions, and returned to the gathers in Penny Stanley's pink confection. She'd tried to tell the girl—diplomatically, of course—that hot pink taffeta and bright red hair wasn't the most flattering combination. However, nothing deterred the freckle-faced teen from her agenda. So hot pink taffeta it was, for Penny.

With a few special stitches at strategic locations.

Zoë smiled secretly to herself and blew her bangs back as the brownies came through with the sweeper again. Everything had to be perfect for Prom Night.

Bernie the brownie paused near Zoë's worktable. "Heard Ted from Make-a-Mortal is going to be a chaperone tonight."

Zoë pricked her finger but carefully buried it in her skirt to prevent staining the pink taffeta. "That's nice," she said without looking up from her work. Once assured she wouldn't stain the fabric, she resumed stitching Penny's gown. "I hope he has a wonderful time."

"Ah, Zoë, lighten up, kid."

Bernie had been around Enchantment Place too long, and he knew too much . . . he was a one-brownie grapevine.

She drew a deep breath, blinked, and met Bernie's gaze. He was a domestic faerie, homely and beautiful in the same interesting ways. The little guy must have seen at least two centuries come and go. "Thank you, but no thank you," she said, knowing he understood her meaning.

"Life's short, kid."

"Except in your case." She grinned, and he shrugged.

Chuckling, the brownie went on about his business, ensuring he and his crew left nothing less than perfection in their wake.

Enchantment Place mandated all shops remain open on Prom Night, so Zoë had hired extra help. She would hang around a few hours later than usual, just to ensure no disasters occurred, but she had no desire to hang around after the music and dancing commenced in the decorated courtyard. She'd already noticed the ice sculpture and chocolate fountain earlier.

"I need a break." She put Penny's finished gown on its hanger and bagged it with the appropriate label. "This is paid in full, Diana. I'll be in my office if anyone needs me."

"Got it, boss."

Zoë headed toward the back of the store, assuring herself she hadn't seen pity in Diana's expression. Surely her longtime friend and employee didn't know Zoë's secret. How foolish for a woman who owned a successful business to mourn a long-lost love and a missed senior prom . . .

By the time she shoved through her office door, her eyes stung from unshed tears, which she immediately attributed to exhaustion and overwork. *Yeah, right.* She knew the truth, but damned if she'd admit it, even to herself.

On some kind of autopilot, she went to the back closet behind her desk, muttered the secret words only she knew that would open the portal. No one else could even see the door to her special closet.

She stepped inside and pulled the door shut behind her, removed her simple ivory linen tunic and trousers, then slipped the violet silk prom dress she'd made over ten years ago over her head. It laced in front—sort of a medieval design—fell off her shoulders with butterfly sleeves, a handkerchief hem, and revealed a hint of cleavage; the deep purple created a stunning contrast between her inky hair, bright blue eyes, and ivory skin.

Ted would have loved seeing her in this . . .

She bit her lower lip and silently cursed herself. Why did she torture herself this way? Well, she knew why.

She'd never moved beyond that lost night in one way, as she'd fallen deeply in love with the gentle werebear. If only things had been different. If only she could have forgiven him for letting her down that night—though she had been able to justify it—and . . . if he'd forgiven himself.

Now they worked a few doors away from each other every day, yet they had rarely spoken since that night she'd waited for him to pick her up for their senior prom.

She stared at herself in the mirror—twenty-eight-years-old, wearing her silly prom dress, and still in love with the boy who'd left her waiting.

"Zoë!" Diana's frantic tone permeated the secret door. "Come quick!"

She didn't want anyone to see her in—or even know about—this dress, but Zoë knew Diana wouldn't use such a frantic tone without good reason. Her protective and service instincts took control, and Zoë emerged from her secret closet, knowing Diana wouldn't see it even now. But she would see the violet prom dress. No way around that now.

"What is it?"

"Tom and Jerry!"

"Oh, no. " A sense of dread settled in the pit of Zoë's stomach. "What now?"

Diana shoved a rolled scroll toward Zoë. "They have Brenna, and they're demanding Mab's magical cloak for ransom."

"No . . ."

"They want to make the exchange tonight at the prom. They sent this, too." She handed Zoë the soft wool beret belonging to Brenna's father. "Maybe you know what it means."

Zoë knew one thing for sure—Brenna never would have relinquished the beret willingly. "I hope she's all right." If the girl hadn't been in her store when the pixie thugs had buzzed through, she never would have fallen in harm's way.

Diana looked at Zoë's dress and her eyes widened. "Wow! Looks like you're already dressed for the ball, Cinderella."

*   *   *

Zoë Zykowski was going to the Prom at Enchantment Place.

Ten years tardy . . .

She tucked the very special cloak she'd constructed for Queen Mab into her evening bag—after all, pixies were tiny. Her Majesty would sense immediately if Zoë failed to provide a magical cloak, so the red velvet with gold braid trim did, indeed, include a few magical stitches along the hem and stand-up collar.

And something more . . .

Zoë could only hope it was enough.

More than enough.

At the entrance to the extravagant courtyard, she drew a deep breath. Thanks to Diana, her make-up and accessories were perfectly coordinated. Go figure . . . It didn't matter. Her mission was simple—deliver the ransom and rescue Brenna.

Nothing more, nothing less.

Even so, she couldn't suppress the small, odd thrill that swept through her as she walked along the red carpet. She didn't need a ticket. She was on the chaperone list. *Thanks, Bernie.* She smiled to herself, knowing the old brownie had something to do with that little miracle.

So where would she meet the kidnappers—the little pixie thugs, who'd obviously used magic to overpower young, innocent Brenna? Zoë squeezed her eyes closed for a moment and drew another deep breath. Captain Hansen's beret was tucked into her bag along with the evil Queen Mab's cloak.

"Zoë?" a rumbling male voice asked. "You look . . . just as I always knew you would . . . that night."

Oh, damn. Zoë counted to five before opening her eyes. "Ted." She'd forgotten that Bernie said he was chaperoning this evening. With all the urgency surrounding Brenna's abduction, it had slipped her mind.

Hadn't it . . . ?

She opened her eyes and was transported—back in time, to the prom that should have been. Not that she should concern herself with any of this, but . . . until

Tom and Jerry contacted her, what else was she to do but pretend she was a chaperone having a good time?

And ogle the boy/man/werebear she'd loved from afar for over a decade?

Ted was still gorgeous. Tall, golden, handsome. Tonight, he wore a chocolate brown tux, and the candlelight danced golden in his hair and beard.

"Is there a full moon tonight?" she whispered, before she could help herself.

He ducked his chin and shook his head. "Wouldn't matter. I'm a big boy now."

I'll say!

Zoë bit the inside of her cheek, reminding herself she was a woman with a mission—one far more important than reliving a prom she'd missed a decade ago.

"I . . . didn't know you were on the chaperone list," he said. "If . . ."

"Doesn't matter."

"Is . . ."

Somehow, Zoë knew what he wanted to ask but hadn't. "Yes, this is the same dress I made for our—er, when we were seniors."

Not our prom . . . That never happened.

"It's gorgeous." He reached for her hand, and she—like a fool—let him take it in his. "And so are you."

And you . . .

"You're chaperoning this year?" he asked, his thumb drawing circles on the back of her hand.

"Um, sorta." Zoë glanced down at her handbag, remembering her mission. Then she knew what she had to do—she had to trust Ted. Furthermore, she *did* trust Ted. She released a long, slow breath.

"Something's wrong."

"Yes." She met his gentle gaze and focused on her mission. Next thing she knew, she'd told him everything—about Tom and Jerry (though every merchant at Enchantment Place knew about them!), about Brenna, her father, the beret, and Queen Mab's cloak. Everything except the special touches she'd added to the cloak . . .

"All you know is they'll contact you here?" he asked, once she'd finished her story.

"Yes." Zoë glanced around the courtyard. "Though I have to tell you it's pretty cool to see so many gowns I designed in one place at one time." She grinned.

He returned her grin. "I'll bet." I don't see any of my Make-a-Mortals here, though."

She had to laugh at that. "I'll bet," she echoed.

Ted's expression grew solemn. "Zoë Zykowski, will you go to the prom with me? Now?"

His expression held such sincerity, such intensity, Zoë's breath caught. All she could do was nod. Barely . . .

"Let's make up for some lost time and dance."

Music she vaguely recognized as hip-hop boomed over the speakers. "Ouch. To that?"

"Well, you have a point." His chuckle resembled a low rumble of a growl, and—before she knew it—he'd pulled her into a gentle, warm bear hug.

"So let's walk around and watch until they play something more suitable, or . . ."

"Until Tom and Jerry show up."

"Right."

With her small hand tucked into Ted's large one, Zoë circuited the courtyard, scanning the crowd for the pixie thugs. Where was Brenna? And Britney was conspicuously absent as well. Of course she wouldn't be here—not with her sister being held for ransom.

And how could this tragedy have finally brought Zoë face-to-face, arm-in-arm, with the man she'd missed for ten years?

Life was blatantly unfair.

After their second circle around the courtyard and Zoë's description of various gowns, their owners, the stories behind the design and making of same, Ted was chuckling more than talking. And squeezing her hand until she felt warm all over . . .

How she'd missed him—missed this elemental connection she'd denied them both for a decade. Why? Punishing herself for something beyond their control?

"Something green and sparkly at eleven o'clock," Ted murmured near her ear near the chocolate fountain.

"Two somethings," Zoë confirmed. Tom and Jerry, no doubt. "They'll find me, since they didn't tell me how to find them, and I have what they want."

"Do you?" Ted tightened his hold on her hand, his emphasis clear. "Be careful, Zoë. They're dangerous."

She remained silent for a few seconds as the green glows came nearer. "I know, but not as dangerous as what could be."

Ted cupped her cheek in his large hand and tilted her face upward to meet his gaze. "You're a wonderful woman, Zoë. You always have been—always will be."

And he kissed her, very briefly—right there at the Prom at Enchantment Place as he should have a decade ago. The right man, the right place, the right dress . . .

She was way, *way* overdue for this, on more ways than one . . .

Wait, wait, wait!

She had Tom and Jerry's pixie pranks with which to deal. She certainly didn't need this distraction. Well, she did, but not now. "Later . . . "

"Count on it." Ted gave her hand a squeeze and they turned together to face the approaching pixies.

Tom and Jerry hovered around her. "You got the cloak?" Jerry finally asked.

"Where's Brenna?" Zoë clutched her evening bag closer to her body. Ted loomed large and comforting at her side.

"Ya think the werebear is gonna scare us, honey?" Tom taunted.

A low, warning rumble came from somewhere deep within Ted's chest. Tom and Jerry hovered closer to Zoë after that, despite their bravado.

"Where's Brenna?"

"Queen Mab has a spell on her house and everybody in it, until you give up the cloak." Jerry held out an open bag. "Just put it in here, and the kid's family will be free."

What choice did she have? Zoë opened her evening

bag and removed the tiny velvet cloak. Hesitating, she stared at Jerry. "Immediately free and unharmed?"

"That's what Mab said."

With a sigh, Zoë placed the garment in the bag. The pixies left the courtyard with their booty immediately. Zoë removed the black beret from her purse, along with her cell phone. "I have to check on Brenna."

Ted followed her into the foyer and remained nearby while Zoë made her call. "No answer." She worried her lower lip until someone shouted her name from the rose-adorned archway near the entrance of the courtyard.

Brenna rushed toward her, followed closely by Britney in her blue silk prom dress and her handsome date.

"Those mean faeries did something weird, and no one could leave the house."

Zoë gave Brenna a hug and handed her the beret. "I believe this belongs to you."

"Thanks. They took that, too." Brenna smiled. "Daddy's coming home. Mom's waiting for me in the car. I wanted to thank you for whatever you did to set us free."

"I'm glad your dad's coming home." Zoë gave Brenna another squeeze and watched the girl dash back out to where her mother waited. She gave Britney a thumbs-up. "You look gorgeous. I think you're a sure bet for prom queen."

Britney shook her head. "I don't care about that anymore. But thank you. I'm just glad Dad's coming home and everybody's safe."

She smiled up at her date, and the handsome couple strolled into the courtyard.

"Tell me something, Zoë." Ted placed his hands on her shoulders and gazed down at her. "I know you didn't really give Mab a powerful cloak, so what did you do?"

"You know me better than I realized." Zoë smiled. "I had to put a bit of magic in it, because I knew Mab would sense if there was none. But . . ."

"But?"

She grinned and gave Ted's hand a tug. "The trim on

the cloak is extra special, with many, many chips of iron carefully distributed through—"

Ted burst out laughing. "Brilliant. Enough to subdue her and her evil ways."

"I think you owe me a dance, werebear."

ANSWERS

Elizabeth A. Vaughan

Elizabeth A. Vaughan is the author of the *Chronicles of the Warlands*, a new fantasy romance trilogy: *Warprize*, *Warsworn*, and *Warlord*. Her short fiction has previously appeared in DAW's *Furry Fantastic*. She's always loved fantasy and science fiction and has been a fantasy role-player since 1981. By day, Beth's secret identity is that of a lawyer, practicing in the area of bankruptcy and financial matters, a role she has maintained since 1985. Beth is owned by three cats and lives in the Northwest Territory, on the outskirts of the Black Swamp, along Mad Anthony's Trail on the banks of the Maumee River.

The sign said "Answers."

It hung from a black iron bracket and was carved of a dark wood, the letters deeply incised and glittering gold. The door of the storefront was the same wood, with glass so you could see inside. There was no display in the windows, just more clear glass.

Amanda had come as soon she got off work. The hours weren't posted on the door, so she peered in, afraid she'd come too late. She used her hand to shade the glare off the glass and caught the faint smell of green peppers. Made her sick to her stomach. Scrub as hard as you could, but you still stank of the stuff when you had to be the one slicing and dicing all day.

The place was empty except for a desk with a computer screen and a keyboard. And an old wooden client chair, sitting there in front, right in the center of the big empty room. The floors were bare hardwood, gleaming in the light from the lamp on the desk.

Amanda hesitated.

This was nuts, of course. There was no way she'd find answers here, just no way. But her friend Mary had done it, hadn't she?

Amanda pulled back from the glass, only to see her reflection. There were worry lines now, and a frown. She tried to smile, to get rid of the lines, but the smile seemed cheap and false. If it weren't for her problem, she'd never have come here.

If it weren't for what Mary had said . . .

Mary'd been dealing with a problem too, a real problem. She'd told Amanda that she'd come here to get an answer. Amanda had asked what kind of help Mary had gotten, but Mary wouldn't tell. "You just have to go and ask," was all she would say. "But be careful, okay? Just remember—one question, one answer."

Mary had been so serious. Amanda scowled at the glass. Of course, she was also a bit of a flake. But Amanda had a feeling in the pit of her stomach that she'd been serious.

The wind picked up and blew through her coat, and Amanda shivered. She felt stupid, just standing there. She should either go or . . .

There was a woman at the desk now.

Amanda leaned forward and squinted. The glass was old and a bit wavy. She could make out the woman's pale face and brown and gray short hair. Glasses, with silver rims. A thick sweater. The woman didn't seem to see her, or if she did see her, she didn't care. Somehow that gave Amanda the courage to open the door.

The door rattled as it shut, and the woman looked up and arched her eyebrow questioningly.

Amanda headed over to the desk. The floor was hardwood, clean and bright, and it creaked as she walked. The woman said nothing as she sat, just lowered her eyebrow and watched her with a neutral expression.

"I'm Amanda Stuart. I've got a problem."

"Sit." The woman gestured to the chair. "One question. One answer."

"I don't—" The chair creaked as Amanda put her weight on it. She smiled nervously. "I don't under—"

The woman didn't smile back. Not that she was rude. Just serious. "One question, one answer for each customer. No more, no less."

Amanda swallowed, looking around at the bare cream colored walls and the floor. There wasn't so much as a dust bunny to mar its surface. "How much do you charge?"

"Is that your question?"

Amanda blinked. "No, of course not."

There was a brief glint of humor in those faded eyes. "No charge." The woman said evenly. "One question. One answer."

Amanda blinked again, her mind spinning. She opened her mouth and then closed it, as a big hole opened in her insides. "I don't . . ."

The woman just looked at her.

"I guess I don't know what my question is exactly." Amanda felt so stupid, but that was the truth.

"You might want to think about it." The woman's blue eyes looked at her mildly. "Carefully."

Amanda rose, clutching her purse. "I'll be back."

The woman shrugged, as if it was of no importance one way or another.

Amanda went back out into the cold, clutching her coat close to her body. She walked along the bright storefronts, unseeing.

What was her question?

"She told me how to fix it." Mary put a mug of coffee in front of Amanda and settled in the chair next to her. "I went there and said that my child support was screwed up, and that the attorney wanted an arm and a leg, and I couldn't afford that. So, I asked her 'What can I do to fix it myself?' ''

Amanda reached for the mug, more for the heat than for the taste of Mary's instant coffee.

"She says, 'Ah.' That was all she said. Next thing I know, she's leaning forward and typing like a demon." Mary looked at Amanda over the rim of her mug. "Then she leans back and says, 'Very well. Here is your answer.'

"Seems my paperwork was on the desk of a clerk who'd died in a car accident about two months back. They'd reassigned the cases, but mine got lost in the shuffle and got shoved in a desk drawer."

Mary shook her head. "She told me to call on Tuesday afternoon and ask for Samantha. Said to give her my case number and tell her that I was sorry to bother her but that I had a problem. She said to say that my attorney wanted an arm and a leg before he'd help me. Said to say I'd have to hire him, if she couldn't help me."

Amanda looked at her. "And that did it?"

Mary chuckled. "Sure did. Seems Samantha knows that lawyer, and he's always hitting on her, what with her being married and all. She tracked it down for me and helped me get the paperwork in order, just to spite the man." Mary smiled. "Ain't that something?"

"I gotta go. I got just enough time to pick up Momma's drugs." Amanda looked glumly at her coffee cup. "I don't know. Seems kinda wrong. Like there's something unholy about it."

Mary shrugged. "I think you could be right, if you're asking the wrong things. Like how to rule the world, or win the lottery." She shook her head. "But for what you want? Seems to me you got a chance to ask a question, you ask it." Mary's eyes were filled with sympathy. "What's the worst that happens?"

The next morning had Amanda standing in front of the store. Mary was right. What was the worst that could happen?

She pushed open the door.

The woman was sitting there, same as before. Amanda walked over the chair, and sat.

"Before I ask my question, I need to know if you know about something."

The woman looked over the edge of her glasses. "I do." It was said with quiet confidence.

Amanda frowned and explained anyway. "My momma's got a cancer. Metastatic carcinoma of unknown primary source. It's a kind of cancer where there's no tumor, so you don't know where it's coming from, and where they don't find it until it's spread through the body already." Amanda paused, careful not to make any of her sentences questions. "Momma's got it in her bones. She's done chemo, and raditation three times, and they're talking about more chemo." Amanda fumbled in her purse, looking for a tissue. Seems all she carried these days was tissue. "Momma does real bad on chemo."

The woman opened a drawer, pulled out a box of tissues, and pushed them across the desk.

Amanda pulled four or five, stalling, trying to get her throat to work.

"I thought to come here and ask you if Momma would live. Or to find out when she got it, and why. Or how much time she had, or if the chemo might take care of it." Amanda choked back her tears.

The woman just waited, as if there was all the time in the world.

Amanda blew her nose. "They're giving Momma an option, whether to have more chemo or not. My brother, Mark, he wants her to do it. Mark's down in Indy. He gets back here about every two weeks to see Momma."

But he wasn't there when that frail body was heaving into a basin or soiling the bedclothes because the chemo left her too weak to move out of the bed. Amanda swallowed the bile in the back of her throat. God above, she hated cancer. Hated it to death. "Momma asked what I thought, and I don't know what to say. If she doesn't do the chemo, they're talking hospice, and that . . ." Amanda's throat closed again, and she fought the tears down enough to keep talking. "That's giving up, in a way."

The woman's face didn't change except that she blinked, and it looked as though she might be breathing.

"We've talked to the hospice people, and they're real nice. They talk about comfort and taking control. About keeping Momma home and no more hospitals." Amanda felt her tears rising again. "I could tell Momma really liked the idea of no more hospitals."

Quiet moments passed. The woman sat silent. Waiting.

"Seems to me there's too many questions, and no good way to pick one to ask." Amanda said quietly. "And maybe no real answer at all, except for God's plan. But I've decided what to ask."

The woman titled her head. Amanda may have imagined it, but there might have been a gleam of respect in her eyes.

Amanda pulled a slip of paper out from her purse, and read it out carefully. "When are they going to find a way to figure out how to find the primary source is, when there's no tumor?"

It was like watching a bulb turn on, Amanda thought, as the woman's eyes went to the monitor and her fingers leaped to the keyboard. As if all she had was the answers, and she lived to find them.

Amanda sat still, clutching her damp tissues in one hand, afraid of disturbing the work. But at last those eyes focused on her, and they gleamed as if from the light of buried treasure.

"In five years, a cancer researcher from California comes to a conference here in Chicago. He will take an interest in this problem and start doing some experiments with the idea of formulating a test to locate the tumors, no matter how small. He won't have much success until two years later, when he attends a college reunion and hooks up with his old football buddy, who works with computer vision detection. They start comparing notes, and within two years, they develop a nonintrusive test that locates cancer cells in the body. They win the Nobel Prize for Medicine a year later."

Amanda caught her breath. "Nine years, then."

The woman nodded her head.

Amanda stood, her knees shaking. 'Thank you. I . . ."
She could not finish the sentence. She just turned and
headed to the door.

"Why that question?" The woman's voice followed
Amanda. It sounded raspy, as if she hadn't asked a question in years.

Amanda turned. "I need to tell Momma what to do,
whether to take more chemo or let go." Amanda swallowed hard. "Whether to fight it or lay down her weary
body and . . ." Her throat closed, and she fought to hold
back the sobs, but she couldn't. Her chest heaved, and
she gulped in air, suddenly so angry at the world, at God,
at everything. She took a step forward, facing the
woman. Her face flushed hot, but her hands were ice.
She let the tears run down her cheeks.

"You tell me," she spat. "You tell me, if you have the
answers. What's the point? Momma worked so hard, and
raised us good, and now the time comes that she can
stop working and rest, she sickens with something we
never heard of. What's the point of living if all we face
is loss and death? Grief and sorrow? You tell me that!"
Amanda's voice rose in a wail that she couldn't control,
a high keening note. Embarrassed, she pressed her fingers over her mouth, feeling her hot tears, and shaking
with the effort of keeping her sobs in her chest.

The woman just looked at her, eyes bright behind her
glasses. "Only you can answer that question, Amanda."

STEEL CRAZY

Laura Hayden

Laura Hayden never met a genre she didn't like and has come to call what she writes, "slasher fiction," i.e. mystery/fantasy or romance/mystery or time travel/Western/comedy and so / "slasher" on. She's written for many major publishers. Her newest endeavor is a political suspense series (no slash necessary) called *Unto Caesar*, published in early 2008. Today she lives in Colorado but thanks to the Air Force, she could live almost any place tomorrow. To learn more about Laura as well as about her new series, visit her website at http://suspense.net or visit her bookstore: http://www.authorauthor.net

Wade Saxon watched his customer carefully. Occum Marsu of the Marsu Clan might be a repeat customer, but that didn't mean he was a welcome one. Occum handled the displays too much, always leaving clumps of hair in his wake. The store's antiodor spell took care of the troll's eye-watering stench, but there was nothing Wade could do about the hair. Or Occum's penchant to arrive five minutes before closing time.

The troll stopped to admire the window display of Excalibur protruding from the stone. The display was the blademaster's equivalent of a barber pole; a universal sign of the profession. When Occum reached out to touch the sword, Wade cleared his throat loudly, and the troll, duly warned, switched his attention to the other merchandise.

"Hmmm . . . new muck swords," Occum rumbled. "That one." He stabbed at the item, leaving a greasy fingerprint on the counter, the mark disappearing a few moments later thanks to the charmed glass. Wade's business partner had installed that along with a host of other time-saving devices. Wade's blade wizardry might be the cornerstone of their business, but his partner, Bard Tinker, was a farking genius when it came to the actual running of the store.

Thanks to Bard's potions, charms and the latest in point-of-sale computerized inventory-management systems, their business ran smoothly enough to make enough money to cover the ungodly overhead cost of a mall location, provide them both a living wage and reinvest into their expanding inventory. They'd even had enough profit to buy a sophisticated security system that blended electronics and enchantments to protect their business to the fullest extent.

Life was good.

Even if it meant selling muck swords to sticky fingered, dung-smelling mountain trolls.

Occum glared at the sword that Wade placed on the counter. "Blade's too small," he complained. "Got any longer ones?"

Wade wasn't surprised. Mountain trolls often preferred heft over finesse, choosing short-handled weapons with long, wide blades for maximum hacking value.

It was a compensation issue.

He remained patient as he catered to the fickle Occum, finally selling the troll an older model muck sword at a discount. Always impatient, Occum wanted an immediate enchantment on the blade, but Wade shook his head and simply said, "RegNine."

WorldLaw Regulation 9.9.9a mandated a two-day waiting period on all weapons and a three-day period on enchanted ones. In Wade's eyes, RegNine was the smartest thing the WorldLaw congress had conjured in the last two decades. It complicated his business, but it eased his conscience. If nothing else, it'd reduced troll-on-troll crime by half.

Occum grumbled, handed over the cash, and pocketed the pick-up receipt. As soon at the troll left, Wade pulled down the security gates and began his nightly closing procedures. Thanks to Bard's ingenious systems, the till counted itself, balanced the amount against the sales, amended the inventory records and self-deposited the money via a monetary transporter spell.

Technology and wizardry, hand in hand.

The brownie cleaning crew knocked on the glass door for admission, and Wade lifted the gate a few inches to allow the cleaners to enter. Fifteen minutes later, the store sparkled, and Occum's clumps of hair were history. Wade signed their time sheet, nodded goodbye and watched them troop to the next store.

After gathering his belongings, Wade let himself out, rearmed the security system, and headed down the empty mall corridor. A few merchants were still puttering around inside their locked stores. As he passed by the toy store, he caught the eye of Wilhelmina Jurvis as she straightened a stack of games. She nodded, blushed then paid inordinate attention to her stacking.

One of these days . . . he thought wistfully.

The trip home was uneventful, and once there, Wade spent the rest of his lonely evening in his workshop, enchanting the weapons sold the day before. He kept only display stock on hand and the rest of the inventory in his own home under security spells that far exceeded those at the mall.

Sales had been brisk lately, and he'd been scrambling every night to keep up with the orders. Bard had suggested more than once that they should hire some counter help, but Wade had resisted the idea. In his opinion, the major appeal of shopping at Steel Crazy was interacting with the artists who understood the range of weaponry and limitations of the blade enchantments.

Even if it meant he had to work with customers like Occum Marsu.

Wade worked on the charming until almost midnight, after which he turned out the workshop lights and went to bed. Morning arrived on time. Normally, that wouldn't have been worth noting, but a couple of college pranksters had managed to make the sun rise early twice the previous month.

After showering, Wade dressed and entered his workshop to pull the completed orders. Rather than haul his night's work to his car, drive in from Lisle, park at the loading dock, and fill out the paperwork for permission to carry dangerous weapons through the mall, he simply performed the point-to-point transportation spell they'd registered with the Teamsters two years ago. It was much like the bank deposit transport but on a much larger scale. It included all the necessary fees to keep the union guys happy and automatic paperwork to fulfill mall safety regulations. Even better, the system allowed Wade to avoid dealing with the ogres who ruled the mall's Barney-Fifedom of rent-a-cops.

Once Wade reached the employee lot, he knew something was up. Something bad. There were Preternatural Division cars—marked and unmarked—at every entrance to the mall. Before he could even get out of his vehicle, two uniforms trotted over to him and asked his name and reason for being there. When he told them, they consulted their list.

"Come with us, sir."

They led him over to a clutch of grim-looking plainclothed Prets. One suit stared stoically at his clipboard. "Saxon. Steel Crazy." He looked up. "Weapons, right?"

"Mostly. What's happened?"

"A gang hit the mall overnight—took some pretty big mojo to get in and even more mojo to get out. I've assigned you an investigator. He'll accompany you so you can identify your losses."

Wade said nothing. Thanks to the sophistication of their security system, he doubted they had losses. As he and the Pret assigned to him walked down the corridor, Wade glanced into the stores along the way, watching managers in deep discussion with their own designated

Prets. He caught sight of Wilhelmina being questioned by a gnome Pret. She looked up and shared a brief "You too?" glance with Wade, then turned back to her inquisitor.

Judging by the glass carnage he saw in passing stores, the thieves must have been more smash and grab types than major spellcasters. Lucky for him, he had been prepar—

Wade stopped in midstep and midthought. There was a gaping hole in his store's security gate. But it was the conspicuous absence from the window display that chilled his blood.

Excalibur was gone.

His heart wedged itself in his throat.

As his blood pressure rose to unmanageable heights, sparks began to form at his fingertips. Clenching his hands, he forced the wayward power to explode into his palms. He hadn't lost control like that since he'd hit puberty. The last thing he wanted to do was reveal to the Prets exactly what level of wizardry he was capable of, not to mention the true value of Excalibur.

"Something wrong, Mr. Saxon?" The Pret wore no expression.

Wade dragged in a deep breath. "I need to talk to your superior. Whoever is in charge."

The Pret raised one of his three eyebrows. "Got something to confess, Mr. Saxon?"

"No. I simply need to talk to the guy in charge," he repeated, now trying to control his anger as well as his magic.

Ten long minutes later, he sat in the mall manager's office, the space evidently seized by the Prets as their command post. The tall blond man who strode in was obviously half-elven and wholly pissed. He wore an ID that identified him simply as "Inspector Phumholtz."

"If you're wasting my time, Saxon, I swear I'll put you in a cage directly beneath the ogres," the halflen threatened.

"Excalibur."

Phumholtz consulted his notebook. "The replica in your store window. Stolen, right?"

"Not exactly."

The halfflen inspector remained perfectly still in the way only a forest elf can. "Which is it? Not stolen or—"

"Not a replica."

Wade's reward for truth was being on the receiving end of a very stern, penetrating gaze. However, Wade had stared down creatures twice as scary, with or without badges.

Finally, Phumholtz spoke. "Explain."

Wade closed his eyes. He'd only repeated the story twice before, once to his mentor and once to his business partner. His mentor had taken the secret to his grave and beyond. And Wade trusted Bard Tinker with his life.

Wade drew a deep breath, then spoke. "You know the various tales about King Arthur, Excalibur and the Lady in the Lake, right? One legend says that Arthur pulled Excalibur from the stone and the other says that he got the sword from the Lady of the Lake. Both are true. He did pull Excalibur from the stone, but it broke in battle when he misused it. He threw the pieces into the lake and the Lady presented him with a second sword that he also named Excalibur."

The inspector looked totally unimpressed. "So?"

"What no one mentions is that the pieces of the first sword were eventually discovered."

"And you have one of them."

Wade hesitated.

Phumholtz wasn't dense. He tapped his pencil against the side of his notebook. "You have both of them."

Wade remained silent.

"That's the stupidest thing I've ever heard. No one in his right mind who owned both halves of one of the most famous power conduits in history would stick one of them in a store window. In public. Where anyone can see it . . ." His air of incredulity faded away. "And automatically assumes it's a replica because no sane creature would . . ."

". . . hide it in plain sight," Wade supplied.

The Pret dropped down into the chair, as if too exhausted by shock to stand. "You took a big risk, pulling a fool stunt like that."

"A calculated risk."

"And you think someone figured this out?"

"Possibly. What was stolen from the other stores?"

The Pret shrugged. "Nothing else of any real value. Trinkets, mostly." The inspector leveled Wade with second penetrating gaze. "You seem to be the only person who lost something of great value. I wonder . . . exactly what do the thieves expect you to do? Rush home and make sure the other half of the sword is safe?"

"Assuming it's in my home . . ."

The manner in which Phumholtz watched Wade suggested that the inspector wasn't merely a halflen but someone more . . . skilled, more dangerous. A fae shapeshifter, maybe? They were known for their legendary powers of observation and attention to detail, both necessary to create a perfect impersonate. Some were even rumored to be able to detect a change in a creature's heart rate at twenty paces. Of course, Wade had never heard of there being any shapeshifters in the Preternatural Division. But why take chances?

He remained in his seat. "Is that what I'm supposed to do? Panic and, in doing so, reveal the second hiding place so it can be stolen as well?"

"If that's the plan, then it's not going to work, eh?" A small smile tugged at the official's lips. On any other creature, the smile might appear harmless, even congenial. However, on a Pret, Wade knew it was a calculated ploy to disarm and engage.

"At least all is not lost," the inspector added.

Another ploy? "How's that?"

"They stole your sword but failed to take the stone . . ."

Realization hit Wade like a brick in the stomach, and he failed to hide his response. "The stone . . ." His mind raced ahead to an unsavory conclusion.

"We found it in Service Corridor B," Phumholtz said,

wearing a small smile of triumph for having broken through Wade's control. "Looks like whoever stole it was tired of carrying it around and left it behind."

At this point, Wade no longer worried about holding his cards close to his chest. Something far more important than his pride was in jeopardy. Without the stabilizing influence of the stone, it wouldn't take long for the sword's unchecked power to grow to lethal levels.

"Do you know what sort of strength it would take to remove the sword from the stone?" he asked quietly.

The inspector stroked his chin and chuckled. "True king of England strength?"

Uncontrolled magic exploded in Wade's clenched fists and traveled up his arms. "It'd take a Class Nine Wizard to separate the two," he said in hoarse whisper.

Phumholtz eyed him. "And you're what? A Class Three?"

Wade tried not to reveal how far off the Pret's guess actually was. As an unregistered Eleven, he'd worked hard to hide his true nature from the Prets. Inviting their interest was never a good thing. The last thing he'd wanted to do was become a government hired wand. His powers were his business and no one else's. But now it might be unavoidable in a sort of End-of-the-World-As-We-Know-It way.

"We're in deep trouble if the sword was forcibly removed without any enchantments," he admitted.

"How deep?"

"The sword is a power source. The stone is a power sink. They were keyed together centuries ago so that now they make a nice little display, enough tingle to surprise and entertain customers but no power build-up, no problems." His seat became suddenly uncomfortable. "But if the sword has been forcibly removed from the stone without being rekeyed to another depletor, the power will start to build, unrestrained. If we don't return the sword to the stone by—" he consulted his watch and made a rough calculation "—midnight, the power will have built to an uncontrollable level. The failsafe mechanism will kick in, and the power overload will be channeled back into the sword. There'll be a hundred-mile wide crater where the sword used to be."

"Then what do we do next?"

"Let me examine the stone."

Less than a minute later, they stood in Corridor B, where Phumholtz excused the technicians who had been dusting the stone for magic residue. Once they left, Wade squatted down and examined it, performing three different revelation incantations to reveal counterspells. But he saw none. Something, someone with enormous physical strength had ripped the sword half from the stone and in doing so had torn the binding spell into shreds, not to mention shattering the power sink spell.

By the time he ran through his repertoire of options, including a variety of locator and time-regression spells, even an illegal psychometric enchantment, he was no closer to an answer and in danger of sapping his personal energy reserves.

"There's no way to guess who did this, much less how," he finally admitted to the inspector.

Phumholtz reached into his pocket and pulled out an illegal vial of Privacy, which he broke, isolating the room from all outside connection and communication.

At Wade's expression of amazement, the Pret shrugged. "You have your secrets. I have mine. Judging by what I just witnessed, you're a Class Nine or higher. I don't care why you hide it. I won't even mention how much trouble you could be in for having a weapon of this magnitude in a public place. All I care is finding it."

"Same here."

"If we can't find a magical trail, let's try some mundane techniques." The Pret punctured the privacy curtain, releasing the spell, and motioned for Wade to follow him. "The security cameras indicate that no one entered or left the mall except through the one loading dock door that wasn't enchanted but was heavily guarded. Or so we think. Maybe you'll see or sense something we missed."

They reached the loading dock.

"We've requested a Class Ten but they said he

wouldn't get here for another hour or so. I don't think we have time to wait. So you're my expert."

Despite his flagging energies, Wade tested the security spells. Following the contrails of the various transportation spells, he managed to backtrack every delivery including his own, proving that no authorized or unwitnessed deliveries or departures had been made.

That meant the sword was still in the mall. Somewhere.

He opened his senses and reached out, tried to pick up a slender silver thread of power that might or might not be the sword.

"I can almost . . . sense it. But the trail is too thin, too delicate to trace."

"Try."

Wade headed back to the main mall corridor, casting out his widest mental net to detect any signs of power. But as he walked through the hallway, he was distracted by similarity in the damages the other stores. In each case, interior shop doors showed evidence to physical breaches. Security spells had been fractured, but not removed.

Phumholtz noticed his interest. "You sense something?"

"Do you have a list of what was taken from every store?"

The inspector turned to the first page in his notebook and read aloud a list.

A bra and two thongs from A Touch of Silk. Blue silk.

A broad spectrum love potion from Bottles, Inc., capable of imparting a mildly amorous effect to anyone from the smallest fairy to the largest ogre.

A pair of walkie-talkies from ElectroShak.

A signed baseball from Bears, Bulls and Cubs, Oh My! the sports store.

"It's as if the thieves hoped to obfuscate their real object of desire by hiding its theft among the more mundane objects."

A subordinate sidled up to them and whispered something to Phumholtz. The inspector handed Wade the list. "I'll be right back."

Wade dropped to a bench and pondered the notes. He must be missing something. Some clue. But what? With his attention riveted to the paper, he didn't notice Wilhelmina Jurvis until she practically stood in front of him. He sprang to his feet to display the manners his mother had shamed into him and managed to dislodge the notes so that pages fluttered to the floor. Wilhelmina leaned over to catch them at the same time he bent over, and they succeeded in knocking heads.

"I'm so sorry," they said simultaneously, rubbing identical knots on their foreheads. "Are you okay? I'm fine," they said in unison.

Wilhelmina tried to smile, but the expression failed to reach her eyes. Instead, she dropped to the bench and released a heavy sigh. "I think I just lost my job."

"How come?"

"Mr. Durst, my manager, thinks the break-in was my fault."

Wade clenched his fist in anticipation of a few errant magic sparks. "That's stupid. Your store wasn't the only one that got hit."

"Still . . ."

He consulted his list. "You lost what? A couple of dolls?"

"Not just dolls—a special shipment of Darbie Dolls. They weren't even supposed to be released to the public until next week." She burst into tears. "Mr. Durst said the manufacturer will probably sue us for violating their date-of-release contract."

Unsure what to do, Wade reached over and awkwardly patted her hand. "It's okay. I'm sure they'll understand. Maybe they have a *force majeure* clause or something like that."

She sniffed in a way that made his heart ache on her behalf. "Mr. Durst doesn't care. He's already told me to pack my things and leave, but the police won't let me go until they've finished their investigation." She glanced around the corridor, which was usually bustling with traffic by this time of the morning. "I have to hang around here until they release us."

Now's your chance, he told himself. *Time to be courageous. Daring. Dashing, even. Time to—*

"Mr. Saxon? My notes?" Phumholtz stood next to them, his hand outstretched.

When Wade handed him the papers, he sensed the slightest residue of magic coating the man's hand. "Where were you just then?"

"Pardon?"

"You've touched something. What was it?"

The inspector raised one eyebrow. "We just recovered some items from Miss Jurvis's store." The eyebrow arched higher. "Several dolls."

"The Darbies?" Wilhelmina asked, hope flooding her face with much needed color.

The inspector nodded. "We just found them stuffed under a bench." He snapped his fingers and a subordinate trotted over and handed him a clear plastic bag which contained two naked Darbie dolls.

The flair of hope on her face faded. "Where are their clothes?"

"We found them this way."

She sat heavily. "I'm still in trouble. It's not the dolls that are important as much as their clothing."

The hairs on the back of Wade's neck prickled. "What were they wearing?"

She released a deep sigh. "These were part of the new High Risk Darbie line—HazMat Darbies."

Wade rose from the bench and grabbed her by the hand to help her up. "You have any left? Can you show me?"

She rose with reluctance. "We have some, but I doubt Mr. Durst will let me back in."

Wade glanced at the inspector. "Can you get us in there?"

Phumholtz narrowed his gaze. "Try to stop me." He pivoted and stalked toward the toy store with Wade and Wilhelmina close behind.

Somehow, it seemed natural for Wade to hold Wilhelmina's hand and even more natural for her to let him. When they approached the closed gate and saw the

daunting Mr. Durst behind it, Wade squeezed her hand
in reassurance.

One flashed badge and Phumholtz not only got them
inside but also short-circuited any comments from Durst.
Moments later, they stared at a brand new mint-in-box
HazMat Darbie. The inspector ripped open the box
which made Durst cringe, then handed the doll to Wilhelmina. "Would you undress the doll, please?"

She complied, and seconds later they had a small pile
of clothing, specifically a full-body jumpsuit in Day-Glo
yellow, matching boots, gloves, and a protective helmet
with clear plastic shield.

"Well?" the inspector asked. "You think . . ."

"Yeah, I do."

"What are you talking about?" Wilhelmina demanded.

"It all makes sense now," Wade said. "The walkie-
talkies. The bra and the thongs. The baseball. And the
love potion was to assure compliance from everyone involved." He held up the tiny hazmat jumpsuit between
his thumb and forefinger. "And this?" He smiled. "To
protect someone who couldn't touch steel."

Confusion fell from Wilhelmina's face. "You mean
fairies? They did this? But why?"

Phumholtz spoke into his radio. "I want every fairy,
every pixie, every—"

"Brownie," Wade supplied.

"Brownie. Every creature in the mall with a height
under twelve inches brought to the center court by the
fountain. ASAP."

"Wait, I need one more thing." Wade turned to
Wilhelmina. "And I need it from you."

She listened to his plan, then turned to the inspector.
"You'll have to talk Mr. Durst into letting me back into
the store."

His lips twitched with a hint of a smile. "With
pleasure."

Ten minutes later, a small crowd assembled in the center court. The mall manager, a pixie named Bastion, flew
toward them, his voice shrill with anger. "On behalf of

the Organization for Equality for Smaller Creatures, I am lodging a complaint against the Preternatural Division for their unfair treatment of—"

"Shut up." Phumholtz brushed Bastion away like an annoying bottle fly. "Everyone, line up over here." He pointed to several wooden benches sitting near the fountain. "Pixies on the first bench. Fairies, the second. Brownies, the third. Everybody else—fourth bench."

The creatures lined up accordingly. The fairies all crowded together at the corner of the bench as far from the fountain as possible, trying to avoid the occasional spray from the dancing spurts of water. The pixies buzzed like an overturned beehive, unable to stand or sit still on the bench. Always industrious and paid by the task, the brownies took the opportunity to polish the bench with tiny cloths while they waited to be questioned. A lone leprechaun sat on the fourth bench by himself.

Wade found an out-of-the-way place to observe the groups as Phumholtz and his men interrogated each group of suspects. But Wade centered his attention on the brownies. They all dressed in the same uniform and had basically the same features, so it was difficult to pick out those six who had been part of the cleaning crew the night before. When Phumholtz reached the brownies, he scowled at the assembled group. "Who was on duty last night as the cleaning crew?"

Five tiny sets of hands went up.

The inspector turned to Wilhelmina. "How many were in your cleaning crew?"

She stared at the small faces. "Five."

"And you?" He turned to Janelle Marsden of the lingerie store.

"Five."

He received a chorus of "Five" from various store managers except Wade, who stepped forward and said in a clear voice, "Six."

Phumholtz bent down to better address his audience. "We seem to have a disagreement."

The crew chief swaggered to the front of the bench in a way that only a ten-inch-high brownie can. "We run five-man crews, Inspector. Always have, always will."

Wade allowed a few sparks of magic to leak from his clenched fist as an obvious threat. "They're lying and I can prove it."

Two of the Prets rushed toward Wade, but one command from Phumholtz stilled them. "Let him continue."

Wade stood over the brownie crew chief, taking full advantage of the difference in their heights. "You ran five man crews everywhere else because you didn't need an inside man to help you break into those stores. They have only the most basic security measures in place. But because we're a weapons shop, we have extremely sophisticated security protocols, meaning the only way you could break into my store was to break out of it. You ran a six-man crew in, but only five departed. You left behind one person to hide until after I left. The rest of you used the stolen items to help the inside man break out and take something with him." He turned to Phumholtz. "May I demonstrate?"

"By all means." The inspector snapped his fingers, and a Pret approached, handing Wade a paper sack and placing a bucket on the floor at Wade's feet.

He fished out the lingerie. The two thongs had been looped around each bra strap. "The slingshot," he announced. Then he reached into the bag and pulled out the baseball. "And the projectile." Using two Prets to hold the thongs, Wade demonstrated by shooting the baseball across the center court. "It's surprisingly accurate. I bet if I practiced, I could consistently hit a spot as small as six by twelve inches." He turned to the crew chief. "Or roughly the size of the ventilation for my store's security gate. Tie a fishing line to the ball and you can use it to pull in a rope or a chain or something strong enough to hoist up Excalibur."

"You're crazy. We run five-man crews. Period. And we don't steal." He puffed up a bit. "It's the brownie code."

"You don't remember because you were all drugged last night." Wade pulled a bottle from the sack. "Love makes you do silly things. Love potions make you do silly things and not remember them. If you allow the inspector to run blood tests, I know it'll show traces of potion in your blood."

The chief looked confused. "Then someone . . ."

"Used your good reputation against you. I didn't think twice about counting how many of you showed up. You come, you always do a great job, and you always leave. We're all used to letting you have free rein."

A chorus of agreements from various managers backed him up.

"And you can touch cold iron. You wouldn't have needed something like this." He pulled the Darbie hazmat suit from the bag. "Only wee folks who couldn't touch steel would need these." He pivoted and stared at the fairies, whose wings blurred with tension.

Wade shot them his cold-steel smile and they collectively shivered. "One of you infiltrated the cleaning crew, dosed them up so they would do whatever you say. You broke out of my store, stealing Excalibur and the stone."

The fairy union steward stepped forward. "You're crazy, man. Even with protection, no fairy is strong enough to lift the sword and the stone."

"You're right. But an ogre could." Wade nodded toward the line of shaggy line of security ogres. "If you test the guards, I think you'll see one of them was dosed, just like the cleaning crew. Trouble is, the potion doesn't work long on larger creatures. But it lasted enough for him to pull the sword and stone up and through the opening and maybe long enough for him to be coerced to tear the sword from the stone. The thief gets the sword, and the ogre carries off the stone."

"We like stones," a voice said from the lineup of security guards.

The fairy shop steward stepped in front of the others. "Mr. Saxon. I swear I can account for everyone here. None of my people did this."

Wade nodded. "I suspect you're correct." He pivoted sharply and glared at the brownies. "I think our bad guy believes in hiding in plain sight."

He kicked over the bucket of water so that it spread across the floor, beneath the bench where the brownies stood. "Well?"

The brownie crew chief balanced his hands on his fists. "Don't we have enough to do around here without you making work for us? C'mon boys." He hopped down as did everyone in his crew, save one.

One brownie remained on the bench, hatred dancing in his eyes. The chief looked up at his remaining crew member, unwilling, or perhaps unable to cross the water.

"Fairies don't just fear cold iron." Wade glanced at the fairies who nonchalantly tried to avoid the side of the bench closest to the fountain. "There's a large segment of them that can't cross water."

He reached into his pocket and pulled out the water pistol that Wilhelmina had retrieved from the toy store stock. He pointed it at the chest of the remaining brownie, a fairy in disguise.

"You don't realize the problems you've caused. The sword needs to be put back into the stone. Immediately. If we don't, everything within a three mile area around it will be gone by midnight."

The fairy shifted uncomfortably. "You're lying."

"No. I'm not. You knew exactly what you were stealing. You knew it wasn't a display but the real thing. And it's still here, in the mall somewhere, isn't it?"

A collective gasp rose from the crowd.

"If you don't want to turn into fairy dust at midnight, then you better tell me where the sword is. Now."

The fairy took almost a minute to work up to an answer, his fear and instinct for survival warring plainly on his face. Finally, he collapsed. "She has it," he whispered.

Phumholtz stepped forward. "She who?"

The fairy glanced over his shoulder. "The Lady."

Phumholtz looked confused, but Wade knew there was only one Lady who mattered.

The air filled suddenly with soft music and the roselike aroma of magic. Everyone around Wade sparkled with magic, then froze in midword and midaction, Phumholtz included. A cloud of mist rose from the water fountain and coalesced into the form of a woman.

"Sir Wade of Saxon," she called out.

Wade immediately fell to one knee. "Here. Might I assume I am addressing the Lady of the Lake?"

"More like the Lady of the Water Fountain." She laughed and it sounded like bells in a waterfall. "The mighty have fallen, indeed."

"It's just a change of venue, ma'am."

"I told myself it was an appropriate place to dwell during the twenty-first century." She looked down at him with sadness in her eyes. "I did not mean to cause you consternation or to endanger these people. I sensed the energy filling your store and feared that your efforts to contain the sword's power had failed. It was an ingenious plan, and I didn't realize how effective it was until my servants freed the sword to be placed in my protective care." Her expression softened into a smile. "That's when I realized the true source of the power I'd sensed."

Wade felt his face flush.

She dipped her hand into the shimmering pool and exposed the missing half of the sword. "This is a powerful relic and could be dangerous in unskilled hands." She lifted it higher, exposing the entire blade, now fully restored. "Yes, I discovered you had the other half as well. However, I am assured that it will remain whole in your possession, unlike its owner before you."

"But the power—"

"—has been restored by the unification of the two halves. It will no longer be an unchecked danger to you or your world."

Unchecked, Wade repeated to himself.

"Its magic can only be wielded by an extraordinarily powerful wizard, someone worthy of its strength, someone with the heart to use it wisely."

Wade struggled to draw in a breath.

"You." She glanced toward the frozen crowd. "Don't worry. We can unwind all this. Set things back to the way they were. You may hide your true identity and the extent of your abilities. No one need know what you can do but yourself." She moved closer to him, holding the sword out, hilt first.

Wade stopped himself from reaching for it. "How will I hide it? Hide myself?"

Her flashing smile filled him with a sudden sense of comfort. "You hide as you always have hidden. In plain sight. With the sword in the window of your shop as it has always been. The only difference is that it is now whole and no longer a danger. Some day, you will be called to use it to unite this world, to bring both magical and mundane creatures together as one voice, one army, and lead them against a common enemy. The sword will not only identify you as their leader but will give you strength."

"W-when will this happen?"

Her smile deepened. "I can't tell you that. I won't even allow you remember this conversation. But know this—when the day comes, you will instinctively reach for Excalibur. And it will not fail you. Or your world."

A fog billowed at her feet, rising from the surface of the fountain. "Sir Wade of Saxon, Master of Blades and of Wizardry, I bid you farewell."

As the mist clouds rose to obscure her, his thoughts grew foggy as well.

Another long day at the store. Wade gathered his belongings, rearmed the security system, and headed down the empty mall corridor. A few merchants were still puttering around inside their locked storefronts. As he passed by the toy store, he caught the eye of Wilhelmina Jurvis as she straightened a stack of games. She nodded, blushed then paid inordinate attention to her stacking.

One of these days . . . he thought wistfully. Then he stopped. *Why not today?*

He rapped on the glass and waved at her. Her resulting smile was sweet, shy and thrilled him to his toes. She walked over and unlocked the door.

"Is there something I can do for you, Mr. Saxon?"

Courage flooded him. "You can call me Wade, and

you can tell me you'll join me for a cup of coffee and a piece of pie."

She blushed a marvelous shade of rosy pink. "I thought you'd never ask."

OUT OF THE FRYING PAN

Diane Duane

Diane Duane has been writing science fiction and fantasy professionally for more than twenty-five years, working on such projects as her continuing *Young Wizards* novel series (now approaching its ninth volume) and licensed properties such as *Star Trek®* (on which she's worked in more forms than anyone else alive). With more than forty novels in print and various television and film works screening worldwide, she somehow also finds time for train travel in urban Europe and hiking in the Alps. She also makes a mean coq au vin.

Editor's Note: This piece and the next one (. . . "And Into the Fire") are written by a husband and wife team and are paired because they involve the same characters and are meant to be read together.

She was arguing with a werewolf about the price of saffron when the veiled woman wandered in.

Veils were presently enjoying one of those small renaissances that the fashion features of bygone years sometimes have, so the shoulder-length sweep of dark gauze by itself wasn't enough to seriously distract Annabelle from the ongoing disagreement. She turned back to Harl and said, "Look, you can't expect to pay super-market prices for this stuff, especially since *this is not a supermarket!* In case you haven't noticed. When you consider what my saffron goes through before it gets here—"

"I know what you *say* it goes through," Harl said, leaning on his elbows on the counter and absently twirling one side of his mustache, "but the prices you're discussing are insane! Only the fact that you're the extremely nice lady that I know you are—for a one-skinner—has kept me from complaining about the markup until now . . ."

Oh boy, Annabelle thought, *here we go, the Witch With A Heart of Gold ploy. Why is it we're all either Good Mommies or Crone Mothers and never anything in between? And next, I bet, comes the not-so-thinly-veiled request for a discount. How many seconds will it take?* She decided not to wait—possibly since Harl had arrived in a middle transitional stage, and his studded biker leathers were starting to come across as increasingly incongruous when taken together with his burgeoning ear hair and the muzzle that Annabelle could swear was lengthening as she watched. "Smile when you call me that," she said. "How would *you* know how many skins I have hanging in the closet?" She pushed some of the small impulse-buy merchandise off to one side of the cash register and leaned on the counter too, while the veiled lady in the dark amber kaftan ambled around the far product island, apparently intent on the cookware. "Harl," Annabelle said, looking up at him, "my markup has a whole lot to do with what my suppliers charge me. We're not talking about scamp short-stigma saffron grown on some vacant lot outside Marbella! We are talking about prime violet-petal *sativus*-x corms containing back-patched genetic material from the original Akkadian *azupiru* heritage strain, planted on a particular south-facing hillside outside a village in the Cevenne hills in the department of Gard in southern France. And it's *not*," and she held up a finger as Harl started drawing breath to say something, "just the corm stock at issue. Before the saffron was planted, that hillside had to be certified safe by the *Insti-*

tut Nationale des Thaumatoxisme, a government regulatory agency that, at great expense that you'd better *believe* gets passed down the line, first cleared the ground of piled-up malign influences. Kind of like dealing with toxic waste, except that toxic waste doesn't normally leap out of the ground in the shape of a blood-colored dragon and twist your head off."

Harl idly picked the lid off the bowl of lollipops by the cash register: Annabelle slapped his hand, took the lid out of it, and replaced it on the bowl. "Do you want to rot your teeth? Stick to Milk-Bones. *Then* the detoxed ground in question got checked over by not one but *two* feng shui agencies, one hired by the grower and one commissioned by the distributor, each of them checking the other and trying hard to find details about the topology that the other geomancer has missed. And that cost got passed down to me too. Along with the labor costs of the nice local people who break their backs picking all those fiddly little stamens out of the flowers on Samhain Eve every year." She sighed, picked up the lid off the bowl, and went burrowing among the lollipops, hunting for one with a chocolate center. Unfortunately, she had eaten them all. She dropped the lid back on the bowl. "So you should *not* be complaining to me that this stuff costs eighty bucks a gram. Because the price means that when you and some nice lady friend who's also in her second skin and also in the mood for luuuuuuve get together at the full of the moon and stick it up your noses, you'll get the desired effect . . . and *not* find yourself stuck in your skins the next morning when you need to change and go to work. Nor will you fail one of those embarrassing random mana tests later in the week. So if you want to pay less, sure, go on, go down the street to Dominick's or the Jewel and pay twenty bucks a gram. What you get'll be either the Marbella vacant-lot saffron or maybe dyed safflower stamens, and you'll deserve it."

Harl rolled his eyes. "Oh, come on, Annabelle, they have to be ripping you off somewhere along the line. If you go online there are bulk-order places that'll cut you a much better deal. All you have to do is . . ." *Blah,*

blah, blah, Annabelle thought, doing her best to look courteously interested but feeling less inclined by the moment to indulge Harl's pouting. This was the third or fourth time this month he'd started giving her grief about prices. The first couple of times, an insufficiently clued-in customer might be allowed to get away with it; but Harl knew perfectly well that the special needs of weres called for a much higher-grade spice than "single skinners" or other varieties of just plain mortal could get away with. *I may lose him as a customer . . .*

Yet Annabelle was finding it harder to bring herself to care. Harl had never referred anyone to her, as far as she could tell, and he frankly didn't buy enough stuff in the course of a month to make it worth her effort to try to hang onto him. Getting more weekday traffic in here was a much bigger issue. She flicked a glance at Ms. Kaftan-and-Veil, who was still eyeing the cookware and now reached up a thin wrinkled hand to touch a pot; cast iron clonged faintly against iron in her wake as she moved away and headed around the far side of the island toward the generic spice racks. *If I could please have about fifty more like you every morning,* Annabelle thought. *More plain-vanilla mortals who can touch cold iron and don't make me order in high-end nonferrous utensils at high-end prices and low-end profit margins . . . I've got to find ways to leverage our advertising to a wider customer base without alienating the supranormal market.* It was just one more aspect of her ongoing problem. The overhead involved in keeping this place going was proving to be higher than she'd thought it would be at first, after the rent increase last year. In fact, after this morning's jolly little visit from the shopping center's unit management agent, who after a look at the store's books had started sweetly insinuating to Annabelle that she really should move downstairs into a smaller unit— *Yeah, off the main drag where I'll get even less walk-in than I get now.* She looked up at Harl again. *Oh, come on, the phone's been ringing all morning with bad news, can't I have a little more, please, just to shut this mouthy wolf up?*

But the phone would not oblige her. *I'll throw a can-*

trip at it, Annabelle thought. *Or* him. *And the Threefold Rede can just go chase itself.* The thought was tempting. *But no.* "Harl," Annabelle said, "the heartbreak of mange is a *terrible* thing. I wouldn't wish it on a dog . . ."

He gave her a sudden horrified look. *See, that's all it takes: I'm the Crone Mommy now. And ask me if I care!*

"Oh, all right," Harl said, checking his watch. "I have to get going or I'll miss my train. Just give me a gram to hold me over."

Train, shmain, Annabelle thought as she pulled out the electronic scale pad and set it on the counter. *Around the curve of the world, the moon's going full, and you have a hot date waiting . . .* She slipped out from behind the counter and made her way to the spice cabinet at the back of the store. It looked very rustically domestic, all distressed oak and diamond-paned glass, but it had better security on it than the cash register did, and a more advanced alarm system than some drugstores. Everything in it would bring street prices in the hundreds of bucks per gram: the saffron was not the most expensive thing in there by a long shot. Darkmoon asafetida, wattleseed, chokepard aconite, king basil, melegueta, calamus, double-detox nightshade, whiplash galangal, pepperbush, forest anise, the usual range of psychotropic mushrooms and chiles, and even the wolfsbane that Harl would probably be scandalized to see sitting in carefully measured sachets right underneath the saffron that was a were's preferred aphrodisiac—they were all here. And dozens more, some genetically tailored for supranormals' use, some for spellwork, some just the best of their kind for whatever purpose. Annabelle prided herself on having the best spice selection in the center city; since she opened up, no practitioner of the Art had to go outside the Loop for that special potion ingredient, for a really good *hiera picra,* or the sixty-six ingredient mithridatium that had won her the silver medal in the *Esoterica* Magazine "Compound Interest" competition last year. Or, for that matter, for tyrannosaurus garlic or a decent pair of oven mitts that went all the way up to your elbows; you

OUT OF THE FRYING PAN

couldn't be expected to spend your day muttering protective spells over *everything*.

She put her right thumb to the particular spot on the woodwork that her witchery had sensitized to her aura and said three words under her breath. The door unlatched, and Annabelle took the precautionary look around her before reaching back for the saffron: she'd had snatch-and-run jobs done on her before. But Harl was leaning on the counter, looking more bored by the moment, and Ms. Veil-And-Kaftan was flipping through a pile of screen-printed Irish linen dishtowels, and nobody else was in the place.

Annabelle picked up the saffron container, checked it the regulation three times, and locked the cabinet up again. Back at the counter she paused a moment to rummage underneath for a shopping bag and a slip of measuring paper. "Harl, how do you want this today?" she said. "Envelope? Capsule?"

"Capsule will be fine," Harl said. Now he was fidgeting and looking eager to be out of there. Annabelle busied herself with the scale, carefully tipping out the little golden threads onto the white measuring paper. The scale spun up to .998 gram, then to 1.004: Annabelle looked at the tangle of saffron, then pulled out a couple of extra threads to bring it up to .005, sealed the service container and put it down.

Harl raised a quizzical and increasingly furry eyebrow at her. "Four's a death number," Annabelle said, and she tapped a button on the scale to bring up the total. "Call my part of it eighty even," she said. "Eighty-six seventy after the City's cut."

"I think we need a new mayor," Harl growled, doing a little shimmy to get his wallet out of the pocket of the very tight leather pants.

"Always thought one more Daley was one too many," Annabelle said. "Especially one who'd just come back from a council-sponsored junket to Haiti. At least for a change *this* politician can't sue when the papers accuse him of being a zombie." She folded the measuring paper scoop-fashion, tipped the saffron into the capsule, snapped its top shut, wrapped the paper around it, reached down and snapped off a length of red antidemon thread from the spool, wound it around the paper and capsule, dropped them both into the little shopping bag. "There you go, Harl. Enjoy!"

"Will do. Thanks." And he was out the door.

"And in Hecate's name, *don't use it in risotto!*" she called after him. But he was already around the corner.

Annabelle sighed. It wasn't as if every word she told him about the production of the saffron wasn't true. Somehow, though, he still thought she was cheating him, and she felt wounded. *This is not the job for me,* Annabelle thought for the hundredth time recently. *I'm too thin-skinned for retail. I should be doing something creative—*

The phone rang. "*Now* you do it," Annabelle said under her breath. "Thanks so much." She picked it up. "A Taste of Spice, good morning, this is Annabelle, how can I help you?"

A busy signal blatted into her ear. Annabelle frowned and hung up a lot more gently then she wanted to. It was one more of what seemed like an endless number of hang-ups that were the legacy of the phone company having typoed her number in the new directory: the swapped digits meant she kept getting calls meant for one of the local massage parlors.

The phone rang again; she picked up. "A Taste of Spice, good morning, this is Annabelle, how can I help you?"

"By not using your I-am-a-stern-mommy-and-*not*-a-dodgy-masseuse phone voice on me?" George Dimitri's voice said.

She grinned and leaned on the counter again, watching Ms. Kaftan turn away from the towels toward the cookbooks. "It was an accident," Annabelle said. "How's business this morning?"

"Three divorces, two injury suits and a C&D letter," George said. He was an old college buddy of Annabelle's, the only one of her fellow freshman biochemistry students who had been completely unfreaked by finding that there was a witch in the class. They had dated briefly, then stopped dating, but they remained fast friends even when their university tracks had wildly diverged, and George had dumped his humanities major and gone prelaw. Now he was a paralegal working out of a shopfront community-services operation in Humboldt Park while he worked on his Masters. His daily prelunch phone call was always a breath of fresh air to someone whose personal universe often seemed bounded on three sides by cookware and on the fourth by mulish rare-herb distributors.

"Busy morning," Annabelle said, watching idly as Ms. Kaftan got down a copy of *The Kitchen Minimalist* and started going through it, head bent. *The problem is that the veil makes it impossible to see what she's thinking. Or looking at. And now that I think of it, there's the kaftan, too . . .*

"You have no idea," George said. "The cease-and-desist was for a ghost."

Annabelle started wondering about that kaftan as she watched the woman wearing it page through the cookbook. *You could hide a lot of things in a kaftan's sleeves,* she thought. *"For* a ghost," Annabelle said, "or *to* a ghost?"

"To."

The woman turned the book's pages carefully. *Clean hands,* Annabelle thought. *And well kept. Not homeless. . . .* Yet you couldn't always tell. *New Bloomingdale's bag . . .* But the bag you were carrying wasn't necessarily a reliable indication of anything, either. "Think it's likely to work?"

"You can never tell. Then again, if the ghost retains counsel, it gets interesting."

"Messy, I bet," Annabelle said.

"Please," George said. "I wasn't going to get into the ectoplasm, so close to lunchtime."

Annabelle chuckled. "What's legal precedent for a dead person countersuing a live one?"

"Depends on the nature of the suit," George said, "but generally, I'd say a good rule would be, try not to get caught in between them."

The veiled woman put the cookbook away and started to make her way toward the counter. "Can I call you in a few?" Annabelle said.

"Sure, no probs. Got time for lunch today, if you do."

"It's been quiet this morning," Annabelle said. "I might take half an hour." The veiled woman stopped in front of the counter, put her bag down. "Talk to you shortly. Bye." She hung up, and as she did, the woman reached up and put back her veil.

Annabelle found herself taking a breath of surprise, one that she tried to keep from being too long or obvious. She wasn't sure exactly what she'd been expecting to see under that veil—someone very old, perhaps, uncertain about their looks, possibly even disfigured—but not this: an astonishingly young-looking face, clean cut, high cheekboned, almost fierce. The hands she had seen as thin from across the room were not, as she'd at first assumed, much wrinkled with age; they were just very slender, very fine boned. But the hands would not long hold anyone's attention while those eyes were on you. They were a brown so dark they were almost black; and though the hair pulled back from the brow above them was long and silver-white, Annabelle somehow felt sure that it had once been nearly the same color, a dark malt brown—maybe with the occasional russet highlight speaking of hours spent out under some southern sun. "How can I help you, ma'am?" Annabelle said.

"Well, I have these—" The lady bent a moment to go rummaging in that bag again. Strange how so Midwestern an accent could come from such an Italianate face, but then there'd been a lot of Italian blood around here for many years. Annabelle found herself looking not at the hands now but the sleeves of the kaftan as the lady rummaged. The garment's color, that nondescript beige, now seemed a lot less important as Annabelle realized it wasn't actually a kaftan at all and was made of some kind of slubbed silk, fabulously lustrous, multiply wrapped and draped. *Vintage,* Annabelle thought. *Or antique*— She was beginning to think that what she had here was one of those wealthy, eccentric older ladies, unmarried scions of trust-fund families, who occasionally escape the keepers in their city penthouses and run off for a few hours to do something, anything, unsupervised.

"Here we are," the lady said, and brought up an armful of rolled-up things that rustled, placing them carefully on the counter.

They were almost the same color as the kaftan; at first glimpse, Annabelle thought they were perhaps rolls of the same silken material. But as she got a better look, she saw she was mistaken. The lady took one of the rolls and spread it out; it crackled softly under her hands. The material was something like a thick, coated, softly glossy, written all over with beautiful abstract patterns— some kind of lovely, nonrepeating linear design. "Oh," Annabelle said. *Old wallpaper?* she thought. But there was no reason not to put the best possible construction on what was before her. "I see. Table runners? Yes, they're very handsome, aren't they?" She stroked the surface of one; the ink or caustic used to produce the dark patterns could be felt as something slightly raised. "But there's not much market for this kind of thing the past couple of years, I'm afraid. Right now the 'naked table' look is all the rage—tablecloths are out, not even placemats are in any more. Napkins are still hanging on, but . . ." She shrugged. It was one of those fads that came and went in home design, and Annabelle for her own part looked forward to the day when it would pass.

"You're not interested, then," the lady said.

Annabelle sighed, unable to simply ignore the disappointment in the voice. Often enough some senior citizen would bring a package of some unidentifiable herb or some attic-derived artifact that he or she thought was rare, trying to make a little money off it or, in some cases, just looking for a little contact with another human being. *Overheads or no overheads,* Annabelle thought, *how much would it cost me to make this lady feel a little happier than she is at the moment?* "Well," Annabelle said, "it would depend on the price, of course—"

"Three hundred and eighty-nine thousand, five hundred and twelve dollars," the lady said. "And seventy-six cents."

Annabelle's eyes widened. "Uh," she said. "Uh, no, ma'am, I'm sorry, I don't think I can quite see my way to spending that much for them. My apologies."

"That's quite all right, dear," the lady said, "quite all right." And she gathered up the armful of rolls again, dropped them into her bag, smiled at Annabelle, and turned away.

Annabelle let out a breath and raised her eyebrows. *And seventy-six cents,* she thought, bemused. Ms. Kaftan had stopped by the cookbook display near the front of the store and was fussing with her bag again, rearranging her rolls. *There's one for the books,* Annabelle thought. *George'll be fascinated to hear about this, I bet. I wonder, does the number mean something, or . . .* But she abruptly lost her train of thought as Ms. Kaftan came up with several of those rolls and a cigarette lighter, flicked the lighter into life, and touched it to one end of the rolls.

"Uh, excuse me, *ma'am?*" Annabelle said, hustling out from behind the counter. But it was already much too late. Mrs. Kaftan dropped the rolls onto the floor and stepped back, watching with a rather clinical interest as they burst enthusiastically into flame. *Dear Lady above us, did she soak those in lighter fluid or something, look at them go—*

A second later the smoke detector began to screech, and the sprinklers directly above the spot where the scrolls lay burning merrily on the floor went off instantly—Annabelle had made sure that they were reset that way after that last time with the fire elemental. But the sprinklers' aim wasn't at all what it should have been, and they managed to soak everything *but* the spot where the flames were rising. Out in the mall, the area fire alarm went off, clanging enthusiastically as Ms. Kaftan turned her back unconcernedly on the burning scrolls and headed out into the concourse.

Annabelle was much too busy stomping on the scrolls to see where the lady went. She shortly became busier still as mall security showed up, and the shopping center's fire officer and his staff, and about half a dozen other people who had no particular business responding to a fire alarm. The crowd wound up taking up most of the front of Annabelle's retail space, but there didn't seem much point in any of them being there—the fire had burnt itself out within a matter of a minute or so. Nothing remained of the scrolls but a few charred scraps and a scatter of soot and ash.

"I can't believe how fast they went up," Annabelle said to the fire officer. "It was as if they were soaked in something—"

"Not much smoke," the fire officer said, looking around thoughtfully. "You got lucky. The ventilators'll clear it out in half an hour or so."

"Random vandalism," said one of his subordinates. "Been seeing too much of that kind of thing lately."

"Or some kind of grudge, maybe," said the center's publicity manager. "Like the people who turned those basilisks loose in Macy's because they're still not over the name change from Marshall Fields."

"Or someone looking for an insurance payout," said the building's business manager, a little pale man in a shiny suit.

Annabelle gave him a look. "What kind of payout?" she said. "Are you suggesting *I* set this up?"

"No, of course not, but—"

"You've never seen this woman before?" the fire officer asked.

Annabelle shook her head. "Never."

"Well, we'll put a banning order on her," said the head security officer. "She won't get back in." He glanced out into the mall, then looked over his shoulder at his assistant. "Get down to the office and pull the recording from the number three and four cameras on this level. One of them will have her."

The assistant disappeared—literally: he was a licensed teleport, as most of the security people were. One by one the interested parties started to go away, leaving Annabelle staring at a sooty, scorched patch of floor and at the business manager, who was looking at Annabelle as if she were just as besmirched. "It's always a problem," he said, "when a business starts attracting the wrong kind of clientele—"

This is the same song that what's-her-name the unit management lady was starting to sing the other day, Annabelle thought with some annoyance. *Begins with a B. Barbara . . . ?* "Mr. Farnsworth," Annabelle said. "This is not a conversation we need to be having right this minute. Right now, I need to scrub this floor."

Farsnworth hastily took himself away, probably not wanting to be associated with any labor so plebeian. But he wasn't through with her yet, as Annabelle discovered about ten minutes later as she finished cleaning the floor up. That was when one of Farnsworth's minions arrived with a stack of papers, the incident report Annabelle had to fill out.

Half an hour later, when George finally arrived, she was still muttering in astonishment at how much paperwork one crazy lady with a few rolls of antiquated wallpaper and a twenty-five-cent lighter could produce. Now it was George's turn to lean over the counter as Harl had done, but with a lot less mustache twirling. For all his six feet of height and what he called his Serious Lawyer suit, George's fresh face and big blue innocent eyes made him look more like an escaped choirboy than anything else. "You're not even going to have time for a sandwich at this rate," he said, watching her start signing the bottoms of the forms.

"Yeah, I will," Annabelle said, glancing out at the concourse. "Wednesdays are usually dead, and this one's deader than usual, fire or no fire. I'll close up for an hour."

"And you never saw this lady before?"

Annabelle shook her head, signed the last form, pushed the paperwork away. "It's all a mystery to me," she said, reaching under the counter to get her purse out of the locked drawer.

"You should do a scrying when you get home," George said, heading out to stand in front of the store while Annabelle pulled out her keys and started the security gate rolling down out of the ceiling above the doors.

She ducked under the gate and stood looking up and down the concourse for a moment while the gate clanged into place. She knelt to spell the padlock closed, then stood up, dusting off her knees. "I've been thinking about that," she said. "Where's lunch?"

"Your choice. Plantain City or Dodo's."

They walked down the north stairway together. "No more pastrami," Annabelle said, "not after last week. What's at Plantain City?"

George went off into one of his patented restaurant reviews, in this case involving much Jamaican food and some spices even Annabelle wasn't entirely sure she could identify. After the fourth or fifth lovingly described entrée, she stopped him, laughing. "I will never understand how such a desperate foodie is working the paralegal side of the street!"

"Because it's a foodie that likes to be able to *afford* being a foodie," George said. "And today was payday, so the jerk chicken's on me. But, seriously, Belle, if Miss Amateur Arson shows up again, call me first and I'll do lawyer magic at her. The last thing you need is to lose all that high-priced stock to some dementia-ridden firebug. Has the insurance company *ever* paid off on that fire elemental thing?"

She sighed as they headed out the center's doors into the street. "Still working on it."

"I told you, you should have called me first. Make sure you *do* it next time!"

She promised him, of course, and she promised him again over the jerk chicken and again on the way back to the store. The afternoon was perhaps mercifully quiet after that: from lunch to closing time Annabelle sold nothing but a cast-iron frying pan, a copy of *Cordon Bleu Cooking For Dummies*, and two ounces of leaf malabathrum—guaranteeing the demure young woman who bought it, at the very least, an extremely interesting bath if she and the friend who might be in the tub with her both knew the cantrip that went with the herb.

Annabelle closed up the store and caught the bus home to South Lawndale, still musing over the veiled woman, who hadn't struck her as anything like a firebug, despite what George might have said. *All right,* Annabelle thought as she headed up the front steps of her condo and got out her house keys, *maybe I'm not a mental health expert, but crazy? She wasn't crazy.* There had been something very thoughtful about those eyes; crazy would have seemed the exact opposite of what was behind them.

She let herself in, shut the front door behind her, and just stood there in the hallway for a moment. But it wasn't the hallway she was seeing. It was those scrolls . . .

Don't ignore your instincts, she remembered her scrying instructor telling her. *When you're seeing, see.* And the advice had paid off often enough.

Annabelle slipped out of her coat, threw it over the coatrack, and went into the living room. There she turned on a couple of lights, for it was starting to get dim outside. *Twilight's always good for scrying,* she thought. *Not quite day, not quite night, both sides of the border visible. When's nautical twilight today?*

Then she shrugged. *Never mind, don't waste time fiddling around in hopes of maximizing the effect.* Annabelle went over to the old maple breakfront, touched her thumb to the keyhole patch on the right-hand door, and pulled it open, rooting around for a moment among the ceramic pots and cups and other bric-a-brac there. *Now where's that mirror?* Normally she kept a small one here in case of situations like this. But it was nowhere to be found. *Did I borrow it from myself to do my makeup the other night? Oh, heck.*

After a second she muttered, "Never mind, it's about time I got some new powder," and went out to the hallway to go rooting in her purse. The compact, at least, was where it was supposed to be. Annabelle went back into the living room, sat down on the couch in front of the coffee table, opened the compact, and put it down on the table, turning it carefully so that when she sat back it would reflect nothing but the white of the ceiling.

Annabelle tucked her legs up under herself and got comfortable, then allowed her gaze to drop gradually to the mirror, as if by accident. That seemed to be the main trick to catroptomancy, at least when Annabelle was doing it: *sneak up on the optic, sneak up on the hidden reality, don't let it see you coming . . .*

But apparently it had seen her already. The mirror went pale, not with the reflection of the ceiling's white paint but with the strange glossy texture of the rolls that Ms. Not-Really-A-Kaftan had spread out for her. *More an ivory color,* Annabelle thought, as the long dark scrawls of the design ran down the mirror—almost as if someone were holding it in her hand, running it down one of the rolled-out scrolls. *Of course. It's not paper—it's parchment. The smooth side of a piece—not the skin side.* She had been fooled into thinking the material was something modern by how excellent its condition had been. *Very carefully kept. For how long, I wonder?*

The view in the mirror didn't change. *And not just designs. Writing.* This too was something you had to sneak up on, being careful not to press too hard. The mirror would show you the truth if the truth was at all accessible; but you had to keep your own preconceptions well away from the scrying, for fear of skewing it. The black writing writhed as Annabelle watched it—paled, shimmered, then shifted. Suddenly it looked like English-language cursive done in a very regular hand; but it was hard to read, having been written with a broad-nibbed pen. Annabelle dared not look too hard at the mirror, but here and there a word became plain as the writing flowed by. *Water . . . irresistible, and . . . the basic human necessity . . . must take time to . . . in the fire, but . . . chicken . . .*

Chicken?? Annabelle thought, incredulous.

And the compact's mirror cracked from side to side.

"Oh, damn," she muttered, "I rushed it." Annabelle sighed and swung her feet down off the couch, picking up the compact. There would be no more scrying today: One a day was her limit. She glanced around to make sure that no splinters of glass had jumped out when the mirror broke, then closed the compact, got up, and headed for the kitchen, pausing only to dump the poor broken compact back into her purse. *I'll get a replacement tomorrow,* she thought. *Meanwhile, just the thought of chicken is making me hungry. Oh, well, make some dinner, think about this . . .*

But dinner didn't help her get any closer to working out exactly what she should be thinking about. Annabelle spent the rest of the evening quietly, then slept on the problem. Sleep didn't help either. She woke up no more enlightened about what she'd seen than she'd been when she went to bed, and she went off to work as usual.

If possible, it was even quieter than it had been the day before. Annabelle occupied herself with casual stock-taking and dusting the cookware on the hanging racks until, about an hour before lunchtime, the phone finally rang. She hastened toward it, oddly pleased. *George, probably. Wait till he hears about that scrying.* "A Taste of Spice, good morning, this is Annabelle, how can I help you?"

"By getting out of retail. It doesn't suit you," her mother said.

Annabelle rolled her eyes. She loved her mother dearly, but the two of them had a gift (as her father put it) for "winding each other up the wrong way." The fact that her mother was telling her exactly what she'd been thinking herself somehow just made matters worse. "Mom," she said. "I thought you said you'd be out getting your hair done this morning."

"They canceled on me. Sheila came down with that bug that's going around. You should be careful you don't catch it too, working in a public place like that."

"I'm fine, Mom," Annabelle said. *It would be really nice if someone came in now, even if they weren't going to buy anything from me. Come on, somebody get in here and make me seem busier than I really am.*

"Besides, it's sales, you're not the kind of person for sales," her mother said, making the word sound as if she was discussing indentured servitude. "If it's spices and food and whatever you want to be working with, you should open a restaurant! Everybody raves about your cooking! Every time we have a dinner party, everybody's always saying, why doesn't Annabelle open a restaurant? But you know best, you had to get yourself into this retail thing, you work terrible hours, evenings and week-ends, how are you ever going to meet a nice—"

Gracious Queen of the Night defend me from this! As if even You could. "Boy, yes, Mom, I *know*, enough about the nice boys! I would love to open a restaurant. It would be delightful. But would you please tell me where I'm supposed to get the money? Especially in this town. And anyway, if you don't want me working in a public place, which by itself would be a pretty good trick, why are you bugging me to open a restaurant? You can't get much more public than that. People crammed into a little tight space, eating at each other and spreading all their germs around—"

This, of course, was just going to make more trouble: Annabelle's mom hated having her own logic used on her as much as Annabelle did. "Now what kind of way is that to talk to your mother!" her mom said. "You know I only want the best for you, but if you just keep on going your own way and never listening to anybody who cares about what you're doing to yourself . . ." Annabelle found herself nodding as if her mother could see her—which wouldn't have been a good thing, since she would also have been able to see the look on Annabelle's face. Just the sight of a shadow falling across the glass of the front display window made her look up in hope. *A customer,* yes! she thought as the woman came in the door. "Mom, I gotta go, I'll call you back," Annabelle said, and she hung up faster than she strictly needed to . . .

. . . and then realized that she was looking at Ms. Kaftan again.

Today the veil was thrown back, and she was in blue.

It actually looks more like a sari, Annabelle thought as she came out from behind the counter and headed for the woman. *And how the heck did she get back in here? I thought Mike said he was going to put up a banspell outside!* But Mike was not a licensed magical professional, having just done one of the standard paramagical programs that security work these days required, and it was all too likely that his spellcast had slipped up somehow. "Ma'am," Annabelle said, "you know I've got to ask you to leave, after that stunt you pulled yesterday—"

"But I was sure you really might want these," the veiled lady said, rummaging around in the bag again. "Even though there are only six of them now."

If you've gotten a little more sensible about the price, I'll buy them just to get you out of here, Annabelle thought. *I can't cope with another of those piles of paperwork!*

"Oh, no, the price is firm," said Ms. Kaftan. "Three hundred eighty-nine thousand, five hundred and twelve dollars and seventy six cents."

Annabelle blinked as the woman dropped the Macy's bag on the floor and stood up with the whole sheaf of rolls in her arms. "For a *limited* time *only!*" Mrs. Kaftan said, giving Annabelle a very sharp look indeed.

"Ma'am, please," Annabelle said, "if I had that kind of money, do you think I'd be working in a shopping mall? And I want to keep on doing that for the moment, anyway, so if you'd please just go before security—"

"Oh, no," Ms. Kaftan said, shaking her head—a touch sadly, Annabelle thought. "I couldn't do *that.*"

Annabelle was opening her mouth to ask why when several of the rolls fell out of her arms onto the floor. This time they burst into flame without a lighter being involved at all.

This time, at least Annabelle had the fire extinguisher unlocked and ready behind the counter. But she couldn't get her hands on it quickly enough to keep the overenthusiastic sprinkler system from going off again. And there was no way to attempt to keep Ms. Kaftan where she was while the fire wasn't yet under control. The veiled woman slipped out the door and wandered casually out of Annabelle's sight. A few minutes later, the burning rolls were nothing but an ugly mess of soot and foam on the floor, and Mike and the fire officer and Mr. Farnsworth and about twenty other people were standing around all talking at once while the sprinklers, finally having being turned off, dripped disconsolately on the cookbook display. And then the phone rang.

"You hung up on me!" Annabelle's mother said.

Annabelle opened her mouth, then closed it before she said something needlessly injurious, and hung up again.

An hour and a half later, as Annabelle was finishing off the last of the paperwork in a now mercifully empty store, George called. "It was your turn to call me today," he said. "What happened?"

"Ms. Kaftan."

"She came back?"

"For a comprehensive repeat performance," Annabelle said, wearily.

"Same deal as yesterday?"

"Same deal. But, Georgie, this is taking on a decidedly supernormal turn. She shows on the security videos, all right. But not coming in, and not going out."

"And the same thing with the scrolls?"

"That's right. And the same fire," Annabelle said, ruefully looking at the spot that she had once again had to scrub; this time the floor covering had blistered. "This time I couldn't keep the water from hitting the cookbooks in the front. Half of them are ruined. And she was even loonier than the last time, George. You'd think she'd have dropped her asking price a little for those scrolls, but no, she wanted the same amount, I think she's fixated on the number for some reason."

George didn't say anything. "Hello?" Annabelle said, wondering if she'd lost the connection.

"No, I'm still here. Belle," George said, "are you saying that she had only—*how* many of those did she have today?"

"Five or six—no, six, she said six."

"And she wanted the same price? You're sure about that?"

"To the penny," Annabelle said. "She was really definite about it. I almost laughed. Her and her seventy-six cents."

George didn't say anything. "George?" Annabelle said.

"Belle," George said, "I have to make a few phone calls. Then you need to close up early. Can you make an excuse?"

"I don't think that would be much of a problem," Annabelle said, for Mr. Farnsworth had just walked by outside again and was giving her one of those odd looks that she suspected was going to mean trouble sooner or later. And right now, later looked good. "But where am I going?"

"We. Out to lunch."

"Isn't it kind of late for that?"

"I'm hoping not," George said.

He actually came to pick her up in his car, which was unusual—George detested driving in the city—and drove her north of Madison. He made inconsequential law-office talk for most of the short drive, discussing the ghost's cease-and-desist letter with the air of someone who was actually thinking hard about something else. "Where we're going," George said finally, as he waited at an intersection for the light to change, "it may get loud. Don't get scared, that's all I can say."

"Scared? Of lunch? Why would I get scared?" Annabelle asked.

He pulled over to the curb and sat looking at a storefront with a frosted plateglass window and a frosted plateglass door. "You'll find out," he said.

They got out of the car, George locked up, and they walked over to that glass door. Only when she saw the tiny clear glass letters set at eye level above the door handle did Annabelle start to understand what was happening. The letters said S P Q R.

Annabelle's mouth dropped open. "Good Lady above," she said, "do you eat *here*?"

"Every Saturday," George said.

"No *wonder* you need to be a lawyer," Annabelle said under her breath. If you could get into the place, which normally meant reserving two months ahead, the prices on SPQR's menu were such that it was rare for mere mortals to be able to afford a meal there without going into escrow.

"It's all right," George said, opening that severely plain door for Annabelle. "I also play poker here every Saturday. And the chef believes in luck . . . which is unfortunate when one of the people at the table is a card counter." George grinned. "In you go."

In Annabelle went. She had seen pictures of that stark interior in the *Tribune*, but the pictures in the *Trib* could not convey the contrast that the glass-and-white starkness made with the lush Italianate aromas that, even after lunchtime was properly over, were still wafting out of that kitchen. Some of those scents Annabelle knew very well: she was one of SPQR's many suppliers. *White marjoram,* she thought, instantly catching the aroma, along with someone else's homegrown oregano. *I can't believe they're putting that in spaghetti sauce. Well, yes, considering the prices, I guess I can.*

She had no more time for critique of a dish she could only smell and not see. The room was empty now, the thick glass tables naked. Back near the stainless-steel front wall of the open kitchen was a large circular table with a very unfashionable linen cloth on it, and at it sat two people: a slender, dark little woman in a trim business suit and a large, broad, tall, man with a mustache that reminded her of Harl's. That man Annabelle knew, if only from Sunday supplements in the *Tribune* and repeats on the local PBS station: Adelio Famagiusta, sorcerer and TV chef, famous all over the Midwest for the chain of restaurants of which SPQR was flagship, as well as for his never ending succession of cookbooks, his relentless self-promotion, his flamboyant lifestyle, and his temper. As they headed for the table, Famagiusta got up to greet them, scowling. "Ah, now," he said, "you bring me a pretty lady, is that all this meeting is about, this big hurry hurry phone call? Don't you know I'm flying out to Napoli this evening?"

"No, I don't," George said, going straight to the chef and hugging him, "and no, you're not, not when you hear what we have to tell you. Annabelle, this is Adelio Famagiusta. Adelio, Annabelle. Let's all sit down."

They sat. There was already wine on the table, and the chef poured Annabelle a glass and pushed it across to her. "Barolo," he said. "Good enough for me, good enough for you. Giorgio, what is this about? You tell me, bring money? I bring money." He nodded at the little dark woman with the long hair.

She smiled at Annabelle, waggled her eyebrows. "Janine Weller," she said. "I'm with Dolph Millett Grond."

It was one of the biggest accountancy firms in the city, suitably lofty to be handling the accounts of a one-man microindustry. Annabelle smiled at her, as much to cover up how at sea she felt as for any reason of mere courtesy.

"Annabelle," George said, "tell Adelio about the lady who came in yesterday morning and again today."

She looked at George, confused. George just closed his eyes and made a "Go on" gesture with his head, so Annabelle told the story. At first Famagiusta had no particular reaction. Neither did Ms. Weller, who just sat between Famagiusta and George doodling on the linen tablecloth with a ballpoint pen, as unconcernedly as if it were a paper placemat. She seemed hardly to be paying all that much attention until Annabelle mentioned the numbers, the price of the scrolls. That figure got jotted down, and the accountant's pen began playing with the numbers, as if of its own accord.

When Annabelle got to the part about Ms. Kaftan setting the scrolls on fire, she was surprised to see the expression that flitted across Famagiusta's face: alarm. "Now," George said, "the scrying." He turned to Annabelle. "Can you reproduce the results of what you saw last night?"

She blinked. "You mean, not a new scrying? Just a repeat? Well, yes."

Annabelle reached into her purse, pulled out the broken compact. "Wine," she said, "that we have. Can I get some water?"

"Still or sparkling?" Adelio said.

"Uh, still, please."

The chef got up, still wearing that faintly alarmed look, and went back into the kitchen. He came back a moment later with a bottle of San Pellegrino. "Enough?"

"Yes, thank you." Annabelle opened the bottle, put a finger into her wine glass, carefully pulled out one drop of wine, a second, a third, and dropped them into the water bottle. Then she said the appropriate spell under her breath, opened the compact, and poured the wine and water mixture onto the mirror.

Water splashed onto the mirror, off onto the tablecloth, and ran right across it. Where it ran, writing as dark as the wine in the glass followed it: cursive lettering, graceful, covering the whole side of the table where Annabelle and George were sitting. Adelio stood up, leaned over the table, his lips moving as he read.

" 'The basic human necessity,' " he said. " 'To eat, to be entranced by what is eaten, to be sustained, to acquire more than sustenance—' " Slowly he sank back down into his seat, staring at the writing on the table.

"It's the story I heard long ago when I was studying Roman myth," George said. "It's the story you told me three years ago when you were plastered, that night. Isn't it?"

After a moment Adelio nodded. His mouth worked as if dry; he took a drink of his wine. "All the rest of it," he said, "recipes, just a few recipes, the first of many. The lost Cumaean scrolls—"

George turned to Annabelle. "The Sibylline Cookbooks," he said.

Her eyes went wide.

"What?" she said.

"They were offered once before," Adelio said. "In ancient days, to the King of Rome. He refused them. Some of them were burned. The Sibyl, the prophetess, went away, came back again, offered them again, six books instead of nine, the same price. Again they were refused, again she burned some. Finally she came back one last time, offered the books. The King of Rome bought them. They held great secrets—but the king could not understand them. He thought they were political tracts, prophecies about something as stupid as politics! They were not about countries, their idiom was completely misunderstood, they were about *food!* And then they were lost. But now she comes again, now she offers again, as was prophesied! A man who had these books, who had such knowledge, could cook dishes whose mere smell would heal the sick, cure the world's troubles—"

"And make the owner seriously, *seriously* rich," George said softly.

That was when it started to get noisy. "I will buy them!" Adelio cried. "I will open such restaurants as will make the world gape with wonder, I will—"

"You won't," George said. "*She* will." He nodded at Annabelle.

"What??" Annabelle and Adelio said in unison.

"You can open all the restaurants you want, but the scrolls are going to belong to *her,"* George said. "The Sibyl came to *her."*

"But why her?" Adelio roared. "Why not the great Adelio, why not someone with some public profile, why a shopgirl with pretensions of spicery?"

Annabelle bristled. George shrugged. "Because she's a witch?" he said. "Because she's another seer?"

"A seer!" Adelio flung his hands in the air.

"It makes sense," George said. "*You* can't see anything but yourself!" Adelio turned red, but he said nothing. "Maybe like calls to like. Or maybe it's because Annabelle was patient and kind to a little old lady. What difference does it make? What you need to do now is make a plan," George said, "because you can't afford to let this opportunity go by. You are going to give her three hundred eighty-nine thousand, five hundred twelve dollars and seventy-six cents."

Even Adelio had to gulp at that, though again, the alarm was brief. "And let her do what? Run off and become famous with my money?"

Annabelle started to get hot under the collar again. "Adelio," she said, "I'm normally a very ethical person. But I won't just sit here and be insulted. I would really regret turning you into a frog. But the regrets would come *afterward*."

Famagiusta stared at Annabelle in brief horror. For a moment he looked so much like Harl had yesterday morning that she could have laughed out loud, but she managed to restrain herself. Then she was shocked in turn when Adelio started laughing.

"You," he said, "you perhaps I could train. We would start you in the kitchen, oh, very low—"

Annabelle grinned at him. "Not too low," she said. "No lower than a frog can jump."

Adelio roared with laughter. "And I keep the store," Annabelle said. "You wouldn't want to lose a good supplier. I'll find an assistant."

"Make notes, we will need contracts," Adelio said to George. "You don't need to do this," he said to Miss Weller, who was still scribbling on the tablecloth. Some of the scribbles were the remains of drawn games of tic tac toe. She had just started another one, but she was now staring at the numbers she had jotted down and at the crossmarks she had just set up. "Wait a minute," she said. "Look—"

She reached out for a napkin, drew a square, subdivided it like a tic-tac-toe board, and wrote in all but one of the squares. Then she turned the napkin around so they could see it.

"Magic square," the accountant said. "All the numbers add up to the same sum, all the way around. The only thing missing—"

Annabelle looked at the square, did some addition in her head, then some subtraction. "Four," she said. "It's a death number."

"There's your amount," the accountant said. "Read the numbers down, then up, then down again. Three hundred eighty nine thousand . . ."

"An omen," Adelio said, his voice hushed. "And death the only thing missing. Life, life and good fortune forever. I take it back, little seer, Anna *la bella!* A check, Janina, *vite, vite, write a check!* Three hundred eighty-nine thousand, five hundred twelve dollars—"

"—And seventy-six cents," Annabelle said, the next morning, under her breath.

The center would not be opening for three hours yet. The thought of what would start happening later when Adelio descended on the place, the media people probably howling in his wake, had filled Annabelle with an urge to get in here and tidy things up. But tidying was going to have to wait. Standing in front of the roll-down gate, waiting for her in a *palla* of golden silk, was "Ms. Kaftan," with the veil once more thrown back and the Bloomingdale's bag over her arm.

"You knew I'd be here now," Annabelle said as she joined the Sibyl outside the store's closed doors.

"I'd be a pretty poor prophetess if I didn't, dear," the Sibyl said. "Do you have it?"

Annabelle reached into her purse, pulled out the check, handed it over. The Sibyl read the check carefully, folded it up, slipped it into one of the sleeves of the palla. Then she handed Annabelle the bag.

"The roast chicken recipe," the Sibyl said, "is particularly good."

Annabelle had to smile. The Sibyl turned to go.

"Just one thing," Annabelle said. "Why me?"

The Sibyl paused. "The eternal question," she said. "We always wind up needing reasons. Kindness to a weird old woman? An old friend repaying old friendship? A life starting itself over? A mother's prayers for her daughter, finally fulfilled?"

"Oh, please," Annabelle said, amused.

"Don't laugh," the Sibyl said. "I had a mother too. But would it be heretical to suggest that sometimes it's

just your turn?—that sometimes the bread *does* fall but-
ter side up, despite all life's attempts to convince us
otherwise?"

"Dangerous theory," Annabelle said.

"Only if you start expecting it to be that way all the
time," said the Sibyl. "But just occasionally, why not let
the universe be kind? And use those," and she glanced
at the bag full of scrolls, "to give you a hand. For food
is life . . ."

And she was gone, just like that.

Annabelle let out a breath, got out her keys, and unlocked the gate, activating the switch to roll it up. There
was no telling what lay beyond it—how many cookbooks,
how many restaurants, how many more stores opening
in what would eventually be her own chain. But for the
moment, this one needed tidying.

Annabelle ducked under the gate, unlocked the inner
doors, and, smiling, went in to start taking inventory of
more than just the spices.

. . . AND INTO THE FIRE

Peter Morwood

Peter Morwood's writing career first took off in the early 1980s while he was working for Her Majesty's Civil Service. As a two-time signee of the UK's Official Secrets act, he is delighted not to be able to discuss exactly what he was doing for Her Majesty (though it seems not to have involved firearms or a double-0 number). The books making up his best-known novel sequence, the *Book of Years* series (*The Horse Lord*, *The Demon Lord*, *The Dragon Lord*, *The War Lord*) remain cult classics, soon to be joined by the forthcoming *The Star Lord*, along with a new TV miniseries—period drama with (no surprise to Peter's readership) a fair amount of swords and blood. He is a recipient of the Polish Silver Star of Merit but is far more famous for his signature pork with chilies and chocolate.

Through the clouds of steam that filled the kitchen at SPQR, through the clang of the pots and the shouts of the staff, one sound, one voice rose above all the others. Annabelle, sweating in her whites, rolled her eyes; she knew what that voice was going to say. It said it at least fifty times a day, and it'd taken this long, barely two weeks, for it to stop being funny.

272

"Who moved my knife?!"

Most of the kitchen staff did what they had been doing ever since Annabelle had arrived three weeks ago—and possibly for as long as the restaurant had been running. They ignored him. Those who had a moment to look up from the plate they were dressing, or whatever they were sautéing or chopping or broiling, simply shouted back, more or less in chorus, "Nobody *touched* your knife, Chef!"

The answer was a splendid and florid outflow of Italian, almost certainly obscene, if Annabelle was any judge. They were a few words she was beginning to know the sound of. One of them sounded something like "gorilla," but she was sure it had nothing to do with primates. Chef meanwhile stormed up and down the kitchen, waving his arms, miraculously avoiding banging his head into the pot rack, dunking one of those seemingly heatproof fingers into Tonino's sauté pan as he went by, sucking the finger clean as he headed down to the sink—Chef was manic about hand hygiene—and then, as he finished washing his hands, sliding gradually back into English as he came around the far end of the prep station and headed back toward Annabelle. There was this about working with a sorcerer who was also a chef: he might turn you into something nasty, but not in the rush before lunch or dinner—only afterward.

"Not enough basil!" Adelio shouted. That was mostly what Adelio did all day: shout. *But then,* Annabelle thought, *by now he probably thinks it's expected of him.* All through his three television series, you could hear that now famous voice upraised, never much more quiet than a 747 revving up its engines for takeoff, excoriating, cajoling, advising, critiquing, praising.

"I put more in, Chef," the sous chef said, nearly as loudly as Adelio, but much more justifiably. "In fact I put in nearly twice as much as you told me to."

"See that, now," Adelio roared, "I tell you what to do and you ignore me! What kind of thing is this, hey? You will never be executive chef anywhere, Tonino, if you keep ignoring me." He bore down on Annabelle.

"And look here now, Anna *la bella*! Since you left it, that fancy spice shop of yours, it's gone to hell! Your assistant, she sends us crap, she gives us regular basil—not the *good* basil you used to get for us—"

Annabelle carefully put down her knife, because there were times when Adelio's behavior would tempt even a saint. "I brought that basil in for you myself, Chef," she said. "It's best white-vein basil from Michigan. The grower is my second cousin, and I taught him everything he knows about herbs for paranormals. So as for any opinion you might have about the basil, I don't want to hear it."

Adelio threw his hands in the air and turned in a circle where he stood, meeting every inquisitive eye in the kitchen. They were many: The staff had been watching Chef's sparring with "the new girl" with some interest, but Annabelle smiled gently. She knew all about the betting pool.

"See how I am disrespected," he shouted, "in my own kitchen! Here is a woman blessed, yes, blessed by the gods, who have sent her me, *me!* Adelio Famagiusta! To be her patron, to give her hundreds of thousands of my good dollars so that she can bring me these recipes from the divine Sibyl. And what is my reward for my kindness?"

"A media coup?" Annabelle said. "Even more money than you had already?"

Adelio paused, astonished, then burst out into the big laugh that Annabelle suspected had really made him so famous and beloved all over the world. His joviality and love of food was practically a tangible thing, and he was also as far from the PR image of the sorcerer as you could get. Too often in the popular consciousness they tended to be seen as saturnine, grim, ascetic people, often overwhelmed by a sense of the importance of their own magic. The only thing that overwhelmed Adelio was a sense of his *own* importance, an absolutely unshakable belief that the universe could not exist in its present form without him. Annabelle thought this was probably true; he was a tremendously talented chef with a gift for making food that people loved—and loved to make at home, which was far more unusual. But it didn't do to let him know you shared his opinion of himself. That was too much like feeding honey to a bear, one who would critique the flavor and the provenance of the honey even while he scoffed it down.

"And what are you looking at?" Adelio shouted at the kitchen staff. "She is better than any of you, Anna *la bella!* All of you get back to work, it's ten thirty already, why isn't prep on the vegetables done? And what about my knife?"

"It's on your cutting board, Chef," said Tonino.

"And the best starsteel too," Adelio said, "so don't let me see any grubby fingerprints on it! I don't care where you found it, someone's wall, someone's knife rack, someone's *back*, that's my business, and you leave it where it is! So now, Anna, come with me, I need to see your chicken."

He made his way back up past the prep stations to the counter and the island that was his own, the station where he worked. All around the kitchen, Annabelle could see and hear the staff breathing little sighs of relief as they got back down to business.

Adelio scowled, pulled the ever present oven cloth off his shoulder and threw it onto the marble pastry slab that covered half his station. "They're all afraid of me, all," he said under his breath, in the exasperated tone of voice he used until he clocked out at the end of the day and sat at the big round table in back of house, cradling a glass of wine as he watched the last patrons of the day. "Not one of them gives me proper respect, looks me in the eye, like you."

"That's because every time they do," Annabelle said, "you yell at them that they're disrespecting you. And then you fire them." She picked up the oven cloth, folding it in halves. The big main stove was right by Adelio's station, a silent indicator to the staff that there was no place too hot in that kitchen for the man who was its master. But there were also legends about Adelio's oven, legends that there was something in there not quite normal—something responsible for the chef's talent with food, rather than the other way around.

Naturally, no one had ever found traces of anything to prove it. Some people had gotten themselves hired into Adelio's kitchen under false pretences, trying to investigate the secret of his oven and his magical food for one rag newspaper or magazine or another. Mostly they'd just gotten themselves fired again directly they were found out—although there *was* that last case. The guy was in the zoo right now. He'd surprised Adelio late at night, when chef was closing up. Someone else might have gone for a gun or a knife.

Adelio was more direct. Bang, shapechange spell, and goodbye wise guy, hello rather handsome chimpanzee. His criminal trespass/breaking-and-entering case was pending, but in the meanwhile the local justiciary saw nothing wrong with letting him spend his remand time fighting off interested lady chimps. The kitchen staff's turnover had decreased somewhat after that.

Annabelle, for her own part, felt that if there was something going on with the oven, it was Chef's business. But it could also be like the story of the violinist who was supposed to have some kind of deal with the devil. *Some people would sooner believe in Hell than in genius,* Annabelle thought. *Their problem, not mine.* But the big shiny oven presented Annabelle with an entirely different problem, since her own station was right on the other side of it. The staff had their own ideas about what this meant. Either Chef didn't trust her—because Annabelle was too new, too ambitious, too threatening—or he trusted her too much, because she was too pretty, too smart . . . Or had put a spell on him.

That particular whisper, when she heard it, always made her frown. *Like my ethics are any worse than any other witch's,* Annabelle thought. *Didn't I pass the screening procedure for my license?* But there would always be those who'd respond, *Sure. Proves you can pull something shady without getting caught.* People who thought that way would be more than willing to think she'd done something underhanded to Adelio. After all, when a famously hardheaded businessman suddenly turned around and gave a third of a million bucks to a woman he'd only known for an hour or so—

Annabelle let out a breath, glanced around. For someone who shouted so much, Adelio could be surprisingly quiet sometimes. Now he was just standing there, humming under his breath, arms folded, looking at the oven as if expecting the door to open by itself. "Sorry," she said, wrapping her hand in the oven cloth, and pulled down the big, heavy oven door.

The genuinely divine scent of roast chicken flowed out of the oven. Even in that kitchen, already full of good smells, all the staff looked up. *Or not quite all of them,* Annabelle thought. Over in the corner of the kitchen, by the back door, one of the very minor assistants—the knife-sharpening guy—sat stolidly at his work in the corner of the rearmost part of the kitchen, steeling one of a pile of the kitchen's no-name knives.

She shrugged and unfolded the oven cloth, pulling the roaster out of the oven, then boosting it up onto the stainless steel counter. Not so long ago a veiled woman standing in the front of her little spice shop in the Center had said, *The chicken is very good.* And of course she was right. But it wasn't just the chicken that made this true, though it *was* custom-bred free-range cornfed neo-Poilane Seriously Happy chicken from Minnesota.

The first recipe on the old scroll—one of the six that survived the incendiary attentions of their former owner—had been for the specific mixture of herbs and spices required to produce this effect. Moonlight thyme, purple stealth capsicum, crossnail clove, and aromatic creeping frogfoot were just the more easily obtainable ones. When these ingredients were prepared in the prescribed way and combined in the correct order, the effect they had on the chicken, and on those who ate it, was not strictly natural.

But then, neither was the clientele of SPQR's front room, which on a normal evening was likely to contain as many weres, vampires, faes and trogs as normals. The only thing all those people had in common was a desire to eat in a famous TV chef's restaurant and the ability to pay a big fat heap of money for the privilege. And a lot of them were waiting for this dish in particular, because the local media had been full of it for the last three weeks.

Once Adelio had produced a translation of the chicken recipe, Annabelle had taken great care over the design of the preparation. All this care had paid off, for on unadvertised test runs, the entrée had made people out in "front of house" push and shove to get at it and had caused some diners to run off with other diners' plates. At the official launch, the *Tribune*'s famously persnickety food critic had eaten not only his own entrée but his companions and had then tried to talk the local CBS affiliate's features reporter out of hers.

That feature reporter, a lady of the Wereish-American persuasion, had taken exception. The *Trib*'s food critic was now reported to be taking solid food again and was expected to make a full recovery, and negotiations between the insurance companies serving the newspaper and the TV station were said to have reached the "frank but productive" stage.

Now Annabelle and Adelio looked at the chicken together, while elsewhere in the kitchen the staff looked in all other possible directions. Annabelle had never understood why people who supposedly liked food so much could suddenly become intent on pretending they weren't noticing *this*: as if when they did, they would somehow lose face. *Their problem.*

Adelio was shaking his head a little.

"What, Chef?" Annabelle asked.

"It smells like Heaven. Angels, I hear them singing. But it looks too plain. The color—is too *ordinary*. They will eat it, they will love it—"

"And they'll complain about the presentation," Annabelle muttered. This was a theme they'd been over and over these past couple of weeks. "What do they want out there? Should the dish glow in the dark? Should it be borne in by identically liveried deepgnomes and flambéed at the table by some lucky server who gets to stand there squeezing a firedrake like a bagpipe? I don't think your insurance'll cover it."

"Showmanship," Adelio said. "Spectacle. Given what we charge for an entrée, they have a right to it."

Annabelle let out an annoyed breath. "Adelio, to a certain extent, yes. But then you have to ask: Is this a restaurant or a circus tent? It's the *food* that's supposed to count! Not flambéing, certainly not flamboyance for its own sake! These recipes are magic, some of the oldest food magic on Earth. They're supposed to fill the heart as well as the mouth and stomach! What was it you said? They would cure the sick, change the world? Give them a chance to do that by themselves, without needing to be pimped up with gimmicks! You're one of the world's most famous restaurateurs; you should be able to start a trend, so why not a *plain* trend instead of the same old fancy one?"

She caught herself waving her arms around. Annabelle stopped, then, and carefully folded her arms, as Chef had done. Besides the fact that mimicking his body language was a smart way to keep him from getting annoyed, it was also the best way to keep herself from starting to pick at the chicken.

He was the one who finally unfolded his arms and picked up a knife to slice the chicken with, rather than just tearing a hunk off. Carefully Adelio lifted one of the drumsticks just enough to slice a sliver of the back meat off. The perfectly crunchy skin glistened; there was not a touch of scorch anywhere. *You could understand,* Annabelle thought as Chef popped the morsel into his mouth and chewed, *why people might think there was something going on with this oven. More likely it's just those thick cast iron walls, the heat's so even—*

He shook his head. "You are right," Adelio said, looking almost sad: "you are right, but, Anna *la bella,* right is not enough. In this naughty world we live in, there is also marketing. I must concentrate on that. And so must you. The food is not enough. We must create a sensation, so the PR will be much, much bigger, so the new restaurant will be a huge success."

She sighed. "All right. We'll work on it. But chef, we need more translations from the scrolls. There are other spice mixtures to translate and analyze, once we've got them, we can swing out, do a few more entrées. And since I can't handle the dialect they're written in—"

Adelio rubbed his face. "Yes, yes. So, all right. Tonight we go to the bank, yes?" He made an expansive gesture in the air. Over the oven the air thickened, went solid, and flattened itself into a credible imitation of a computer terminal, showing his schedule for the next three days. He tapped the square of light with one finger, then paused to study that evening's schedule. "Those interview people," he said, highlighting one schedule-block at the bottom of his schedule, "I tell them to come back next week. This is more important. We go check the scrolls, we make some copies of what we need . . ."

"At least three more entrées," Annabelle said. "I can get Monica working on the basic spice acquisitions and start work on the more involved parts of the mixtures myself. And," she said, and gave him a small wicked smile, "we can leak part of one of them to the press."

His initial shocked look turned to a sly expression. "Oh, bad creature! Then we deny everything, oh so vehemently, and the recipe spreads everywhere, and there is so much publicity, so soon before the opening!" His eyes got that slightly feral twinkle. "Publicity like you could not buy; even I don't have that much money."

"Why waste it, Chef?" Annabelle said. "When they'll give it to you free?"

He patted her on the shoulder. "Tonight," he said. "I send the car. Six o'clock? I call Mystislav." Mystislav was his long-suffering bank manager at First Trust, who'd seen so much of Adelio since the Sibylline scrolls went into its vault that he occasionally threatened to transfer them to a large enough deposit box that he could lock up Chef and scrolls together.

"Sounds good."

"And this chicken, it worked out fine; we make some

very, very upscale sandwiches for lunch today, eh? Maybe with some bruschetta. Morris," he shouted at the commis chef who doubled as their bread baker, "get the yeast, I need some bruschetta. Hurry now." He waved at the intercom spell that was buried in his appointments screen, and the face of the restaurant's upstairs receptionist appeared. "Daniela, listen, be quick, call a courier. And the *Tribune*. The new food critic, not the old one. Oh, why not, the old one too. I send them both a nice sandwich. Mystislav can have one too, it will make him happy—"

Annabelle left him to what he was doing and took off her apron. There was no point in her staying here over the lunchtime rush—she would just be in the way. As she hung her apron up and put her little kitchen worker's hat on the hook at the front of the kitchen, Annabelle looked toward the back, where the knife guy was still busy with the sharpening steel. Tonino, heading past her with a pan for the dishwashing guy, paused and threw a glance that way. "Think he might stick one of those in you some time?" he asked, and grinned, not a very nice look.

Annabelle shook her head. "Not sure what I think," she said. "Come to think of it, I don't even know his name."

"Bob or something," Tonino said. He shrugged. "Nobody here ever calls him that, though. Just 'the knife guy.' He was one of chef's charities. Some mercy hire."

"You could make a case that I was too."

"You?" Tonino said. "Not a chance. Too much money changed hands." Annabelle wondered, there, for moment, if she had seen a quick shadow of jealousy flicker across Tonino's features. *Just me being paranoid, maybe.* But in this environment everybody was on the take or on the make; this was one of the hottest kitchens in the city and a stepping-stone to bigger, better work elsewhere.

Annabelle glanced back at the knife guy, who didn't look up, just kept sharpening knives. There *was* something faintly creepy about him; she became resolved not to turn her back on him. *But I still ought to say hi, get to know him. Later . . .*

She headed out to the front of the house. Helen, the front-of-house manager, was standing at the podium by the front door, scribbling away in the big reservations book. Next to her, very softly, the phone was doing what it had been doing nonstop for nearly three weeks now: ringing. As Annabelle headed for the front door, Helen glanced up with a weary look. "Going or coming?" she asked.

Annabelle shook her head. "Feels like both," she said. "But then it has for days. I'm going over to the new place, but I'll stop at A Taste of Spice first." She reached under the podium and got out her tote bag. "If Chef needs anything, give me a call on the mobile—I'll bring some fresh stuff back."

"Sounds good . . ."

Outside the severely plain, frosted-glass front door was the dark car that Adelio kept waiting. This was another useful perk of being associated with a world-famous and wealthy restaurateur—the chauffeur driven cars, people fighting for a chance to talk to you or meet with you. Annabelle had been working to take it all lightly, but it was difficult. The stories in the newspapers about her involvement with Adelio had been lavish, extravagant; some of the media had been touting her as some kind of new creative force behind SPQR and had produced all kinds of intrigue, whispering, and backbiting in the food world.

Some of Adelio's fans took very ill to the concept that anyone could surpass him or possibly supplant him. Additionally, a significant portion of that fandom was female—and when news got out that he was opening a new restaurant in cooperation with a woman from Chicago, there was uproar. Annabelle had had to change her e-mail address three times in as many weeks; the hate mail from the most rabid Adelio-groupies had been surprisingly vitriolic. She'd been accused of being a talentless and unscrupulous gold digger—and those had been the *kindest* descriptions.

Annabelle opened the door of the waiting black sedan, slipped in, closed the door, then sagged against the back seat. "That bad?" said big, dark Malachi, the driver, folding up his newspaper and looking over his shoulder at her.

Annabelle shook her head. "Just getting started, Mal," she said. "A Taste of Spice first, and then let's go over to the new place. All I want to know is that the front floor's finally in."

Malachi started the engine. "I hate to say this," he said, revving the motor, "but I don't think you're going to see any action in that department."

"Why on earth not?"

"Not on earth," Malachi said. "Under it."

"Oh, my God. Don't tell me. The dwarves *did* go on strike."

"Last night." Malachi checked his mirrors and pulled away from the curb. "Management wouldn't come back to the table."

Annabelle fastened her seat belt, then closed her eyes and rubbed them, feeling a headache already starting. Of all the paranormal groups, dwarves were probably the most unionized; after an early flirtation with the Teamsters, they had finally broken away to set up their own trade union—one famous for heavy bargaining, strikes of terrifying unanimity, and the ability to bring whole industries to their knees if the dwarves felt the need. Only their skill at any possible handcraft—especially stonework, which was what Adelio had hired them for— could counterbalance such intransigence.

As they pulled onto the main drag that ran that down to the Enchantment Mall, Annabelle took a long breath, tried to compose herself a little. *It's been a couple of days since I've been in there. The floors might be in, it* might *be all right . . .* She straightened up, opened her eyes, took a long breath.

"Got a Plan B if the floor's not in?" Malachi asked.

Annabelle chuckled. "Go insane?" she said. "Bang my head against the wall?"

"First option might be less painful." As they turned

the corner into the rear approach to the shopping center, Annabelle's phone rang inside her purse. She sighed, reached in, pulled it out. Malachi saw the face she made as she looked at the phone. "Chef?" he asked.

"Oh no, no," Annabelle said. "Much worse." She flipped the phone open. "Hi, Mom."

"You didn't call me last night," her mother said. "What happened?"

"Work, Mama," Annabelle said as they stopped in one of the parking spaces near the elevators to the main level. "I told you, I wasn't going to call you any time I got off work after twelve."

"He works bad hours, that man," Annabelle's mother said. "I don't care how rich he is. Or, on the other hand, maybe I see how he got as rich as he is. Taking advantage of people! You were always too good-natured, you never knew how to keep people from taking advantage of you—"

Or how to get you to stop nagging. One of these days . . . "Mom," Annabelle said as Malachi turned the engine off, "he doesn't work me any harder than he works himself. Or any of the other staff." She wiggled her eyebrows at Malachi in the rearview mirror. He raised his own eyebrows at her, picked up his newspaper and started reading; he'd heard her side of these conversations too many times before and had shared some long discussions about how he handled his own mom. The fact she was a ghost only made the situation more amusing. "They all go to the same nagging school," he'd said, and Annabelle was beginning to agree with him.

"—and I don't care how hard he works, he's probably cheating them too. If you would just—"

"Mama," Annabelle said, but it was far too late; she was on a roll.

"How'd do you think he got that rich, anyway? You people let him push you around, you should be tougher, stand up for yourselves, unionize like those dwarves did, that's the way to do it—"

Dwarves, Annabelle thought, and took a long breath.

"Mama," she said "was this about anything in particular? I have to go to the shop."

"And another thing," her mom said. Annabelle shook her head wearily at Malachi, held up a hand with fingers spread to suggest "five minutes," and got out of the car. "That girl you've got working up there now," her mother said as Annabelle got into the elevator, "she was so rude to me the other day. I called the shop to see if you were there, and she said that you—"

"—aren't in the shop except on Tuesdays and Fridays, and then only in the afternoons," Annabelle said as the elevator doors closed on her. She punched the button for the second level. "And you know that perfectly well, mama, because I've told you at least four times now. There's no *point* in calling me at the shop. Mostly I'm not there. You're the one who's been telling me for the last five years that I should get out of sales and start a restaurant, and now that's what's happening! And as for Monica, she came very highly recommended because *Norman* recommended her, and you've always told me that I should listen more to his advice." Norman was an old friend of her mother's, a lawyer with offices along the south side. "And if Monica was brief with you, that's because she has to be brief with people. We had so much business at the shop the last three weeks—"

The elevator doors opened. Annabelle strolled out onto the second level, where A Taste of Spice was located. There seemed to be an unusual buzz for so early in the mall's day. As she walked down one side of the atrium aisle toward the shop, she could see that there was actually a line outside: people, lots of them. She had to smile at the sight. *Three weeks ago, I would have killed for this. And now it's just something else to worry about, because how is our stock holding up?*

"Mom," she said, "gotta go. Was there anything this was about, or were you just checking up on me?"

"I'm always checking up on my little girl," her mother said in a faintly wounded tone of voice. "You watch out, because there's all kinds of people who'll want to be hanging around with you, now they see you as somebody rich and fancy, someone who's on the radio and the TV all the time."

"Oh, Mom," Annabelle muttered, "please, I am *not* on TV all the time. Gotta go now. Love you." She hung up quickly, before her mother could find a way to slap some kind of commentary onto that statement as well.

As she walked into A Taste of Spice, Annabelle began wondering if there might be something to what her mom was saying. Heads turned, people in the line nudged each other and stared. Annabelle smiled and nodded at them as she passed; no reason not to be friendly with people, even though their interest was purely for notoriety's sake.

In the middle of the front of the store, she stopped briefly, glanced around, trying to keep the concern off her face. Monica had been moving some of the cookbook tables around, and one of them had been seriously rearranged—no cookbooks on it except those by Adelio Famagiusta. Worse, there was a picture of *her* perched on top of the piles of books. Annabelle raised her eyebrows, not sure she liked that. *It looks too—commercial, somehow. Then again, maybe I'm just not used to this self-promotion thing yet.*

She went over to the main counter, up at the front and off to the left-hand side. Monica was ringing up a purchase, all efficiency: a very sharply dressed, intelligent-looking young woman, skirt-suited, with long dark hair pulled back tightly, and fierce green eyes. Her face was sharp, sharper than strictly normal for a human. But then, Annabelle had planned from the start to hire a were, whose sensitive nose would be useful for more than just analyzing spice blends and assessing the quality of the arcane herbs that were the shop's stock in trade. A were could also smell a shoplifter halfway out into the mall, if she'd had the right training; and Monica, like a lot of other werefolk, had done some security work in the beginning of her career.

As Annabelle approached, Monica looked up and smiled at her. "Thanks for your purchase," she said to the extremely tall and handsome Asian woman she'd been serving. The woman, dressed in Korean silks, took her bag, smiled at Monica, and stepped away from the counter. Annabelle smiled at the next lady in line, a small round woman with a Russian-*babushka* look to her. "Madame, would you excuse us? Just for a moment, if you would."

She nodded Monica off to one side of the register. Looking after the departing customer, Monica said, "That's the third dragon this morning, boss. Do we have some kind of promotion going for the Asian community? One Chinese, one Japanese, one Korean, all in a row, just like that."

"What are they buying?" Annabelle asked, getting out her cellphone, flipping it to its PDA screen and starting to make notes.

"Lifestyle herbs," Monica said. "Scale sheen, jasmine basil—things like that. A lot of the basil, now I think of it. Three ounces just this morning."

"Okay," Annabelle said, "better reorder that. You do the phones this morning?" Monica nodded. "Any problems with distributors?"

Monica shook her head. "Nothing serious," she said. "Denzel over at HerbCo says that they're running low on idiopathic nutmeg, but we're stocked up on that. Oh, and SPQR wanted more of the butterfly marjoram. I just couriered them a package."

Annabelle nodded. It was one of the arcane herbs needed for the chicken recipe; possibly Adelio wanted to have another run at it after lunch. "How's the cookware moving?"

"Better," Monica said. "That big nonferrous stockpot that's been there since I came? Gone."

"Good riddance. We can hang three, maybe four pots in that space. And the cookbooks?"

"Moving a lot of them, boss."

"Good." Annabelle looked back over her shoulder at that table. "But does my picture have to be there?"

"I didn't like to take it away." Monica smiled slyly. "Your mother put it there."

"Oh, Goddess, she's diabolical. Just hide it for the time being. If she comes in, tell her, I don't know, tell her you're cleaning it or something." Then the phone on the counter rang. "It doesn't stop, does it?"

Monica shook her head. "A lot of people trying to reach you personally," she said. "Not just your mother. Media contacts, people trying to get at the Big Man through you." Now her smile went slightly feral, something that would come naturally to a were. "I give them the bum's rush, mostly. But people have been calling, asking when's she gonna be in the shop, I have a special order, I need the owner's attention, blah blah blah."

"You've been feeding them the party line?" Annabelle said.

"Tuesdays to Fridays, one to three, leave your details, and she'll get back to you."

"Make me a list, and I'll deal with them later in the week. Any more crazy fangirls?"

Monica deliberately showed a gleaming inch of her incisors. "A few. They don't linger."

"Okay. Call me if you need anything. I'm on my way to the new place." Annabelle turned, smiling again at the *babushka* lady at the head of the line. "Thanks for waiting, ma'am."

"Did you hear about the dwarves?" Monica asked.

Annabelle sighed. "Am I likely to hear about anything *else* today?" she said. "Pray to the Wolf-Father for an early settlement. See you."

Down in the parking structure, Malachi was still deep in his newspaper when she knocked on the window. He popped the lock open for her, and Annabelle got into the back seat, shut the door and stretched her legs out wearily. "The new place now?" he said.

"Yup."

It was no more than a five-minute drive from here, a location that Adelio had liked specifically because of its closeness to the Mall. Annabelle leaned back against the soft leather seat and tried to get her thoughts in order. *If the floor isn't in,* she thought, *what* do *we do? This can't wait more than a day or two.* All the cellarage work had been done by dwarves. But there were a lot of other people who had been doing specialty work for the new restaurant. All the cabinetry, for example, was being done by gnomes, as far as Annabelle knew.

Adelio had purposely decided to go very much against the design stream of his main restaurant, intending to emphasize the more traditional, more ancient side of the cuisine that was going to be served at SPQR2. Instead of all the glass and gloss and lacquer, the new place would have a much more rustic look: quarry tile, antique Alpine softwoods, stucco walls limewashed in soft spattered pastels. *So the question is,* Annabelle thought, *do gnomes do stone floors?* Or did they have some kind of obscure craft agreement with the dwarves so that neither side would intrude on the other's contract work? *Well, I'm going to find out now.*

They turned into the new place's street, and Annabelle looked two blocks down and saw a sight that chilled her heart: The front of SPQR2 *without* four different workmen's vans sitting in front of it.

"Oh no," she said softly. Malachi pulled the sedan up in front. "Mal, you may want to just dump me here and go back to the restaurant. This might take a while."

"Okay. You call, I'll come right back. Chef doesn't usually need me till after lunch."

"Thanks. Just wait here for half a sec, I want to have a quick look." The front window was next to useless, being covered on the inside with white butcher paper, and this front door wasn't sleek glass like SPQR but instead a beautiful old knotty pine, the *arvenholz* of the Italian Alps, with a few discreet panes of bubbly, antique glass set into it. Annabelle peered through the topmost of these, squinting. It was always hard to see in; dust from the construction work usually wound up obscuring the views somewhat. But then, through the dimness, Annabelle could see that there *was* actually a floor inside. White marble, all the big slabs laid down, and as far as she could tell, the sealing work had been done as well.

"Thank you, Goddess," she said under her breath: "I owe You a cookie." What a relief to see that done. There was no movement inside; it was too early for the dwarf workmen to take their lunch break, so she had to assume that they were off work, here as everywhere else. Annabelle fished around in her purse for the front door keys, came up with them, unlocked the top and bottom locks, and then put her hand on the single hexed panel on the door.

The spell lock came undone; the edges of the door shivered, disassociating themselves from the doorjamb. Annabelle pulled on the door to make sure it was open, then went back to the car. As she bent down toward the window, Malachi hit the button to roll it down and look out at her. "It's not as bad as I thought," she said. "You go ahead. There are some things I should be doing here anyway."

"No problem," Malachi said. A second later he had executed a neat U-turn in the middle of the street and was heading back toward SPQR.

Annabelle headed back to the door, pulled it open and slipped in. The door squeaked as it fell closed behind her. *Brand new, and it already needs oil? One more thing for the to-do list,* She stood there in the dim, creamy light filtering through the papered-over window, looking around at the bare, bright space. It was hard to imagine how it would be when it was ready—filled with furniture, the tapestries and woodwork up on the walls, the accent lighting installed, here and there a painting, maybe one of Adelio's trademark bronzes possibly near the entrance. But right now, there was nothing but a shiny floor and shiny white walls. *And a cellar,* she thought after a moment. *We'll have a look at that shortly.*

She made her way toward the back of the restaurant-to-be. Right now, the front room's back wall was defined by a waist-high wall of glass blocks, and on the right side, a wide doorway that would lead to the men's and women's and others' rooms, while at the back of the kitchen was the access to private staff storage, the wine cellar, and other cold storage. The door to the restroom area hadn't yet been hung, but the flooring was complete all the way back. The secure door to the cellarage hadn't been hung yet, either; there was just an empty doorway, and the stairs beyond, leading down toward the cellar.

For the time being, her main interest was the kitchen. Annabelle went in through the door to one side, standing by the pass-through into the main dining room. This would be her place, the space in which she would rise or fall as a chef. It was a scary, scary concept. People who had never seen or heard of her would be watching her every move, studying what she did, writing about it, talking about it on television . . . It was something she was just going to have to get used to. *Mom,* she thought, *is going to love it. I don't care what she says.* Any excuse to brag about her daughter was something that Annabelle's mom would extract maximum value from. *While still nagging me,* Annabelle thought, *about being too public.*

Right on cue, her phone rang. But the ring tone was Adelio's "Pines of Rome" melody, full of marching legionaries, rather than her mom's Nutcracker music. Annabelle snapped the phone open. "Adelio?"

"You are there?" he said.

"I am here," she said, looking out toward the main room, "and what's more, the floor is here."

"*Bene!* I sacrifice a goat in Vulcan's honor."

"Save me some," Annabelle said. "I'm going to deal with the racking downstairs, a few other things."

"How long do you think?"

"A couple of hours. Oh, and that marjoram's coming along from the shop for you."

"*Bene. Ciao, bella.*"

She hung up, put the phone away, and looked around again. The space was intimidating even when empty. It was going to make a big difference that she would have some of Adelio's most talented kitchen help with her. She stood there, looking at the blank, black floor—in here it was rubberized rather than marble and has been done last week—and the side islands that had already been installed. *Hot table,* she thought walking toward the back of the long room; *fry station, sauté station, assembly. Plating island. Sauce stove, cold station—no, of course, that has to go on the opposite side of the room, right across from the assembly island.* And right at the back, closest to the emergency exit—she smiled, just a little grimly—*chef's station. My station. Right next to the biggest stove; the hot seat . . .*

The stove, of course, was in already. There was a clear view down the length of the kitchen to it. In its way it was center stage of SPQR2—the biggest piece of equipment in the kitchen, the heaviest, introduced to the space before the back wall had even been sealed up. Eight gas burners above and below, three ovens, side by side—purposely oversized, more for showmanship's sake than anything else. *What on earth are our fuel bills going to look like?* Annabelle wondered, making her way down to the massive thing, running a hand along the spotless upper surface.

It gleamed. *And it's going to take endless work to keep it doing that,* Annabelle thought, remembering the looks of loathing that all the other restaurant staff had displayed when they'd visited the space and seen it. The stove wasn't surfaced in honest brushed stainless but chrome, and it would be an incredible nuisance to keep clean. Adelio, though, had been adamant. "The patrons, they will want to see this, it's reaction," he'd shouted down the phone at his interior designer. "The front of house flies in face of the fashion too much right now, eh? Too much natural stuff out front, the back has to be sleek, otherwise they think we're old fashioned, and we lose all this good money I spent—"

Annabelle let out an amused breath, paused to lean against the cold stove. *You and I,* she thought, *we're going to have to come to terms.* But all the other stations were as yet blank canvases, shining but otherwise identical stretches of stainless steel yet to be customized. Their accessories would be shuffled around until Annabelle and the rest of the kitchen staff found a combination of stations that worked best for the space.

The sudden squeak of the front-of-house door brought her head around. *Got to fix that before it drives me nuts,*

Annabelle thought. She stepped hurriedly out to the glass-block pass-through.

There her eyes widened slightly. Standing in the doorway was the knife guy. And for some reason, the hair stood up right on the back of Annabelle's neck. *Think he might leave one of those in you some time?* said Tonino's voice in her ear.

Annabelle pushed the nasty thought away. The guy was standing there in the doorway with an armful of boxes, looking frankly scared and upset: she wondered why. "Hi there," Annabelle said. "Come on in—"

I still don't know his name, she thought. *Must do something about that.* The knife guy edged into the room, still wearing his grungy whites and even grungier checked pants, looking around the empty shining place as if he were afraid Chef was going to emerge from a wall and start shouting. *He's so skinny,* Annabelle thought, suddenly concerned. *And he looks so scared. Why does he look scared?*

"Come on in, it's all right," she said. "What have you got for me?"

"Please, miss," the knife guy said, in a voice that managed to be both hoarse and squeaky at the same time, "knives. And utensils, and a lot of pots and things." He edged a little further into the front room.

"That's good," Annabelle said, trying to sound calming, since there was something about his voice that suggested he might break and run on the spot. "And you don't have to call me 'miss!' I'm Annabelle."

He actually blushed as he started fumbling around with the boxes. *What a sweet kid,* she thought, *and really shy, poor guy.* "No, don't put them down there! Come on in, bring them back into the kitchen. That's where we'll be needing them."

She went back in, looking around at the vast stretches of stainless steel to see if she could spot any drawer or sliding storage that looked as though it had been intended for this purpose. Down between the sous chef's station and the fry bay, she spotted an overhead storage cabinet with sliding stainless steel doors. She slid one open, glanced in. *Good deep shelves. The stuff can go there for the time being; it's going to be a few days before the kitchen is ready enough even for dry runs.*

The knife guy came shuffling in. *He really is very thin,* Annabelle thought, as he came in under the unforgiving fluorescents. *And so pasty looking. Does he ever get any exercise outside? Poor kid.* "I'm sorry," she said, "I've been in Chef's kitchen for days and days, and I don't even know your name."

"Bob," the knife guy said as he came over to her. Just for that second, as he said the word, his eyes flickered up to meet Annabelle's. They were blue, blue as sky. Unaccountably, she flushed hot at the look. Direct the glance might have been, but there was still something naked and unnerved about it, something Annabelle had a sudden and embarrassing sense that she shouldn't have seen. She looked away, and so did he.

"Bob. Good to meet you officially." She smiled toward him, rather than at him, afraid somehow that she might upset him by forcing another glance. "Why don't you put the knives up there. Are they in rolls, or loose?"

"Rolls," Bob said, sounding scandalized. "Never loose. Chef wouldn't like it."

"I believe you there," Annabelle said, turning away toward the counter a little further down in the kitchen, reaching under to a drawer and pulling it open. She knew in a general way that every chef had his own foibles and preferences, but Adelio seemed to have more than his share. Possibly it went with being so famous—people expected your personality to be bigger than life, whether it was or not. *Showmanship.* "There's room for more of them here. Pots can go further back—plenty of over-counter storage, for a change. Chef insisted."

Annabelle smiled again, remembering Chef's multiple noisy phone-borne rages on the subject: "What, because I'm a sorcerer, you think I have energy to waste on storage spells, holes in space, such garbage! I need my power for my genius, for my food!"

Bob looked around, gulped. She saw his Adam's apple

go up and down, somehow further emphasizing that skinny, scared look. "You go ahead," Annabelle said. "I have some things to do here."

Bob nodded, put his first load of boxes down, and started unpacking the topmost. "Do you want me to do anything after I've got all the boxes in?" Bob said. "I could sharpen the knives."

"What did Chef tell you to do?"

"He just said to take the boxes over to the new place."

"Okay," Annabelle said. "The knives can always use sharpening."

She turned away, thinking about the next thing on the to-do list: the racking downstairs. She went back to the cellar entrance, down the first flight to the landing that turned the corner toward the cellar proper. The stairs hadn't been tiled yet; that would have to wait until the dwarves got back, probably.

Annabelle's footsteps rang hollowly in the bare stairway; another fourteen steps down brought her out into the main cellarage level. Here was another place where walls and floors were mostly bare of fittings, but it was full of boxes, crates, piles of linen from the old place, due to be recycled here; napkins, tablecloths, runners, who knew what. Just over to her left was the cage area that would be the wine cellar: not her problem right now, until the main delivery of wine came in next week. *But all the rest of this has to be sorted out by the end of this week at the latest. Maybe this is a blessing in disguise, the dwarves not being here today.*

She started unpacking some of the boxes, stacking the linen in the wire racks that lined either side of the basement. It was quite a long basement for a city building—*must go right out under the street,* she thought. She paused, listening. She could hear no car noise, only upstairs, the clatter of metal against metal as Bob the knife guy unpacked the contents of more boxes into the kitchen storage. *Never mind.* Look *at all these tablecloths! Better start taking a count.*

Maybe two hours later she straightened up, hands pressing into the small of her back, trying to work a kink

out of it. The last of the boxes was unpacked. Five or
six times at least, now, Annabelle had heard Bob pick
up his empty boxes, go outside, and after a pause come
back in with more, unpacking them in turn. *Adelio must
have had him fill that whole van,* she thought. *Maybe he
wanted to get the kid out of the kitchen for a little while.*
She smiled slightly. Word about Adelio's charity work
always seemed to get out, though he swore and blustered
when it did; a lot of money from the restaurant and the
cookbooks went into farms and sheltered accommoda-
tion for people with special needs, and Annabelle—
coming to know Adelio as she now was—felt fairly sure
that he wasn't doing this just for the tax breaks. It was
entirely possible that Bob-the-knife-guy was indeed what
Tonino had so crassly described as a "mercy hire," but
there would have been a lot more than just mercy behind
it—

She heard the upstairs door go *squeeeak!* one more
time. *Enough of that,* she thought. *It's making me crazy.
I know I saw a can of oil down here. But poor Bob! How
many more boxes?* Then Annabelle grinned, since that
was a question she'd been asking herself down here.
*Well, now that everything's racked, we can get started
bringing in the sealed staples and the other nonperisha-
ble consumables.*

She headed up the stairs, trailing a hand along the
concrete wall, since there was no stair rail yet, eyeing
the steps as she went. The concrete seemed a little crumbly at some of the stair edges. *Well, that probably doesn't
matter: the tiles will cover it.* As she headed for the landing where the stairway turned, looking up she caught
sight of a shadow lying across the landing. *Bob, wanting
to know if he can go back to the restaurant,* Annabelle
thought—until the shadow moved, the person producing
it stepped down onto the landing, and Annabelle, astonished, found herself staring into the muzzle of a gun.

"Back downstairs, lady," the man growled.

Her mouth went dry in what seemed about a second.
Annabelle froze where she was, terrified, and furious
with herself for being that way. She didn't want to turn

her back on the man; she felt backwards with one foot for the stair behind her, stepped down on it, then carefully down on the next three.

At the bottom of the stairs, she kept backing up and did her best to size the man up without being too obvious about it. Maybe five ten, stocky without being fat, dark hair, big broad round face, florid, maybe of Irish descent. Little eyes, narrow-set. A pugnacious look, the kind of face you wouldn't want to meet in a dark alley. *Or in a basement, with no way to get anyone's attention and let them know what's happening with you—*

Her hand crept into her pocket, and instantly the gun was pointed at her eyes. "Not another inch," the man said sharply. "Get that hand out of there. Boss? Lady's got a phone."

"Very good, Charlie," said another voice from upstairs. "That will make things simpler."

Another man came down the stairs, paused in the doorway, and looked at Annabelle. The newcomer was at least six feet tall, thin, and gray: dark gray for the suit, light gray for the hair, pale gray for the eyes; even the skin had a grayish cast. *Some troll blood in there,* Annabelle thought. *Why on earth would any woman in her right mind bed with a troll?* Though she had an idea. Gold would be an impetus . . . and so might the troll's physical powers, which a woman would share with her partner for a short time after they coupled. Afterward, the full-blood trolls would be only too glad to take the halfling child off the woman's hands, for it too would have abilities that would make it worthwhile later to all kinds of people. *Like whoever hired this one,* Annabelle thought.

"I don't have any money," Annabelle said, trying hard not to let her terror show as the first man came toward her. She shrank from him, but she didn't dare move as he put his hand into her pocket, came up with the phone, glanced at it, then pocketed it himself.

"Of course you don't, madam," said the gray man, not moving any closer to her. He was looking around the cellar with a chilly interest. "But some people you know do. And some of them possess things that are worth much, much more than mere money."

Annabelle went cold, then hot with fury as she realized that she was not these men's intended target. They were after Adelio, and she was going to be the puppet they'd use to get at him.

"When he does not hear otherwise from you, he will come to meet you here," said the gray man, standing quite still, looking at her as if he could see through her . . . and maybe he could. Trolls could see through stone; flesh would hardly be an obstacle. *But a halfling could see more,* Annabelle thought, and got goosebumps. *Someone thought this through. They know I'm not an offensively powered witch and can't do much of anything without the right equipment. There's been plenty in the papers about how weird it is for me to get involved in food services since I'm just a seer.* Her glance flickered around. Water, mirrors, anything reflective, those were the heart of her art; but there was nothing down here that would be even remotely useful. *And even if there* were *something down here I could use to scry something useful about this situation, what could I do about it? Mister Bouncer there has the gun.*

She looked at the gray man. "This is about the scrolls, then," Annabelle said.

The gray eyes were nearly colorless; looking into them made Annabelle feel vaguely faint, for the power they contained was similar to her own, and meeting them produced an effect much like feedback. She looked away at almost exactly the same moment the gray man did. "Do not do that again," he said, cold voiced. "I would regret damaging you, but it would not reduce your usefulness to us. Go sit down on that box, and don't meet my eyes again."

Annabelle was almost relieved to do so. *Still, it's worth knowing that if I started to see something, it'd affect him. Feedback.* "About twenty minutes," said the first man to the second.

"How do you know that?" Annabelle said.

The first man simply chuckled. Annabelle scowled.

Now that she thought of it, there were probably a hundred ways for someone to know, or find out: phonetap, scrying spell, underhearing. *Or a tipoff from someone in-house,* Annabelle suddenly thought. She blanched a little at the thought of the treachery. *Someone who worked for Adelio and saw a way to make a little extra on the side. Who? Someone in the kitchen? One of the clerical support staff?*

A sudden thought occurred to her and made her go cold. That upstairs door had opened and closed many times while she'd been working down here, and her assumption about who had been doing it was plainly wrong. "What did you do with the knife guy?" she said.

"Who?" said the first man.

"The runner from SPQR," Annabelle said. "He's been here most of the afternoon, unpacking things."

Another of those silences. Faintly, Annabelle could feel the gray man looking up through the structure of the building to see whether there were any aura traces on local spacetime that would confirm her story. "Gone some time now," he said after a moment. "Substandard intelligence. Not a problem. Meanwhile, Annabelle, I now think better of you. I could not understand why you would have left the front door open so that anyone could simply walk in. For surely it has occurred to you that your personal value has significantly increased."

She kept quiet. It had occurred to her, but it hadn't occurred that anyone would actually *do* something about it. Then, *Am I crazy?* she thought. *This is Chicago! There's* always *someone willing to do something like this. And these guys are plainly very sure they're not going to get caught.* The chill ran down her back as this led her to the next, more obvious, conclusion. *Since they've let me see them, they don't intend to keep me alive any longer than—*

She purposely turned her attention away from the thought. *Be a little dumb,* she thought, *a little panicky, let them think* that *hasn't occurred to you yet.* "You're going to hold me here to make him go to the bank and get out the scrolls," she said.

The gray man chuckled softly: not a pleasant sound at all. "Such things are better held in more ambitious hands," he said. "Think what the big multinationals will pay for the formulae for food additives capable of *forcing* any sentient being to eat a product containing them, repeatedly, obsessively. Yet all these 'herbs and spices' have been approved by the FDA for use by humans. As an addictive agent, even tobacco will be shouldered aside by these compounds once the food chemists have had time to isolate their key ingredients and reproduce and recombine them in more potent forms. Much more effective, wouldn't you say, than merely coating chickens in them to make people 'happy'?"

The calm scorn he added to the word infuriated Annabelle. She concentrated on keeping her fury out of her face, on looking scared. *Probably not hard at this point.*

The gray man checked his watch. "About now will do very well," he said to his opposite number, and reached out a hand. "Give me her phone."

A moment or so later he had flipped it open, was dialing. Someone picked up; Annabelle could hear a faint squeaking coming from the other end.

"I'm afraid Annabelle can't come to the phone right now," said the gray man. "We have her."

There was a silence. After that Adelio's response was so loud that Annabelle could hear it even though the phone wasn't on speaker, and the gray man held it away from his ear, wincing slightly. When it stopped, he smiled just slightly. Annabelle swallowed, for the look was astonishingly cruel.

"She's quite safe, and nothing will happen to her," said the gray man, "as long as you do exactly as you're told. You were originally planning to go to the bank from here, and that's just what you're going to do. But your colleague won't be going with you. One of us will. The other one will stay here to make sure that you pick up the items from the bank without any fuss. Once you've turned them over to us, we'll turn her loose."

There was a pause. Annabelle kept her face quite still,

knowing from the man's tone of voice that this was a
flat lie. *What can I do? There must be something.* Think!

"I warn you," the gray man said, "any slightest attempt by you to warn the police, and we'll know. We
have people in your place who're watching your every
move. Make one wrong move, and you won't see her
again until a few weeks from now, when somebody fishes
what's left out of the river."

A pause again. She couldn't hear anything that was
being said. Finally, the gray man said, "Good. Fifteen
minutes."

And they waited.

Annabelle's mind went around and around in circles
all that little while. *It's true what they say about relativity,*
she thought, maybe three minutes into the process. *This
is a small eternity right here, and I'm not using it well.*
But she couldn't think what else she might do. There
were no reflective surfaces down here to work with. Also,
there was the minor matter of composure. It was hard
to get into the right state of mind in a situation like
this—

The front door squeaked. *Oh no,* Annabelle thought,
too soon, Adelio, too soon! She got up.

"Stand still," said the gray man. "You're not going
anywhere."

"Annabelle!" Adelio shouted from upstairs.

"She's quite safe, Signor Famagiusta," the gray man
called back. "Go with my colleague. Do as you've been
told, and nothing bad will happen."

"I go nowhere," said that big angry voice, "do nothing,
until I see her safe."

"No," said the gray man.

A pause. "You do not understand," Adelio said, and
this time, his voice was as cold as the gray man's. "This
is business, a business deal. If the scrolls are merchandise, then so is she, eh?" Annabelle's eyes widened at
that. Then she thought, *Never mind what he seems to be
calling you. Let's get out of this first, and you can yell at
him later!* "If this is a trade, I see what I am trading for

first. I did not get to be worth so much money by being stupid! So you do a little thing, nothing important: You let me see her. Then we go and do your silliness, no trouble. I have what I want from the scrolls now, and if this is going to happen, happen, happen all the time, better I should be rid of them. As good a way as any, and the insurance company, they don't care, they'll pay all right, they cannot afford the bad publicity of a lawsuit with *me*, Adelio Famagiusta!''

The gray man stood silent for a moment, smiling slightly. "He does think well of himself, doesn't he?" he said.

Even in this extremity, Annabelle found it impossible to keep from rolling her eyes a bit as she muttered, "You have no idea."

That smile got more edged, more amused. *And nastier*, Annabelle thought; *who'd have thought it was possible?* But somehow the tension had broken slightly. "Charlie," said the gray man, "go upstairs and make sure the area's secure." As Charlie disappeared, the gray man too produced a gun. "Nothing sudden, miss," he said.

She shook her head dumbly, concentrating on looking thoroughly scared. After a moment, Charlie said, "All clear."

The gray man gestured with the gun. "Up the stairs," he said. "Take your time."

Annabelle went, again most unwilling to turn her back on him but not seeing any way around it. Her mind was racing. *Up in the kitchen*, she thought. *What's up there that could change the game in our favor? I might not be able to move around much, but—*

She came to the landing, put a hand out to the wall to steady herself. Suddenly that gun was pushing into the small of her back. "Nothing amusing, little witch," said the cold gray voice from behind her. "Watch what you touch. You go within arm's reach of water or glass, and a second later your spine will be in two pieces."

Annabelle gulped, nodded, headed on up. *Water or glass! The water's not even connected yet*, she thought, desperate. *And there's no glass but the glass block up in*

front, too wavy, too far away, no good for what I'd need.
Near the back of the kitchen, by the oven, Charlie was
standing with his gun out: as she came up, he grabbed
her by one arm. At the other end of the kitchen, by the
glass-block partition, Adelio was standing, in his whites.
His face was composed, his eyes absolutely unrevealing;
he looked as though he were waiting for a bus.

The oven! Annabelle thought. *That nasty, shiny, polished chrome!*

"So," Adelio said.

"You see now," said the gray man. "She is perfectly
safe. All you have to do now is go quietly with Charlie
to the bank."

Charlie was pushing Annabelle past the front of the
oven, toward the far side of the kitchen, across from the
stairs, while his boss passed behind them and headed
toward Adelio. *Now or never!* Annabelle thought. On
Charlie's next push, she stumbled, went down to her
knees, grabbed the oven door's handrail, stared into her
own reflection in the stainless surface and willed it away.
*No time for setup, no time for fancy ritual. Show me
something, anything, just enough to blind the gray man
for a second . . .*

Then Annabelle gasped. The realization that, impossi-
bly, the oven was *hot,* came simultaneously with the vision, blinding her with the temporary primacy of the
unseen reality over the seen. What Annabelle saw for
that flicker of a moment was an utterly unexpected blaze
of light, a compact thing, a core, burning, ravening blue:
an impact like a blow on her brain. But also, *eyes.* Looking back at her. Blue eyes, scared; and again she felt that
hot flush as something perceived her own fear, flared up
in fury—

Goddess! she thought. Annabelle fell over sideways,
blinking her tearing eyes and cursing, for her hand was
scorched. But now she knew what to do. "Adelio," she
shouted, *"look out!"* Then she yanked the oven door all
the way open, and threw herself out of its way.

The roar, the rush of fire right past her scorched Annabelle's face, filled the air around her with a hot-ironing

smell of her whites, suddenly lightly browned by the blue-white blaze that leaped from the oven and at Charlie, who had whipped around with his gun and was even now reaching down toward Annabelle to jerk her to her feet or possibly put a bullet in her.

He never had time. That storm of licking blue flames burst in front of him like a firework, wrapped itself around him in wings of fire, ate straight through him. Annabelle, horrified but transfixed by the violence of the moment, saw skin and muscle go up like paper under the ministrations of a blowtorch, saw the bones briefly glow pink-red like an electric element before calcining to ash.

The gray man held up his hands and cried out something that made the floor crack open at his feet, right through the rubberized surface to the concrete beneath. That crack now strained wider as the gray man began to shimmer, going the color of the concrete, his essence already warping and flowing toward this opening gateway to somewhere else.

But a second later, without warning, a glittering object flew unerringly from Adelio's end of the room and wedged itself into that crack, abruptly stopping its spread—a knife, the biggest starsteel knife from SPQR's kitchen. The untouched Widmanstaetten lines in the back of the blade flared up in an eye-hurting crisscross of fire as Adelio shouted something in Italian.

The gray man shimmered harder, but there was no more time for whatever he was trying to do. A second later, the bolt of blue fire had arched away from the greasy scorched spot where Charlie had been toward the gray man. Now it fastened on him in turn, wrapped around him. There was a struggle, a strange crackling noise like stone heating, cooling, heating again. Then the scream.

Annabelle gulped, got to her feet. After those few seconds, there was no more left of the gray man than there was of Charlie: less grease, though, and more ash, like stone burned to powder. Adelio stood there, stony faced, as the whirl of eye-hurting fire leaped toward him. He didn't move as it circled him once, then darted away from him, back toward Annabelle, past her, and into the oven.

"Better shut it," Adelio said.

Annabelle nodded, reached out for the rail—much cooler than it had been just a few seconds before—and tipped the door shut. A second later, it seemed, Adelio had grabbed hold of her and was shaking her. "They didn't hurt you? You're all right?"

She nodded, gulping, suddenly finding it hard to talk. Adelio was always grabbing and shaking people—he was very physical, and it was one of the reasons why some people, who couldn't get to grips with it, didn't last long in his kitchen—but he had never done it to *her* before.

"I'm fine," she said. "No, really, I'm fine!" She shook him back a little bit, to demonstrate this, and then turned her attention back to his oven. "But this—"

"Never mind that," Adelio said. "You know, you *do* know, those things I said, they were garbage? I had to make them bring you up. I had to know—"

"I know," Annabelle said. But it still warmed her to hear him say it. "Adelio, a couple of people just got killed here, we have to call the police! They have to—"

"The police will be here soon," Adelio said. "They know. How not? Should someone try kidnapping, extortion, maybe murder, on *me,* Adelio Famagiusta, and get away with it?"

He sounded more outraged at the slight to his intelligence or his reputation than at any attempted crime. Annabelle didn't know whether she wanted to burst out laughing or just cry. Finally it seemed that laughter was smartest. "But, Adelio," she said, "the oven. All along, there really *has* been something going on with your oven."

Adelio did something Annabelle never would have suspected she'd see: he boosted himself up onto one of the counters and sat there, swinging his legs. "Anna *la bella,*" he said, "it's a simple thing. You have something very valuable, you don't send it somewhere in an armored car. You give it to a courier in torn jeans and a hoodie, eh? Sure, everybody is curious about the famous oven in SPQR, everybody's suspicious, everybody looks to see me do some big magic with it, sorcery, something special, the secret of my genius!"

He laughed. The laugh was genuine but also sly, like a child relishing the secret he's known for a long time, and relishing—finally—sharing it. "But they miss the point. I don't use sorcery in my food. Sorcery is the great power, the High Art! For more than just food. With that, a long time ago, when I was just starting out, I went in search of the best heat to cook with, the fire that would make any food magical. And I found it, in the volcano, in Vesuvius: the real Phoenix, the true fire that burns forever. Nothing unusual—many have found it! Some have even survived. Though always, you get burned." He studied those heatproof-seeming hands, and for the first time Annabelle really registered the scar tissue and realized that it might be from something less prosaic than fishing around in sauté pans. "But I understood what the others didn't. That it didn't want to be just a tool, a puppet. That always it wanted to be useful under its own power, of its own free will, eh? Doesn't everybody want that? To make the difference, to be worth something? It had just been an elemental until then. But when I found it, it discovered that it could be more. And finally,"—he dropped his voice quite low—"finally, when it trusted me, when it was happy, it reproduced. A little before the scrolls came."

"And when it did, 'Bob,' the knife . . . *guy* . . . " Now she understood that strange flush of heat that had washed over her at the mere glimpse of fire-blue eyes. "Bob had another Bob, a *baby* Bob?"

Adelio nodded. "Sometimes," Adelio said, "he complains to me, he says, Hey, Chef, I'm bored with being safe inside now, I want to come out, I want to be human! He is not shapefast: he's fire, he's change itself. So he wants to look like a human, sure, it's no problem! But *being* human, that's work." Adelio gave her a sidewise look. "He's still getting the hang of it, so he has trouble, he walks weird, doesn't talk much, hey, it's okay, when you're not people to start with, sometimes the people skills take time! I tell him, you sit there, do the knives, watch people. What they do, what they say."

He squirmed a little where he sat on the counter. "But you, Anna *la bella*, you have good people skills. That's how the scrolls came to you, ne? He's your friend now. So he will be in your kitchen for a while and learn more about people. And his brother, or clone, who lives in my oven now, he's a little further along, and anyway they pass what they learn back and forth, they're the same fire after all."

"But then all the fires are the same, aren't they?" Annabelle said. It was something that had come up in her third year of training, the interdisciplinary year. "The candle, the star . . ."

"The elemental," Adelio said, "the passion. All the same. Us, we just keep the fire burning, serve at the altar."

"Serve," Annabelle said. "My Goddess, Chef, shouldn't you be at SPQR? Who's cooking?"

Adelio smiled, and this time the smile was more purely wicked. "Mike," he said.

"Not Tonino?" Annabelle said, and then her eyes widened as she realized what had happened.

"Tonino got fired."

Annabelle's eyes went wider still, for there were presently too many things that could mean.

"No, no, nothing like that. I just caught him making a call to someone he shouldn't have, this bad gray man. Jealousy is a terrible thing; it burns and does no good. So after the police are done with him, he will go find himself some other kitchen to be jealous in, probably a prison kitchen, and will count himself lucky I do not set all my lawyers on him. Little toad."

Annabelle nodded. "Chef," she said, "only one thing." She was looking at the TV vans that had pulled up outside: three of them, and here came a fourth, U-turning out in the middle of the street. "Tonino made his call and got fired. But somebody else seems to have made another call. What are all *these* people doing here all of a sudden? Before the police and their own seer arrive?"

"There's no such thing as bad publicity, eh?" Adelio said, and slipped down from the counter. "Pull your hair back, Anna *la bella,* my partner. You must look good for the cameras or they won't respect you!"

He sauntered off toward the empty front of house. Annabelle, briefly shocked by the word "partner," which he had never used to her before, now stared after him in infuriated comprehension. "Adelio," she shouted, *"you set this up?!"*

He paused, looked back at her, and grinned that bad-child grin again. "Everybody talks to me, Anna *la bella,*" he said. "Over the wine, late at night, they tell me everything, back at my round table when the lights are low. Sometimes I do not even have to put things into the wine to help me find out."

She stared at him, suddenly realizing why SPQR's orders for butterfly marjoram were so hefty. It had culinary uses, yes, but also ones that the witches' licensing board would have frowned on, especially when used on normals. *But being a chef,* she thought, *is the perfect cover.*

"And I hear all kinds of things," Adelio said. "Sometimes they tell me accidentally, sometimes on purpose. When you are big money, there are a lot of people who want to take it, a lot of people who want to be friends with it. Sometimes they get in each other's way, you put one piece of news together with another." He shrugged. "The bad men, they made their plan, they were waiting for their chance," Adelio said, "but once I found out what they would do—how, and where, and when . . . Why waste? Why wait? Let them convince themselves never to try this again—on you or me. And let there be a mystery about it—not to the police, of course, they will know, but to the public. Mystery is good for business, eh? Now come on, if we hurry we will be live in the features slot at the end of the six o'clock news."

He headed for the door, pulled it open. It squeaked. Astounded, touched, Annabelle stood there for a moment longer, watching as the blaze of TV lights abruptly came awake outside. She paused for just a moment to pull the oven door open a crack, and look inside, and smile.

Then she shut it and followed Adelio into the light.

THE POOP THIEF

Kristine Kathryn Rusch

Usually, Kristine Kathryn Rusch hides her sense
of humor behind her romance byline, Kristine
Grayson. But Rusch doubts Grayson would use
the word "poop" so liberally. Rusch is a multiple award-winning author and editor whose latest book is *The Recovery Man*. She also writes
as Kristine Grayson and Kris Nelscott and a
whole bunch of other names too numerous to
mention.

"Okay, this is just weird."
        The voice came from the back of the store. It
belonged to my Tuesday/Thursday assistant, Carmen.
High school student, daughter of two mages, Carmen had
no real talent herself, but she was earnest, and she loved
creatures, and I loved her enthusiasm.

"I mean it, Miss Meadows, this is weird."

Oddly enough, weird is not a word people often use in
Enchantment Place. Employees expect weird. Customers
demand it. What's weird here is normal everywhere
else—or so I thought until that Tuesday in late May.

"Miss Meadows. . . ."

"Hold on, Carmen," I said. "I'm with a client."

The client was a repeat whom I did not like. I'm duty
bound at Familiar Faces to provide mages with the
proper familiars—the ones that will help them augment

their talents and help them remain on the right path (doing no harm, avoiding evil, remaining true to the cause, all that crap). I do my best, but some people try my patience.

People like Zhakeline Jones. She was a zaftig woman who wore flowing green scarves, carried a cigarette in a cigarette holder, and called everyone "darling." Even me.

I called her Jackie, and ignored the "It's Zhakeline, dahling." Actually, it was Jacqueline back when we were in high school and then only from the teachers. The rest of us called her Jackie, and her friends—what few she had—called her Jack.

Whenever she came in, I cringed. I knew the store would smell like cigarettes and Emeraude perfume for days afterward. I didn't let her smoke in here— Enchantment Place, for all its oddities, was regulated by the City of Chicago, and the City of Chicago had banned smoking in all public places—but that didn't stop the smell from radiating off her.

Most of my creatures vacated the front of the store when she arrived. Only the lioness remained at my feet, curled around my ankles as if I were a tree and Zhakeline her prey. A few of the mice looked down on Zhakeline from a shelf (sitting next to the books on specialty cheeses that I'd ordered just for them), and a couple of the birds sat like fat and sassy gargoyles in the room's corners.

Nothing wanted to go home with Zhakeline, and I didn't blame them. She'd brought back the last three familiars because the creatures had the audacity to sneeze when they entered her house (and silly me, I had thought that cobras couldn't sneeze, but apparently they do—especially when they don't want to stay in a place where the air is purple). We were going to have to find her something appropriate and tolerant, something I was beginning to believe impossible to do.

On the wall beside me, lights shimmered from all over the spectrum, then Carmen appeared. Actually, she'd stepped through the portal from the back room to the shop's front, but I'd specifically designed the magical effect to impress the civilians.

Sometimes it impressed me.

Carmen was a slender girl who hadn't yet grown into her looks. One day, her dramatic bone structure would accent her African heritage. But right now, it made her look like someone had glued an adult's cheekbones onto a child's face.

"Miss Meadows, really, my parents say you shouldn't ignore a magical problem, and I think this is a magical problem, even though I don't know for sure, but I'm pretty certain, and I'm sorry to bother you, but jeez, I think you have to look at this."

All spoken in a breathless rush, with her gaze on Zhakeline instead of on me.

Zhakeline smiled sympathetically and waved a hand in dismissal. Bangles that had been stuck to her skin loosened and clanked discordantly.

"This hasn't really been working, Portia." Zhakeline said with a tilt of the head. She probably meant that as sympathy too. "I've been thinking of going to that London store—what do they call it?"

"The Olde Familiar." I spoke with enough sarcasm to sound disapproving. Actually, my heart was pounding. I would love it if Zhakeline went elsewhere. Then the unhappy familiar—whoever the poor creature might be—wouldn't be my responsibility.

"Yes, the Olde Familiar." She smiled and put that cigarette holder between her teeth. She bit the damn thing like a feral F.D.R. "I think that would be best, don't you?"

I couldn't say yes, because I wasn't supposed to turn down mage business, and I could get reported. But I didn't want to say no because I would love to lose Zhakeline's business.

So I said, "You might try that store in Johannesburg too, Unfamiliar Familiars. You can see all kinds of exotics. But remember, importing can be a problem."

"I'm sure you'll help with that," she said.

"Legally I can't. But you're always welcome here if their wares don't work out."

The mice chittered above me, probably at the word "wares." They weren't wares, and they weren't animals. They were sentient beings with magic of their own, subject only to the whims of the magical gods when it came to pairings.

The whims of the magical gods and Zhakeline's eccentricities.

"I'll do that," she said. Then she turned to Carmen. "I hope you settle your weirdness, darling. And for the record, your parents *are* right. The sooner you focus on a magical problem, the less trouble it can be."

With that, she swept out of the store. Two chimpanzees crawled through the cat doors on either side of the portal holding identical cans of Fabreeze.

"No," I said. "The last time you did that we had to vacate the premises. Or don't you remember?"

They sighed in unison and vanished into the back. I didn't blame them. The smell was awful. But Fabreeze interacted with the Emeraude, leading me to believe that what Zhakeline wore wasn't the stuff sold over the counter but something she mixed on her own.

Without a familiar, which was probably why the stupid stuff lingered for days.

"Miss Meadows." Carmen tugged on my sleeve. "Please?"

I waved an arm so that the store fans turned on high. I also uttered an incantation for fresh ocean breezes. (I'd learned not to ask for wind off Lake Michigan; that nearly chilled us out of the store one afternoon). Then I followed Carmen into the back.

Walking through the portal is a bit disconcerting, especially the first time you do it. You are walking into another dimension. I explain to civilian friends that the back room is my Tardis. Those friends who don't watch *Doctor Who* look at me like I'm crazy; the rest laugh and nod.

My back room should be a windowless 10x20 storage

area. Instead, it's the size of Madison Square Garden. Or two Madison Square Gardens. Or three, depending on what I need.

Most of my wannabe familiars live here, most of them in their own personal habitats. The habitats have a maximum requirement, all mandated by the mage gods and tailored to a particular species. Each bee has a football-sized habitat; each tiger has about a half an acre. Most creatures may not be housed with others of their kind, unless they're a socially needy type like herding dogs or alpha male cats. The creatures have to learn how to live with their mage counterparts—not always an easy thing to do—and its best not to let them interact too much with other members of their species.

Theoretically, I get the creatures after they complete five years of familiar training (and yes, you're right; very few familiars live their normal lifespan. Insects get what to them seems like millions of years, and dogs get an extra two decades; only elephants, parrots, and a few other exceptionally long-lived species live a normal span).

That day, I had too many monkeys of various varieties, one parrot return who'd managed to learn every foul word in every language known to man (and I mean that) during his aborted tenure with his new owner, several large predatory cats, twenty-seven butterflies, five gazelle, sixteen North American deer, eight white wolves, one black bear, one grizzly return, one hundred domestic cats, five hundred sixty-five dogs, and dozens of other creatures I generally forgot when I made a mental list.

Not every animal was for sale. Some were flawed returns—meaning they couldn't remember spells or they misquoted incantations or they were temperamentally suited to such a high-stress job. Some were whim returns, brought back by the mage who either bought on a whim or returned on a whim. And the rest were protest returns. These creatures left their mage in protest, either of their treatment or their living conditions.

All three of Zhakeline's returns had been protest returns although she tried to pass the first off as a flaw return and the other two as whim returns. It gets hard for a mage after a few rejections. Eventually she gets a reputation as a familiarly challenged individual and might never get a magical companion.

And if she goes without for too long, she'll have her powers suspended until she goes through some kind of rehab.

Fortunately, that's never my decision. I'd seen too many mages fight to save their powers just before a suspension: I never want all that angry magic directed at me.

Carmen was standing on the edge of the habitats. They extended as far as the eye could see. My high school assistants didn't tend the habitats the way that civilian high school assistants would tend cages at, say, a vet's office. Instead, they made sure that the attendants that I hired from various parts of the globe (at great expense) actually did their jobs.

Each attendant had to log in stats: food consumed, creature health readings, and how often each habitat was entered, inspected, and cleaned. Then they'd log in the video footage for the past day—after inspecting it, of course, for magical incursions, failed spells, or escape attempts.

Carmen had called up our stats on the clear computer screen I'd overlaid over the habitat viewing area. She zoomed in on one stat—product for resale.

I frowned at the numbers. They were broken down by category. The whim returns and most of the protest returns were listed, of course, along with byproducts—methane from the cows (to be used in various potions), shed peacock feathers (for quills), and honey from the bees that had convinced the mage gods to make them hive familiars, not individual familiars.

Those bees only went to special clients—those who could prove they weren't allergic and who could handle several personality types all speaking through their fearless leader, the sluggish queen.

"See?" Carmen asked, waving a hand at the numbers. "This week's just weird."

I didn't see. But I didn't have as much experience with

the numbers as she did. And, truth be told, I didn't think her powers were in spell-casting. I believed they were in numerology—not as powerful a magic, but a useful one.

"I'm sorry," I said, feeling dense, as I often did when staring at rows of facts and figures. "What am I supposed to see?"

She poked her finger at one of the columns. The lighted numbers vanished, then reappeared in red.

"Available fertilizer," she said. "See?"

I stared at the category. Available Fertilizer. Our biggest seller because we undercut the competition, mostly so we could get rid of the crap quickly and easily.

"There's no number there," I said.

"Zero is a number," Carmen said with dripping disdain that only a teenager could muster.

"E . . . yeah . . . okay." I knew I was stammering, but the big honking nothingness made no sense. "The assistants haven't been cleaning the habitats?"

She pressed the screen, drawing down the earlier statistics. Cleanings had gone on as usual.

"So what happened to the fertilizer?"

"I have no idea where the fertilizer went," she said. "I'm not even sure it came out of the cages. I mean, habitats."

I had planned to give her a tour of the back, but I hadn't yet. So she always made the "cages/habitat" mistake, something she'd never say if she actually saw the piece of the Serengeti plain that Fiona, the lioness who liked to sleep under my cash register and Roy, the lion who supposedly headed her pride, had conjured up to remind themselves of home.

Cleaning the habitats was a major job, especially for the larger animals, and usually required extra labor. Entire families came in for an hour or two a night to clean grizzly's mountainside, especially during blackberry season.

I moved Carmen aside, pressed some keys only visible to me, and looked at several of the previous day's vids in fast motion. Habitat cleaning happened in all of them. Habitat cleaners weren't required to log in what they cleaned unless the item was marketable, which poop generally was. Animal poop that is. There's never a big market for insect poop.

Animal poop (ground up into a product called Familiar Fertilizer) had a wide variety of uses. Mages bought it for their herb gardens. In addition to being the Miracle-Gro of the magical world, it also made sure that wolf's bane and all the other herbal ingredients of a really good potion, magical spell, or "natural" remedy was extra powerful. Some mages vowed that anything fertilized with familiar poop could be safely sold with a money-back guarantee—especially (oddly enough) love spells.

"Must be a computer glitch," I said and stabbed a few more buttons.

"Let me." Carmen got to the correct screens quicker, without me even asking. She knew I wanted to check all that basic stuff—how many pounds of poop got ground into fertilizer at the nearby processing plant, how many pounds of fertilizer got shipped, and how many of our magical feed-and-seed brethren paid for shipments that arrived this week.

Each category had a big fat zero in the poundage column.

"I don't like this," I said. "You just noticed this?"

I tried to keep the accusation out of my voice. It wasn't her job to keep track of my shipments and my various product lines. She was a high school student working two days a week part-time after school.

I was the person in charge.

"I was going over the manifests like you taught," she said. "I let you know the minute I saw it."

Which was—I checked the digital readout on the see-through computer screen—half an hour ago, one hour after Carmen arrived.

Pretty dang fast, considering.

"I mean, everything was fine on Thursday."

Thursday. The last day she worked.

My lunch—an indulgent slice of Chicago pan-style pizza—turned into a gelatinous ball in my stomach. "Can you quickly check the previous four days?"

"Already on it." She pressed a few keys.

I watched numbers flash in front of my eyes—too quickly for my number-challenged brain to follow. I could have spelled the whole thing, looked for patterns, but I had Carmen. She was better than any magical incantation.

"Wow," she said after a few minutes. "Those animals haven't pooped since Friday."

The gelatinous ball became concrete. I reached for the screen to look at health history, then stopped. A few of those creatures would have died if they hadn't pooped in three days. Some internal systems were less efficiently designed than others.

Still, I had her double-check the health records just to make sure.

"Okay," she said after looking at health records from Thursday to Tuesday. "So they all have normal bowel readings. What does this mean?"

"It means that your parents are right," I said.

"Huh?" She looked at me sideways, all teenager again. She hated hearing that Mom and Dad were right.

"Magical problems become bigger when they are allowed to fester."

"This is a magical problem?" she asked.

"The worst," I said.

She continued to stare at me in confusion, so I clarified.

"We have a poop thief."

You find poop thieves throughout magical literature. Heck, you even find them in fairy tales.

Of course, they're never called poop thieves. They're "tricksters" who steal their victims' "essence." They're evil wizards who rob their enemies of their "life force."

Most scholars believe that these references are to sperm, which simply tells me that magical scholarship has been dominated too long by males. (Those inept male scholars don't seem to be able to read either; a lot of the victims are women, who are, of course, spermless creatures one and all.)

The scholars are right in that "life force" and "essence" are often composed of bodily fluids. Some (female) scholars have assumed that this essence is blood, but blood is a lot harder to obtain than the simplest of bodily fluids—pee.

Pee, though, is like all other water. It seeps into the ground. It's difficult to get unless someone pees into a cup or a bottle or a box. (Unless you've magicked the chamberpot, and there are a few of those stories as well (Those Brothers Grimm didn't like the chamberpot stories and so kept them out of the official compilation.)

Poop, on the other hand . . .

Poop, actually, on either hand is a lot easier to obtain.

Poop, like pee, blood, and yes, sperm, is a life essence. Even in its nonmagical form it has magical powers. It gets discarded only to be spread on a fallow field. The nutrients in the waste material break down, enriching the soil, which is often used to grow plants—plants that later become food. The food nourishes the person who eats it. The person's body processes the food into energy and vitamins and all sorts of other good stuff, and the leftovers become waste yet again.

Most of the nonmagical have no idea of the power held in a single turd.

Hell, most of the magical didn't either.

But the ones who did, well, they were all damn dangerous.

And I'd already lost too much time.

It seemed odd to call Mall Security at a time like this, but that was the first thing I did. Mine wasn't the only store with magical creatures.

If someone was stealing from me, then maybe he was stealing from the pet store down the way, the organ grinder monkey show just outside the food court, and the various holiday setups with their real Easter bunnies and Christmas reindeer and Halloween bats. Not to mention all the working familiars accompanying every single mage who walked into the place.

I let Carmen talk to security. She was young enough

and naïve enough to think they were sexy. She had no idea that most of them were failed magical enforcers or inept warlocks who'd been demoted from city-wide security patrol to Enchantment Place.

I stayed in the back room, bending a few rules because this was an emergency. Anyone who took that much poop had a plan. A big plan—or a need for a lot of power.

At first, I figured this thief simply wanted the magical support of a familiar without actually getting a familiar. Magical crime blotters were full of minor poop thieves who stole rather than get a new familiar of their own. They'd mine someone else's familiar, using the poop as a tool with which to obtain the magic, and no one would notice until that familiar got sick from putting out too much magical energy.

Maybe what we had here was a more sophisticated version of the neighborhood poop snatcher.

Which made Zhakeline a prime suspect.

But Zhakeline's magic had always been shaky at best, even when she had a familiar. That was why she looked so exotic and had so many affectations.

She had to appeal to the civilians who think we're all weird. She mostly sold her small magic services to them. If she predicted the future and was wrong or if she made a love potion that didn't work, the civilian would simply shrug and think to himself *Ah, well, magic doesn't really work after all.*

But the magical, we know when someone can't perform all of the spells in the year-one playbook. Zhakeline barely passed year one (charity on the part of the instructor) and shouldn't have passed from that point on. But that happened during the years when telling a kid that she had failed was tantamount to murdering her (or so the parents thought), and Zhakeline got pushed from instructor to instructor without learning anything.

Which was one of the many reasons I didn't want to give her another familiar.

And that was beside the point.

The point was that Zhakeline, and mages like her—

the ones who needed the magical power of familiar
poop—didn't have the ability to conduct a theft on this
massive scale, at least not alone.

And even if they tried, they'd be better off going to
the back yard of a mage with a canine familiar. There
was always a constant poop supply, and it provided
enough power—consistent power (from the same source)
that the thief might become a slightly less inept mage,
for a while, anyway.

Next I investigated my assistants. Most had no magical
powers of their own but had come from magical families.
They knew that magic existed—and not in that hopeful
I wish it were so way that a civilian had but in a *this is
a business* way that led them to peripheral jobs in the
magical field.

They worked hard, most had a love of animals, insects
or reptiles, and they often had a specialty, whether it was
cooking the right kind of pet food or calming a petulant hyena.

I couldn't believe any of the assistants would be doing
something like this because they would have to be working for someone else.

The nonmagical don't gain magic just by wishing on a
powerful piece of poop.

I scanned records and employment histories. I scanned
bank accounts (yes, that's illegal, but remember—
emergency. A few rules needed to be bent), cash stashes
and (embarrassingly) the last 48 hours of their lives.
Which, viewed at the speed of an hour per every ten
seconds, looked like silent movies watched at double
fast-forward.

I saw nothing suspicious. And believe me, I knew what
to look for.

Although I wished I didn't.

You see, I got this job, not because I have a particular
affinity with animals or I'm altruistic and love pairing the
right mage with the right familiar.

I got it because I have experience.

I know how to look for mages heading dark or mages

who should retire or mages who mistreat their magic (and hence their familiars). I know how to take care of these mages quietly, efficiently, and with a minimum of fuss.

It didn't used to be this way. In the past, places like Familiar Faces existed on side streets and had just a handful of creatures, few of them exotic. Only in the last few years have the megastores come into existence at high-end malls like Enchantment Place.

And even though we're supervised by the rules of the mage gods like all other familiar stores, we're run and subsidized by Homeland Security-Magical Branch.

(Not everyone knows there's a Homeland Security-Magical Branch, including the so-called "head" of Homeland Security. Hell, I even doubt the president knows. Why tell the person who's going to be out in four or eight years one of the world's most important secrets. Knowing this crew, they'd probably try to co-opt the Magical Branch into something dark. Better to keep quiet and protect us all.

(Which I do. Most of the time.)

My job here is to watch for exactly this kind of incursion. Technically, I'm supposed to report it and then wait for the guys with badges to show up.

But I didn't wait for the guys with badges. I doubted we would have time.

(And, truth be told, I did want the glory. I was demoted to this position—you guessed that already, right?—for asking too many questions and for the classic corporate mistake, proving that the boss was an idiot in front of his employees. I'm a government employee and as such can't be fired without lots and lots of red tape—even in the magical world—so I was sent here, to Chicago, where I grew up, to Enchantment Place, where I have to put up with the likes of Zhakeline with a smile and a shrug and a rather pointed—and sometimes magically directed—suggestion.)

I toyed with rewinding time in all of the habitats—another no-no, but it would have been protected under the Patriot Act, like most no-nos these days. But rewinding time takes time, time I didn't really want to waste looking at creatures moping in their personal space.

Instead, I did some old-fashioned police work.

I went back out front, where Carmen was still flirting with some generic security guard (and the mice were leaning over so far to watch that I was afraid one of them would fall down the poor man's ill-fitting shirt), and beckoned the lioness, Fiona.

She frowned at me, then rose slowly, stretched in that boneless way common to all cats, and padded through the portal ahead of me.

When I got back to the back, she was sitting on her haunches and cleaning her ears, as if she had meant to join me all along.

"We have a poop thief," I said, "and I think you know who it is."

She methodically washed her left ear, then she started to lick her left paw in preparation for cleaning her right ear.

"Fiona," I said, "if I don't solve this, something bad will happen. You might not get a home of any kind, and none of the other familiars will be of use to anyone. You might all have to be put down."

I usually don't use euphemisms, and Fiona knew it. But she didn't know the reason that I used it this time.

I couldn't face killing all these wannabe familiars. And it would be my job to do so. I'd get blamed for the theft(s), and I'd have to put down the creatures affected. It was the only way to negate the power of their poop.

She put her newly cleaned paw down on the concrete floor. "You couldn't 'put us down.'" She used great sarcasm on the phrase. "It would set the magical world back more than a hundred years. There wouldn't be enough of us to help your precious mages perform their silly little spells."

"Which might be the point of this attack," I said. "So tell me what you saw the last few days."

And why you never said a word, I almost added, but didn't.

"I'm not supposed to tell you anything. I'm not even supposed to talk with you."

Technically true. Familiars are only supposed to talk to their personal mages. But I get to hear every one of them speak when they come into the store to make sure they really are familiars and not just plain old unmagical creatures looking for a free handout.

But Fiona had spoken to me before, mostly sarcastic comments about the store patrons. I'd tried pairing her up with a few, but she always had an under-the-breath comment that convinced me she and that mage wouldn't be a good match.

"I haven't seen anything," she said.

"What have you heard, then?" I asked.

"Nothing," she said. "The system is working just fine."

That sarcasm again, which lead me to believe she was leaving out a detail or two deliberately, hoping I would catch it.

Damn lions. They're just giant cats. They toy with everything.

And at that moment, Fiona was toying with me.

"But something's bothering you," I said.

"Not me so much." She picked up that clean paw, turned it over, and examined the claws. "Roy."

Roy was the lion to her lioness. He wasn't head of the pride because there was no pride. We knew better than to get an entire pride of lions into that small habitat. No one would ever be able to see their individual natures— and no mage was tough enough to get that many catly familiars.

"What's bothering Roy?" I asked.

"Ask him."

"Fiona . . ."

She nibbled on one of the claws, then set her paw down again. "There was—oh, let me see if I can find the phrase in your language—an overpowering scent of ammonia."

"Ammonia?"

"And a very bright light."

"An explosion?" I asked. Fertilizer mixed with the right chemicals, including ammonia, created the same thing in both the magical and the nonmagical world.

A bomb.

Only the magical bomb made of this kind of fertilizer didn't just destroy lives and property, it also cut through dimensions.

"It's not an explosion yet," she said. "He claims he has a sixth sense about things. Or did he say he can see the future? I forget exactly. But it was something like that."

"Or maybe he just knows something," I snapped.

"Or maybe he just knows something." She sounded bored. "He does say that because he's king of the jungle, the wannabes tell him things."

Which was the most annoying thing about Roy. He really believed that king of the jungle crap. Too much Kipling as a cub—or maybe too many viewings of the *Lion King*.

"I should really send you back to the habitat until this is resolved," I said to Fiona.

She hacked as if she had a hairball, a sound she (sort of) learned from me. She thought it was the equivalent of my very Chicago, very dismissive "ach."

"I'd rather be out front, watching the floor show," she said.

And I sent her back out there because I had a soft spot for Fiona. Technically, I don't need a familiar. I have more than a thousand of them.

But if I did need one, I'd pick Fiona.

She knew it, and she played on it all the damn time.

I waited until she was through that little curtain of light before I stepped through the hidden door into the habitat area.

It was always surprisingly quiet inside there. The first time I went in, I expected chirping birds and chittering monkeys and barking dogs—a cacophony of creature voices expressing displeasure or loneliness or sheer cussedness.

Instead, the area was so quiet that I could hear myself breathe.

It also had no smell—unless you counted that dry scent of air conditioning. The animal smells—from the pungent odor of penguins to the rancid scent of coyote—existed only in the individual habitats.

Just as the noises did.

If I went through the membrane on my left (and only I could go through those membranes—or someone I had approved, like the assistants), I would find myself in a cold dark cave that smelled of rodent and musty water. If I looked up, I'd see the twenty-seven bats currently in inventory.

We were always understocked on bats. Mages, particularly young ones raised in Goth culture, wanted bats first, wolves second, and cats a distant third. I'd given up trying to tell those kids to get some imagination.

I'd given up trying to tell the kids anything.

If I went through the membrane on my right, I'd slide on polar ice. Here the ice caps weren't melting. Here, my six polar bears happily fished and scampered and did all those things polar bears do—except that they didn't attack me. They didn't even bare their fangs at me.

I stopped between the two membranes and frowned. Whoever took the poop hadn't taken it from inside the habitats. It was simply too dangerous for the unapproved guest.

Hell, it was often dangerous for the assistants. I'd had more than one assistant mauled by a creature that didn't like the way he was looking at it.

And the poop was not registered as collected either. So whoever had taken it had spelled it out between gathering and delivery into the outside system.

I walked between dozens of habitats, trying to ignore the curious faces watching me.

I did feel for the wannabes. They were like children in an old-fashioned orphans' home. They hoped that someone would come to adopt them. They prayed that someone would come to adopt them. They were afraid that someone had come to adopt them.

And the only way they would know was if I brought them out of the habitat to the front of the store. (Except in the case of the dangerous exotics or the biting/stinging insects. In those cases, the mage had to enter the habitat without fear. *That* rarely happened either.)

Finally I got to the Serengeti Plain.

Or what passed for it in Roy and Fiona's habitat. It was kind of an amalgam of the best parts of a lion's world minus the worst part. Lots of water, lots of space to run, lots of space to hide. A great deal of sunshine and never, ever any rain.

I slipped through the membrane and, because of my past experience, paused.

The first step into Roy's world was overwhelming. The heat (about twenty degrees higher than I ever liked, even in the summer), the smell (giant cat mixed with dry grass and rotting meat from the latest kill), and the sunlight (so bright that my best sunglasses were no match for it—and, as usual, I had forgotten any sunglasses) all made for a heady first step into this habitat.

More than one assistant had been so disoriented by the first step that Roy was able to tackle, stand on, and threaten him or her in the first few seconds. After you've had several hundred pounds of lion standing on your chest, with his face inches from yours—so close you could see the pieces of raw meat still hanging from his fangs—you'd never want to go back into that habitat either.

Unless you're me, of course. I expected Roy to scare me that first time.

I didn't expect him to catch me off guard.

So when he did, I congratulated him, told him he was quite impressive, and warned him that if he hurt a human, he'd never graduate from wannabe to familiar.

And from that point on, he never jumped on me again.

But he always snuck up on me.

On this day, he wrapped his giant mouth around my calf. His teeth scraped against my skin, his hot breath moist and redolent of cat vomit. He'd been eating grass again. We were going to have change his diet.

"Hey, Roy," I said. "I hear you have a sixth sense."

He tightened his jaw just enough that the edges of

those sharp teeth would leave dents in my flesh—not quite bites, not quite bruises—for days. Then he licked the injured area—probably an apology, or maybe just a taste for salt (I was instant sweat any time I came into this place).

Finally, he circled around me and climbed a nearby rock so that he would tower over me. If I weren't so used to his power games, he'd make me nervous.

"It's not a sixth sense," he said in an upper-class British accent. That accent had startled me when we were introduced. "So much as a finely honed sense of the possible."

"I see," I said, because I wasn't sure how to respond. I hadn't even been certain he would talk to me, and he'd done so almost immediately.

Which led me to believe the king of the jungle was more terrified than he wanted to admit.

"You realize I am only speaking to you," he said with an uncanny ability to read my mind (or maybe it was just that finely honed sense of what I might possibly be thinking), "because great evil is afoot, and I have no magical counterpart with which to fight it."

I almost said, *It's not your job to fight it*, but I didn't. I didn't want to insult the poor beast. Instead, I said, "That's precisely why I'm here. I figured you know what was going on."

"Bosh," he said. "Fiona told you. She has a thing for you, you know."

"A thing?" I asked.

"She wants to be your familiar." He opened his mouth in a cat-grin. "She doesn't understand—or perhaps she doesn't believe—that you have hundreds of us and therefore do not need her."

I nodded because I wasn't sure what else to do. And because I was already thirsty. I'd forgotten not just my sunglasses but my bottle of water as well.

"Well," I said, "you do know what's happening, right?"

"Oh, bombmaking, dimension hopping, familiar murder—all the various possibilities." He lay down and crossed his front paws as if none of that bothered him. "And just you here because you seem to believe that you can save the world all by your own small self."

"With the help of your finely honed sense of the possible."

"That too." He tilted his massive head and looked at me through those slanted brown eyes.

My heart rate increased. Occasionally I still did feel like prey around him.

"Well?" I asked.

"Have you ever thought that your culprit isn't human?"

"No," I said. "Demons don't care about familiars. Only mages do."

"Really." He extended the word as if it were four. "Humans generally ignore scat, don't they?"

"Generally," I said. "We try not to think about it."

"And yet those of us in the animal kingdom find within it a wealth of information."

"Yes," I said. "But the amount of power it would take to complete this spell tends to rule out anything that isn't human."

He made the same hairball sound that Fiona did. They were closer than they liked to admit.

"You humans are such species-est creatures. It doesn't help that the mage gods allow you the choices, and we have to wait until you make them. It leads me to believe that the mage gods are human—or were, at one point."

I wasn't there to discuss religion. "You're telling me, then, that your finely honed sense of the possible leads you to the conclusion that a familiar has done this."

"I didn't say that."

"A creature then. A magical creature of some kind."

He slitted his eyes, the feline equivalent of yes.

"But you have no evidence," I said.

"I have plenty of evidence. Consider the timeline. It took you forever to discover this theft, and yet no bomb has exploded. No one has made threats, and no mage has suddenly gained unwarranted power."

"That's not evidence. That's supposition."

He lifted his majestic head. "Is it?"

"So who do you suppose has stolen the poop—and why?"

He rested his head on his paws and continued to stare at me. "That's for you to work out."

"In other words, you don't know."

"That's correct. I don't really know."

"But you're not worried."

"Why should I worry? From my perspective, removing the scat is a prudent thing to do."

I hadn't expected him to say that. "What do you mean?"

He heaved a heavy, smelly sigh. "I'm a cat who lives in the wild. Think it through."

Then he jumped, and I cringed as he headed right toward me. He landed beside me, chuckled and vanished through the tall grass.

He'd gotten me again. He loved that. He'd probably been planning to jump near me through the entire conversation, his back feet tucked beneath him and poised, even though his front half looked relaxed.

He wasn't going to give me any more. He felt he didn't need to.

Cats in the wild.

Cat poop in the wild.

Hell, cat poop in the house. Cats were all the same.

They buried their poop so no one could track them.

The problem wasn't the poop thief.

The poop thief was protecting the wannabes from something else. Something that tracked through scat.

Something that wasn't human.

I swore and bolted out of the habitat.

I needed my research computer, and I needed it now.

Very few things targeted familiars—or perhaps I should say very few nonhuman things. And I'd never heard of anything that targeted wannabes, because a wannabe's power, while considerable, wasn't really honed.

Wannabes were, for lack of a better term, the virgins of the familiar world.

And nothing targeted virgins (not even those stupid civilian terrorists. They got virgins as a *reward*).

So when I got out of the habitat, I had the computer search for strange creatures or things that targeted virgins. I got nothing.

Except the search engine, asking me a pointed electronic question:

Do you mean things that prefer *virgins?*

And I, on a frustrated whim, typed *yes.*

What I got was unicorns. Unicorns preferred virgins. In fact, unicorns would only appear to virgins. In fact, unicorns drew their magic from virgins.

But the magic was pure and sweet and hearts and flowers and Hello Kitty and anything else treacly that you could think of.

Except if the unicorn had become rabid.

I clicked on the link, found several scholarly articles on rabies in unicorns. Rabid unicorns were slightly crazed. But more than that, they had no powers because no virgin (no matter how stupid) was going to go near a horse-sized creature that shouted obscenities and foamed at the mouth.

That was stage one of the rabies. Unlike rabies in no-magical creatures, rabies in unicorns (and centaurs and minotaurs and any other magical animal) manifested in temporary insanity, followed by darkness and pure evil.

The craziness, in other words, went away, leaving nastiness in its wake.

Minotaurs, centaurs, and other such creatures attacked each other. They stole from the nearest mage—or enthralled him, stealing his magic before they killed him.

But unicorns . . .

Unicorns still needed virgins.

And the only solution was to steal the powers of wannabe familiars.

Provided, of course, that the unicorn could find them.

And unicorns, like most other animals, hunted by scat.

*   *   *

I wish I could say I got my giant unicorn-killing musket out of mothballs and carried it through an enchanted forest, hunting a brilliant yet evil unicorn that wanted to devour the untamed magic of wannabe familiars.

I wish I could say I was the one who shot that unicorn with a bullet of pure silver and then got photographed with one foot on its side and the other on the ground, leaning on my musket like hunters of old.

I wish I could say I was the one who cut off its horn, then snapped the thing in half, watching the dark magic dissipate as if it never was.

But I can't.

Technically, I'm not allowed to leave the store.

So I had to call in the Homeland Security-Magical Branch anyway. I could have called the local mage police, but I wasn't sure where this unicorn was operating, and HS—MB had contacts worldwide.

They found four rabid unicorns all in the same forest, somewhere in Russia, along with a few rabid squirrels (probably the source of the infection) and a rabid magical faun that was going around murdering all the bears for sport.

The unicorns died along with the squirrels and that faun. The poop reappeared in my computer system and went back through the normal channels. That week, we made double our money on magical fertilizer, which was good since we'd made none the week before.

All seemed right with the magical world.

Except one thing.

I dragged Fiona to her habitat so I could confront both her and Roy.

They usually didn't spend much time together. They blamed it on not really having a pride, but I knew the problem was Fiona. She hated having to hunt for him, then watch him eat the best parts.

She hated most things about feline life and once muttered, as yet another well adjusted young mage took a domestic cat as her familiar, that she wished she were small and cute and cuddly.

She had to fetch Roy. He wasn't going to come. He hadn't even attacked me as I entered the habitat—probably because Fiona was with me.

I waited as he climbed to the top of his rock, then assumed the same position he'd been in before he jumped at me. Only this time I was prepared. I had my sunglasses and my water bottle.

I also stood a few feet to the right of my previous position, a place he couldn't get to from the top of that rock.

Fiona sat at the base of the rock, beneath the outcropping, in the only stretch of shade in this part of the plain.

"You want to tell me how you did it?" I asked when Roy finally got comfortable. He sent me an annoyed look when he realized that I had stationed myself outside of his range. "You knew that there was a rabid unicorn after wannabes, and you somehow got the entire group at Familiar Faces to cooperate with you, all without leaving your habitat."

Then I looked at Fiona. She had left the habitat. She left it every single day.

The tip of her tail twitched, and she tilted her head ever so slightly, her eyes twinkling. But she said nothing.

Roy preened. He licked a paw, then wiped his face. Finally he looked at me, the hairs of his mane in place, looking as majestic as a lion should.

"I am king of the jungle," he said.

This is a plain, I wanted to point out, but I didn't for fear of silencing him. Instead I said, "Yet some of the other familiars don't live in habitats like yours. The snakes, for example."

He yawned. "The unicorn wasn't after them."

"But the animals?" I asked.

He closed his great mouth, then leaned his head downward, so that his gaze met mine. "The Russian Blues are refugees. You didn't know that, did you?"

I have two domestic cats—purebred Russian Blues. Most purebred cats aren't familiars—they have the magic bred out of them with all the other mixed genes—but

these Blues were amazing. And pretty. And not that willing to talk, even when they knew it was the price of
gaining a mage.

"Refugees?" I said. "They were adopted before?"

"Their mages were murdered by the new secret police
for being terrorists. I thought you checked all of this
out."

I tried to, but I never could. Animal histories weren't
always that easy to find.

"They'd heard rumors about something rabid getting
into an enchanted forest somewhere in deepest darkest
Russia. Then some young familiars—what you call
wannabes—withered and died as their powers were
sucked from them over a period of months."

He tilted his head, as if I could finish his thought.

And I could.

"So the Blues suspected unicorns," I said.

"There were always rumors of unicorns in that forest,"
he said, "but, of course, none of us had ever seen them.
For normal unicorns, you need virginal humans. None of
us had encountered abnormal unicorns before."

I did the math. The Blues had arrived last Thursday,
which was the last day Carmen had worked before Tuesday, when she discovered the problem.

"You went into protect mode immediately," I said.

"It is my pride, whether you admit it or not."

I didn't admit it, but I understood how he thought so.
He needed a tribe to rule, so he invented one.

"I still don't understand what happened. You don't
have the magic to make other animals' poop disappear."

"But they do," he said.

"I know that." I tried not to sound annoyed. He was
toying with me again. I hated being a victim of cat
playfulness.

"So how did you tell them what to do?"

He opened his mouth slightly, in that cat-grin of his.
Then he got up, shook his mane, and walked back down
the rock. He vanished in the tall grass, disappearing
against its browness as if he had never been.

"He could tell me," I said.

"No, he can't." Fiona hadn't moved.

I let out a small sigh. He hadn't been toying with me. She had.

"You did it," I said.

"Me and the bees," she said. "They're creating quite a little communications network with those hive minds of theirs. They send little scouts into the other habitats every single time you go from one to the other. The ants too. You really should be more careful."

I felt a little frisson of worry. I had had no idea. I didn't want the bees to get delusions of grandeur. I already had to deal with Roy.

"You told them to spread the word."

She nodded.

"And you told them how the animals could hide their poop."

She inclined her head as regally—more regally—than Roy ever could.

"Why?" I asked. "You had no guarantee of a threat."

"This is the biggest gathering of the Hopeful on the globe," she said. "Of course we are a target."

She was right. I sighed, took a sip from my water bottle, and frowned. This entire event had opened my eyes to a lot of scary possibilities, things I had never considered.

We were going to have to rethink the way we handled waste. We were going to have to protect the poop somehow, and I didn't want to consult HS-MB about that. They'd have to hold hearings, and the wrong someone could be sitting in.

I didn't want us to become a magical terrorism target, nor did I want us to be a target for every rabid unicorn in the world.

I would have to set up the systems myself.

"You need me," Fiona said, "whether you like it or not. You can't have pretend familiars. You need a real one."

She was making a pitch. Cats never did that. Or they only did so if they believed something was important.

"Why here?" I asked. "I've found you some pretty

spectacular possible mage partners, and you've turned them down."

She wrapped her tail around her paws and stared at me. For a moment, I thought she wasn't going to answer.

Then she said, "This is my pride. Roy might think it his, but he's a typical lion. He thinks he's in charge, when I do all the work."

She raised her chin. That tuft of hair that all lionesses had beneath looked more like a mane in the shade than it ever had. It made her look regal.

"Well," she added, "I'm not a typical lioness, content to hunt for her man and to feel happy when he fathers a litter of kittens on her only to run them out when they threaten his little kingdom. I don't want children. And I want to eat first."

"You can do that with other mages," I said.

"But I won't have a pride. Don't you see? I'm the one who spoke to the Blues. I'm the one who keeps track of those silly mice—even though I want to eat them—and I'm the one who calms the elephant whenever she has the vapors. No one credits me for it, of course, but it's time they should."

No one, meaning me. I hadn't noticed, and Fiona was bitter. Or maybe she just felt that I wasn't holding up my end of the bargain.

"Besides," she said, "it's hot in here. Can we go back to the air conditioning?"

I laughed and stepped out of the habitat. She followed.

"I'll petition the mage gods," I said.

"I already did." She was walking beside me as we headed toward the front room. "They said yes. I put their response under the cash register."

We went through the portal. The mice were having a party on top of the cheese books. One of the snakes was dancing too, trying to come out of its basket like a charmed snake from the movies. The dance was a bit pathetic, since the snake was the wrong kind. It was the tiniest of my garden snakes.

They all stopped when they saw me. I looked toward

mall's interior. The customer door was closed and locked and the main lights were off. The closed sign sat in the window.

Carmen had gone home long ago.

I went to the cash register and felt underneath it. Some dust, some old gum—and yes, a response from the mage gods, dated months ago.

"You took a long time to tell me this," I said to Fiona. She wrapped herself around the counter. "You should clean more."

Come to think of it, a few months before was when she really started muttering her protests out loud. In English. She was doing everything felinely possible except blurting it out that she was now my familiar.

I had never heard of a familiar picking a mage.

Although that wasn't really true. The familiars always made their preferences known. I knew how to read the signs. For everyone, it seemed, but me.

"Do you regret this?" Fiona asked quietly.

"Hell, no," I said. "Your brilliance averted a major international incident and saved the lives of hundreds of familiars."

"Don't you think that makes me deserving of some salmon?"

I almost said *I think that makes you deserving of anything you damn well please*, and then I remembered that I was talking to a cat. A large, independent-minded, magical cat, but a cat all the same.

"Salmon it is," I said and snapped a finger. A plate appeared with the thickest, juiciest salmon steak I could conjure.

I set it down next to her.

"Next time," she said, "you're taking me out."

"Restaurants don't allow animals," I said. "At least, not in Chicago."

"I wasn't talking about a restaurant," she said. "I meant a salmon fishery or perhaps one of those spawning grounds in the wild. I heard there's a species of lion who hunts those grounds."

"Sea lions," I said. "You're not related."

She chuckled, then wrapped her tail around my legs, nearly knocking me over. Affection from my lioness.

From my familiar.

However I had expected my day to end, it hadn't been like this.

Carmen was right. This day had been weird.

But good.

"So are you going to promise to take me to a fishery after the next time I save lives?" Fiona asked.

"I suppose," I said, wondering what I had gotten myself into.

Fiona licked her lips and closed her eyes. The mice started dancing all over again, and chimpanzees came out of the back to see what the commotion was.

After a weird day, a normal night.

And I found, to my surprise, that I preferred normal to weird.

Maybe I was getting soft.

Maybe I was getting older.

Or maybe I had just realized that I was a mage with a familiar, a powerful smart familiar, one I could appreciate.

One who would keep me and my animals safe.

One who would rule her pride with efficiency and not a little playfulness.

I could live with that.

I had a hunch she could too.

Sherwood Smith

Inda

"A powerful beginning to a very promising series by a writer who is making her bid to be a major fantasist. By the time I finished, I was so captured by this book that it lingered for days afterward. I had lived inside these characters, inside this world, and I was unwilling to let go of it. That, I think, is the mark of a major work of fiction...you owe it to yourself to read *Inda*." -Orson Scott Card

INDA

0-7564-0422-2

New in Paperback!

THE FOX

0-7564-0483-3

Now Available in Hardcover

THE KING'S SHIELD

0-7564-0500-7

To Order Call: 1-800-788-6262
www.dawboks.com

Jennifer Roberson

The **Karavans** series

"The first volume in a new fantasy saga from
Roberson establishes a universe teeming with
fascinating humans, demons and demigods.
Promises to be a story of epic proportions."
—*Publishers Weekly*

"High-quality action fantasy." —*Booklist*

"Roberson's prose is compelling, the book's
premise is well-presented, and the pages almost
seem to turn themselves." —*Romantic Times*

"Set in one of the most vividly described and
downright intriguing fantasy realms to come
along in years, *Karavans* is arguably Roberson's
best work to date..This is a "must-read" fantasy
if there ever was one.
—*The Barnes & Noble Review*

KARAVANS	978-07564-0409-6
DEEPWOOD	978-07564-0482-6

To Order Call: 1-800-788-6262
www.dawbooks.com

P.R. Frost

The Tess Noncoiré Adventures

"Frost's fantasy debut series introduces a charming protagonist, both strong and vulnerable, and her cheeky companion. An intriguing plot and a well-developed warrior sisterhood make this a good choice for fans of the urban fantasy of Tanya Huff, Jim Butcher, and Charles deLint."
—*Library Journal*

New in Paperback!
HOUNDING THE MOON
0-7564-0425-3

Now Available in Hardcover
MOON IN THE MIRROR
0-7564-0424-6

To Order Call: 1-800-788-6262
www.dawboks.com

Kristen Britain

The **GREEN RIDER** series

"Wonderfully captivating...a truly
enjoyable read." —Terry Goodkind

"A fresh, well-organized fantasy debut,
with a spirited heroine and a reliable
supporting cast." —*Kirkus*

"The author's skill at world building and her feel
for dramatic storytelling make this first-rate
fantasy a good choice." —*Library Journal*

"Britain keeps the excitement high from beginning to end, balancing epic magical battles with
the humor and camaraderie of Karigan and her
fellow Riders." —*Publishers Weekly*

GREEN RIDER   0-88677-858-1
FIRST RIDER'S CALL   0-7564-0209-3
and now available in hardcover:
THE HIGH KING'S TOMB 0-7564-0209-3

To Order Call: 1-800-788-6262
www.dawbooks.com

The Novels of
Tad Williams

To Order Call: 1-800-788-6262
www.dawbooks.com

DAW 102

Patrick Rothfuss
THE NAME OF THE WIND
The Kingkiller Chronicle: Day One

"It is a rare and great pleasure to come on some-body writing not only with the kind of accuracy of language that seems to me absolutely essential to fantasy-making, but with real music in the words as well.... Oh, joy!" —Ursula K. Le Guin

"Amazon.com's Best of the Year...So Far Pick for 2007: Full of music, magic, love, and loss, Patrick Rothfuss's vivid and engaging debut fantasy knocked our socks off." —Amazon.com

"One of the best stories told in any medium in a decade. Shelve it beside *The Lord of the Rings* ...and look forward to the day when it's mentioned in the same breath, perhaps as first among equals." —*The Onion*

"[Rothfuss is] the great new fantasy writer we've been waiting for, and this is an astonishing book." —Orson Scott Card

0-7564-0474-1

To Order Call: 1-800-788-6262
www.dawbooks.com